Siloam

Siloam

Keepers of the Spring

CHUCK COOPER

RESOURCE *Publications* · Eugene, Oregon

SILOAM
Keepers of the Spring

Resource Publications
An Imprint of Wipf and Stock Publishers
199 W. 8th Ave., Suite 3
Eugene, OR 97401

www.wipfandstock.com

PAPERBACK ISBN: 978-1-5326-6082-5
HARDCOVER ISBN: 978-1-5326-6083-2
EBOOK ISBN: 978-1-5326-6084-9

Manufactured in the U.S.A.   01/10/19

For All the Saints, William W. Howe, 1864, Public Domain

The Battle Hymn of the Republic, Julia Ward Howe, 1861, Public Domain

In loving memory of my wife's parents, Thomas and Alice Pickett, who accepted me as their own, unconditionally, and with love.

I want to express deep appreciation to my wife, Dr. Patty Pickett-Cooper, for her constant support of my writing, and for editing this book.

Major Characters
in Alphabetical Order

Doc Clyde Bailey: Local physician

Nate Beard: Owner of Salty Dog Fishing Cruises (engaged to Sally)

Buddy and Caitlin Beard: Nate's children

Carmelita Biffle: Chief of Police

Blessed John: Mysterious Nomadic Being

Shirley Boley: Administrative Assistant to Police Chief, Married to Jens.

Marlene Brooker: Local Realtor

Father Francis Callaghan: Priest at Our Lady of the Harbor

Carla Chavez: Letter Carrier

Rev. Jimmie Crackers: Evangelist/flim-flam artist

Minnie Belle Crackers: Wife of Jimmie Crackers

Georgia Curry: Cook on Nate's fishing boat

Evita DuPont: Mysterious older woman, patron of Joe's Diner

Roy Edgefield: Troublesome citizen, friend of Jens

Ruth Edgefield-Martin: Nurse, brother of Roy, mother of Little Therese

Little Therese Edgefield-Martin: Teen-age mystic, daughter of Ruth

Rev. Stewart Grenville: Cook at Joe's Diner, Lighthouse keeper, husband of Katye

Caleb Habibi: Newly arrived physician, Spouse of Liz

Liz Habibi: Community organizer, daughter of Hope and Lou, Spouse of Caleb

Marshall Hale: Deputy

Sally Hankins: Manager of Joe's Diner (engaged to Nate)

Homer Hill: Evangelist, operator of criminal enterprise

Bartosh Honecker: New owner of the bank

Susanna Kappos: Owner of the Argostoli Art Gallery

Rocky and Magdalena Joplin: Leaders of the Unsettlement

Mrs. McCarthy: Cook at Our Lady of the Harbor rectory

Joe Magnus: Founder of Joe's Diner

Ruby Malone: Head of Tribal Confederation Council

Jens Marsden: Rehabilitated ne'er-do-well, Husband of Shirley

Katye Puckett: Community Leader, Dean of the Community College, wife of Stewart

Samir Salah: Photographer, partner of Jeremy Woods

Frances Saugus: Retired School Principal

Lou Schofield: Mayor of Safety Harbor, husband of Hope, father of Liz

Hope Schofield: Teacher, Spouse of Lou, Mother of Liz

Raven Sinclair: Representative of Bread from Stone Inc.

Meriwether Starhawk: Spiritual Leader of Mystical Waters Spiritual Community

Silo Sulsberger: Teenage boy

Hobe Watson: Co-owner of the Old Eighty

Georgette Watson: Co-owner of the Old Eighty

Jeremy Woods: Owner, Jeremy's Coffee Shop and Book Store

Preface

IT HAS BEEN FOUR years, since we have been in Safety Harbor. During that time, much has changed. Relationships have developed. Children are growing up. Life situations have evolved. People we have not met before, have moved to town.

In this story, the people face the challenge of the discovery of the breaking through of an ancient spring, just outside of town. It has been dormant, for more than a century, its location long forgotten. While the spring, in former times, provided water for every-day living, it also contained healing powers. Now, dark and malevolent forces wish to take it over, for their own purposes. The struggle to preserve the spring to be used for good, and not for evil intent, is what forms the basis of this story, which captured me and would not let me go, until I had written the very last word.

While *Siloam: Keeper of the Spring*, is a sequel to *Safety Harbor: Keepers of the Light*, I have done my best to make it possible for those of you who have not read the first book, more easily to take in this story. I am including a list of the characters at the beginning of the book, and I have done my best to orient the reader to their circumstances within the text. I hope, when you finish this book, that you will want to read *Safety Harbor*, if you have not yet done so.

We are the offspring of stars. Each of our lives is a microcosm of the cosmos, as it struggles, on the one hand to be born and to develop, and, on the other hand, as it resists giving way to the inevitability of time. So, we too, are always being born anew, and we are always living under the sentence of our own mortality.

What happens between our beginning and our end, is the stuff of our life. It is our story. All through our lives there are signs, metaphors, if we can see them, that call us to be our best selves, that call us to live beyond ourselves, to invest ourselves in something bigger than our own solitary life. When we do this, community naturally forms, and we are no longer alone. We are not meant to be on our own. We are meant to be with, we are meant to be for, one another.

For the people of Safety Harbor [and their neighboring community, the Unsettlement]. the newly discovered spring becomes a metaphor, a sign, and an invitation to participate in a more fully human life that transcends long-standing barriers, long-held grudges and hatred, and yes, and the ways religion is used to divide and not to unite.

There is one, two-fold common human purpose in life, and that is to love and to serve. Everything else perishes. I hope that this story will enable you to reflect upon your own life, to perceive the signs and symbols that point you to your own vocation in life, where you may best love the world, and serve within it, and where you may be a source of healing to all who inhabit it.

Chapter 1

"THERE COMES A TIME in everyone's life, Hobart, when you just have to start letting go of stuff!"

There was a finality in his wife's voice, and Hobe knew, right then and there, that his resistance to moving from the home where they had lived for forty years, effectively, was over. The Watsons put the house up for sale, the next day. Georgette had been thinking about this for over a year, so, when the time came, she had her ducks in a row. The house was ready for show, and the realtor was ready to pounce.

Georgette had been gentle with her husband about the move, at first. But, when she saw that he didn't take her seriously, she began to use logic. When logic didn't work, she knew that she would have to do it another way.

Finally, one day, she said, "For God's sake, Hobe, if you die ahead of me, I'm not going to be left out in the country, in this big house, to wander around, with every nook and cranny and corner reminding me of you! And if I die before you, you'll be lost. I've waited on you, hand and foot, and you'd starve to death, here, waiting for somebody to bring the groceries home!"

Hobe didn't say anything then, but when she brought it up this last time, he surrendered. He'd miss the old place, his shop, all the stuff, as Georgette put it, that had collected over the years. His Uncle Benjamin had given him an old set of tools which he hadn't used in years, but still, they had sat there on one of the shelves of the shop, all this time. They'd provided comfort to him and a reminder of an earlier day when things seemed simpler and more innocent, even if they weren't. And, there was the ancient chainsaw that his daddy had used to cut up logs to chop for firewood for the house, this house, this very house, where he was born, where he had grown up, reared his family, and now, had lived into his old age.

When he had brought his bride-to-be home, his parents, John and Ella, approved right away, and urged them to move into his childhood home with them. Hobe had resisted, but, Georgette had urged him to reconsider.

"Can't you see, honey? They are asking us to move in and take care of them! Your daddy is a big man and he's not so healthy anymore. Your momma is a little thing and she won't be able to dress him and see to his personal needs, when the time comes."

Hobe knew that he had found a good woman in Georgette. She'd taken care of them lovingly and patiently, especially when old John had a stroke and became, as his wife, Ella, had put it, "a mean and ornery old cuss."

After John died, Ella had lived on for years, and Hobe had joked with her that she was going to outlive him. She was with them through the rearing of their four children, and she had been there when they lost their youngest boy, John, to cancer, when he was only eight years old. Every week, for the rest of her life, as long as she was able, she'd go to visit his grave, even when the others couldn't, or didn't.

She died at ninety-six. One night, she just went to sleep and didn't wake up.

Tears rolled down Hobe's cheeks as he thought back on those days when his momma had helped them with the kids.

And, my Lord, how she had loved her chickens!

"Good grief, Momma!" he said one day. "I don't know who you love more, those chickens, or us!"

She said she didn't know either, and Hobe couldn't tell if she was kidding or not. You couldn't tell with momma, that way. Life had been hard for her, and Daddy said that the smile had been wiped from her face early, when she was a little girl. It had never come back. He didn't know what had happened.

Hobe surveyed his shop, turning slowly, gazing at every last bit of it. It had been his sanctuary all these years. There was an old potholder over there in the corner, hanging just above Grandpa's tool box, that Grandma Ella had made. His daughter, Glenda, had hung it on the wall in the shop when she was eight. When Ella missed it, Hobe told her what Glenda had done with it. Had it been anybody else, she would have insisted that he get it, and put it back where it belonged. But, Glenda could do no wrong in her grandmother's eyes, so, there it had stayed all these years, covered now, with ages of dust.

Hobe had never been a man to cry, but he felt a lump in his throat that he thought might be a precursor to a tear; he quickly turned away from the scene, and walked back toward the house. Tomorrow was the auction, when, all of these things that had defined his life, had to go, including his tractor, his riding lawn mower, his lathe, all his power tools, many of the things that told a man of his ilk, that he was a man.

That, and the land. The eighty acres. He was nothing without it. He could feel it right now, solid, beneath his feet, as he walked out toward one of his hay fields. Damn! If he was going to cry, it wouldn't be in front of anybody, that's for sure.

That night, he lay in his bed. Georgette was sleeping soundly beside him, with ever so slight a snore in her breathing.

"My God!" he thought. "The secrets these walls know!"

He thought of the conversations that must have taken place between his dad and momma all the time their kids were growing up. He had given them a hard time, running wild for a couple of years, as his grandma had described it, "with the wrong bunch." Momma must have shed her tears here, in this bed, at night, wondering what would become of him. He knew that Georgette and he had spent many a wakeful night, raising Glenda and her three older brothers.

Hobe, his four brothers and one sister, had been conceived in this very room. His four children, too, although Hobe had teased Georgette that the oldest could have gotten his start up in the grove behind the barn.

He couldn't sleep. He didn't want to sleep. When he opened his eyes, in the morning, it would be time for the auction. He crept out of bed, quietly, and pulled his pants on. Stepping into his shoes, he opened the side door of the farm house to survey the old place again. Everywhere he looked was a memory. Before the night was over, he would walk the perimeter of the entire eighty acres.

On that moon-lit summer night, the trees and the nocturnal creatures could hear a man crying, as if his heart would break.

Chapter 2

IT WAS THE FOURTH day of their cross-country drive. Caleb and Liz decided that, rather than arrive, exhausted, in Safety Harbor, they would stay the night in Portland. Then, fully rested, tomorrow, about midmorning, they would drive the final sixty-five miles home. It would be a surprise to Liz's parents, Lou and Hope, who thought they were coming the following week.

Doc Bailey had cooperated with them in their conspiracy. He agreed that Caleb would have a week for Liz and him to get settled, before he began working at Harbor View General as its first hospitalist. Doc was thinking about retiring but he wasn't ready to quit, until he knew that the people of Safety Harbor were "in good hands," as he put it. Working at the hospital would give Caleb a full experience of every aspect of Doc's general practice.

Caleb Habibi had graduated from Boston School of Medicine, and had just finished his residency in Internal Medicine with the Hadassah Medical Organization in Palestine. Mostly, he had spent the three years of his time in East Jerusalem, with a few months in Gaza, and a few weeks in the West Bank.

He was a native of Ramallah. His family had moved to the United States when he was twelve, and he spent the rest of his growing up years in Paterson, New Jersey. From there, it was on to Boston University.

Liz and Caleb met just before his last year of school in Boston. She was up from New York for the Berklee Middle Eastern Festival. Caleb had noticed her at one of the concerts and had asked her if she wanted to go out for a drink. Liz refused him outright. Not one to give up, he had given her his business card, and asked her to call him if she changed her mind.

She did change her mind, about five minutes later. Caleb's cell phone rang and from that time on, they had seen each other, exclusively. Each had a year of education to finish up, but theirs was a determined commuter relationship.

The next summer, they were married in Safety Harbor. It was one of the biggest events that had ever happened in the little town. Caleb's old family priest came from Ramallah to celebrate the wedding Mass with Father Callaghan. The Habibi family, and a hundred distant cousins, it seemed, came from Paterson, New Jersey, Ramallah, and East Jerusalem. Liz's family drove from Arkansas, Ohio, and Florida, some of whom they hadn't seen in decades, and some of whom they suspected might be of suspicious lineage.

Many of their college friends attended. July 11th, their wedding day, was in the middle of tourist season. Hotels were filled to the brim and that meant that many of the wedding party had to be put up in homes. Lou and Hope insisted that Caleb's parents, George and Nadia, stay with them.

There were so many in the wedding party, that they extended across the chancel, and poured over into the side aisles. Seven groomsmen and seven bridesmaids. Meriwether had offered to get the Country Club for the reception, but Sally had insisted that it be held at Joe's.

Lou and Hope, Sally's parents, who were putting on the affair, agreed.

"Practicality be damned," Lou said. "Joe's is small, but we can set up tents in the back yard and close Newman Street, if we have to. It isn't every day the mayor's daughter gets married!"

And so, they did. By decree, the mayor closed Newman Street, that ran past Joe's; and the diner, somehow, throughout the day, accommodated over five hundred people. People said it was the biggest thing that had happened in town since Joe had been rescued, when everybody turned out to see the boat, limping into the harbor, the year before.

Caleb Habibi and Liz Schofield-Habibi had now been married for three years. During the week that they spent in Safety Harbor for their wedding, Caleb had fallen in love with the town. He was charmed by its beauty, its simplicity, and the basic goodness of the people. When they left, he could think of nothing else than having a medical practice there. Liz tried to talk him out of it.

"What appears to be on the surface isn't always so, in reality," she said. "Small towns are deceptive. There's always a shadow side to them!"

"Besides," she had said, "your people need you more than my people do. Safety Harbor can always get a doctor or drive to the next town."

Caleb would have it no other way. He would fulfill his responsibilities as a resident, and then, he would move to his wife's home town. Doc Bailey wasn't getting any younger.

Three months before they were to arrive, Liz was thrilled to receive a text from Rock and Magdalena, asking her to consider helping them out at the Unsettlement, the transient community near Safety Harbor Rock, with community organizing. Rock told her that they had reached a point where they were going to have to become an honest-to-God town, or close it all down. It would be a real job. They had found some funds to pay a community organizer. They wanted her to be the one.

Tonight, here they were, at the Hatfield Hotel in downtown Portland, having dinner, before their new life began in Safety Harbor, tomorrow.

"Are you sure about this, Caleb, dear?"

"It's a little late to be asking that question now, isn't it?"

He smiled wryly.

"I've been asking you this for months, now. You know that!"

She reached over and took his hand, in order to mitigate her words, that carried with them a certain tone that might be mistaken for peevishness.

"You know," she continued, with her voice considerably softened, "my little town is provincial, by any standards. You and I are coming here from pretty exciting places, where things are happening all the time. And you! You come from far flung places in the world from Ramallah to Rome! Once you get here, you're stuck, at least for the three years you've promised Doc Bailey!"

"Well, for that matter, so are you!"

"So am I, what?"

"Stuck! Same as I am!"

"I'm happy to be stuck with you anywhere!" she said.

"Yeah, but you'll be in your own home town where you're the Liz everybody saw grow up, and the person defined by your relationship with your parents."

"That changed at the wedding!"

"Maybe it did. Maybe it didn't. Probably, it didn't!"

Her hand squeezed his tighter, now. "We're about to find out, aren't we?"

"Are you going to eat that piece of toast?"

"Oh, yes, I had plans for that piece of toast, but if you want it, Caleb, dear!" She feigned a martyr's face.

He snatched it from her plate, broke it into two, applied a generous helping of jam, and handed her one of the pieces.

After they'd finished, he raised his half-empty coffee cup as if to offer a toast. Liz raised her cup as well.

"Here's to our future!" he said.

"And here's to making our home in Safety Harbor!" she said.

The cups clinked, as if to offer the final punctuation on their breakfast conversation.

Chapter 3

HOBE AWAKENED TO THE sounds and smells of Georgette getting breakfast ready, as she did every morning.

He stirred. Now, he realized that his head had been resting on his arms, and he was sitting at the large kitchen table in the old farmhouse. He remembered, now. He had fallen asleep at the table, last night, after his long trek around the Old Eighty, as his father had called the farmland, and his father before him.

"You couldn't have slept very well in that position!" said Georgette as she firmly placed a cup of coffee in front of him.

"I didn't. I didn't sleep well, all night."

"I know."

"I don't want to do it. I don't want to do this day. I'd like to die here. Why can't I die here like Momma and Papa did?"

We've been over this, Hobart. There's nobody here to take care of us like we did with your folks. None of the kids want to come back and live here. We're on our own. And, when one of us goes, the other is alone. That's it. Oh, the kids and grandkids will come and cry at the funeral, and then, they'll be gone, back to their busy lives. They'll phone once in a while when they think of it. But, all we have, really, are each other, and our friends, in Safety Harbor!"

"I know you're right, Georgette."

She put his plate down in front of him. The Women's Missionary Society from Always Sunny Freewill Holiness Church was providing the auction lunch. She knew it was his last meal in the house, before everything changed. She didn't say it. She wasn't given to sentimentality, but, she noticed things, and she knew what he'd want.

They ate in silence. The sounds of birds singing, were all around them. A slight breeze stirred the curtains, providing a rustle in the leaves.

It was as if nature knew the occasion, and was providing them with an especially sweet farewell symphony, for their last meal of the old era.

After all of these years, the house was one with all that was around it. The little seedlings that Hobe's grandpappy had planted alongside the long driveway, were towering Oaks. The Maple, whose branches Hobe had played in, was now a burgeoning creature, that had spread itself over the front yard, as a protecting hen.

Hobe swore it was the prettiest time of the year. The front yard was sewn with bluegrass, with an occasional dandelion here and there. Hobe's daddy had always said that this wasn't a fancy farm, and a few weeds among the grass was a good thing. Especially, if they flowered. Like dandelions. Georgette's large flower garden was just to the north side the front yard, located where it could get just the right amount of sun and shade. Hobe's vegetable garden was out back behind the barn, in the old cattle lot, rich with natural fertilizer from the sixty years of dairy farming.

"There's a couple of motorcycle engines I can hear coming up the driveway. That must be Roy and Jens, here to help get the heavy stuff out, where people can see all of it. They have a few more of their friends coming, too."

Hobe didn't want to move from the chair. He knew he had to do this. He stirred himself, drank the last dregs of the coffee from the bottom of the cup, stood up, and said "Well, that's it, then."

He went out to face the day. Georgette could hear him talking to the newly arrived movers outside, with a forced cheerfulness.

Now that he was gone, she could let down her guard.

She wept.

Chapter 4

"I've got five, um-bud-ah five, five, five, um-bud-ah five, um-bud-ah five! Who'll give me ten, ten, ten dollahs, um-bud-ah ten, ten, ten, for this fine post hole digger? Tennnn, now tennnn, now ten, um-bud-ah ten. I've got ten, um-bud-ah ten, now fifteen, for this hardly ever used tool!"

"Hey!" Hobe called out. "I used that, plenty!"

The auctioneer looked over at him good naturedly and broke his rhythmic chant. "I'm doin' the best I can for you, Hobe!"

There was good-natured laughter in the crowd.

"Fifteen, fifteen, who'll gimme fifteen! Now, twunny, twunny, twunny. Sold, to the gentlemen, over there, in the red cap!"

The man moved forward to the make-shift desk, constructed of sawhorses and an old door, where he paid for his merchandise, and moved on out of the crowd.

No one there could have known that Caleb and Liz were just four miles out of Safety Harbor.

"Well, here we go, husband! I hope it's the life you wanted!"

"I want it to be the life we want!"

"I'm happy to be with you; and my working at the Unsettlement just puts the cherry on the sundae!" she said.

"Must be a lot of fishin' going on today along the creek!" said Caleb. "Look at all the cars!"

"There's always a lot of fishing here. It's tourist season, on top of that!"

The cars parked along the road got closer and closer together and pretty soon they were double-parked.

"This's gotta be more than fishing, Liz."

"I wonder what?"

They rounded the corner. There were signs about every hundred feet until they approached one that announced, "Watson Estate Sale Here."

"Hobey and Georgette! They're selling! Oh, no!"

"Hobey?" Caleb smiled.

"When I was a little girl, I used to call him Uncle Hobey. He always smelled good, like cedar wood, since he worked at the lumber yard, and he always had lollipops in his pocket for kids! I was good friends with his daughter, Glenda. I spent many a happy day there. I overnighted in their house, in the summer. We'd camp outside, under the Maple tree, in a little tent that Uncle Hobey would put up for us! Georgette could cook too! Wow! My momma just isn't a cook, but I guess you know that!"

"Well, since you mentioned it!"

"Oh, now you say it, when we're married, and it's safe!"

"You know, you are right!"

"I s'pose Mom and Dad are there! In fact, I know they are. They wouldn't miss something like this! We'll have to stop, Caleb!"

"We've missed all the parking spaces."

"Looks as if everybody is double parking, the closer we get!"

"I don't want to get off on the wrong foot with someone, right off the bat!"

"Look! There's Momma and Daddy's car. Double parked, right next to them. Dad won't leave, until the last prospective voter has gone from the premises!"

"You're cynical!"

"No, I just know my dad. Believe me, we're safe here."

"As long as Carmelita or Marshall don't start writing tickets!"

"They can't! We're out of the city limits here!"

"You're somethin' else!" he said.

They walked up the long driveway, hand in hand.

"Hey! Maybe we could buy this house!" said Caleb.

"It sure would be nice! I love it. So many happy memories!

They slipped into the crowd, unnoticed, at first. It was when they went up to the Always Sunny lunch table, that Liz noticed her mother talking with one of the women, from the Missionary Society.

She looked at Caleb, mischief in her eyes.

She went up behind her mother and hugged her.

"Liz?" she asked.

"What of it?"

Hope turned around, stunned.

"Liz! It's you, My God! It's really you! And Caleb, dear boy!"

She was clearly, at once, overjoyed and flustered.

"Welcome home, dear ones! Oh, I can't believe you are here! I can't! I just can't!"

Caleb extended his hand. "Mrs. Schofield."

"I'll have none of that. I'm Mom and that's the end of it. No hand-shake. Come here and give me a hug! Come here, both of you! Lou! Lou? Where is that man? Always gone when you need him!"

"He's bidding on a table, Hope," somebody said.

"Well, somebody stop him! We can't put another thing in our house! Tell him to come over here and see the kids! They're home a week early!"

A crowd gathered around the three of them.

Susanna and Sally were the first to greet them.

"Gosh, we've missed you! We've so been looking forward to your moving here!"

"So have we, Susanna!" said Liz. "Oh my! Is that Caitlin over there?"

"Yes, it is. She won't be seen with her brother, anymore. She's four-teen now, and will hardly acknowledge anyone that isn't her age, espe-cially her despicable younger brother, Buddy!" said Sally.

"I'd be disappointed if she were any other way! She's a normal teen-ager!" said Liz.

"Oh, she'd probably be seen with you two! You're from out of town and have been out in the big world! We're too small for her, now. She's on to bigger and better things than Safety Harbor!"

"Caitlin! Over here!" Liz called out.

The young teenager came running over, arms open.

"Liz! Caleb! So good to see you!"

She gave them each air kisses on both cheeks.

"This is my friend, Alicia," she announced, introducing a young woman of her age.

"Where's Buddy?" asked Caleb.

"Somewhere. I don't keep track of him." She said it with more than a trace of sibling disdain.

"He's helping Hobe with the auction. He's good in math, and Hobe wanted to make sure the auctioneer gets his figures right!"

Just then, the auctioneer announced a lunch break.

"Oh, dear, there's Daddy, always ready to grab the mike!"

"Ladies and gentlemen, I'd like all of you to notice that my daughter, Liz, and her husband, Caleb, have arrived home!"

"How did he know?" asked Caleb, in amazement.

"Daddy's got his sources!"

"He hasn't even. . .."

"I know, Caleb, dear. He hasn't even come to greet us yet."

"You have a lot to learn about your father-in-law!" exclaimed Hope.

"He'll be here soon!" said Liz. "He just can't resist being the first to announce that we are here!"

His proclamation was met with cheers and applause, among those who knew them. Soon enough, Lou was there, putting Liz in a vice grip hug, and shaking Caleb's hand, profusely.

"Let's get some lunch, kids!" said Lou.

They made their way to the long tables, set up by Always Sunny.

"Give these kids whatever they want! It's the last time I'm buyin' anything for 'em!" he joked. "In fact, Sally, Susanna, Caitlin, Alicia, go ahead and grab whatever you want. It's on me!"

Buddy walked up, in the company of Hobe and Georgette.

"Well, hello there, Buddy!" said Liz.

"Hi, Liz! Hi Caleb! We weren't expecting you until next week!"

Liz noticed how he had grown into an adolescent, from the little boy that was at her wedding. He had lost many of his childish ways.

"We decided to surprise you all, and arrive early. We wanted to get here, and settle in a little, before Caleb got started at the hospital. And, I'm excited about getting started at the Unsettlement!"

"We're excited to get you started!"

It was Magdalena who had approached the table, just out of Liz's sight. Liz turned and embraced her.

"So good to see you!" said Magdalena, embracing her.

Rock was just behind her, smiling.

"Hi!" he said, giving her a hand wave.

"That won't do!" said Liz. "Get over here and give me a hug!"

Liz pulled Caleb into the mix and the four of them stood in a circle with their arms locked together.

"I can't believe you are really here!" said Magdalena. "We never thought we'd be lucky enough to get you back!"

"We're the lucky ones," said Caleb. "I'm so fortunate to be invited to be a part of such a wonderful little town!"

"We'll see what you think six months from now!" said Sally.

"He'll love it, even more!" said the mayor. "He'll love it here, more every year! I know that I do!"

Chapter 5

IT WAS NOW LATE afternoon. The crowd was drifting away. There was still some machinery to be sold, down by the barn. The auctioneer called a break, and those who wanted to bid, slowly ambled their way toward the barn, grabbing a cold drink, or a late afternoon sandwich.

It was in the middle of the sale of Hobe's old Allis-Chalmers tractor, that a little boy, who appeared to be about five years of age, came running up to his father. No one local knew who they were.

"Dad! Dad! There's a hole in the ground, behind the barn! There's a hole in the ground!"

His father picked him up and tried to quiet him.

"But, there is, Dad! There is! There's a big hole in the ground! You have to come see it! I almost fell in!"

The last words alarmed his father, and he slipped away from the auction, to see what it was that so excited his son.

Hobe had overheard it all, but couldn't imagine, for the life of him, what it could be. He knew of no hole in the ground, behind the barn, and he had lived here for nearly seventy-three years, except for his stint in the army. He made his way down the side path that led to his garden, located behind the large red barn, in which he had spent at least as much time as his own house. He noticed out of the corner of his eye, that the paint was starting to fade in places and blister in others.

"Gonna have to take care of that, next year1" he said, aloud, to himself.

Then, he realized that he wouldn't be here, and the thought of it overwhelmed him, like an unexpected sickening jolt of a riptide that he had experienced as a boy. It had nearly taken him under; and this wave, too, seemed for a moment, to overwhelm him so much, that he staggered.

He righted himself and lifted up his head. He saw that, about fifty paces away, the boy and his dad were standing, staring down at the ground. Hobe moved quickly now, to see what it was that these two strangers had spotted, that he had not seen, on this, his own land.

More people were now moving down toward the man and his son. Hobart wondered if anyone was left behind to buy the rest of the machinery.

In fact, there was a well, right where the boy had spotted what he called a hole in the ground. Hobe was amazed. Four roughly hewn boards covered it over and made a platform for it. The wood had rotted to the point that the whole frail construct was nearly ready to fall in the well. It was clearly dangerous and Hobe would have to do something about it.

The auction had been all but stopped by this scene. The auctioneer approached Hobe and told him so.

"What do you wanna do, Hobe?"

"How much is left to sell?"

"Your riding lawn mower, your plow, hay rake, and hay bailer, the old Allis Chalmers and Ford tractors, and a few other small things."

"I'm keepin' the garden tools. Whoever buys this house is gonna hafta put up with me in this garden, until she's harvested. I can sell the rest of the stuff, easy enough."

They decided to call it a day, as far as the auction was concerned. They could never get people back together now, because most everyone who remained was down by the well.

Hobe had some lumber stacked behind the house from an old building project. Roy and Jens brought enough boards down, to cover the well and make it safe.

"I think we just ought to take those old railroad ties off there, Hobe!" said Jens. "They are rotten. You don't know when they'll give way and fall in."

"I think you're right!" said Hobe.

"He's always right, Hobe!" said Roy. "Just ask him!"

"You boys'll never change, will you?" Georgette laughed heartily.

Hobe hadn't seen her behind him and he, uncharacteristically, took her hand and pulled her up alongside him.

"Well, the old place is still surprising us, dear!" he said.

"I can't believe you have never seen it down here, or your father, any of your family . . . or, just anybody, all of these years."

"Yet, there it is!" said Hobe.

"Well, at least, we can say that we have another source of water when we sell the place!" said Georgette.

"Oh, it's probably dry after all these years."

Well, we won't know until we find out, will we?" she said, squeezing his hand.

Chapter 6

The discovery of the well was the main topic of conversation at Joe's, the morning after the auction.

Hobe and Georgette joined the regular crew at the diner. It was the first day in their marriage that Georgette had not cooked Hobe's breakfast, except for a vacation, here and there, for forty years. Hobe used to come in, with his brother, Johnny, for coffee, first thing in the morning, but then, he'd go home to Georgette's good cooking. They were greeted, enthusiastically.

"Come over and join us!" said Father Callaghan. "It's about time you two got yourselves in here!"

Georgette could not help but notice the Stone of Gleaming that everyone had talked about. She had always intended to come by, but she never had taken the time. Now, she saw what everyone meant when they said you had to see it, that there was no describing it. An inexplicable soft glow of light emanated from the stone. It was a simple, ordinary boulder, from down the coast, at Clever; but, buried deep inside it was the luminous stone, that had come from Gemma. It was said that human eyes couldn't look directly on the stone, without losing one's sight. The rock from Clever shielded the light, so that creaturely eyes could take it in.

Hobe noticed a sense of well-being and happiness as he approached the stone. His sadness and heaviness of heart departed from him, while he was near it.

Father Callaghan, Hope and Lou, Jeremy and Samir, along with young Reverend Cecil Bainbridge, the new pastor at Always Sunny, were all sitting at the long Wisdom Table, that could accommodate twelve to fifteen people. Sally had found a book of recommendations in Joe's desk that he had bequeathed to them. Among his other writings, Joe had recommended what he called the Wisdom Table. If anyone had a question or a problem to ponder, it would be given over to the collective wisdom of those who had chosen to assemble there. The question could be presented informally, or a special meeting could be called, for the purpose of considering it. Sometimes. there would be an ongoing conversation about a particular challenge, that might continue over two or three days.

Most of the time, the Wisdom Table was just a place for conversation, as it was this morning. Hobe and Georgette were soon joined by Caleb and Liz, who were given a standing ovation of welcome home. They found themselves sitting across from Hobe and Georgette. Nate joined them just long enough, he said, to get his order to-go, as business was waiting at the dock.

Yes, it was uncanny, Hobe was saying, that the well had been there all that time on his property and he had never seen it, never noticed it before this. It took a little boy to find it, and then, it was lucky for everybody that the kid didn't fall in the well, what with the weak platform.

"There's plenty of room over here!" called out Jeremy, to Susanna, as she made her entrance. "Sally, Susanna's here! She's ready for her breakfast!"

Sally had now brought breakfast out to the entire table.

"Record time, I'd say, dear Sally! I don't know about the rest of you, but my breakfast is delicious!" said Father.

He began to clap his hands and nodded to the rest of them.

"Maybe if we applaud we can coax the cooks out of the kitchen for a 'thank you.'"

The table followed on and spread around the entire diner, even to those who had no idea what they were applauding. Stewart and Luther appeared in the dining room and made low, exaggerated bows.

Chapter 7

THE CONVERSATION AT THE long table broke into three separate ones. Caleb and Liz were sitting across from Georgette and Hobe.

"Tough day yesterday, Uncle Hobey," said Liz. "I know it must be really hard to leave the farm."

"You don't know the half of it," said Hobe.

His eyes welled up a bit, and Georgette reached over and placed her hand over his.

"Momma and Daddy lived there, all of their lives. When they went there, it was just a little hut, more or less of a log cabin. Fact is, people didn't know, for sure, what it was. A little plywood here, a few two-by-fours there, a few rough-hewn logs, and maybe even a little cardboard. The kitchen was the only thing that was stable. Daddy took his time building, 'cause he knew Momma. If she had her kitchen, she was happy. He was smart that way. We were as poor as church mice, but they saved and saved and built the place right.

"They were still building on it for all the time I was in school, right up to graduation. My room moved three times, during that build! Actually, I had to share a room with Johnny for a while. God, I hated that! He was squirrely, even in those days. He would never go to sleep at night. He'd wake me up at three in the morning.

"He'd come over to my bed. 'Hobe!' he'd holler. And when I pretended not to hear him, he would come over to my bed and yell, 'Hoooh—-barrrt'! He'd wake the entire house.

"It was always some cockamamie something or other that didn't amount to anything, but, I couldn't get back to sleep. I had to get up early to do chores, before I went to school, but Johnny did chores at night; so, when I left the room, he was sawing logs! God, I hated my brother! Only when I got to the war did I realize how much I loved him. I would've

19

traded a three o'clock in the morning wake-up by Johnny to any morning I woke up in 'Nam.'"

Georgette squeezed his hand, as a signal that he had talked enough. For a minute, there was a respectful silence, allowing Hobe's cathartic conversation, a space of its own.

"You've done a lot of work out there, too, Uncle," said Liz. "Daddy often said he wished your farm was in the city limits, so he could get some taxes out of you!"

"That may be comin'," said Georgette, "with so many people wantin' to live here, what with our famous diner and all. People love the Story of Joe and just want to live here where it all took place!"

"Like a holy city!" said Caleb.

"Yeah!" said Hobe, "like a holy city."

"While I have the floor. . ." said Caleb.

"Oh, I'm sorry I talked so long!"

"Caleb!" said Liz. "Uncle Hobe doesn't talk very much!"

She kicked his leg under the table. She had been noticing lately how much Caleb reminded her of her father.

Georgette recognized it too.

"Good Lord!" she said. "You two remind me of Lou and Hope!"

"Don't say that!" said Liz. "I already know that, and I said I would never turn into them when I got married!"

"You could have done worse in having a Daddy! You were . . . you are . . . the apple of his eye!"

"I know. He's the best in the world. And Momma too."

"You've been awful good to them to come home in the summer between college years," said Georgette. "I know you had to go by rules that weren't your own any more, when you did that. It takes a lot of effort to come home and live, after you've had your own independence!"

Liz sighed.

"I wish I could say that it was easy, but it wasn't. Fortunately, most of the time, I held my tongue. When I didn't, I know Daddy felt bad, and I always regretted it. Momma understood, I think, but not Daddy. I've told Caleb that I'll always be Daddy's girl, even after we've been married for twenty years!"

"Liz and I have been talking," Caleb said, lowering his voice a little so as to minimize the chances of what he was about to say being over heard. "We'd like to buy your place. We want to live in the house, but, if you want, you could continue to grow your vegetable garden and farm the place, and we could split the profits, fifty-fifty."

Clearly, Hobart and Georgette were stunned.

"I don't know what to say, Caleb!" said Hobe.

"You two sure you want to live in our old house after all the places you've been and all the things you've seen and done?" asked Georgette.

"Absolutely!" said Liz.

"You can think about it!" said Caleb.

"The only thing is, Georgette wants me to take it easier. I'm not the man I used to be."

"On the other hand, I don't know what Hobe is going to do with himself. He doesn't golf. He doesn't have any hobbies. That farm has been his life. He is already grieving it, and we're not even gone from the place."

"Well, think about it."

"I hate to ask," said Georgette, "but, can you two afford to buy the place?"

"Caleb has inherited a considerable amount of money," said Liz. "We don't want to spend it all in one place, so to speak, but we know we have enough for a down payment."

Hobe's mischievousness emerged.

"How do you know you can afford it? You don't know what I am asking for it!"

"Well, here's the deal. We would give you half of whatever we settle on, as a down payment, in cash. You would stay working the farm and take my half of the profits of the farm while you work it, in payment for the year. I know we can handle it."

"We'll go home and sleep on it!" said Hobe.

"Yes, we'll have to adjust our thinking to do this," said Georgette. "I want to travel, and Hobe will stay right here, if he can get away with it."

"You can always plant crops that will let you get away in the winter to warmer climes!" said Liz.

"Call you tomorrow!" said Georgette. "Give me your cell phone number, dear."

And with that, the conversation melded back together, with the rest of the group, sitting at the Wisdom Table.

Chapter 8

THE LAND AROUND SAFETY Harbor had not been open to settlement, until the turn of the twentieth century. Lincoln County had been established in 1893, but not much was there, at the time. That didn't last long. Fishing industries began to develop quickly, all up and down the coast. Towns were established. Churches were built. Lighthouses sprang up. Post offices appeared. It was clear that the area had a future for those who were coming to live here, although the good fortune of many was at the cost of the indigenous people, especially the Siletz tribe around Safety Harbor.

The farm, that the Watson family had lived on for three generations, was known to the long-timers in town as the old Harrison place. A fellow by the name of Cyrus Harrison had come out from Portland with the fancy idea of creating a waystation for travelers, from Portland and Salem, to the coast. He would have a couple of log cabins for the more well-to-do traveler and a few tents for those who wanted to go, economy class.

The only problem was that Cyrus established his "hotel" two miles off the main road, while it was only a mile and a half, on into Safety Harbor, from the main road. The weary travelers from Portland and Salem, already on the road for three days, calculated that it would be better, just to get on in to town. Those who did come to the encampment, discovered that the tents soon gave way to mud and rain in the winter and offered no real shelter, from the heat in the summer. The traveler assumed that there was food and water to be had. Most were low on supplies, if not out, entirely. But, Cyrus was not a business man. He had not thought that far ahead, and word quickly spread that the waystation was not worth the trouble.

It took two years for Cyrus to realize that he had miscalculated. His dream was not going to happen. But, he couldn't go back home and admit failure. His daddy would not accept any failure among his sons.

Rather than cutting his losses, he went to Bartholomew Grundy, who had grabbed up most of the land, from five miles inland, to the central west coast, and bought eighty adjacent acres, of what Grundy called farmland. If he could not be an innkeeper of sorts, he would be a farmer. Only later, he would discover that about twenty acres of it was farmland. and the rest was all in timber.

Cyrus was about as good a farmer as he was a hotelier. He didn't know what to plant. On top of that, he had no equipment to farm! Once again, he hadn't thought ahead.

Then, he realized that he had sixty acres of harvestable timber. He could sell that! Yes, he could! He went to the lumber company in Mapleton, owned by Bartholomew Grundy, of course. Within two years, the land was a clear-cut scar against the forest that grew around it.

But, Cyrus had his money and he fled the place overnight, leaving behind him a mountain of debt, including the mortgage payment, which was behind by six months.

When Earl Watson came to the area about two years later, he picked up the foreclosed property for a song. It was just in time. Literally, a few months later, property values started to skyrocket, as more people came to town. It was 1926.

When he brought his wife, Winifred, out from McMinnville, to show her the place, she was stunned. There wasn't much there and what was there, wasn't much! Earl had not been able to make a start as a dry goods merchant. There were already two such places in McMinnville, and his never got off the ground. Unlike Cyrus, he knew when to cut his losses. He went looking for work on the coast and ended up in Safety Harbor, where he was told of the availability of the old Harrison place. Now, here they were, just Winnie and him, to make of the place what it would be.

The land had stayed in the Watson family now, for three generations; but of all the children born in the current generation, not one soul was interested in taking over the operation, which, by now, had grown into a successful and prosperous enterprise. For Hobe and Georgette, who had invested their hearts and souls in the whole thing, the demise of the Watson era was a bitter pill to swallow.

That's why it was a welcome offer that had come from Caleb and Liz. Hobe could continue to stay close to the land that he knew even better than the back of his hand, and, at the same time he could be rid of the financial responsibilities, and the upkeep necessary, to keep the place in top condition.

Hobe and Georgette discussed it, on the way home, and called Caleb and Liz that evening, asking them to come out first thing in the morning. Georgette would cook breakfast for everybody, and then, they could get down to the terms of the transaction.

Chapter 9

Bartosh Honecker had purchased the bank from the Cone family about a year and a half after Wendell died. His unusual name had been given him by using the surnames of his parents, Diarmaid Honecker and Hilda Bartosh. Both families boasted of deep roots, in the history of the country. The Bartosh family arrived in Texas around 1850 and the first recorded Honecker stepped onto American soil in 1795.

He was born when his parents were older, after the last of his siblings were grown and gone. His grandmother on his mother's side, never one for subtlety or diplomacy, told him, when she was rocking him on her knee on day, when he was five, that he was an "accident."

"Your parents didn't intend to have any more children. They were ready to enjoy the rest of their lives, and then you came along!" she said.

"Momma," little Bartie said one day, not long after the unfortunate conversation, "am I an accident?"

"Where did you get that idea?"

"Grammy says I was an accident, that you didn't really want me to be born."

Bartosh remembered to this day how, at first, his mother's face turned white, then red, and then, some kind of combination of purple and a color he had never before seen.

"Your grandma doesn't always know what she's talking about," said Hilda. "I think she must have misunderstood what I said."

"What did you say, Momma?"

"Why, I said you were a surprise!"

A s'prise? Why was I a s'prise? You mean, kind of like a present at Christmas time!"

Hilda looked relieved. "Why yes!" she said. "That very thing is true! You were like a Christmas present that we opened, and were delighted with the gift. You are a gift, little Bartie. Yes! That's what you are! A gift!"

Still, the memory of being on his grandmother's knee, telling him he was an accident, had stayed with him, for life. Somehow, he knew that there was more to it than his being a wonderful surprise, as his mother had said. As he grew older, he noticed the age of his parents, compared to those of his friends, and he realized that he had changed all of his parents' plans when he came along. They were the same age as some of his high school friends' grandparents.

And they had doted on him like grandparents, to the consternation of his older siblings. They bought him a car when he was sixteen. They sent him to Austria for his senior year of high school where he stayed with some of his mother's family. Diarmaid had some influence at Harvard and got Bartie into the School of Business.

He lived with great expectations from his parents, and great resentment from his siblings. He wasn't sure he was cut out to have a career in business. He loved history, and thought that he might want to be a teacher. But, the Honecker and the Bartosh families both had roots in the economy of the communities in which they lived, and beyond. As the youngest of the family, doted on and protected, Bartie wasn't sure how to live in the world, without those built-in advantages, and a constant safety net.

Diarmaid got him a job as a business consultant in Chicago, at a law firm that specialized in corporate law. Every day, he went up the elevator a hundred and one floors in the Sears Tower, to his job. And every evening, he went a hundred and one floors down. He did this for five years.

One day, when Diarmaid was in town from their home in Corpus Christi, he had lunch with Bartie.

"Something on your mind, Dad?"

"Well, yes, there is, Bartie."

"What is it?"

His dad hesitated.

"Shoot, Dad! You know we can talk about anything."

"Well, okay." He hesitated a moment more and then he blurted out, "Bartie, are you gay?"

Bart was dumbfounded.

"Well, no, I'm not, but if I was, what's the difference? What would make you ask that, Dad?"

"Are you sure?"

"Yes!"

"Very sure?"

"Quite sure, Dad. Who's spreading this rumor?"

"Your brother, Tad, was in town this last week, and stayed with us, overnight. During dinner, he began to remark about how you have no girlfriends, and how by the time he was thirty, he had three kids!"

My eldest brother has always thought he knew what I should do with my life!"

"Are you dating?"

"Dating? No!" he smiled, trying to laugh the conversation off.

"Why?" asked his father.

"Why what?"

"Why aren't you married, or at least dating?"

"I haven't met anybody yet that I want to marry, and if I wouldn't want to marry them, why would I date them?"

"Well, you won't find anybody if you don't go out, once in a while. You're a good-looking boy. You have money. You have a good future. Why, the women ought to be climbing in the windows of the hundred and first floor to meet you!"

"I want a marriage like Mom's and yours, Dad. I know Tad found a woman right away, or soon enough, anyway. But Alice and he don't really get along. They aren't happy!"

"Your mother and I had our rough patches."

"You mean, like when I was born?"

His father blanched.

"That's still a sore subject in our house. Your mother never forgave Grammy for what she said to you when you were but a wee boy."

"Maybe it bothers Momma because it's true."

"That you were an accident? Why, that's a figure of speech, Bartie, for parents who think their child rearing days are over, only to be surprised, when they turn up expecting. But an accident? No. You were no accident. Why, believe it or not, we were both still so in love that we wanted to make up for lost time, once your older brothers and sisters were out of the house!"

"That's getting close to TMI, Dad!"

"What's TMI?"

"Too much information!"

"Well, it's true. You were born out of your mother's and my deep and passionate love for one another!"

"Then, all at once, you had another screaming baby keeping you awake all hours of the night!"

"We found ways!"

"Now, that *is* too much information, Dad!"

Six months after the conversation, both of his parents were gone. Momma died first. She fell down some stairs, at his sister, Eleanor's house, and never came home from the hospital. Daddy, so grieved at her passing, died of a stroke not a week after she was buried.

The will treated Bartosh generously. He had enough money to leave his job, which he had never liked in the first place. Suddenly, he had the freedom to do whatever he wanted, with no expectations. Of all the places he had been, he had never been to California and the west coast. He had seldom needed a car in Chicago, and when he did, he took a cab, but he knew enough to know that you can't get anywhere in California, or most anyplace in the West, with the exception of Seattle and San Francisco maybe, without your own wheels. So, he bought a car.

He loved Los Angeles, but not its traffic, and he knew he must travel on. Santa Barbara was beautiful, and Santa Maria, too. He went on to Morrow Bay, Big Sur, Monterey, Santa Cruz, and then, headed for San Francisco. He stayed a week. This might be the place, he thought. It might fit his style, being considerably more sophisticated than sprawling Los Angeles. Still, he wanted to see the entire coast.

He drove north casually, and his third day out from San Francisco, he stopped for lunch in a little town called Safety Harbor at a place called Joe's Fine Dine-ing, according to the sign. What an unsophisticated place! People couldn't even spell here. He'd get a sandwich-to-go, hope it was palatable, and then, hightail it, right on out of here.

As he entered, he noticed the interior seemed to be flooded with light, although there weren't any more light fixtures than normal. Oddly enough, the light seemed to be emanating from that rather large stone, almost a boulder, placed to the right of the entrance. A fine piece of art. He wondered how the artist created that kind of effect. Maybe this town isn't so bad, after all.

Then, his eyes lighted upon what he thought was the most beautiful woman he had ever seen! Maybe he'd stay for lunch, after all! There were no seats available, except for one at the long table, where the beautiful woman was sitting. A man, who looked to be in his late fifties, motioned him on over.

"Welcome! Welcome! This is a community table and anybody can sit here! Take this seat right here, if you don't mind sitting by this pretty woman!"

It was Mayor Lou, of course, along with Hope, Father Callaghan, Jeremy, Doc Bailey, Meriwether, Carla, and Mrs. Saugus.

The woman, over which Bartosh had become instantly smitten, was Susanna Kappos the lovely brunette owner of the Argostoli Art Gallery, who had lost her husband, a few years ago. He didn't know if he could sit by her, without shaking. He suddenly became lost for words, knowing that, in a few seconds, he would be incredibly close to this stunning creature. But, he summoned the courage, walked over, and sat down.

"Mayor Lou Schofield!" Lou extended his hand.

"Bartosh Honecker! "But, you can call me Bart!

There was a palpable relief at the table and laughter too. Everyone went around and told him their names. He feigned interest, but couldn't wait to hear her name.

"Susanna," she said, as she extended her hand.

"Susanna!" he said slowly in reply.

"No, I'm Susanna. You're Bartosh!" She laughed.

The woman looked amused, as if she knew he was taken with her, and that it embarrassed him. He felt like he was back in Middle School again. Their eyes met and for a moment, everything around Bartosh stood still. He couldn't tell how much time had passed but, he suddenly realized that, most likely, he had been holding the woman's hand too long, maybe even way too long.

"Susanna is the only cultured person in town," said Lou.

"Speak for yourself, Mayor," said Father Callaghan. "Your wife leaves you in the dust when it comes to culture."

"That's right, Mayor!" said Mrs. Saugus.

"Well, she does own the art gallery!" Hope had said. "I'll give my husband that!"

So, not only beautiful, but cultured! He tried to see if she was wearing a wedding ring.

"And she's not married!" said Sally, coming up behind them to take Bartosh's order. Did she see him peering at her left hand? Uncanny!

"Sally!" said Susanna in a mock scolding tone.

When he heard her voice again, he thought he would faint.

"May I recommend Susanna's Special?" asked Sally, sensing the stranger's attraction to her friend.

Susanna turned and rolled her eyes at Sally, but Sally did not let up.

"Susanna recommended it, and now, we serve it all day!"

Bartosh did not know whether he could find his voice or not.

"Sure! That'll be fine!"

"Susanna's Special it is!" she said.

Bartosh did not remember the rest of the conversation, so near was the woman, for whom he had instantly fallen, head over heels. He didn't want the meal to end. He had hoped Susanna and he might have some time to talk, but, she turned to go. Immediately, he felt let down, thinking that he would never see her again.

Maybe he would take a little look around town and see what the place was like. Maybe he would even find the art gallery. He was delighted to find that such a small community seemed so self-contained. Everything you needed was right here. He decided to stop at Marlene Brooker's Real Estate and Antiques, to see what might be for sale.

Chapter 10

MARLENE BROOKER WAS A middle-aged, well-dressed, friendly, but all-business kind of person. She had well-coiffed hair and wore a powerful perfume, the latter of which practically filled her office. She had an intensity that indicated she was ready to sell anything at a moment's notice. For the discriminating customer, she had just the thing for you, whether it was a house, a condo, a business, or a fine piece of furniture of impeccable provenance, that had been owned by somebody's great-great grandmother, and came west on the Oregon Trail.

She showed great interest in Bartosh. She could always smell money.

"Welcome to Brooker's! How may I help you?"

She extended her hand and took Bart's hand firmly in hers, now sandwiching it with her other hand.

"Are you interested in real estate, antiques, or both?"

"I just had lunch at Joe's on my way to Seattle. Your little town is interesting, so I thought I'd take a little look around, afterward."

"Are you thinking about moving? Where is your home now?"

"Well, I don't really have a home. I'm just traveling the West, to see where I might want to land, or maybe I'll just go back to Chicago. I don't know yet."

"Safety Harbor is a good place to live, and we have several good homes available, and even a couple of businesses."

"What kind of businesses?"

"Well, there is a fitness gym for sale."

She didn't tell him that the owner of the business couldn't make a go of it, and was going through foreclosure. She'd seen businesses brought back from the brink before in this town.

"And, the bank is for sale too!"

Bartosh jumped at the chance of buying the bank. Marlene and he spent the afternoon together. She introduced him to the interim president of the bank, and they looked at three rentals and two homes that were for sale.

"I'll sleep on it," he said.

"Why don't you sleep on it, right here in town?" she had asked.

"It's the height of tourist season. I doubt there'll be a place to sleep around here!"

"I have connections!"

He spent the night on Nate's houseboat as his guest. Nate and the two kids gave him a warm welcome. He spent some time with Nate when Caitlin and Buddy had gone to sleep. After they had talked a couple of hours, he knew that he wouldn't need to sleep on his decision.

The next morning, he went to Brooker's, rented a condo, and arranged to buy the bank.

That had been over two years ago, now. Seattle would have to wait.

Chapter 11

THE EVENING OF THE day that Caleb and Liz had talked to Hobe and Georgette about buying the Old Eighty, Rock and Magdalena joined them for dinner, at Lou and Hope's. They gathered in the back yard. Hope had spread a welcoming table on the patio. Lou was barbequing steaks. As they sizzled, they sat under the shade of the old oak tree, that Liz had climbed when she was a girl.

"Gee, it's good to have you kids all together again. It's like old times!" said Lou.

"Someday, these will be the good old days, Daddy!" said Liz.

"They are all good days as long as you are with us!" said Hope.

"You know, there's a new fellow in town who owns the bank. His name is Bartimaeus Holnecker, or something like that."

"Bartosh Honecker, Mr. Mayor," said Rock, with a slight smile and a sideways glance at Liz.

"We've had him down to the Unsettlement for dinner, he and Susanna," said Magdalena.

"Susanna? Susanna!" Liz fairly screamed.

"Yes, Susanna," said Magdalena. "Bartosh, or Bart, as we call him, stopped by Joe's for lunch on his way through town. He met Susanna and never left!"

"Susanna took some persuading," said Hope. "She wasn't sure she was ready, but Bartosh was persistent. I'll give him credit for that. He treated her with such respect and deference that, finally, she could no longer resist. They've been an item now for about a year."

"Well, the thing is," said Lou, "I've invited them to join us for dinner."

"I'm sorry, kids," said Hope. "He did that without consulting me! He just sprang that on me, tonight!"

"Oh, that's fine, Mrs. Schofield, uh, Mom," Caleb smiled. "We may need a banker before we're through talking tonight!"

"And, of course, I've invited Frank as well," said Lou

The doorbell rang. Soon, Hope returned with Susanna and Bart.

When Magdalena and Liz saw Bart, they looked at one another approvingly.

There were hugs and hearty greetings all around.

Lou called everyone to attention and said, "Caleb and Liz, I'd like to introduce you to Bar . . . Bar. . ."

"Bartosh, Mr. Schofield," said Bart, patiently."Bartosh Honecker."

Liz whispered in Susanna's ear. "Ya done good!"

Susanna smiled. "Ya think?"

"Oh, yeah, I think!"

"Now, say, where's Frank, for God's sake? I've never known him to miss a meal!" exclaimed Lou.

"Right here, Mr. Mayor," Father Callaghan had let himself in, and performed his usual exaggerated bow.

"Would you like a glass of wine, Father?" asked Liz.

"I could never turn it down, the fine quality of wine you serve here!"

The group naturally formed a circle. There was congenial small talk for about another half hour, after which Hope called them to the table.

"Bless us, O Lord. . ." Lou said the blessing.

"Daddy, I've never heard you pray before!" said Liz.

"It's my good influence on him!" Father's eyes twinkled.

Lou became suddenly serious. "Well, that's partly true, Frank, but I have to give a lot of credit to my illness."

"How are you, Lou? asked Susanna.

"I've been better. I've been worse. Right now, Doc says my tumors have shrunk, but they're not gone. Not completely. Not yet anyway. They may never leave, but they're under control.

"You know, the evening of the day after Joe left us, that night, I was standing in my office watching Nate's new boat, sailing across the waters, and the backdrop of the beautiful sunset, I heard Wendell's voice say to me, 'Don't waste any time, Lou, not any time at all'. I heard it as plain as if he had been standing there, right behind me. In a way, you might say I've gotten religion, of a sort. Yes, you might say so!"

Then his demeanor changed suddenly. He was always uncomfortable talking about such things.

"Well, that's enough of that. Somebody pass the potatoes, will ya?"

The group silently passed food around the table. Liz and Hope's eyes were wet. A tear flowed down Susanna's cheek.

"I'm anxious to hear about the Unsettlement!" said Liz.

There was a moment of silence before Rocky began.

"The real truth of the matter, the thing is. . ."

"What he's trying to say, Liz, is that we're in trouble!

"In trouble?"

"We've got about six weeks to get our act together, or we're going to be closed down. We've got the grant for you, but we don't have much of any other money. We have no choice. The county is evicting us, and, so far, there is no place to go."

Well!" said Liz. "It looks as if I have my work cut out for me!"

"I'm so sorry, Liz. I wanted to tell you, but I worried that if I told you, you wouldn't come; and if you didn't come, well then, I knew there'd be no chance!"

"I would have come anyway," said Liz, "and I'm especially glad that I'm here now, because I've got some skills to help you with this, and [she smiled], "I still have few connections around town!"

Then, without missing a beat, she said, "Caleb and I are in serious discussions with Uncle Hobey and Georgette to buy their place!"

Lou looked as if he had swallowed a bird. "All of it? The whole thing? You mean the house, or all of it?"

"We want to buy it all. We're going out to see them in the morning, and we're going to find out!"

"What's he asking for it?"

"Lou!" Hope scolded. "That's none of our business!"

"Oh, that's okay, Mom!" said Caleb. "We haven't signed papers and when we do, you can ask again."

Liz was amazed. He was good with her dad. He had just let him off the hook and, at the same time, had told him nothing!

Chapter 12

THE NEXT MORNING, CALEB and Liz joined Hobe and Georgette, at the Old Eighty.

"The first thing you should know," said Georgette, "is that we've signed a real estate contract with Marlene Brooker in town, so any deal we make will have to go through her."

"Yes, but I think we can work out the details here and let her know what they are. She doesn't care as long as she gets the commission!"

"Hobart!"

"It's true! Yes, it is!"

"I've been looking at the values of property around the area," said Caleb, "and you've got a very valuable piece of land here, especially with the house and farm buildings. Have you talked to. . .

"Marlene?"

"Yes, Marlene, about what the asking price ought to be?"

"She hasn't put an ad out on it yet, but I think she had two different sales in mind. She thought we could get more, if I sold the land and the buildings, separate."

"Well, you probably could, Uncle Hobey."

"Yes, we probably could," said Georgette, "but the opportunity for Hobe to stay on the land . . . that, and knowing that it will be taken care of, especially my house, especially my kitchen, is worth some money. You never know. A developer could buy this land, cut it up in pieces, and demolish the house. Nobody would ever know all of this had ever been here!"

They settled on a million dollars for the eighty acres of land, and three hundred thousand for the house and buildings. Hobe would call Marlene later in the morning, and let her know the details. Caleb and Liz would go and see Bart Honecker, at the bank, as soon as they could get an appointment.

After breakfast and an extended conversation, around the breakfast table, the four of them went out to take a look at what two of them had sold, and the other two had purchased.

"There's only one thing that I'm concerned about."

"What's that, Uncle Hobey?"

"That well. I can't believe I didn't know about it all of these years, but I never saw it there. I can't believe one of the livestock didn't stumble and fall into it. You'll see the problem in a minute."

They went through the passageway the cattle use to go into the barn.

"Watch your step!" said Hobe, smiling.

"By the way, we'll have those cattle and all the other creatures around here sold, well before you get here," said Georgette.

"Take your time with that," said Liz. "Maybe we'll want to keep an active farm!"

"My Hobe is retiring from the cattle business, and that's final!" said Georgette.

"I think she means it, Uncle Hobey!" said Liz.

Hobe, pointed to the well, which was now in sight. "The water has risen, and it's flowing over the top of the new platform. Now, a spring has started flowing just on the other side of the well. I don't know what we're going to do about it, if this continues. The water has to go somewhere."

They walked closer.

"That spring has gotten stronger, since just last night," said Hobe.

"Good heavens! I hope it's not going to flow toward the house," said Georgette.

"No," said Hobe. "The incline is downhill from the house. It's going to head toward Safety Harbor, unless it's diverted. It will take a while to get there, but if this continues. . ."

"What are you thinking, Caleb?" asked Liz. "I can always tell when those wheels are turning!"

"I am thinking about the Gihon Springs, back home, in the Kidron Valley."

"Oh yes, the one that fed the Pool of Siloam! Your people call it the Virgin's Fountain!'"

"That's the one! This reminds me of it, for some reason."

"I don't think this is going away anytime soon," said Hobe. "The flow is getting stronger."

Chapter 13

Stewart and Katye now lived in the old lighthouse keeper's residence. It had been restored to its original condition by the Cone Foundation, and donated to the City of Safety Harbor.

With Stewart's history in the lighthouse, in the Time of Joe, he was asked to be the attendant at the lighthouse, and to schedule times for it to be open to the public.

Early each morning, Stewart would climb the spiral steps of the lighthouse, leading to the watch room, where he had waited for the return of the pilgrims, who had gone to search for Joe. It gave him comfort and a sense of connection to the time, that many now viewed as Sacred Time, or simply Joe Time, as Little Therese called it. The image of the little boat with tattered sails containing Joe and the pilgrims, coming into harbor, was marked, indelibly, upon his mind.

He found peace here, albeit for a few moments of the day. He breathed in the fresh salt air, around him. It replenished his being. Mostly, he would sit quietly, with his eyes closed. He had learned from Little Therese that one could see as much, without seeing, and sometimes more. The watch room was suspended, between heaven and earth. The holy fire had been installed in the lamp of this lighthouse and he realized that, whatever he did here, whatever he thought here, whatever he felt here, whatever he spoke here, was sacred. Joe had not visited him, as in the old Sacred Time, although he hoped and longed for it.

His rituals were ones of the cycle of nature, as the sun rose each morning, as the tides rolled in and out. He took note of his own inward cycles, as well. He had never noticed them, before this. He had been too busy tending to others.

"Now is all there is," he had once overheard someone say.

He was almost sure he overheard it, or perhaps, the voice came from within his own head.

As for Katye, she had become the Dean of Students at Coast Range Community College. Her popularity continued to grow, and her cheerful heart won her the affection of many.

It was no surprise, then, that she had been asked to be the permanent organizer of the city parade, which, by now, had become known as the Joe Parade. Each year she asked the now-retired school principal, Mrs. Saugus to be her assistant.

Susanna had taken seriously, her assignment to be in charge of beauty in the Gate of Light City. She had approached each merchant and store owner about what they could do to improve the attractiveness of their property. She employed Marlene Brooker to help with what Marlene called "curb appeal." Susanna established a fund to provide money and resources to those who could not afford to improve their property. As a result, some estimated that three times as many flowers were growing in town. Each store had a new paint job. Bright colors had often been chosen, and, the whole city literally gleamed when the sun was out. The diner remained white with red trim around its three bay windows. When the sun was not out, the gloomy days, of which there were plenty, were brightened by the bold and blazing mix of colors, that was Safety Harbor.

The Joe Team, composed of all of those who were deeply involved in the search, and the subsequent finding of Joe, met in the diner, as needed. Not everyone could come every time but whoever showed up was considered a quorum. Their agenda was to ensure that they were being faithful to Joe's Plan for the community, to be a Gate of Light.

There could be no doubt that, in four short years, that Safety Harbor had become a different place, an even better place than it ever had been.

Chapter 14

THE THIRD DAY AFTER Caleb and Liz arrived in Safety Harbor, they traveled to the Unsettlement. A large number of the population had assembled to meet them, in the community tent, where a generous breakfast waited to be consumed.

"This is amazing!" said Liz, hugging Magdalena.

"Yes, thanks very much!" said Caleb, opening his arms wide for a group hug with Rock, Magdalena, and Liz. Others gathered around to greet the couple, even before they got into the tent.

"Welcome!" said Magdalena. "We are so glad you are here. We are going to introduce you to this crowd, before breakfast. Come on up to the microphone."

"Good people!" said Rock, addressing the crowd. "We are welcoming our new community organizer and her husband this morning. Will you come forward, Liz and Caleb?"

They were greeted with a standing ovation.

"As you know," said Magdalena, moving behind the microphone, "we are facing some critical challenges in the next few weeks. We are so glad Liz is among us now, to help us.

Rock continued. "Magdalena and I will be meeting with Caleb and Liz, this morning, after breakfast, to talk about our future. You are welcome to sit in, if you can afford the time. We'll ask you to hold your questions and comments until later, when we have another meeting."

"I want to say what a great privilege it is to be with you," Liz began. "As you know, I grew up not far from here, and came home each summer, from college and grad school, until I married this man! We've been in Palestine and Israel over the last three years. working among the people. But, once we'd been here for the wedding three years ago, Caleb fell in love with Safety Harbor, and the Unsettlement as well.

"We always wanted to come back. So, when you asked me to come as your community organizer, I was overjoyed. Just two weeks before Magdalena called, Doc Bailey and Dr. Habibi [That's my Caleb!] had talked on the phone, and Caleb agreed to come out and help at the hospital. The timing couldn't have been better!

"I know you . . .we. . .are in a bit of trouble right now. The best thing we can do is to face reality, and work with the hand we have been dealt, together. We'll keep you all informed, and we will be completely transparent in all we do. Thank you."

On the way home, Liz said to Caleb, "We are going to have to work fast on this. Rock and Magdalena are inspirational leaders, but they need a lot of help, when it comes to details. I don't know if we can pull this out or not."

"You keep saying 'we', I notice!" Caleb smiled.

God, she loved it when he smiled!

"Don't smile like that if you want me to talk seriously with you!"

"What do you want? A frown?"

"Just a regular face so I can keep my mind on things!"

"Okay. Here it is." He made a face.

She cracked up and pretended to slap him, playfully.

"Hey! I have to drive! Watch it!" he said, smiling again. "Seriously, do you have a plan in mind?"

"Right now, I haven't the slightest idea what to do! But we won't let anybody know that, will we?"

Chapter 15

AFTER THEIR DIVORCE, WHICH had been filled with spite and umbrage, Jens and Shirley had come back together, during the time of the search for Joe. They lived together three years, before asking Meriwether to re-tie the knot last year. They had held off until Shirley was as certain as she could be, that Jens's days of drinking and womanizing were in the past. One slip and he was out, she had told him.

They had purchased a triple-wide mobile home, and had set it on some land that was owned by Shirley's uncle, on the north side of town, just beyond the golf course. Shirley had planted flowers in front of the house. Jens planted some trees that lined both sides of the driveway, along with three lilac bushes, about ten yards out from the front of the house, setting the house off from the rest of the acreage. The house was situated back from the road, affording them the privacy that they so craved.

Shirley continued to work at the police station as receptionist, administrative assistant, and dispatcher. Jens had signed on as an over-the-road hauler, and was gone sometimes for ten or fifteen days at a time, and then, was home, for five or six. Shirley had remarked to Carmelita that this worked out fine for her, since, when he was underfoot for very long, they had their troubles.

"I'm always glad when he comes home, and I'm just as glad when he leaves!" she confided.

Jens continued to be clean and sober, Shirley said. At least he claimed to be.

When Jens went back to Shirley, Roy lost his roommate. He had moved in with his sister, Ruth, and his niece, Little Therese. He had made some improvements, especially since Jens was back with Shirley. Drinking, for Roy, was social, and if he didn't have anyone to drink with, he usually didn't drink. Then, too, he had found a job, as a fork-lift operator, at the lumber yard in Mapleton. He was tired when he came home.

Little Therese was still a mediating influence on his behavior. Ever since the parade, when she had unwittingly shamed him into doing the right thing, they had been tight. She had always seemed to have wisdom beyond her age. She never offered him advice, directly, but he found after talking to her, at times, he not only became a better person, he wanted to be a better person.

The School for the Blind had closed two years ago, and the students went back to their communities, to be mainstreamed into the local school system. Little Therese, already a celebrity, of sorts, made friends easily in her new school.

Chapter 16

WHEN THEY GOT BACK from the Unsettlement, Caleb and Liz met Hobe and Georgette, out at the Old Eighty, to sign papers.

"Before we get down to business," said Marlene, "let's take a tour of the place."

They got in Marlene's Ford Explorer.

"Hobe, I'll depend upon you to give me directions, around the farm."

At Marlene's insistence, they went over every known road on the Old Eighty.

"By Jiminy, Marlene, I saw things about the place I hadn't ever stopped long enough to see before! I must say, you are good at your job." said Hobe.

"Oh, we still have to look at the buildings," she said. "That's very important."

"I think it's at least important that we look at the old well," said Caleb.

"After we look at the buildings!"

"Oh, sure!" said Liz, casting an eye at Caleb. "I think you are right, Marlene," said Liz. "The buildings are relevant to the sale. The well isn't!"

"The well sure is going to be important," said Caleb. "It's going to be ours to live with for a long time. What's going on with it right now, Hobe?"

Let's get through the buildings first," said Marlene. "Then, we'll look at the well. After all, I have to earn my money!"

To the northeast, adjacent to the large lawn behind the house, was Hobe's oversized tool shed, and a one car garage. The first thing you noticed when you headed south of the house toward the farm buildings was the working windmill. Behind it was a horse tank, a small pasture, and a stable, where Hobe kept his horses. An old corn crib, probably one of the few still operative anywhere around, was directly south of that. A hog house was right behind it, which Hobe used to store small hay bales, to feed the horses. By now, the large barn, clearly the most prominent building on the farm other than the house, loomed ahead. The haymow took up the second floor. The large door on the second story was open, with bales of hay stored upstairs, clearly visible.

"I'm probably the last holdout on using the old-style square bales," said Hobe. "I have a hay baler my daddy bought, and I enjoy using it. I resisted the big round bales, and now I resist those little junior square bales they're making. I do like my farm toys, but Georgette has kept me on the straight and narrow. If a piece of equipment still works, we use it. Why, I've got an old Ford tractor over there that just had its fifty-second birthday!"

Hobe pointed toward the large metal machine shop and farm equipment storage, the only metal building on the place. All the others were wood, and had been kept up well.

They proceeded behind the barn. The well and the spring were in plain view.

Chapter 17

EARLY THE NEXT MORNING, when Hobe went out to look at the well and the spring, the volume of water had increased significantly, since last night. The ground around it had become completely saturated, and a pool was now forming within the pasture, just to the west.

Within another fifty yards, the land began a significant downward grade, and the water would, predictably, continue to flow toward the path of least resistance. At this rate, by tomorrow, the water could very well reach Mrs. Saugus's property. The make-up of the topography was mostly rock and bedrock, and remained largely unused. The land continued its rather steep descent, until it reached the foothills which cradled Safety Harbor, as it stretched toward the city.

His first thought was to call Caleb and Liz.

"You might want to come out and take a look," Hobe said to Liz. "One of you, at least. There's more water all the time."

Caleb and Liz asked Hope and Lou to accompany them. The four arrived at the farm around ten thirty. Lou and Hope arrived at the same time.

"Now, how did he know we were meeting?" asked Caleb, incredulously.

"He's been this way all his life," said Liz. "I quit trying to figure it out!"

Hobe met them, at the car.

"I wanted you to see this," said Hobe. "It's going to change things completely around here. Very soon, this won't be the same land that you bought only a few hours ago."

"Oh, we still want the place," said Caleb. "We'll see what we have to do to fix this."

"The thing is," said Hobe," that well just seemed to appear, out of nowhere. I didn't know it was there, and I grew up on this place. I never heard anybody talk about a well, and Georgette and I haven't known of it, all the years we lived on the place. When we did discover it, during the sale, it was dry and nearly wide open. I am sure thankful that little boy didn't fall in. It had to be here, all this time, but, how could we have missed it? I don't know!"

"It looks as if the well and the spring are gradually becoming one flow of water," said Liz.

"I see what you mean," said Lou.

"There are several things to be concerned about here, it seems to me," said Liz.

"What are you thinking, honey?" her husband asked.

"It all depends, of course, on whether the spring keeps flowing."

"I think we have to assume it will," said Georgette, who had joined them by now. "If it doesn't, we have no problem. But, we need to be prepared."

So, what are you thinking, Liz?" her husband asked again.

"There is the entire question of all of this water on our property; then the two properties between Safety Harbor and us; and finally, if it reaches Safety Harbor. Then, that's Daddy's problem," she said.

"Who owns the property between here and Safety Harbor?" asked Caleb.

"Frances Saugus lives on the property, adjacent to us," said Hobe. "Bill and she moved there years ago. He died a decade ago. The other one is owned by some outfit, from out of town."

"We'd better let her know about this, right away!" said Georgette.

"Hope and I will stop there on our way home to let her know," said Lou. "And I'll ask Pinna, my able administrative assistant, to call the county and see who owns that other property."

"Let Frances know she is welcome to come up and take a look at what's going on here, anytime she wants," said Georgette. "Tell her to call ahead though. We're getting our condo ready in town, and we're not here as much as we used to be."

"I still can't figure out why none of us have ever seen this before. How could we have missed it?" Hobe slapped himself on the forehead.

You know," said Lou, "somebody ought to get hold of Ruby and ask her if any of her people know anything about this. They were here long before any of us were."

"Ruby?" asked Caleb.

"Ruby Malone," said Hope. "Lou knows her well. She's one of the leaders of the Siletz Confederation. I'll make sure he calls her. He's got so much to do all ready. The election is coming up in November, you know, and several people are thinking about running."

"For mayor?" asked Georgette. "How can they even think about running against you, Lou?"

"That's what I wonder." Lou smiled. "You'll be in town by then. Make sure you vote for me! Hobe too!"

"Oh, you can be sure of that, Mr. Mayor!" said Georgette. "I'll be looking for something to do. Maybe I can volunteer!"

"Let's get going!" said Liz. "We all have work to do!"

Chapter 18

THE NEXT MORNING, AROUND 10:00 a.m., Lou went to the Siletz Confederation Museum and Gift Shop.

"Ruby!" he said. "I was hoping to find you here!"

"What more could you white people possibly want from us?" she said, only half-jokingly. "You have everything, all ready!"

"I need to talk. I have some questions to ask you, and they are of an urgent nature."

"Do we need to go somewhere else?"

"Can you get free?"

"I have my day clerk here. I'll put her in charge."

"Let's go to Joe's!"

"Let's walk, Lou. It's good for you!"

As they began their ascent from the museum near the beach, Ruby asked, "What's on your mind, Lou?"

She walked with an easy gait, while Lou struggled to catch his breath.

"Do you know how steep this climb is, Ruby? A true friend would not ask me to walk and talk at the same time under these circumstances!"

"You're going to have to get in better shape, Lou! The white intruders never would have beaten us, if they had all been in your condition!"

He smiled good-naturedly. He had been slow to come around to Hope's and Liz's health food cooking. He was doing better, but sometime he'd go into the pastry shop about once a week, and ask, "Any free samples here, Ari? If Hope asks if I'm spending money on good stuff like this, I want to be able to tell her 'No'!"

They sat down at the Wisdom Table.

"What'll you have?" asked Sally.

"What's healthy?" asked Lou, smiling good-naturedly. "Then, I can choose something else!"

They both settled on coffee and a bagel.

"What's on your mind, Lou? I can't be gone too long."

"Do you know anything about the old Harrison place where the Watsons have lived now for several generations?"

"I might. Depends on what you're asking."

"Do you know anything about an old well on the place?"

"How do you know about it?"

"So, you do have some information about it?

"That well's been lost for years. Those who knew where it was are now long gone to the ancestors. As early as the time Harrison was on that land, he didn't know anything about it, or maybe he wouldn't have gone out of business."

"What's the story, friend?" asked Lou.

"Before I answer that question, why do you ask?"

"The day of the auction, somebody, a little boy, I think, discovered what he called a 'hole in the ground'! When he took his dad to see it, he recognized it as an old well. It was covered over with a wood platform, but it was so rickety, it's a wonder the kid didn't fall in."

"Where is it, Lou?"

"It's up behind the barn. The thing is, Hobe was going to just cover it over, but the next morning, after the sale, he went up to look at it again, and found water spilling out of it."

"Go on, Lou. Go on."

"Well, it was the next day, I think, when Hobe noticed a spring bubbling up just about six feet from the well."

Ruby did not respond for a moment, but, when she did, she asked, "May we go see it, Lou?

"Sure, you can go and see it anytime. I'm sure Hobe and Georgette won't mind."

"No, Lou, I mean right now. You and me."

"Well, of course we can go, Ruby. I should have driven up here, though. Now, we'll have to walk back and get the car."

"You can go get your car! It'll be good for you! I'll wait here! I haven't finished my coffee yet."

Lou pulled out a ten-dollar bill.

"I'm payin'."

"Okay," she said. "See you soon!"

He called Hope on the way down to get his car.

"I'm going out to the Old Eighty."

"What for?"

"I am taking Ruby out there. I think we might be onto something!"

"What does that mean, Dear?"

"It means that I'm a hundred and one percent sure that Ruby knows something about that well, and the spring right next to it."

"Do you want some company?"

"Oh, that would be just fine! I'll stop and pick you up. Is Liz there?"

"No, she's gone down to the Unsettlement. And Caleb is at the hospital."

"Well, it'll be just you and me, then. And Ruby, of course. I always forget everyone else when I'm around you!"

"You think that works, do you?"

He could feel her smiling.

"It has so far!"

"You're a dog, Lou Schofield!"

"I'm out in front of the house. Come on out or I'm coming in for you!"

Chapter 19

WITH THE COUNTY'S REFUSAL to budge on the six-week notice given to the Unsettlement, Liz would have to have a 'come to Jesus' talk with Rock and Magdalena, about the real possibility of their experiment having to come to an end, if there was no alternative location to be found. She headed down to the Unsettlement to give the bad news to them.

"I just find it hard to admit that I haven't been able to bring myself to tell the people that they could be on their own. I know I should have," said Magdalena.

"I think it's that we were hoping when you got here, things would be better. I have to admit that for myself, at least," said Rock.

"I wish it were that simple," said Liz.

"We know it's not, Liz. We know that."

Their conversation was interrupted by Liz's phone.

"It's Daddy," she said.

"Hello, Liz?"

"Can you hear me?"

"Of course, I can hear you, Daddy! What do you want, Daddy?"

"Can't I just call my daughter because I love her?"

"Yes, you may. But, somehow I don't you called for that reason."

"Well, not entirely, anyway."

"I'm talking to Rock and Magdalena right now, about the future of the Unsettlement. So, if you could get to the point, dear Daddy, I'd be grateful."

"Give them my best! They are wonderful kids! We love them, Hope and I do."

"I'll do that, Daddy. Now, to your point?"

"I'd like to know if you could meet us up at your new home. Your mother and I are headed up there, along with Ruby."

"Ruby?"

"Yes, she may have some insight on that spring out behind the barn that seems to be growing in volume, by the hour. Can you come?"

"In a few minutes. I think we're about through here."

"Well, come as quick as you can. Where's Caleb?"

"He's either at the bank or the hospital. I'm not sure."

"See if he can come."

"Okay. But he may not be available on such short notice. I'll see."

"Hurry! We're almost there!"

"Soon as I can, Daddy. Soon as I can!"

On a whim, she asked Rock and Magdalena if they wanted to accompany her.

"It'll be good to get away from all this for a little while," said Magdalena.

The three of them got into Liz's car, and headed toward the Old Eighty.

Chapter 20

The Watsons were waiting in the front yard.

Liz, Magdalena, and Rock arrived, soon after Lou, Hope, and Ruby.

"You must have flown low!" said Lou.

Liz chose to ignore him.

Folks," said Lou, "allow me to introduce you to Ruby. Ruby Malone. She manages the Siletz Confederation Museum and Gift Shop in Safety Harbor, and she's some big mucky-muck for the Confederation, too!"

"To be precise, I'm the Assistant General Manager of the Confederated Tribes and I serve as an attorney for the confederation."

"Mucky-muck, Daddy! Honestly, I think we've met before, Ruby," she said, "when you were involved in the search for Joe."

"Ruby thinks she might have some idea of what that well and spring is all about," said Lou.

"Sure," said Hobe. "Let's go on out there! I'll tell you, the amount of water coming out of that spring is considerably more than last night! It's growing, all the time."

Liz noticed that Ruby's face countenance had begun to shine.

"What is it, Ruby?"

"We are near the Sacred Spring. I can feel it!" she said.

They walked into the cattle pen, beside the barn, and then, beyond it.

Liz was startled at what she saw. The volume of water coming out of the spring must have increased three or four times.

Ruby rushed up to the spring ahead of the others. She stood before it as transfixed. Liz thought she might be bowing ever slightly.

"This is it! It has to be it!" exclaimed Ruby.

"What is it?" asked Lou.

"It's the long lost legendary Sacred Spring of our people! It has to be!"

"How do you know that?" asked Georgette. "I have lived here all our married life, and Hobe, for all of his adult life. None of us have ever seen the well and certainly knew of no spring, around here! The wildlife coming out of the woods, would have certainly found the water, if it had been here."

"I think you are right, Georgette," said Lou.

"Well, it is here now!" said Liz. "But Ruby, I'm anxious to find out if there is story attached to this site."

"If this is the place, then, there is. Yes."

"How will you know?"

"There's an old storyteller by the name of Roy Legband. He lives way out in the woods, by himself. Only comes in for food and to gamble a little, sometimes. He's squatting, out on some land. He says he isn't squatting because, as he puts it, 'How can you squat on something that was yours in the first place?' He claims to be the heir of earlier storytellers, who chose him to commit the tribe's stories to memory. But, he's a little crazy and nobody knows for sure whether some of the stories are true. I'd listen to him every year when we got together for pow-wow. The story of the Sacred Spring: he's always told that story, and it hasn't changed at all over the years. I almost have it memorized, myself."

"Tell us, Ruby! Tell us," said Liz.

Ruby stood in front of the spring and the stream that led away from it, as if she were involved in some kind of well-practiced and oft-repeated ritual.

Chapter 21

THE EARLIEST WHITE PEOPLE *to arrive in the territory, were those who intended to change our connection to the earth and to the sky, and to bring to us what they called 'civilization'. The white men's ways were unknown to us, and we did not take kindly to their efforts to change us. But, they were very powerful, because of their weapons; and just a few of them could overcome us. It was clear that they wanted our land, and would take it from us, by any means. The man who took our spring was Zechariah Dodge.*

One day, a party of white people came through, on their way to what is now known as the Willamette Valley. Zechariah Dodge stayed on. He decided he wanted the land where the great spring bubbled up out of the ground, that watered all that was around it, making it a lush and prosperous place. Animals came there to drink, vegetation grew all around it, and our people drew from its great abundance.

One evening, when the women of the tribe had come to get water from the spring, they were met by six white men with drawn guns. They would not allow the women to take any water back with them. The spring was closed off to every living thing, except the white men, and their horses.

In a short time, the Sacred Spring began to dry up. Soon, there was no water coming out of the ground at all. This angered Dodge and his men, as they had made all of their plans around the spring. They dug a well beside the dried-up spring, but, it was folly. The well was dry. No water could be found. Soon, they moved away.

The disappearance of the Sacred Spring meant that the water, that was once there for all living things, was gone. So, we had to leave the immediate area and go down and live by the Tutuni River. No one inhabited the area of the sacred spring; and in two generations, no one remembered where the spring was, anymore. It was lost, to all succeeding generations.

Our ancestors tell us that a great flood came one Spring and the heavy rain washed rich land from the forests down into the bottomland all over the area we once inhabited. Any chance that the spring might be seen, or that Dodge's well would be found, was gone.

But, our story-tellers say, there will come a day when the Sacred Spring will reappear. It will be when the hearts of people are no longer hardened toward one another, and the springs of love and compassion, from an open heart, will flow once more in the land.

After Ruby had told her story, there was silence, as everyone realized the profound significance of this event, and of this place, where they were standing. The Siletz story said that the spring would come back when the hearts of people were open to one another. Was this such a time? Could such a thing really be, after all these years? Could there be, now, an era of peace and harmony among people, among the people of Safety Harbor, and all of those who lived in and around her?

Liz broke the silence. "I am deeply moved by your story, Ruby. I know all of us are. What a privilege it is to see the Sacred Spring come to life again."

Chapter 22

THE NEXT MORNING. THE Wisdom Table was filled. Caleb and Liz, Hope and Lou, Hobe and Georgette, Rock and Magdalena, Jeremy and Samir, Bart and Susanna, Ruby Malone, Father Callaghan, and Marlene Brooker, were all there. Frances Saugus was absent.

Sally's eyes showed absolute panic as she saw them all assembling together in such a short time.

"No worries, Sally," said Carla. "We're gonna be here a while. Take your time!"

Katye emerged from the kitchen.

"Hey!" said Magdalena. "We didn't know you were here!"

"Oh, Stewart is pitiful this morning! I thought I would come down and give the boys a hand!"

"Speak for Stewart only!" called out Luther.

"Oh, I am! I am!"

People noticed, and were grateful to see that the easy way there had once been between Stewart and Katye, was now returning. They were on the mend.

Sally had just finished taking all of their orders, after maneuvering her way between conversations.

"I'll be back with these as soon as I can!"

"With Katye in the kitchen, I'm sure that's true," said Lou. "Otherwise, if the erstwhile clergy, Luther and Stewart, were the only cooks, I'd be skeptical!

"Now, the reason we are here . . ."

Liz placed her hand firmly on one of Lou's hands while Liz placed one of her feet, firmly, on his.

"I think we should start with Ruby," said Hobe. "Her people go back a lot farther than we do on this land."

Ruby had been silent since the gathering began.

"I've asked our old story-teller, Roy Legband to join us, but he doesn't always pick up his messages at the store. He stays away from modern conveniences so that he can experience life as it was when our ancestors lived here, he says. We respect Roy for his intentions. and no one else has all the stories from the past."

"All of us know that a well was discovered during the Watson auction. A spring developed a day or so later, just a few feet from the well. The Sacred Spring is in Roy Legband's collection of stories, and I believe it is the same spring that dried up, long ago, when white intruders took over the area around the spring, and drove us out."

Between Sally and Katye, breakfast was distributed and coffee replenished.

"Could I have an orange juice, please?" asked Samir.

He motioned for Liz to go ask Katye if she could come and join the conversation.

"And by the way, Marlene" said Lou, ever the politician, "I'm buying your breakfast."

"Thank you, Mr. Mayor," she said. "You are very kind."

Truth be told, she was lonely. Her husband, Claude, was quiet, in contrast to Marlene's outgoing personality. He was content to come home from his job at Ripple's Market where he kept the books, settle down for a long night of TV, many times without speaking a word to her all evening. She amused herself, sometimes, by imagining a number of plots to murder him, which she, of course, would never do. She didn't think so, anyway.

So, she kept up her professional persona, and lost herself in her work. She came to town too late to meet Joe or to be a part of the search, but she had heard the stories that some believed and some did not. She did not know which category she was in.

"What do you know about the property next to Frances, Marlene?" asked Georgette.

"I know it's owned by a corporation called BFS Inc. I manage the property. It goes all the way down the hill from Mrs. Saugus's place to the city limits, you know. The Grundy family used to own it, but BFS bought it right after. . .well. . . right after Joe left us. I managed the sale for the family. Sold it through a man who introduced himself as Raven. Raven Sinclair."

"I see."

Father became silent.

"I will contact him this morning and see if we can connect in order to have a conversation about this."

"Is there anyone else?" asked Father.

"Not that I know of. It's always been Raven I have talked to."

She looked at him quizzically. He looked away, appearing to be lost in thought, and said nothing more.

Chapter 23

MARLENE'S FIRST THOUGHT, ORDINARILY, would have been to call the police. But, she experienced an immediate and powerful attraction to the stranger waiting for her, in her office. This left her confused, and a little disoriented. She was not frightened. Her first impulse was, shamelessly, to walk across the floor of her office, and kiss him, passionately. Fortunately, she shook herself out of the stupor that had suddenly overtaken her.

Still, she did not follow through with caution, but walked right up to him. Instead of asking, "What are you doing at my desk, and by the way, how did you get in here?" she said, "Well, hello! Who do I thank for the pleasure of your company?"

"Please forgive me, dear Madam, for my sudden appearance, without notice."

He did not apologize for breaking and entering, or for placing himself at her desk, where there were many personal files of her clients.

She did not care. Thoughts popped into and around in her head, like spontaneous fireworks. She wished she had dropped that thirty-five pounds. She wished she had worn a more attractive dress. She wished she wasn't married. Maybe she'd just have an affair!

"Don't give it a thought," she said, extending her hand, relieved that he held it too long, and not resisting, when he placed both hands over hers.

He stood, came around to the front of the desk. He bowed low, and kissed her hand. She vowed, like some junior high girl, never to wash that hand. She giggled, unbecomingly. God! She wished she had popped a mint after that breakfast of huevos rancheros!

"Have we met before?" she asked.

"Yes, as a matter of fact, we have."

"Oh, you are so handsome, I'm sure I would remember!"

"You were with your husband, then. Claude, I believe."

"Oh, yes, Claude."

"I am Raven Sinclair, Mrs. Brooker."

"Oh, call me Marlene! Please!" she said.

"Marlene, then," he said, flashing a bright and toothy smile. "Of course."

He reached up, and, seemingly absent-mindedly, twisted the corner of his mustache and stroked his well-groomed beard. Marlene thought she was going to pass out. He could see this, and was, obviously, amused.

"Well," she said, laughing nervously, "we've got to quit meeting like this."

Totally inappropriate, totally unprofessional, she thought. But she didn't care.

"I represent the corporation who owns the land, just adjacent to your fair city!"

"I have just been assigned to call you about the property."

"I know."

"You know?" she asked. "How could you know? I just found out minutes ago that I was assigned to get in touch with you."

"My dear Madame," he said, with a kind of old-world flavor in his voice, "there are many ways to know things."

God! she thought. His low velvet voice fairly reeks of testosterone.

He continued. "We are aware that the spring, on the old Harrison place, has returned. I arrived last night and I, myself, went out to the farm."

"Yes, the land has been sold to a young couple in town, the mayor's daughter and her husband, who is a doctor."

"I'm sure everything can be worked out, dear lady."

The voice! She couldn't stand it!

"Oh, I am so pleased! Maybe you and I can work on it together?"

He came closer. The smell of his cologne nearly made her faint.

"Marlene, I would be happy to work on anything with you! Anything!"

She thought he was going to kiss her but he backed up just enough to make that unlikely.

"Oh, good!" she said.

"BFS Inc. wants the spring," he said, suddenly, his voice turning darker.

Their conversation was interrupted by the squeak of the front door opening. She resented the intrusion, whoever it was. It was Frank Callaghan.

"Oh, hello Father! How can I help you?"

"I was just coming to follow up on our visit earlier, but I can see that you are busy."

"Not at all," said Raven. "I was just leaving."

"Oh, no! Don't do that!" Marlene fairly shouted. "We will need to talk some more, after Father Callaghan has gone."

"That is true," he said. "But, I do not want to interrupt."

"I'm sure you won't! Father probably doesn't have much to say, do you, Father?"

"How long have you lived in Safety Harbor, Marlene?"

"Three years."

"And, you haven't yet learned that the Catholic priest, in town, has never been lost for words?"

Father smiled, and Marlene returned a forced smile. He was definitely picking up some weird energy in the air, that caused him to perceive the attraction she had for the stranger and, on the other hand, the danger that exuded from him. Marlene needed him to be there with them, in this moment, more than she knew.

"Father, this is Raven Sinclair and his visit is fortuitous. He represents the company that owns the land between Mrs. Saugus's place and the city limits."

"Fortuitous, indeed!" said Frank. "How convenient that he is here waiting for you, when you open your office!"

His message was directed more to Raven than to Marlene.

"I understand there is a crisis brewing in your fair community," said Raven, ignoring the priest's sarcasm.

"Well, not a crisis, but an unexpected blessing, and, as with so many blessings, we have to figure out what to do with it!"

The air fairly bristled with electricity, as Frank felt resistance from Raven.

""How long are you going to be in our fair city?"

"As long as I am needed, Mr. Callaghan."

"That's Father Callaghan!"

"Yes, Father," said Raven with polite, but unmistakable sarcasm.

Marlene's attraction to Raven did not decrease, but Frank's presence brought her back down to earth.

"Perhaps the interested parties could assemble at Joe's in the morning, Marlene."

"Yes, maybe we could. Although Raven and I will have to do some planning before that."

"Yes," said Raven. "We will need to . . . consult!"

Father had noticed Raven's face become pale when he suggested Joe's as a meeting place, so he was not surprised when Raven said, "Isn't there somewhere other than Joe's we could meet?"

"Oh, it's clearly the place in town to be," Father goaded him.

"Why ever would you object to meeting at Joe's, Raven?" asked Marlene.

"Well, it's just that Joe's is busy all the time, and the noise will prevent us from hearing one another, clearly. I want to make sure we are on the same page, when we finish our meeting."

"There is Jeremy's Coffee and Books," said Marlene. "Maybe we could meet there."

"I am sure Jeremy would appreciate the business! All right," said Father. "Let's meet there, say at ten o'clock tomorrow morning? Many of us will have to have our Joe's Fine Dine-ing breakfast before that."

"Raven," Father goaded him, "you are most welcome at the diner earlier for breakfast."

"I am sure I will be tired."

He smiled slyly at Marlene.

"I am sure we will be meeting quite late into the evening."

Marlene blushed.

"Don't meet too late," said Father. "Claude gets worried about you when you are out late at night."

"Oh, yes, Claude," said Raven. "We had almost forgotten about him, hadn't we, Marlene?"

"She never forgets about her Claude!" said Father. "Do you, Marlene?"

"No, I suppose I don't."

"How long have you two been married now?"

"Seventeen years."

"Sev-en-*teeen* years!" Father exaggeratedly drew out the number so as to emphasize it. "That's a long time to be faithful to one another!"

God, she wished he would just shut up!

"Yes, it is Father."

Some would say too long, she thought to herself.

"Do you trust Claude?" Father asked.

"Of course, I trust him."

"And I know he trusts you, completely. He's told me how lucky he was to have you, how he felt you were above him, and how he is humbled by your marrying him."

Message received, she thought. Loud and clear.

When they looked up from their conversation, Raven Sinclair was nowhere to be seen.

Chapter 24

THAT EVENING, MARLENE TOLD Claude the cover story that she had to go out and meet a client. She felt guilty about it, but not guilty enough not to go.

Claude knew that Marlene did not always go where she said she was going. She was forty-five and he was fifty-nine. He was slowing down and thinking about retirement. His libido wasn't as strong as it used to be.

It was always something, most often a client, that she said she needed to see. But, Claude knew that there just weren't that many houses for sale in Safety Harbor or even in Clever, for that matter. Sometimes, she sold a house in Lincoln City, but not many. The local real estate people had that pretty well sewed up. It could be nothing, but, if it was something, there wasn't anything he could do about it. She always came home, although sometimes her "meetings" ran quite late. Claude accepted her explanations, although he seldom believed them. He was just glad she was home and safe. He loved her and he forgave her, even when she didn't ask to be forgiven.

"I have to go to Lincoln City tonight. It's a meeting between some of us in real estate and potential . . . clients. There'll be a light meal and refreshments and lots of talk, so don't wait up. I've left your dinner in the fridge."

"Okay," said Claude.

"Aren't you going to ask me when I will be home?"

"No."

"Why not?"

"I figger you'll be home when your finished . . . with whatever you are doing!"

"Won't you miss me?"

He didn't answer.

He had missed her for quite a few years now, since she had started going out at night for reasons which often belied belief, and sleeping on the far side of their bed. Lately, he had begun not to feel much of anything at all about it. He used to stay awake, tossing and turning until she got home, at which time he pretended to be asleep. But now, he went to bed and slept like a baby. Sometimes, he didn't even wake up, when she got home. He just hoped she didn't get herself in any trouble. He knew that if she was hurt, or worse, he would get a call from someone.

Deep inside, Claude had always known that he was the strong one. Even though Marlene put on a professional and sometimes blustery persona, inside, she was frightened and insecure. He was sure that was why she sought out other assignations, and new, and sometimes dangerous experiences.

He believed that she would not leave him. She needed him. She knew it and he knew it. Claude just hoped she would give it up, and come home for good, before so much time went by, that there was nothing but a shadow of a man to greet her, when she did.

Chapter 25

THE NEXT MORNING. RUBY brought Roy Legband to the spring. As he was walking through the farmyard, approaching the side of the barn, just before they would come out on the other side, where the spring awaited them, he began to sob. Then, he bent over, and moaned. Those around him were worried that he was in pain, or was having a heart attack.

But when he straightened up, they discovered that he was smiling now, almost laughing, and broke out in a run to get to the stream before them.

"I have often had visions of the Sacred Spring," he said. "It is just as my visions told me that it was!"

"This is it, then, Roy?"

"Yes, Ruby, this is the Sacred Spring, the one our ancestors lost to the cruelty and greed of the white man, generations ago. This is the spring that dried up, because the white people killed our people, drove them out, starved them, and tried to destroy our ways and our heritage."

"But, what is it that has brought the spring back to us, Roy?" asked Ruby.

"This must be the work of the Maker, who once walked the earth, but has now gone up to the sky, and lives with many people who have gone there with him. Most of the time he does not interfere with human life, but there are times when he comes and helps us in order to make our lives, our world, better. When the Sacred Spring dried up, our holy people told us that, in that day when people came together in harmony and peace, the Sacred Spring would be restored."

The word had spread of the visit of the Shaman to the Old Eighty. Lou and Hope had arrived on the scene by now, along with Bart Honecker and Luther.

The old holy man continued.

"In our ancestors' teachings, the earth is flat and floats on water. The water, coming up through the Sacred Spring, comes from a hallowed place, from the water that bears us up and keeps this earth-boat afloat, so that we can live."

"Sort of like the ark, then!" said Luther.

"Your stories are your stories and our stories are our stories," said Roy Legband. "We have heard your stories for many generations now. We have discovered that we cannot live without our stories, just as you cannot live without yours.

"Now, the time is coming when we shall draw together with our hearts. This can only happen when white people begin to learn our stories and respect them. Then, our hearts will open, fully, one to the other, and we shall see ourselves as human beings, all of us. There must be no hate or vengeance among us. The Maker has come to us and has blessed us, once again, with the Sacred Spring. We must live up to the responsibilities given to us."

Chapter 26

LIZ WAS ON HER way, once again, to the Unsettlement.

She thought about their dilemma, as she drove south, on Highway 101. Where could they go? Magdalena had told her of the close relationships that had developed, and the community that had formed in the past few years that they had been together.

"This kind of closeness and connection," Magdalena had said, "is the envy of many of our friends, and others, who work with those on the margins. When they visit, they are amazed at the way the people work together so easily."

As ideas about where they could go floated in and out of her head, she didn't want to lose them. She pulled over, in order to put some of her thoughts on her i-phone. Fortunately, the coast road offered a way off the highway to Devil's Churn, and the accompanying gift shop.

As she sat, deep in thought, making notes to herself, she became startled, becoming immediately aware, of her surroundings. She was parked on the edge of a cliff that jutted abruptly down into the sea, with the bumper of her car snugged up against the four-foot fence that served as a barrier to prevent vehicles and people from careening off into the ocean. A few people were standing up against the fence to get the closest view possible, down the cliff, to the waves that crashed against it. Two teenagers watched as a third companion climbed over the fence, and inched toward the edge of the cliff, suddenly standing up and waving furiously to his friends.

Stupid, stupid boy, she thought.

Her eye landed upon a man, who stood out from the rest of the tourists. He carried himself, she thought, with a cosmopolitan air. His dark hair and mustache stood out, in contrast to his skin, which, she thought, had just a hint of a glow about it. Even in the warm and sunny weather, he was wearing an over garment that reminded her of Father Callaghan's cassock. He carried with him a kind of rugged, yet somehow, smooth handsomeness that was, at once, appealing and at the same time, made a woman want to protect herself.

He walked toward her. Surely, he would walk on, past her car. He did not. He approached her window, which was down, about half way. Immediately, she rolled her window up, and stared straight ahead, as if she were focused on the panorama, ahead of her.

He did not go away, but continued to stand by her car. His eyes were slightly averted, but she could tell that he was staring at her, even then. She started the car, and began to back out. She looked behind her. He was standing behind the car. Good God! Hadn't she seen him in the front of the car a few minutes ago? How did he get there?

He was, clearly, trying to prevent her from leaving. Her next instinct was to call 911, but there was no cell phone service on this part of the road.

She sat there, in a stand-off with the formidable figure standing, directly, behind her. What did he want? How she wished that Rock was here. But, no one was around to come to her aid. No one at all. What could she do? The panic arose, for a moment.

Then, she remembered what Caleb had taught her about living in Ramallah and Jerusalem. Show no fear! Suddenly, the fear departed and was replaced with anger and annoyance. What right did this intruder have to detain her?

"What do you want?" she demanded through the closed window.

The stranger's voice was deep, and his words oozed out like honey, dripping over the edge of corn bread.

"I apologize for the inconvenience, dear lady."

She struggled not to be mesmerized by the sound and tenor of his voice. Each vowel had a place in each word and every consonant served as a frame around every vowel.

"What do you want?" demanded.

"I was just admiring your car," he said. "It is beautiful indeed. I would like to inquire as to where you got it?"

"It belongs to my parents. Usually they buy their cars in Lincoln City."

"I am here on business," he said.

"Are you now?"

She did not hide her annoyance.

"What difference does that make to me?"

"It should make a lot of difference. I represent the company that owns the property just down the hill from your new home."

A chill ran up her spine.

"How do you know who I am?"

"Oh, I believe we have met before somewhere. Elizabeth, isn't it? Yes, I know we have."

"Well, I don't remember you at all, and I'm uncomfortable talking with you, without my husband."

The stranger looked genuinely hurt.

"Oh, I am sorry, dear Elizabeth. Please forgive me, if I have frightened you."

His voice was so seductive, she was inclined drop her guard, but then, she thought better of it.

She began to back her car up, once again. This time, he did not prevent her from leaving. As she approached the highway, she looked in her rearview. He was waving at her. She did not wave back. Instead, she gunned the gas feed, and drove, ever faster, out of the parking lot. She turned to look at his car, parked at the edge of the lot, close to the highway.

Good God! That looked like Marlene Brooker in the passenger seat! What was she doing here, with this stranger? She decided that she did not want to know.

She turned her car south, toward the Unsettlement.

Chapter 27

WHEN SILO SULZBERGER WAS twelve years old, his mother sold him to Homer Hill. Silo had watched as Homer counted out five crisp one hundred dollars bills, and gave them to his mother.

Sensing Silo's sadness and confusion, Homer said, "Suck it up, young man. You are one lucky kid. Opportunities await you that you only have, by coming with me."

"Did my mother sell me, Mr. Hill?"

"No, I didn't buy you and your mother didn't sell you. The money was for her . . . expenses."

Homer, a corrupt, self-proclaimed prophet, lived in a slightly-run-down two-story house, with an attic. The neighborhood had once been considered one of the better parts of Muncie, Indiana. But now, it was going downhill fast, and Homer had been able to buy it cheap, two years ago. He had paid cash, which made his deal even better. This house was for his ministry, he said, the Homer Hill Healing Waters Evangelistic Association, which was a front for his criminal enterprise.

Every Sunday morning Homer would hold his church service on the first floor of what had once been the parlor, now converted into a chapel.

Homer ran what he called "The School of the Prophets" every week-night from 7:00 pm to 10:00 p.m. in the attic. The same three men were always in attendance.

Silo expected that he would be going to the private school that Homer had told his mother he ran, but Homer told him that school was not in session, right now. Only the School of Hard Knocks, as he put it. After three months, Silo realized that there wasn't going to be any school, at all.

Homer had bought himself a child slave. He put Silo to work, im-mediately, cleaning the house. After it was all finished, Homer set him to painting the interior walls, except for the attic. He was not allowed to go there.

"Mr. Hill, may I join a baseball league or something? Any sport. I love sports."

"Son, the Lord has called you out of the world. He doesn't want you participating in the sinful activities of the Devil. You stay here and give yourself to this ministry. God will reward you, I promise."

Each morning Silo had a breakfast of warmed-over whatever-was left over from dinner. Homer was often not around during the day. Silo was not allowed to get into the refrigerator or the cupboards, or to go into the pantry. Often, both of them were locked. Many times, it wasn't until evening that Silo had anything to eat again. He worked hard, and, over those first three months, he lost weight, and he was all ready thin.

After the house had been cleaned six times, Homer told him that he had passed the test to continue in his current position. However, his work responsibilities would expand and he would be called on to carry out errands for Healing Waters House. He loaned Silo a bicycle which, he said, belonged to the ministry, but Silo would have the honor of using it while he worked for the Lord.

One day, while he had gone on an errand to the bank, he got up the courage and rode the bicycle back to his mother's house. But, when he tried to open the front door, he found it locked.

He knocked.

"Mom!" he called out.

A stranger came to the door. She was not happy.

"Is my mother home?"

"Young man," the woman said sternly, "I don't know who you are or what you are even talking about. But, if you do not leave, immediately, I am going to call the police!"

Tears came to his eyes, as he realized that his mother truly had abandoned him. She would not be back for him. He may never see her or his brother and sister again. He went back to Homer's house, quietly sobbing, all of the way.

One evening, he heard a lot of commotion upstairs, and eased his way up to the second floor, then, quietly up the ladder, that led to the attic. All four men were counting money. Lots of it.

When he asked Homer about it, his face turned a deep red.

"You disobeyed the rules!" he said. "You are never to go up there again!"

Then, Silo was shocked when Homer backhanded him. The rage on Homer's contorted face frightened him. He didn't look like the same man, as he claimed to be.

"Now, go to your room until morning, boy!"

Silo only had breakfast that day and he could not go to sleep for his hunger pangs. He began to wonder if Brother Hill really was a man of God.

Two weeks later, Homer informed him that he would be going on a trip to Oregon.

"The ministry needs a new start," he said. "The ground here in Muncie has been burned over, and we need new fields to bring forth the harvest. I'm going to trust you to take care of the house, while I am gone. I know you won't run away, because God has called you to this ministry, and should you leave it, well, all I can say is, may God have mercy on your soul."

Sometimes, Silo believed Homer, although he could not understand why his life had to be so hard, while he was working for the Lord. But, he was now, Homer had told him, a valuable asset to the work. If he left, Homer said, he did not know what he would do without him.

Every day that Homer was gone, Silo faithfully carried out his duties, as he would if Homer were home. The second week, he took some liberties and rode the bike around the neighborhood, but he didn't stay long, lest Homer come home early, and find him neglecting his duties.

The last day before Homer was scheduled to be home, Silo worked up the courage to go up to the attic. The room was full of boxes, cases, and plastic tubs. He could see right through the tubs. They were full of cash. He opened a few boxes and found them full of cash, too. All of it was cash, in all denominations.

"Brother Hill must be bringing in a lot of offerings!" he heard himself say.

He climbed down quickly from the attic.

Chapter 28

WHEN HOMER RETURNED, SILO was given a new task. Every day, he was to go to the bank with ten rolls of quarters, and bring home a hundred dollars, in paper money. He would go to a different bank, each day of the week, and then, start all over again.

After six weeks, one of the cashiers on his Monday route, noticed that Silo was also going into the bank, across the street, every Tuesday. The bank manager called his colleague. They determined that Silo was asking the same thing, of both banks.

The next Monday when Silo appeared at Mutual Trust and Savings the manager asked him if he'd like a candy bar. Silo hesitated, but then, he said that he thought it would be all right. He hadn't had candy in a long time. Bad for your health and my pocket book, Homer had said.

"Come over to my desk, son, and I'll see that you get your favorite."

He asked Silo where he lived, and who was sending him on this weekly errand. He asked him why he wasn't in school, and how old he was. Although he knew Homer wouldn't like it, Silo told the truth. After all, it wasn't right to lie, was it?

That night, the Muncie police came to the house. Homer went outside and closed the door behind him. Standing nearby, Silo could hear Homer's voice become louder. From what he could overhear, the police wanted to come in and search the house, but Homer told them they would need a warrant.

When he came back in, Homer's face was ashen.

"We have to go! Right away!"

"Where are going?"

"Away. To Oregon."

"Now!"

"Now?"

"Pack your clothes!"

He could hear Homer on the phone talking in low, but urgent, tones.

Within an hour, a large rental truck showed up along with the students at the School of the Prophets Sunday School class.

"Come up here. We need your help!"

This time, it was okay for Silo to be in the attic. For the next two hours, the five of them loaded boxes full of cash into the U-Haul.

"Come to the basement, now!" said Homer.

Below, were five, fifty-gallon drums. Before Homer sealed the last drum, Silo saw that it was filled with rolls of quarters. Wow! If all the barrels were full of quarters, this was thousands of dollars!

One of the men, at Homer's direction, brought the moving dolly downstairs and loaded one of the barrels on it. Halfway up the steps, the stairs collapsed. No one was hurt, but, the drum was now ensconced in the tangle of wood that lay, twisted, on the basement floor. It took them fifteen minutes to extricate it.

"We are losing time!" Homer fairly screamed at the others.

Silo couldn't believe it when he saw their solution. One of the basement windows was slightly larger than the rest of them.

"We're gonna take 'em up through this window!"

For the next three hours, the men pulled and tugged with ropes and chains, to get the drums through the window. It was five o'clock in the morning, when they finished.

"Let's hightail it out of here right now!" said Homer. "They're fixin' to come back here with a warrant."

"What about your congregation, Brother Hill?" asked Silo.

"To hell with the congregation!" he said.

Silo decided at that moment that Homer was not a good man.

"I'm starved, Homer!" said one of the men. "We've been working all night!"

"No time to eat now! You want us to get caught? When they find we're not home, they'll come lookin' for us. They're probably all ready on the look-out! They'll expect us to run."

They didn't stop until they got into Illinois. From there, they took back roads, all of the way west to Oregon. Each night, they would stop and rent two hotel rooms among them. Silo stayed with Homer and Homer's gang was in the other. Silo heard the doors of the hotel room next door open and close several times a night.

Three nights later, they stayed in Omaha. Homer decided it was time for celebration. They had avoided the law, up to this point, and he was feeling less paranoid. They went to dinner at a large steak house, where they had prime rib, and drank a lot of Scotch and Vodka.

Talk got pretty loose and before the evening was over, it was clear to Silo that all of the quarters in the fifty-gallon drums were from the gang robbing parking meters. He remembered, vaguely, seeing something on one of the televisions in one of the banks, while he was exchanging quarters for paper money. Parking meters in surrounding small towns, like Berne, St. Mary's, and Celina, who still had cash-only meters, were being robbed. Now, he knew who it was that had been carrying it out. and why Homer had to leave town so quickly; and why, even now, they were "on the lam."

But, where could he go and what could he do? He decided he would not try to run away on the trip west. He would bide his time until they got to Oregon.

They had been traveling the Oregon Coast road, for about two hours, through Lincoln City, and down through a little burg called Safety Harbor. About ten minutes south of Safety Harbor, Homer slowed down, and pulled the rental truck over to the side of the road. He pointed to an old neglected building, largely made of glass and steel, extending well out over the water. Then, he drew Silo's attention to three small cabins that were next door, looking every bit as dilapidated as the glass building.

"This is the new home of the ministry," said Homer. "It's fixer-upper property, I know, but the ministry has the money and we'll be up and running, in no time. When I took my first trip to Oregon, I got all of this for a song. Now, we have a lot of unloading to do and we have to get that rental truck back to Lincoln City, pronto. Let's get to work!"

Chapter 29

"Hopey, I've got an idea that'll knock your socks off! It's about the Unsettlement, and where they could move, at least, temporarily."

"Have you run this past Liz?"

"No! I just thought of it!"

"Well, it may be a good idea, but, you need to check it out with our daughter, before you go running off and carrying out your ideas, without her. I know. It's difficult for me. too. Just a few years ago, she was a teenager, in high school. But, she's a grown woman, now. She's in charge of an important project. She's a leader. She takes after you, Lou! She looks like me, but, when it comes to her personality and abilities, she's a chip off the old block.

"Of course, you're right, Hopey. You're always right. It's just that . . ."

"I know, dear husband. You miss being center stage."

"I fear I'm getting old, and people will see me as a has-been."

"That is not Liz's problem. If you have a good idea, make the suggestion, but, don't interfere with her work."

Suddenly, he looked like a small boy.

"But, it is a good idea, honey. I'll call her! Yes, that's it, by God! I'll call her!"

Liz sighed. She was always in a losing battle with her husband about his language, but it didn't stop her from trying.

"Don't you mean 'Jove'!"

"What?"

"I mean, don't you mean 'by Jove' instead of what you said?"

"Oh, yeah. By Jove. That's it. By Jove."

He was already calling Liz.

Chapter 30

NATE AND SALLY HAD asked for some time with Father Callaghan. He was always glad to have people over for dinner. The Rectory could get lonely in the evening, and the sound of human voices in the priest's home was often a thing of comfort to him. Father Callaghan suggested that they come over for dinner that evening.

"You haven't even asked us what this is about, Father," said Sally.

"Well, I figured it must be something about your wedding."

"You always know everything, don't you?" she said, smiling.

"I like to make people think so. It gives me an air of mystery."

"So, what is this meeting about?"

"Glad you asked, Father," said Nate.

He looked at Sally and she gave him a nod, as if to say, "Go ahead!"

"We want to move the wedding date up," said Sally.

"Well, of course!" Frank was a little surprised. "You've gone through the necessary marriage preparation, so it's fine. Can you tell me why?"

"We are concerned that Carrie Lynn, the kids' mother, may come back to town, just to make trouble, just to stir things up and ruin the wedding," said Nate.

"Anything make you think that?"

"Just some stuff she's said to the kids," said Sally. "She's dropped some hints."

"I won't pry."

"Thank you," said Sally. "We have an idea we'd like to present to you."

Chapter 31

"WHY, DADDY, THAT'S A wonderful idea!"

"I know. It would be temporary, but, it's something."

"Your Dad's not modest, you know!" said Hope.

"Well, it is a good idea! A damned good idea! I've talked to Jens and Shirley . . . I hope you don't mind."

Lou was smiling, ear to ear.

"But. will it work?" his daughter asked.

"We have to tie all the strings together, but once we do, it ought to go smoothly!"

"I wish I'd had some time to give a heads-up to Rock and Magdalena." said Liz.

"Well, your dad just had this idea, and worked it out in a hurry. I'm sure, once they know the context, they'll be all right, dear," said Hope.

"It'll be important to present to the group as an idea for them to buy into, rather than as a done deal. We don't want to be patronizing."

"I've never been patronizing a day in my life, Liz!" said Lou.

The two women rolled their eyes.

"I really think this is a good idea, and that you handled it well, sir," said Caleb.

"Thanks, Caleb!" said Lou, looking from his daughter to his wife with bright dancing eyes.

Lou always appreciated praise, no matter who it might be, even though Hope often said that he didn't recognize the difference between praise and being damned with faint praise. It wasn't so much ego as it was that Lou wanted to help people. He really did. Lou was a public servant, in the best sense. And when he heard that he had "done good" as he described it, he was happy.

Although he never said anything about it, Hope knew that some of the need for praise came from his childhood.

"She had told him one time, "You know, your dad is a real SOB!"

"Why, Hopey!" Lou had said. "You'd kill me for using language like that!"

"I don't think I've ever used that word before, and I don't think I'll ever use it again. But, it's the only word I can think of to describe Harry," Hope had said to Lou about her father-in-law.

"Lou is always a day late and a dollar short," his Dad would say within hearing distance of his son.

After Lou and Hope were married, when Harry and Maude would come for a visit, they would always complain that the town had no conveniences like they had in St. Louis.

"Back home" Harry would say, "you can get anything you want, and more. Why anyone would want to live in a little town like this, I don't know."

"They like it here!" Maude would say. "This is their choice, even though it would not be ours. No, not by a long shot."

These words were spoken, without fail, as ritual, on the first night of each visit they made to Safety Harbor.

Hope always gave them the master bedroom. Lou and Hope used the "Hide A Bed" in the living room. Harry always smoked a cigar in the evening, after dinner. Hope requested that he smoke it outside. He always began there, but, inevitably, he would come in, halfway through his smoke, pour himself a Scotch, and just not go back outside. He did this without saying a word about it. By the end of the first evening, Hope was seething with resentment. It was always a long week. Mostly, it hurt her the way they treated her husband.

Hope knew that, whenever Lou went ahead and did something that she might otherwise call "pulling a stunt," he just wanted to make people happier, to make their lives better. Why, if he could perform miracles, he would do them for others and not ask one for himself! Sometimes, she had to smooth the way, quietly, behind the scenes. They were loving actions by a wife for her husband, who, often, never knew what she had done.

Chapter 32

WHEN LIZ HAD SEEN Marlene in the car, with the stranger, they were headed to a remote landing strip, just south of the Unsettlement, where Raven kept his personal jet. They arrived at a small inlet, well hidden from the road, and guarded by a generous row of trees. The strip could remain hidden here, for a long time, without anyone ever seeing it.

"I never knew this place was here, and I thought I knew every inch of land, for a hundred miles, around Safety Harbor."

"Ah, dear lady!" said Raven. "This place wasn't here until just recently. I had it made, especially, for my time here."

"You did? Who owns the land?"

"BFS Inc., of course! We have always operated on the principle that the whole planet belongs to us, and we're just renting it out to others!"

Raven looked over at her to get her reaction. When he saw the perplexity on her face, he began to laugh. It was deep and piercing.

"Stop!" she pleaded. "Stop laughing at me!"

He pulled the car over to the side, and parked it in a parking space, beside the strip. Raven had invited Marlene to dinner, at the Governor Hotel, in Portland. They were headed there, now.

"I've never flown in a small plane before!" said Marlene.

Raven helped her up into the front passenger seat. His hand held her firmly and yet, somehow, gently, as she made her way into the small aircraft. He started the engine. The sound of the engines, immediately, made it difficult to hear.

"In a small plane. You feel every bump and every twist of the wind. It's as if you had your own personal wings, and you are flying as the birds. If the air is just right, it's rather . . . sensuous."

She couldn't tell if he was kidding. She looked over at him and saw him looking at her with amusement. She was beginning to realize that she usually always felt just a little "off" around Raven. She never knew whether to take him literally or not. She could not tell whether he liked her or whether he was just playing her, just having fun, at her expense.

The flight into Portland was a smooth one, in Raven's jet, only about forty minutes, including take-off and landing. The limousine was awaiting them. Raven placed his hand over hers. But, as they reached downtown, his touch began to feel more like a restraint. With some effort, she moved his hand. But, when he looked over, seeming obviously hurt, she took his hand again. and locked fingers with him. They rode silently.

Downtown Portland was busy and full of energy. The air was warmer here, seventy miles inland from the sea. She felt her small-town-ness.

Raven sensed this.

"Dear lady, you look elegant! I would pick you out of all the women within my sight."

"What about the ones that aren't within your sight!"

"I am afraid, dear one, that you have me at a disadvantage!"

She was feeling better already.

Raven took her by the hand and, together, they walked into the hotel. There was an old elegance about it. They went to the dining room, where Raven had reserved a small table for them in the corner, by the window.

"This is . . . this is wonderful!" said Marlene, as Raven helped her be seated. He adjusted her chair until she was comfortable.

"I'm glad you like it," said Raven. "This hotel is my headquarters, while I am here on business."

"It is? I just assumed you were staying at one of the Safety Harbor motels!"

An unmistakable look of disdain came over Raven's face, which he managed to remove quickly, but, not before Marlene had noticed it.

"I guess you're used to the big important places, where lots of important people carry on their business! That's certainly not our life, in Safety Harbor. Sometimes, it's so every-day, I just want to scream! Nobody understands my ambition to make money, and lots of it. I mean, if you're going to make money, why not make as much as you can?"

"You and I understand each other, dear Marlene. In fact, you are the perfect representative for us, in Safety Harbor."

"I am? Oh goodness!"

"In fact, you are, my dear; which gets me down to business."

A waiter came by, and Raven ordered martinis for both of them.

"About this spring business. BFS Inc. is very concerned about what is happening there. The water has healing components. Whoever owns it will have serious power. We need to find a way to obtain this property. This must be done at any cost. You are the key person in helping us to get the property. We are depending upon you. I will work with you, very closely. We will have many wonderful opportunities to get to know one another."

After dinner and a liqueur, they returned to the plane. Raven held her hand all the way home. So bold was he, that, as he dropped her off at her home, he planted a firm kiss on the lips. Marlene offered no resistance.

"You must go now, dear Marlene. Claude will be waiting, and worried about you!"

"Yes, there's Claude."

Raven opened the passenger seat for her and escorted her to the door. Fumbling with her keys, she opened the door as quietly as she could. She was sure she had not awakened him. Claude remained silent and still, so as not to disabuse her of her erroneous conclusion.

Chapter 33

THE PARADE COMMITTEE MET at Joe's. Liz asked for a fifteen-minute delay, so that she could fill Rock and Magdalena in on the latest possibilities for the Unsettlement.

"We can get started on some of the details without you, can't we?" asked Bartosh.

"Oh, sure!" said Liz. "I'm not the chair!"

Stewart and Katye walked in, just then.

"I'm sorry we're late, guys!"

"Saved by the bell!" said Father Callaghan. "It's not like you! We were getting a bit worried. I was about to call."

"We got a bit off schedule at home," said Katye.

"Well, at least we can get started," said Bartosh, who had never quite slowed down, to the small-town ways of Safety Harbor.

"I've got coffee, tea, and some pastries from the bakery!" announced Sally.

She had brought out carafes and put them on one of the tables and pastries on the table, alongside.

"Good! Thanks! Now, come along and sit down." said Father Callaghan.

The meeting in the corner was finally over and Rock, and Magdalena, along with Lou, joined them at the Wisdom Table.

"I need a minute with Katye!" said Liz.

"Go ahead and get started without us!" said Katye.

Flummoxed, Father Callaghan mused out loud, "I guess the fates are against me."

"To say nothing of the rest of us, Frank!' said Lou.

"It won't take long!" said Liz.

Just then, the diner door opened once again. It was Marlene.

"Is this an exclusive meeting?"

"Oh no! Anyone is welcome!" said Frank.

"Let's get started," grumbled Bart. "Every time another mouth comes through the door, the meeting gets fifteen minutes longer!"

"Why, dear, you don't have to stay!" said Susanna. "We can get this done without you, if you have something else to do!"

Anything Susanna said to him in the mildest tone of irritation crushed him.

"I'm sorry, darling."

"Remember, you're in Safety Harbor now!"

"Yes, honey, I am sorry. I always forget that Safety Harbor is in its own time zone!"

"That's the price of getting the girl of your dreams!" said Mrs. Saugus.

Many at the table looked at one another, and smiled, faintly. Since those last days with Joe, Frances Saugus had changed. Somehow, she was less reserved and seemed to speak penetrating truths, such as this one, whenever the opportunity presented itself and she deemed them needed.

"It's a small price to pay, Mrs. Saugus."

"Let's get started!" said Katye.

The conversation between Katye and Liz had finished, by now.

"Room for one more?" It was Doc Riley.

"Well, Doc! We don't expect you at such meetings. Usually you are up the hill, tending the sick!"

"I've put Caleb to work!" said Doc. "Everybody at Harbor View is in good hands. You may expect me to have more free time from now on, I hope!"

Katye began.

"Before we go on with our general business, Liz has something to say that may well change our plans a bit, here and there. It's what we've been talking about earlier, while you were patiently waiting. Liz was bringing some people on board, so that it wouldn't be a surprise to them."

"Oh! Just a surprise for rest of us!" said Father Callaghan, good-naturedly.

Katye chose to ignore him, and Father gave up.

"I'm going to turn this over to Liz, so that she can fill you in. I think what she has to talk about is very exciting! You know that every year since the Search for Joe days, our parade has taken on new dimensions. The Siletz Confederation has now joined the event. More and more people with disabilities join us each year from all over. Schools and clubs are asking to come."

"Yes, and more and more politicians, too!" said Lou.

"And we already have one of those, which is quite enough!

It was Mrs. Saugus, bringing down a ringer for the second time, in an hour.

"I'm glad you think one is enough, Mrs. Saugus," said Lou, "just as long as it is yours truly!"

"Alright! Let's get on with it!" said Katye. "Liz?"

"Friends, I must admit that Daddy has been up to mischief again, but this time, I think he may have come up with something that will really work!"

Lou feigned a sad look, which, quickly, changed to one of almost adolescent excitement when Liz said, "Since this was his idea, I am going to turn it over to him to tell you about it."

"Idea? I thought this was a done deal!"

"Daddy, nothing is a done deal until everyone gets on board!"

"Process, Mr. Mayor! Process!" said Magdalena with a good-natured smile and an elbow in his ribs.

She had found a place to sit beside him. A friendship and understanding had grown up between them, especially since Liz had gotten married and had gone away. It was as if they had become adopted father and daughter. Lou would call her for advice on some city problem and she, in turn, would sometimes share with him her own troubles and anxieties.

"Well, I'm sure that when everyone hears this idea, they will think it is great!"

Hope went into eye-rolling mode.

"Here's the thing!" Lou began. "I was sitting in my chair one evening, by my beloved. I had even almost dozed off. Then, it all came to me, how we could work out a number of things all together. I'm going to let Jens and Shirley tell you the next part."

Shirley spoke up.

"As you know, we have five acres of wide open space, with just a mobile home on it. Lou came over one night and made a proposal."

"An offer we couldn't refuse, you might say," said Jens.

"He asked us," Shirley continued, "whether or not we would consider allowing the people from the Unsettlement to come and live temporarily on our grounds, until they find a permanent place to live."

"The people of Safety Harbor have been so good to me . . ." said Jens.

". . . to us!" added Shirley.

"We just didn't feel that we could turn the request down."

"Kind of like a way to pay it forward!" said Jeremy.

"Exactly!" said the mayor.

Hope gave him her look, planted one hand on his leg, and one of her feet, directly upon one of his shoes!

"So, that's exactly why we are saying 'Yes' to this. The people of the Unsettlement are most welcome to come and be with us, until they find another place."

There was a general hum of excitement as each person reacted to this, some of them making signs of approval or saying something positive to a neighbor on either side of them or across the table."

"Now, there will be some challenges," said Liz.

"Among them are some zoning issues," said Lou. "But I think I'll manage to have the county go along with us on this one!"

"Won't it be crowded?" asked Nate.

"Yes, it will," said Shirley. "But, my uncle has a pasture that goes mostly, unused. We are going to talk to him about opening his gate, temporarily.

"What about water?"

"The place has a well on it!" said Jens. "There was once a farm house on the place."

"That's how we get our water, now," said Rock. "And we use porta potties, all ready."

"How are the people going to get up here?" asked Nate. "It's going to be quite a job gettin' everybody up here."

Lou clapped his hands together!

"This is the best part of all!" said Lou. "This was the best idea that came to me. We extend the parade to the Unsettlement!"

"How do we use the highway without causing a helluva traffic problem?" asked Nate.

"We close it!"

"What did you say, Mr. Mayor?" asked Father.

"We close it!"

"How?" asked Jeremy.

"Simple. I persuade the state to close it, temporarily, for our parade."

"Impossible!" called out Marlene. "That's the main road, up the coast!"

"All things are possible!" said Father.

"Here's the thing," said Lou. "We're pretty well known, in a lot of places. I can go to the media and tell them our story, which is compelling. It will put pressure on the state. Besides, I hate to say it, but they want those folks off that property."

"This is going to have to be done in a hurry!" said Katye.

"It will take all of us," said Liz.

"All of us, and more!" said Hope.

"Remember," said Magdalena, "the people of the Unsettlement want to be equal partners in anything we do. There are a lot of them that are willing to help out."

"Won't you have to get their okay on this?" asked Susanna.

"Yes, we will need to have a special meeting about this tomorrow night. And remember," said Katye, "we haven't given our go-ahead."

"I can't see any of us opposing this," said Stewart, speaking up for the first time.

"I say we pass it by unanimous consent!" said Father.

"Any objections?" asked Katye.

There were none.

"Done and done!" she said.

Chapter 34

CARMELITA HAD BEEN TO Portland on police business. Halfway home, she pulled over at the Ice Cream King. It was mid-afternoon, and she was going to treat this cop to a chocolate sundae.

Afterward, as she started the car, out of the corner of her eye, she noticed a man who was walking up to the driver's side window.

"May I help you?" she called out.

He continued to approach.

"I hope so," he said.

He was a bulky man. There was a gentle look to his be-whiskered face. His ample head of hair was tousled and white.

"I see that you are from Safety Harbor. I was wondering if I might hitch a ride with you."

"Are you having car trouble?"

"No, I don't own a car. I mostly walk where I'm going. But, sometimes, I get lonely and want to find an excuse to talk to somebody. I saw your squad car sign indicating that you are from Safety Harbor, I thought it was fortuitous, since I am going there."

"Where did you come from?" she asked. "I didn't see you in the Ice Cream King. I didn't see you walking on the road."

"Oh, I don't always follow the road. Sometimes I take an alternate path, here and there."

"You mean, like trespassing?"

She smiled faintly. Her sense of the man, by now, was that he was a harmless eccentric.

"Oh, no, officer, nothing like that!" he said. "Not intentionally, anyway. But, I love the wildflowers, the lilies of the field, and the wonders of nature; and when I see them, I depart from the road, just to look at them, and marvel. 'From whence comes such beauty'? I ask myself. 'How is it that they do nothing but live within the splendor of the creation'? So many flowers bloom and no one is ever there to see them. 'I must go and lay eyes on them,' I say. It seems that, when I do, they see me, as well. Have you ever felt that nature is looking back at you?"

"I can't say that I have, sir. Come on. Get in. I've got to get home."

"Thank you, ma'am. I'm much obliged."

Much obliged. The only time she had ever heard that was from her husband, Cliff's father, and he was almost a hundred years old.

"So, where are you from?" she asked.

"Oh, that's difficult to say. I just feel comfortable, everywhere."

"I'm sure you'll like it in Safety Harbor," she said.

"Oh, I know I will," he said.

"Why are you coming to our town?"

"Oh, sometimes I just go somewhere because I feel like I need to be there."

"Excuse me, sir, but you must be retired. If I may be so bold, how do you afford to stay on the road? Do you have an income?"

"Well, yes, so to speak, I do," he said, without further explanation. She did not push it.

The time passed by quickly. Carmelita could not recall what they talked about or all that he had said, but, she knew that it had been wonderful.

When they arrived home, she said, "I'm going to need to stop at the Old Eighty. They've been having some water problems."

'I am happy to accompany you."

"You are most welcome . . . what do they call you, sir?"

"They call me Blessed John."

"Blessed John. Well, that is what I will call you, then."

He smiled the smile of a man, weary of the world, yet, still happy to be in it.

Carmelita parked the car and they walked across toward and then, behind the barn, where the ever- growing stream was, by now, creating the makings of a veritable flood.

Blessed John's face was practically glowing. He looked at the spring as if he were greeting an old friend.

"Ah yes!" he said. "At last."

Chapter 35

"Hello, Chief!" Roy called out to Carmelita.

"Hi boys!" said. "What are you doin'? Oh, I'm sorry. This is Blessed John. He rode out to Safety Harbor with me."

Roy, Caleb, and Hobe who had been chatting near the spring, looked puzzled. Caleb came forward and shook his hand.

"Blessed John, I am Caleb."

"Pleased to meet you, Caleb!"

The other two followed suit.

"What are your plans here?" asked the newly-arrived traveler.

"It's a long story, Blessed John!" said Roy.

Hobe spoke up.

"This spring appeared here just a few days ago. We're trying to figure out, among other things, how to contain it."

"So, you need to build something that both contains the water and can let it out at the same time. Do you have plans sketched out?" asked Blessed John.

"This spring only appeared in the last three days!" he said. "We haven't had much time to put something together."

"I am pretty good at designing things. Would you like me to sketch something out?'

"We'd be grateful," said Hobe.

"I'll need some paper and a pencil. May I use your work shack?"

"Sure!" answered Hobe.

As Blessed John walked away with Hobe, Caleb asked, "Where did you find him?"

'He asked me for a ride when we met up at the Ice Cream King."

"What's he doin' out here?"

"He said he's come for the parade."

"What's with the Blessed John business?"

"When I asked him his name, that's the name he gave me. I think he's harmless."

When Caleb saw the sketch that Blessed John offered them, he was amazed.

"This very much resembles the ancient Pool of Siloam in Jerusalem!" he said.

When Hobe took a look at the plans, he was astounded.

"This will cost a lot of money!" he exclaimed. "We could put something together much cheaper than this! We don't need a big pool! We just need something to direct the water down the hill. and into the ocean. What would we ever do with this?"

Caleb had to agree with Hobe. It would be expensive. But, he was drawn to the idea. They found Blessed John at the mouth of the spring.

"We like your idea, but it would be too spendy," said Caleb.

"What is it your priest says? 'All things are possible'?"

"Do you know Father Callaghan?" asked Georgette.

"I know him. I am not sure that he knows me. Not yet, at least."

The Habibis and the Watsons hired Roy to contain and channel the water, from the spring. Ray Ripple, of Ripple's Grocery, was now in the rental business, as well as running the grocery store. He would bring a front-end loader out to the farm, at no cost.

"Hobe," said Roy, as they stood together, waiting for the equipment, to arrive "they say that you'd never seen the well or the spring before, until the kid found it at the auction, when he was out wandering around."

"Yes, that's true. Now, that's a mystery, Roy. I know every crevice of that land. I don't think it was, that I never noticed it. I don't think it was there, at all."

"Well, I am not very smart about things beyond engines and machinery, but I have to tell you, I don't know how something isn't there, and then, all at once, it is."

"I'll tell you, Roy, living on this farm, on this good earth, has taught me a lot of things. How does that seed, that you put in the ground. . .I mean, you bury it Roy! . . . how does it just lay there in the darkness, out of the sunshine, and turn into something else? Every doggoned corn stalk or punkin' or watermelon or grapevine or fruit tree gets its start with one small seed! I mean, everybody knows this! But when you are there, right alongside that cornstalk, when it pushes its way up through the earth . . . I mean, it changes you, Roy! You never get used to it. People talk about nature as opposed to magic, but I believe something quite as natural as a seed being buried and producing a tree or something . . . that natural event is magical!"

"Well, when you put it that way . . ."

Roy was now lost for words, because he didn't know where to take the conversation any longer. Hobe sensed it and suggested that they had better get to work. Ray Ripple rented that frontend loader out by the day and they were going to have to move right along to get the job done.

Chapter 36

THE WORD HAD SPREAD, throughout Safety Harbor, and beyond, about the new spring on the Old Eighty. There were many, on Saturday morning, who came by Hobe and Georgette's, asking if they could take a look. When enough cars had accumulated in the yard, people no longer asked permission. They just parked and went straight to the spring.

Mid-day, Blessed John walked up behind the by-now gushing stream and called out to the crowds that were gathering.

"There will come a time," he called out, over the noise of the water, "when those who drink from this water will never be thirsty again!"

"Who's the babbling old man up there?" asked an onlooker.

The question went unanswered.

Ruby escorted Roy Legband. to stand beside Blessed John.

"This Sacred Spring was known to our people before it was taken from us. It dried up because of the violence of the white man. My grandfather, a great shaman, said that it would return when humans were ready to be at peace and in harmony with one another."

"I dreamed last night," called out Little Therese, "and I have dreamed before, that this water shall free thousands of souls."

"What does she mean by that?" asked one of the curiosity-seekers.

"Who is this young girl and what does she know about such things?" asked another.

While they were murmuring among themselves, the mysterious old woman, Evita DuPont, spoke up.

"What is happening among us," said Ms. DuPont, who, it seemed, was always around at sacred moments, "is nothing less than the holy, stirring of the waters beneath us, to come forth, to bless us, and to heal us."

Chapter 37

THE SCENE AT THE Unsettlement was chaotic, as they prepared to move the next day. Liz, Rocky, and Magdalena were everywhere. it seemed, loading tables and chairs on pickups, moving some of the makeshift shelters, changing a flat tire, moving utensils, and generally clearing up the inevitable debris. It wouldn't be long until they were at their new digs.

Like an exodus of old, at nine o'clock in the morning of July 5th, now designated as Joe Day, the population came pouring out of the area once known as the Unsettlement.

People happening by, might have guessed it was a contemporary re-make of *Grapes of Wrath*. Some walked. Some rode their bicycles, some rode in cars, piling in as many as were legal, and then some. Still others came in their motorized wheel chairs. One had a manual chair. People traded off, pushing him. It was hot, and some of the more fragile among them, were being transported on an air-conditioned bus, provided by Bartosh.

Rock and Magdalena were leading the crowd, walking ahead of them, attending to those who needed help, from time to time. Marshall rode back and forth, up and down, along the side of the road, on a horse provided for the occasion, to spot any possibilities of danger or trouble. His western attire did not go unnoticed, for better or worse. Liz and Caleb brought up the rear.

The band of ragamuffin refugees continued, slowly, up the Pacific Coast Highway. Children and teenagers had to be watched, so as not to get too close to the cliffs that jutted out, over the water. There would be no forgiveness for one false move. Water stations had been set up at every mile.

Rocky began to sing and play his guitar. Voices joined gradually, and then, more and more joined in. Up from behind them, appeared Blessed John, employing his voice, with abandon. He continued his swifter gate, so that, within a few moments, he was walking alongside the pilgrims, in the midst of the parade. As he passed by the glass house, where Homer had his headquarters, Blessed John saw Silo, watching from the front step. He reached out and took the young teenager by the hand.

Leading him ever so gently, but firmly and swiftly, he said, "Come on, son. You are coming with us. Your long ordeal is over."

The last mile of the way into town, Mayor Lou and Hope joined them, while scores of local townspeople and tourists waited to welcome them. Always Sunny Church offered free sandwiches and cookies.

Blessed John asked Silo what he would like to eat from the food trucks. It was the first time that Silo had been treated like the boy that he was, in so long, if ever. He pointed to the foot-long hotdog with tears in his eyes.

"Soft drink? Lemonade? Milk?"

"Yes!" said Silo. All three. Then, could I have some pizza?"

Blessed John laughed from the bottom of his ample belly.

"Of course, you may, son! Of course, you may! But, the parade starts soon, and we're in it. So, hurry!"

Chapter 38

MRS. SAUGUS, THE PARADE Marshall for this year, got into the designated car, with her two invited guests, Evita DuPont [the mysterious and gentle woman, who had come to town, several years ago, as the benefactor of Joe's Diner], and Little Therese.

"Look!" said Nate, to no one in particular. "Mrs. Saugus is taking that cussed bullhorn into the car with her! It's like it's an extension of her arm!!"

Just as he made the remark, she handed it out the window, to Carmelita.

The parade had doubled in population, over the years. The Unsettlement had joined the parade, led by Rock and Magdalena, who had led off the parade, for several years, now. The rest of the participants took their places, behind the little transient community. Lou couldn't help but get into the act and, after a few steps, it was impossible to tell who was in the lead. Magdalena locked arms with him, so as to not allow Lou to dominate the scene. Then, as had become the custom, Roy and Jens appeared with their motorcycle engines racing, ready to lead the little band of pilgrims on into the park, as they had, at that memorable moment, several years ago.

At the first Joe Parade, Little Therese had, quite spontaneously, introduced Mayor Lou for his speech. Since then, it had become a tradition. Some of the things she had said that first year, had become a part of the annual script, and people began to anticipate the lines. The laughter often began, even before the line was spoken. Little Therese became sophisticated enough to begin to mix up the lines in order to fool Lou. Each year, there would be speculation by some about what she would do, next. She provided a perfect foil for Lou's self-deprecating humor and his many variations on the dead pan look, that he did so well.

After the community singing came to a close, Father Frank came to the front of the stage and announced that everyone was invited to stay on, for one more event. Just after the last performance, the men in the wedding party began to carve out a middle aisle. The local chamber orchestra assembled itself on the stage.

Father Callaghan came to the front of the stage and said, "Ladies and Gentlemen, I present to you the nuptial vows of Nathaniel Xavier Beard and Sarah June Hankins!"

It had been the best-kept secret in town, and the audience clapped and howled with approval.

"About time!" somebody called out.

There was a second round of clapping and cheering. The chamber orchestra opened, with music by Mozart.

Buddy and Caitlin started forward as ring bearer and flower girl. Buddy looked clumsy, as if he hoped to escape. Caitlin looked as if she was liberated for the first time as a teen-ager, being allowed to dress as a woman.

Meriwether, then Katye, Susanna, and Sally were bridesmaids. Each of the groomsmen escorted each bridesmaid to the makeshift altar.

Finally, as Mendelssohn's Wedding March began, Sally began her triumphant walk up the aisle, formed by the crowd splitting like the Red Sea. On each side of her, were Lou and Hope. Lou had a surprised look on his face, as if he was, permanently, in shock. He was obviously briefed on this only at the last minute. The wedding was coming off as the surprise it was meant to be.

"Dearly Beloved . . . "

Just to the side of the crowd, not far away from Archbishop Malarkey, who was looking on, stood an ample older man. Nearby him was a young boy.

After the vows and before the benediction, Mrs. Glover sang a solo.

The ceremony lasted about thirty-five minutes, By the time it was over, a splendid exhaustion had set in all through the crowd. The Unsettlement still had to move across the street. Carmelita set up a crossing from the park, across Pacific Coast Highway, and within a half an hour, the whole crowd, several hundred, it would be said, had made their way there, helping themselves to the ample food from the food trucks.

The people of the Unsettlement were home. Temporarily.

Jens and Shirley were a long way from going to bed after all of the festivities. Their little house was now right smack dab in the middle of the new location for the Unsettlement. The intensity of the noise outside, along with the celebrating, the music, and the general sense of well- being among the citizens, provided a cacophony of human happiness and joy.

"It has been a magical night, dear wife," said Jens, holding Shirley close. "I'm sure there won't be another one like it in many years, if ever."

"And we both have to go to work in the morning."

The doorbell rang.

"I am Blessed John," said the man. "This is Silo. I am wondering if he could have a place to stay for the night."

"Well . . . sure, but, who are you?"

"Oh, I am sorry. I am Blessed John. Please call Chief Biffle, for a confirmation of my veracity."

Carmelita vouched for him.

And that is how Silo had come to live with Jens and Shirley.

Chapter 39

THREE MIRACLES OF PHYSICAL healing had been reported at the spring. Rumors of the miracles spread, not only to surrounding towns, but throughout the media, which began to call it the Lourdes of the Oregon Coast.

Hobe and Georgia, and Caleb and Liz met the evening of the reports of the first miracles, around Hobe and Georgia's large kitchen table. When Lou got wind of the meeting, through Liz, he insisted upon being present. The crowds in town had increased, substantially. With reports of the miracles, further increase in the numbers of those who would be visiting the place, was inevitable.

At the last minute, Blessed John knocked on the door and asked if he might join them. Liz gave him a warm welcome at the door.

"If I may be forgiven for being intrepid, among strangers, may I begin this meeting?"

This, of course, was difficult for Lou, as he had the entire agenda worked out in his own mind. But, there was general assent among those present. As they began, there was another knock on the door. It was Father Callaghan and Meriwether.

Lou shaded his eyes and turned away.

"Will no one rid me of this troublesome priest?"

Meriwether responded, "I've come to keep the priest in line!"

Blessed John smiled, arose, and greeted them warmly.

Georgette served coffee, and Caleb offered to help her get the baked goods on the table.

"I swear, Georgette!" said Frank. "These are going to be the death of me one day! Nevertheless, until then, one must live!"

He helped himself to three of the available pastries with such gusto that Lou accused him of hoarding. Meriwether grimaced.

"You and I are going to have to talk, Father!"

"Right after dessert! Right after dessert!" he said. "I'm a celibate, not an ascetic!"

The tone turned serious, as Blessed John began.

"You in Safety Harbor have been given the gift of being a Gate of Light city. Now, you have been further blest by the revival of the Sacred Spring. This very day, three miracles have been reported by those who have come in contact with the water. The vision of your child prophet, Little Therese, is coming true. This is a healing stream for body, mind, and spirit. In the future, it will be, for thousands of souls. This place, Caleb and Liz, is no longer yours alone. It is a land to be held in trust for all those souls who come here to find healing and strength. You have been chosen to be its stewards. In the past, this community has been chosen to be Keepers of the Light. Now, you must also be Keepers of the Spring."

With that, Blessed John stood, extended his hand in blessing, and disappeared from their sight.

Chapter 40

CARMELITA'S AND MARSHALL'S INVESTIGATION into Silo's background had yielded much. They had received good cooperation from the Muncie Police and the Indiana Highway Patrol, along with some other smaller towns in Indiana where he had picked up on the trail of Silo's mother.

The truth was more awful than they had imagined. Silo was not the son of the woman, who had sold him to Homer. She, in fact, had stolen him from the nursery in the hospital, when he was only a few hours old. She had kept this secret, for all these years, but, when she was given a tip that the cops were onto her, she sold him quickly, and made her way out of town. Right now, the FBI was investigating as to whether the other three children in her possession, were, in fact, hers, or whether she had stolen them from other people and places. They were looking for Silo's birth mother, as well.

CPS allowed his new foster parents to tell Silo of his family history. Jens placed his arm around the young teenager.

"Silo, I have a story to tell you."

Chapter 41

WHEN RAVEN HEARD OF Homer and his Sunday School class moving into the glass house, he had gone to meet them. He knew, in five minutes, that they would work well together. Now, this morning, the day after the parade, he had called them together, at Marlene's and his office.

"Friends," Raven began, "I'd like to take you to Headquarters. and give you a good look into the inner workings of BFS Inc."

"That sounds exciting!" said Homer.

"When do we go?" asked Marlene.

"Immediately."

"Good. I'll go home and get packed."

"No time for packing," he said. "You will be given everything you need, there."

"Where is it?" asked Shadrach, one of the three members of the Sunday School.

"I'm afraid that I must blindfold you. The location of BFS is a secret, known only to its innermost circle. We're going to get on my private plane at the landing strip."

When they boarded the plane, they were immediately blindfolded, and secured to their seats.

Marlene observed that they couldn't get away if they tried. They felt the plane lift off and its jet engines surge, allowing the metal bird, quickly, to escape the earth, and to move, almost straight up into the air, it seemed. It was difficult to know how much time had passed. The plane landed, as a helicopter would come down out of the air. Marlene felt intense heat coming from below.

The plane came to a stop. The jet engines whined as they wound down. The five of them heard a voice for the first time since they began their journey. It was Raven.

"This is the end of our trip. I have asked my Assistant, Willie, to drive you to headquarters from here. I will meet you there."

They were silently escorted, one by one, off the plane, and placed into what felt like a large car. Had any of the people present at the time of the Search for Joe been there, they would have recognized the sound of the engine as that of the Car of Doom, driven by Willie Bowers, one of the Assistants at BFS Inc., who was now doing a tour of duty at headquarters. Eventually, Willie pulled over, and said, "This will be it, folks. You've arrived. Please wait to be escorted to your destination."

Marlene was surprised to hear Raven's voice next to her.

She felt him begin to loosen the cover from her eyes. Someone was removing the blindfolds from Homer and his Sunday School class.

"Now, stand perfectly still, friends," said Raven.

"This place has never been penetrated by light in any form," said Raven. "Since your eyes respond to light only, you will need a special ability to able to see and to move around here."

Suddenly, they began to be able to see, indeed, if one could call it seeing. They were in a large room.

"This is the center of our operations."

Marlene was surprised to see that there wasn't a sign of high tech anywhere.

"Ah!" said Raven, as if reading her mind. "We do not need technology, that has been created for humans and by humans. Our ways here are beyond your understanding."

They watched, transfixed, as a creature, resembling neither human nor beast, made his way into the room. With their new eyes, they were able to see, in the unearthly darkness, that the creature was moving, gracefully, toward a throne, in the center of the room.

"Ah! We have visitors, do we, Raven?"

When the creature spoke, it penetrated everything around it. All the senses were awakened. There was music. A powerful fragrance filled the room. The experience was overwhelming. Momentarily, there was a loss of the sense of a distinct self. They were attracted to this creature, and simultaneously, repulsed.

"To what fortunate circumstance may I give credit for this auspicious occasion?" asked the creature.

"These are my helpers from Safety Harbor where we now have a stream with healing properties running not far from town. Miracles have been reported."

"This is most serious!"

"And why is that, sir?" Marlene ventured a courageous question.

The creature's once pleasant visage turned dark and foreboding.

"But . . . "

Marlene looked to Raven for help. She had a feeling she should be calling this creature something other than "sir."

"Your Excellency," interjected Raven.

"Your Excellency," she continued, "there are many fountains and streams and caves where people claim to be healed by water. Yet, they have posed no threat to anyone. Why is the stream in Safety Harbor any different?"

"A very astute question. Raven, you must keep her around! The spring was dried up, according to the Indian holy man, when the hearts of men and women became hard, and their greed destroyed it. It has begun to flow again because Safety Harbor, as a Gate of Light, has reached a point of openness and generosity toward one another, as Joe taught them. The miracles are a confirmation of this. Miracles always make our work more difficult. We must gain ownership of the spring, cap it off, and be rid of it. Selfishness, greed, hardness of heart, and wounded spirits are what keep us going."

"Thank you, Your Excellency," said Raven. "We must not take any more of your time. With your permission, I am going to take these good people for a tour of the place."

"Please do. Take your time. They are our guests for dinner."

"Please," said Raven. "Allow your Sunday School class to go to the dining hall. It is most important that Marlene and you receive the tour. Willie, please take them to the dining hall."

Marlene counted nine floors. The entire center of the building was open, with balconies around each floor. A long, ornate staircase went, from the courtyard below, to the top floor. Large doors opened, out, from each room. Most of them were closed. A few people walked along the balconies from several floors, but most all of the courtyard was silent and empty.

"Let us go to the third floor."

They got in the elevator, and it moved, without any instruction from Raven. It opened silently, and the three exited onto the balcony.

"Each floor is dedicated to at least one thing we do in the world. Let us enter this room, for instance."

At his word, the door opened and inside, Marlene and Homer were amazed at what they saw.

"This is our Department of War, Chaos, and Violence," said Raven. As you see, we boast of some of the most famous of history's figures of war and violence here. Genghis Kahn. Caligula. Oh, and right over there is Goebbels. Yes, and Stalin too, although we keep them on separate sides of the room. There are many, many lesser lights here, but these are a few of our celebrities."

"What do they *do*? What do you *do* here?" asked Homer, as if he was, perhaps, a bit envious.

"They use all of their skills and their cunning to inspire today's leaders of hatred and confusion in the world. It is our own war college."

"Sheesh!" said Marlene.

"Let's go walking!" said Raven.

Pointing to each door, he pointed out the name of the departments. "The Department of Domestic Violence. The Department of Genocide. The Department of Alienation. The Department of Human Pain and Suffering. Here is Famine and Poverty. Over here is Addiction and Fear."

"You really are an evil organization!" said Marlene.

"Just practical. We know the heart of human beings. They love the darkness, and the things that come from the darkness. Here, in this darkness beyond the comprehension of even the greatest lovers of darkness in the world, we are able to continue to inspire the evil leaders of your time, through the inspiration of the heroes of old, who work for us, right here."

"Heroes, huh?" Marlene spoke between her teeth. "I had no idea that such a place existed."

"Well, it doesn't!" said Raven, smiling. "Not in your world, the world of light."

"Why have you shown us this?" asked Marlene.

"So that you may see what is at stake. We cannot have such a fountain in the world, that begins to heal old wounds between enemies, that causes miracles in human bodies and human spirits, that brings humans back into touch with the earth. Peace would give humans more time to work on improving the world, human life span, and so forth. Gemma says that humans are basically good. We at Bread from Stone say no; humans are basically evil. Hence, they make great allies for our organization."

"So, you believe I am basically evil" asked Marlene.

"What are you doing here if you are not? Why have you been un-faithful to your husband? Why are you willing to go against your own people for a stranger whom you find attractive? What else could it be?"

"Ab-so-loot-ley!" said Homer. "The prophet says, 'We have all gone astray like sheep, all following our own way.' Isaiah 53:6. I know my Bible!"

Raven chose not to argue with Homer about his point . . . going astray and being evil aren't close to being the same . . . He had found that those who were most sure about their theology actually know very little of it. Homer was, in fact, evil to the bone. He wore his religion with an intent to prey on others. He was proud, way beyond justification. But, all of this could benefit BFS. Evil, but overconfident. This kind are subject to flattery and manipulation.

"I am going to have to go home and talk to Claude and see what to make of all of this."

"Claude, eh? A little late, isn't it? I am afraid, my dear, that once you have experienced the discordant light . . .

"What's the discordant light?"

"It is the light that you are in right now, the light in the darkness that has never been penetrated by light. It is unfriendly to what people recognize as light. It is this darkness that many love. There is no way out now."

"I haven't signed a contract."

"Contracts aren't only signed on paper. Sometimes they are signed when you have surrendered yourself to a person or a cause."

She remained silent.

"There is definitely money to be made here," said Homer.

"Ah yes, money! How much we love money and wealth. It is our sustenance, our life line!" answered Raven.

The two of them shook hands as if they had a private deal.

That night, upon returning from Bread from Stone Headquarters, Marlene slipped into bed beside Claude, and held him more tightly than she had, in years.

Chapter 42

IT WAS 10:00 A.M. when Marlene opened her eyes. Claude had been awake for hours, and was at work at Ripple's. He had left coffee for her.

Did yesterday really happen or had it all been a bad dream? As if to answer her question, she got a call from Raven.

"Are you coming into the office or are you overtired from yesterday?"

"Yesterday?"

"My dear, have you so soon forgotten? Rub the cobwebs from your eyes. Clear your brain. Come into the office. We have much to talk about, after yesterday's visit."

Marlene thought it sounded inviting to stay in her pajamas. On the other hand, she did not trust Raven in the office, alone. She savored few sips of coffee, before jumping in the shower. She did not arrive at the office, until noon.

Raven was clearly irritated with her late arrival.

After a few moments of silence. he said, "I've heard from Headquarters this morning and they are very happy with you."

"Thank you!" said Marlene. "I think!"

Raven smiled slightly as he spoke the last three words.

"One of the reasons I took you there was so that Human Resources and Assets could look you over and decide whether you all qualify for the task ahead."

"Human Resources and Assets?"

"Yes, dear."

She was beginning to hate his patronizing.

"We have all kinds of resources available to us. Among them are human beings."

"What other kinds of resources?"

"That would take another trip to Headquarters."

"I can wait."

Chapter 43

GEORGETTE BEGAN PACKING BY boxing up knick-knacks and small photos. She knew her husband couldn't bear to do it, especially when it came to the pictures of his parents and family. Hobe had gone over to the lumberyard, to take the place of someone who called in sick. It was one way he could hold on to something that wasn't changing.

She stood in front of the mantel, and was stopped short. Various photos of Glenda at different ages and eras stared her in the face. The three boys' photos were there, too. They lost their youngest, Eugene, when he was only eight. Then, there was the photo of Hobe's and her twenty-fifth wedding anniversary. She heard herself chuckle, out loud. They thought they were getting old by then, but didn't know how young they still were. John and Ella's photo was right in the middle. Every year those two looked quainter, somehow, more removed from the present.

Georgia sat down in the rocking chair handed down from her family that was said to have come west on the Oregon Trail. She looked around her. It had been a good life in this house. Each space held a kaleidoscope of memories. They had made a lot of changes. They had replaced the old wood burning stove with a fireplace. The house was trimmed with paint, and the rest was wallpaper that she had changed every two years. She wished she knew how many times she had dusted and swept and changed the table cloths and picked flowers in her garden to put on the table for dinner.

She knew this much. Everything she had done here had been an act of love for her husband and family. Then, of course, during the early years she took care of John and Ella. Ella was loving, but never easy. It was ten years before she trusted Georgette alone in the kitchen.

"Leave her alone and come sit with me, Ella," John would say. "Let Georgette cook supper tonight."

"Soon as she's ready! Soon as she's ready," Ella would say.

Georgette smiled and put her head back, looking up at the ceiling. Slowly, she rocked in the chair until she heard Hobe come in for lunch.

Chapter 44

AT HIS LUNCH HOUR, the next day, Caleb found himself out at the Old Eighty. He walked into the woods. He hadn't gone very far, when he heard the crack of what sounded to be like someone walking on a fallen twig or branch. Through the trees and brush, he thought he saw the outline of a human. As the figure approached, he could hear someone whistling. As the man came out into the open he looked up at Caleb in surprise.

"Good afternoon to you sir!"

"Aren't you Blessed John?"

"Why, yes I am! And you are Caleb! Go ahead, ask me what I'm doing here!"

"There are lots of people on this land who haven't been invited!" Caleb said, with a grim smile.

"It is a beautiful place you have here. Hills and valleys. Trees and open land."

They began to walk an unseen path that seemed familiar to Blessed John, who moved with confidence, as if the woods were his own

"Come. I'd like to show you something."

Caleb was amazed that a man of Blessed John's size and apparent age could move so quickly, and with such stealth. They nearly ran up the hill. The grade was steeper than it had looked to Caleb, as he had viewed it from the barn. By the time they reached the top, Caleb was winded, but Blessed John was breathing, as if he had expended no energy at all.

There, appearing among the trees, was what appeared to be an old forest ranger lookout station.

"Come. let's climb to the top. I want to show you something."

"Is it solid enough?"

Caleb did not feel reassured, but followed Uncle John, who seemed confident in the structure's soundness. As he reached the top, Blessed John reached down and pulled him up the rest of the way. They stood together on the narrow platform.

"Look! Over this way! You can see your entire property from here."

Caleb was amazed. Blessed John was not exaggerating. There in the far distance, the road they had come into town on, and the stream in parallel with it, came into view. The big house, the farmstead, even some of the unsold machinery was recognizable. Then, like a shimmering and numinous living thing, the spring sparkled with light. It stood out from everything around it, which became background to its splendor. From here, it was not something to control and to limit, but a thing of beauty to behold.

He could feel Blessed John's eyes upon him as he stood, stunned by the scene.

"This is no normal spring."

"No, it isn't. It is a gift to all of you, to make you a custodian of this chalice of healing. Wherever the water from this spring is distributed, it will bring healing. Angels will stir up the waters, and those who come to it will experience miracles."

"When Liz and I bought this place only a few days ago, we had visions of settling in and making this place our own. Now . . ."

It was as if Blessed John didn't hear him. He spoke words which would change everything for the future.

"*Look below again, Caleb. What do you see? I mean, what do you see, beyond what is to be seen with the natural eye?*"

"I see an open plain between the pond and the trees."

"Yes, and what else do you see?"

"I see people."

"And what are these people doing?"

"Why, they are building!"

"What are they building?"

"Houses, it seems."

"Yes, they are."

"Take a closer look. Focus in just on one."

"Why, it's Rock and Magdalena!"

It suddenly dawned upon him. It was the Unsettlement. They were building permanent housing, in the clearing. The Unsettlement was settling in at the Old Eighty!

"This you have seen, dear Caleb, not with your natural sight, but with your vision for the future, that tells you what is possible. Does this vision fill your heart? Does it give you a thrill of hope, or does it make you anxious and afraid?"

"Yes, Blessed John! All of that. But once you have seen such a vision, you can't un-see it."

"That is true, lad. The question is always 'What can you see that is beyond what is to be seen with the natural eye?' When you can see this kind of thing, then, the way can be open to see that vision come true. It is not to say there would not be hurdles and obstacles. It may become so difficult that you will question your judgment. But, as long as you can see the vision, you are on the right track."

"I'm not sure what Liz will think. I wish we could have talked about this together, all three of us. We always approach things together."

"Liz and you can still do this. Our paths crossing today was not random. The same One who has given us the spring for refreshment has seen to it that we had conversation. Mostly, I find that I meet people, while they are 'on the way'. My life is that of a wanderer, traveling through the world, drinking in the beauty of the earth, becoming drunk on the wine of Creation. I have no permanent dwelling place. Sometimes it is only clear to me what I am to do, where I am to go, and with whom I am to converse, minutes before the time."

"We were going to have dinner tonight at LeRoy's Blue Whale to talk about the use of the Old Eighty. This is perfect timing."

"Share the vision with Liz," said Blessed John. "Ponder these things. Both of you. Ponder them in your hearts."

Caleb was now at his desk. He did not recall leaving Blessed John, or driving back to the hospital. Had it been real or had it all been a dream?

Chapter 45

"Yes, I wish he would have consulted us together, too, Liz. But, he explained to me that's not how he does things. He encounters people, 'along the way," said Caleb. "Fact is, Liz, I don't know whether it was a real experience, or not. I could have been dreaming. I mean, I don't remember coming back from the Old Eighty. I just sort of 'woke up' at my desk. But 'real' or not, his proposal made such good sense, that I have really been excited to share it with you."

"Things are moving so quickly, Caleb. We are both just trying to get a grip on our jobs and suddenly, we are hit with all of this. Hard to believe it's all because of a spring. Sometimes, I just want to turn the clock back and say to everyone, 'This is *our* farm. Everybody go away. We plan to spend years of our lives here, to begin our family, and to enjoy the good land and the crisp air. We want to look at the stars at night and marvel at them, in peace. We have given our lives in service all ready. Now, it's our time!"

"We could do that."

"Yes, we could."

"What is keeping us from just sending everybody home?"

"Ever since Roy Legband came, and sobbed and moaned so deeply because he now saw the spring that had been taken from them so cruelly, all those years ago, we have felt that the place wasn't ours, not entirely. Blessed John told us the land is not our own."

"Yes, then there have been those miracles. They may or may not not pass a scientific test, but, at least some are finding their lives changed by the stream, spiritually, psychologically or physically, or all three."

"I think we would be happy to share our place . . . I know I would, at least . . . but, at the moment, there is so much chaos, so much unsettledness, that I just want to let it all go back to Hobe and Georgette."

"Well, that's not going to be possible, of course, so we just have to figure out what we're gonna do. The suggestions Blessed John made, seemed so right in the moment."

The summer nights were long, with lots of daylight at the end. The couple decided that they would go out to the farm after dinner. They ate hurriedly at LeRoy's and drove to the Old Eighty, with dispatch.

Chapter 46

LIZ PARKED THE CAR in the driveway. They approached the house and Hobe came out to meet them.

"We thought we would take a walk in the woods on this beautiful summer night," said Caleb. "That is, if you don't mind. The place is still yours."

"Our home is your home" said Hobe.

"We are going up to the summit of the hill," said Liz. "Caleb was up there last night and he wanted to show me the view."

"There isn't much of a view from the top. All the trees keep you from seeing beyond them."

"I ran into Blessed John in the woods yesterday. He took me to the top and showed me the view from the old Forest Service tower."

"That's odd," said Hobe.

"Honey!" he called out.

Georgette came out the front door and greeted them warmly.

"Sorry I didn't get out here earlier," she said. "*Somebody's* got to finish the dishes!"

She gave Hobe a light elbowing. He gasped and feigned deep pain. Liz noticed how gentle the couple were with one another, even in their teasing. She hoped Caleb and she could develop that kind of relationship.

"Have you ever heard of an old Forest Service tower on the property? The kids say that Caleb met Blessed John in the woods yesterday evening, and he took him to this tower, and showed him the view of the whole place, from the top."

"No, I remember no such thing. I'm sure I'd remember it, if I had seen it."

"Maybe I was dreaming," said Caleb.

"Maybe you were!" said Hobe.

Liz, having learned from watching her mother smooth things over from Lou's comments, said, "Yes! He's my dreamer!" She patted him on the shoulder.

Then, she turned and said, "We're off to the hills!"

"You two have a good time up there!" said Georgette.

They walked across the yard toward the path beside the barn that led to the spring. They could hear it now, before they saw it. There was a mist in the air, coming off the water. A few people were standing along the banks. Children were there. One of the men was helping a little girl into the stream. Still another, Caleb guessed to be a young man who had a war injury, and was being carried by friends or family or both, to the water. Caleb and Liz watched as some people, who obviously loved him, lifted him from his chair and gently lowered him into the water.

They were deeply moved by this scene. No words seemed adequate as a response. It was best met with holy silence.

They moved on.

"Where is the trail to the top of the hill?"

"There is no trail that I know of. Blessed John seemed to know the way, and I followed."

Liz was momentarily exasperated.

"Well, husband, how many acres of woods do we have?"

"Sixty. Sixty acres."

"Enough to get lost!"

"I think we can manage it. I really do."

He took her by the hand. As they entered the woods and were taken in by its beauty, they soon forgot their conversation about getting lost.

"I can feel my way along," said Caleb. "I can almost feel Blessed John leading me ahead, to the top."

"I'll have to trust that."

Time passed quickly. Time past slowly. Time stood still.

"We are in an enchanted forest, I do believe," said Liz.

They could hear someone whistling in the distance.

"Someone else is here, enjoying our enchanted forest," said Caleb. "And I have an idea about who it is!"

"Who?"

"Come and see," he said.

The whistling became louder and clearer.

"Look up, friends!"

There, on top the old Forest Service tower was Blessed John.

"Come! Come and join me!"

"I knew it was there! I just knew it!" said Caleb.

"I know you did!"

"Be careful," said Caleb. "The tower is old, but it seems to be solid."

The two climbed toward the top of the tower, and Blessed John helped them up on the platform.

After Liz caught her balance, she began to look around.

"Oh yes, Caleb. I see what you see! How different it looks from where we stand, here, rather than close up, on the ground!"

"Yes, one can see an order to it all from here, a plan, even."

"From this point of view, I don't feel that anxiety that I had constantly, since the spring burst open. Until now, I have had a growing 'What are we going to do?' question in my mind, pretty much all the time. Now . . . "

"Now," Caleb finished her sentence, "we can ask, 'How do we go about doing all that this land, this spring, calls us to do?'"

"Your vision is becoming clearer and clearer." said Blessed John. "The answers to the dilemmas you face are all found in this land, this place, this spring; that, and your selfless sharing with those who are in the most need. You will find that your problems turn into plans, and confusion becomes clarity."

"But, is it really that simple, Blessed John?"

"This place can be a microcosm of healing for the whole world, an example of what can be done if the human heart turns toward generosity and compassion."

"I'd love to see what that looks like, Uncle John, in real time, and in real life."

"This will develop over time. Be anxious about nothing. When your hearts are at peace, all that you are called to do and to be will make itself known."

As they walked down the hill from the tower, Blessed John said, "There will be those who oppose your work here. Some are envious of your good fortune in having this place. Others want to profit from it, especially since the spring has reappeared."

"What do they want with the spring?" asked Liz. "We have been overwhelmed by this unexpected complication."

"There are miracles taking place. The world is full of those who try to profit from spiritual phenomena. They want to use universal human suffering and anxiety, and the deep human need to be freed from isolation and loneliness, as a way to profit, to seek fame, admiration, and power."

"What are we to do?"

"Don't be afraid. You are being accompanied by angels who will bear you up in time of trouble."

"Are you an angel, Blessed John?"

"I am, like you, a creation of God. I am called to roam the earth, laying my eyes on all of the beauty that I can, helping the inhabitants of the planet to see their own beauty, and the beauty of others."

As they left the woods behind, they stepped out into the clearing.

"Let's rest a moment," said Blessed John.

They sat together on one of the limbs of a fallen tree.

"Look at all we have been given!" said Liz.

"Oh, we're paying for it!" chuckled Caleb.

"I mean the opportunities, husband. We have an opportunity for a whole new life. The spring has brought us many blessings."

"There is one vision that Uncle John has for the place where we are sitting."

"A cow pasture? What could possibly be done with a cow pasture?"

"A good place for the Unsettlement, don't you think?" asked Uncle John.

There was a moment of silence.

Liz was stunned. Of course! This was it! This was the answer she was looking for and it had been before her all the time.

"Yes!" said Liz. "I feel good about that. Can it be worked out?"

"With all of the talents and people of good hearts who wish only good, all around you, you have every chance of being successful. And another thing . . . I hope you do no not think I am precocious. . . I hope that you will consult the Joe Team. They will help you with putting a mission together out of your vision. It is your property, but it is the work of everyone."

"We will consider all you say to us, and take it to heart," said Caleb.

When he did not answer, they looked and he was gone.

Chapter 47

A MEETING OF THE Joe Team had been called for the next day, at 6:30 p.m., at Joe's. Stewart and Luther offered to provide a light dinner. They made sliders and potato salad, topped off by a generous helping of ice cream.

Father approved of the meal, declaring it to be worthy of Mrs. McCarthy, his housekeeper's cooking. Everyone knew that Father loved sliders, from his attendance at Friday night football games, but Mrs. McCarthy would not make them because she had declared them to be too unhealthy.

In the last year, there had been more interest among those who had not known Joe and were not present when he was among them or when he was rescued. In response, the Joe Team provided a place for observers. It was clear from Joe's suggestions that only those who had been with Joe should serve on the Team. But, their procedure must be transparent, said Sally. For that reason, anyone could attend.

A dozen chairs had been set up around the Wisdom Table, one of which was occupied by Marlene, who was still on her mission for Raven, to sabotage the goings-on at the Spring. Father took notice of her change in attitude since Raven had come to town. She was less outgoing. She seemed furtive, even secretive. She had her iPad out and was clearly intending to take notes.

Sally opened the meeting. Everyone was present except for Doc Bailey who, Sally had announced, was making a house call.

"Now, I will declare this meeting to be in session. We have asked members of the Siletz Confederation to be a part of this meeting. We welcome them as our special guests, who also will be invited to join in the conversations, for reasons that will be obvious, later."

"Madame Leader," said Mayor Lou, 'what is the purpose of this meeting?"

"Caleb and Liz have asked for a consultation with the team."

Lou looked surprised.

Liz began.

"As you know . . . at least, I think everybody knows . . . that Caleb and I have bought Hobe and Georgette's property known as the Old Eighty. You also know that a legendary old spring has made its way back up through the earth, and is putting a lot of water on the land. We have been struggling to know what to do with it."

"If this was just an ordinary spring," Caleb continued, "it would be difficult enough to know how to deal with it, but, our friends, who were here long before we ever were, inform us that this spring was once available to them and then stopped flowing after it was taken by greedy white men, for themselves. Ruby, will you fill us in?"

Ruby came forward and stood near the Stone of Gleaming. Then, she began.

"Our shaman, Roy Legband, tells us of how this spring is sacred to our people, and that it has healing powers. The Creator has said that the Sacred Spring would begin flowing again, when the hearts and minds of people are open to love. The shaman tells us that this is the time that was predicted by the ancestors, who prophesied when the spring went dry. Now, he goes every day to the spring, offers prayers, and burns sage. We want to be a part of what happens to this Sacred Spring. After all, it was ours and in a real way, it still is."

Liz continued.

"A number of people have claimed that drinking the water, touching the water, pouring the water over them, or stepping into the water has resulted in miracles for them. Just last night when Caleb and I walked past the stream, three separate families were, in some way, seeking a miracle from the water. We were on our way to do some hiking in the hills, when we came upon Blessed John, standing high on an old Forest Service tower. He showed us all of the Old Eighty. From that height, we could see the whole place. On the ground, all that has happened has seemed so chaotic and confusing, but from our vantage point we could envision a purpose for everything that we saw."

Caleb added to his wife's account.

"We want to share our vision with you, to seek your advice and counsel, and your blessing for our plans. We are also open to any questions you may have."

"Sally," said Georgette, "may I add a few words?"

"By all means."

"Hobe and I have become convinced that the spring is a sign to us of the sacredness of the Old Eighty. Hobe has been on this land for over seventy years and I have been with him for fifty of them. Neither of us ever knew of the well. Fact is, we're convinced that it wasn't there. We would have to have seen it, or tripped over it, or the cattle would have stepped on it and with their weight, they would have broken through the platform and fallen into the well.

"Instead it was discovered by a little boy. We don't know who he was and he was never seen, again. As for the Forest Service tower, I have never seen one on the place. But both Caleb and Liz claim to have stood on the tower with the man who calls himself Blessed John."

"And just who is this Blessed John?" asked Jeremy. "Where did he come from? Why is he here? How can a stranger be so trusted in such a short time?"

"I don't think anyone knows who he is," said Father. "Maybe he is just himself, someone just like us, except very eccentric."

"Maybe he was sent to us," said Georgia.

"Yes, but, by whom?" asked Magdalena?

"Perhaps Joe sent him," said Jeremy.

"All I know," said Liz, "is that a human being can't just disappear!"

"He did?" asked Jens.

"He did," said Caleb.

"All things are possible," said Father. "Maybe he is a man. Maybe he is an angel. Maybe he's of some other creation that we don't know about."

"Now you're spookin' me out, Father," said Nate.

"Time will tell," said Georgia. "Until we know, just go with the flow. Something, someone is leading us right now."

"The reason we are here," said Liz, "is to let you know, after our conversation with Blessed John, we have decided what we want to do with the property; but, we want your input, and if possible, your blessing."

"Well, let's hear it," said Jens. "I'm dyin' to hear this."

"We saw from the vantage point of the tower, that we are the owners of the property, but that it does not belong to us. The Sacred Spring is a sign to us; and the sign is confirmed by the miracles that are taking place," said Liz.

"Tell us your plans," said Magdalena. "We really want to know them."

"We want the land to be used in several ways," said. "First of all, the farmhouse. That is reserved for Caleb and me. We have always dreamed of a home just like the one on the Old Eighty. We hope to have a family and raise our children in a place that has heard the voices and sounds of three generations of little ones. The house holds wonderful memories for me when I came to visit Uncle Hobey and Aunt Georgette, as I grew up with their daughter, Glenda.

"As for the well . . . the spring . . . it was there for our indigenous brothers and sisters before we appeared here, in this land. It is available to you anytime you want to hold a ceremony or a celebration."

"Blessed John has given us suggested plans for the pool into which the water will flow. The spring will have a small platform of steps leading up to it, or, if you are at the spring, the steps descend into the pool. The plans Blessed John gave us, resemble very much what archaeologists believe the recently discovered Pool of Siloam in Jerusalem looked like. As with the Pool of Siloam, in the time of the Bible, our pool evidently has healing capacities as well. We want to make sure that it is available to the public. The spring is a gift to the world and we want those who want to do so, to come and bathe in its waters, or come to take some water home with them."

"Now, for our surprise!" said Liz. "We are offering the rather extensive cow pasture as a place for the Unsettlement to make their permanent home. It will take some time to draw up the plans, and, of course, it must be accepted by our friends at the Unsettlement."

There was utter silence.

Father was the first to speak.

"What you are proposing to do with your land is very generous, indeed."

"We can do no other, Father," said Caleb. "The Sacred Spring is a gift to us all and to who knows how many other people?"

"What do you need from us?" asked Georgia. "It sounds as if you have thought out your plans well."

"Well, as I said, Georgia, we want, we need your blessing. Blessed John was clear with us that the Joe Team should be consulted."

"We're overwhelmed, of course, at your generous offer," said Magdalena. "I am sure our community will consent to moving to the Old Eighty."

Silo had accompanied Jens and Shirley to the meeting. He raised his hand.

"You will need some money. I know where there's lots of money, out at the glass house!"

"You do?" asked Jens. "We'll talk more about this at home."

"Silo is right," said Jeremy. "This will take a lot of money, especially with the building of the fountain steps and the pool. This will take all of us. I ask that we, as the Joe Team, open our hearts and our resources to help with this great project."

"Yes!" said Ruth. "By all means!"

"Part of what we can do," said the mayor, "is to figure out, with Caleb and Liz, all that needs to be done, so that we know what our part is in this."

"Some of us have very little money to offer," said Carla.

"Oh, it isn't the money," said Little Therese. "It's the bounty that each of us have to share, from what has been given to us."

Hope mouthed the word to Liz, silently, "Bounty?"

Then she said to Lou, "Where does she get those words? They are way beyond her vocabulary, at this age."

"Blessed John made it very clear that there will be opposition to what we are doing." said Little Therese. "There are some who want the spring for themselves, and will go to any lengths to get it."

"There are some who would use the spring to make money." said Little Therese, "because of its healing powers."

Caitlin raised her hand. Sally recognized her.

"I have a question."

"Yes, Caitlin."

"Are there really miracles taking place at the spring?"

"We know that people are saying that they are experiencing miracles," said Father.

"Shouldn't we evaluate those and decide whether they are genuine or not?" asked Nate.

"It is not within our purview to judge whether or not people have experienced a miracle," said Father. "It is between them and the Holy."

"What's a purview?" asked Buddy.

"Maybe I should have said 'It's none of our business', Buddy. It is not within our understanding, so it's not our business to judge."

"Thanks, Father," said Buddy.

"You are most welcome, Buddy."

"Madame Leader, I would like to honor the Watsons for all they are going through, right now. They have a good two weeks left in their home while escrow is taking place," said Liz.

"We are happy that someone will be doing something with the land besides dividing it up and selling it off in lots. You are going to let Hobe continue to raise a garden and he'll still be planting crops. That'll get him out of our condo, once in a while," said Georgette.

There was general laughter.

Bart raised his hand. "I think when you get to a point that you know what you need, that you should consult the Cone Foundation."

"What would this town be like had we not had Wendell and Irene been with us?" asked the mayor, wistfully.

He turned away as a tear spilled down one cheek.

"How can we help you, from this point?" asked Sally.

"We have a lot of talking to do, especially with the Unsettlement. May we be back in touch, as things develop?"

"There are many of us who stand ready to help, I am sure," said Katye.

"We want to use everybody's know-how!" said Caleb.

Father noticed that Marlene had been taking copious notes on her iPad, looking up only when it seemed to him that she must be hearing something for the first time.

"Marlene," he called out. "would you be willing to share your notes as a part of the record?"

She squirmed.

"Oh, these notes are for my own use. They aren't really minutes, or anything like that."

At the risk of taking the positive edge off the meeting, he continued to press her. He was convinced she was working for Raven.

"And what will you use them for?" he asked.

"Oh, just business,"

She laughed nervously.

"I do have interest in the property, since I am the agent who sold it, and it is still in escrow."

Father chose not to take it any farther.

Chapter 48

THE NEXT MORNING, THE meeting at Marlene's office was tense. Raven was not pleased.

"How will you stop them?"

At first, Marlene believed that she only thought this, but then, she heard herself say the last few words. Suddenly, she realized she was afraid of Raven. She had been intimidated all along. He had known her weakness, her vulnerability, her loneliness, and he had taken advantage of her. She knew that, now. But, she felt trapped. Raven had the goods on her. They were in the midst of an affair. At least she thought so. At times, he brought her close, and then, he would act as if they knew each other casually. It kept her off balance. Still, she felt she had to leave things the way they were. She wouldn't put it past Raven to let it be known that they had a relationship, if that's what it was. It would affect her reputation and hurt her business, to say nothing of her marriage.

Up to now, her excursions to Lincoln City and Portland had amounted only to flirtations, sometimes allowing certain men liberties, much of the time depending upon the amount of her consumption of alcohol. Many nights, she came home from these situations still lonely, suffering from guilt, and shame. She had learned how to put it all behind her by the next morning, and moved on, as if it hadn't happened. Claude conspired with her in this denial.

She was jerked back to the present, by the precise and sharp enunciation of Raven's voice.

"Mrs. Brooker, [this was going to be a day when he keeps his distance, she thought] what is the latest from the spring? Do you have your report available on the Joe Team yet?"

She lied.

"Almost. I'll finish up from my notes, right after our meeting!"

The front door opened. It was Father Callaghan.

"Oh, am I interrupting something?" he asked.

Raven tensed up immediately.

"We were just finishing up, Father," said Marlene, seeing a possible way of temporary escape.

"Good!" he said.

Pulling a young couple up to his side, he said, "Marlene, these are two of my new parishioners. They were just married, at Our Lady, a couple of weeks ago. They are back from their honeymoon, and they are looking to buy their first home right here in Safety Harbor. Can you find them a place?"

"By all means, Father."

Marlene could feel herself coming back into her body.

"We have finished our business," she said.

"And of course, you know Raven."

Raven refused eye contact.

"Hello, priest!" he said.

"Yes, we've met," said Father, without acknowledging him at all.

Chapter 49

FRANCIS WAS A YOUNG seminarian during the last year of the Second Vatican Council. Some of his cohorts and he traveled to Rome, in 1963. Those were heady days. Vatican City itself seemed to exude a dynamic energy. Major changes were ahead. This was exciting for young candidates for the priesthood, whose entire careers were ahead of them. They walked the halls of power, eavesdropped on conversations, and met other seminarians, from around the world, some of whom became lifelong friends.

Rules on serving alcohol were less stringent in those days, and it was easy for young persons to get a beer in the evenings, at one of the bars close to the hostel, where they were staying. After a long theological discussion, fueled by the alcohol, he left his friends behind, to go to bed early. As he was walking down the street, a man he had seen in the bar, began to walk beside him.

"Pardon me, if you don't mind. May I walk with you?

"I don't see why not."

"I couldn't help but overhear your conversation back there. The fruit of the vine and the nectar of the grain, are at the source of much theology!"

"Just two beers for me! I'm done. It's been a long day and another big day is coming. I want to be clear-eyed to take in all that is going on."

"I understand that. A very sober and mature decision on your part, I must say, for such a young man, and very intelligent, as well."

"Thank you. Are you a delegate to the Council?"

"You might say so."

"Where are you from?"

"We have offices around the world. After the Council, I will be going to the United States. You are an American. Right?

"Yes. I am at Notre Dame."

"Ah yes! Our Lady! How we love her, eh?"

"Yes, we do. By the way, what is your organization?"

"We are called Bread from Stone. You know, when the Savior was being tempted, it was suggested that he make bread from the stones in the desert, when he was hungry."

"But, he wasn't hungry, until afterward."

"Do you believe that for a minute? How can someone not be hungry after only a few hours? Thirsty too. It only stands to reason that he would be. Our organization tries to make people use their heads, to believe what is believable. After all, much of what Jesus is supposed to have said, he probably didn't say. Much of what he was supposed to have done, he probably didn't do."

"What do you want to accomplish?"

"We believe healthy religion is sensible religion. We want to see Christianity settle down in the world as another philosophy. Religion is a lot better when it is tame. We don't want to do away with it. We just want it to become palatable and reasonable. We want it to give up its efforts to convert the world. It is just an effort to get power. We want the church to quit its power. After all, do not the Scriptures say, 'My strength is made perfect in weakness'?"

"What does Bread from Stone want the world to be?"

"We believe that we can do a good job at running it."

"So, you want world domination?"

"Not domination. We just want to set up a system that will make the world a better place."

"I see. So, nothing here about God being in charge?"

"I ask you, Francis [May I call you Francis?], what has God done for you lately? God has done a pretty piss-poor job [if you'll excuse my language] of running the world, if you ask me. People have lived as if God is coming to earth to rule things. Do you really want the God who lets babies suffer and die of hunger, and old people malinger, and wars kill and maim and destroy, in complete charge? No, we do not! Some people even say [and I think this is the voice of reason] that there isn't a God and that we are on our own. That would be all the better because we don't have a Big Guy to blame or please, and we can make our own world.

"And look at the Church right here in Rome. Look at all the high-hatted and high minded leaders up there, parading around in obscenely ridiculous costumes, as if their getup gives them some kind of authority and piety and respectability. They have thoughts just as lustful and common as the rest of us. They lie. All the time. They commit adultery. They steal from the church coffers. They get lonely and frightened, as you and I do. That is the kind of club you are thinking about joining, Francis. It is a waste of your life. We have need of thoughtful young people such as yourself. Maybe we could have another beer. Oh look! Here is another refreshment station right here! May I buy you a drink, my good man?"

Time became irrelevant, as Raven poured on the alcohol and talked, convincingly, about Bread from Stone. Francis sort of remembered resisting signing the contract and asking Raven to give him overnight to think about it.

In an unplanned buzz, and with a disturbed mind, Francis tossed and turned all night. The man, who had introduced himself simply as Raven, had brought him to a crisis. How could his faith be shaken so quickly, after a lifetime of devotion? How could he become unhinged so quickly? He tossed and turned, and then, overslept for the Council session, where he had obtained a pass for the morning. He hated himself.

He rubbed his eyes. On the stand, next to the bed, was Raven's card. He dressed and, absent mindedly, put the card in his shirt pocket. Then, he walked quickly down the street to the Vatican, to see if he could find a way into the proceedings, by stealth.

He did not see Raven all that day. That evening, he was, however, at the same bar as last night, where Francis and his cohort had met. Francis tried to avoid eye contact, hoping that their conversation could be forgotten. But was not to be. Raven was persistent.

"May I join you gentlemen?" he asked, approaching the table.

There was a clumsy moment. Many would have seen from the body language that this was a closed table. But, that didn't stop Raven. He was in recruiting mode.

Raven had forced his hand.

"Friends, this is Raven. We met last night, when I was walking home from the bar."

He was invited to sit down, but before long, one by one, Francis's colleagues left the table, leaving only Francis and Raven.

Francis was annoyed. He was making good friends. Resentment arose within his chest. He did his best to hide it.

"Have you given thought to what I offered you last night?"

"As much as I can remember. You fed me some pretty strong alcohol, I'm leaning toward saying 'No.'"

"That's too bad. What will you do?"

"I am going to continue toward preparing for my vocation."

"You are turning down a wonderful opportunity. Besides a chance to see the world, you would find your work to be very lucrative."

"I have been troubled by many things in my dreams last night. All I could see was darkness. I could hear your voice calling me, and yet, I could not see you for the pitch blackness."

"It's silly, Francis. Why would you base your decision on an alcohol-induced dream?"

"The dream just confirmed for me what I'd been thinking consciously. My vocation means more to me than anything. I cannot abandon it."

Raven's face turned dark.

"Your choice is unfortunate."

"Why is that?"

"The call to work for Bread from Stone is an irrevocable calling. You will remain on our list as a recruit. You may well hear from us at different times in your life. In fact, you can bank on it."

Francis had the distinct sense that he should call a cab, rather than walk to the hostel. This he did; and although he kept an eye out, he did not see Raven again, in Rome.

Ten years later, he was serving as Assistant Pastor at St. Ita's in the little town of Portraine, Ireland. He was in the midst of a baptism when he noticed Raven among the family members gathered round the baptismal font. Raven nodded to him and smiled faintly. Father was startled and temporarily knocked off balance.

Two years later, Raven appeared to him in a dream.

"You have not forgotten the call you have to work for Bread from Stone, have you?" he asked Francis.

"I have not forgotten that you *claim* that I have a call. However, my vocation to God's work was with me long before your claim on my life. I have no desire to work for Bread from Stone."

Then, in the dream, Francis found himself flying to where, he knew not. He was brought down at the door of Bread from Stone Headquarters. There, Raven showed him all of the things he would later introduce to Marlene, Homer, and his three followers, including the snake-like Creature, perched on a throne, that Raven announced as in charge of the whole enterprise.

"You can be a part of all of this," said Raven. "You can have your own department and have people work for you, or as we say here, 'do your bidding'. All you have to do is sign the contract."

Francis bolted, and fled the place. He awakened in a cold sweat.

The last time he had seen Raven, before his appearance in Safety Harbor, was when he had taken a stint as a chaplain in the war in Iraq. He spent much of his time at Al Karkh General Hospital, in Baghdad. He heard countless confessions, baptized those who asked, and offered anointing to those who were dying. He offered solace and counsel to atheists, and fed little children.

He became well known to some, beloved to others, and hated by those who fueled their lives by despising the enemy. He was accused by a group of military officers of "giving aid and comfort" to the enemy. More specifically, the charge was that he had been undermining the morale of the military by speaking of peace in his homilies, and by speaking his mind to prisoners of war about the evils of war and violence. He had also pleaded the case of several prisoners, for reunification with their families.

It was Raven, among others, who stood as one of his accusers, in that awful moment when he was brought before a disciplinary committee; and it was Raven who, eventually, came to his defense by changing his mind and talked the others into withdrawing the charges.

"Now, you owe me, Francis. You would have been in the brig had it not been for my intervention."

"None of this would have happened without your bringing charges in the first place."

"As you may well surmise, Bread from Stone is here to get what we can from violence. We don't think it's a bad thing. In fact, it's a good thing. It is slow, but we are taking over the world, one step at a time. It's time for you to come on home, now, to your real calling. You are just what we need, a trusted person of impeccable character."

"If I joined you, my impeccable character would be gone."

Raven's eyes narrowed.

"I will come for you, and when I do, it will be pay day!"

Now that Raven was in Safety Harbor, whatever his agenda, Father Francis Callaghan knew that Raven did not plan on leaving town until he had found a way to take him out.

He shuddered.

Chapter 50

FATHER CALLAGHAN HAD BEEN gone for a few days, to an Archdiocesan meeting. When he returned to the rectory, Mrs. McCarthy was back, full time. She was making him a welcome-home meal, his favorite fish and chips dish dinner, to celebrate his return.

"You have guests in the living room, Father. They have been waiting to see you for some time now."

"No rest for the wicked!" said Father.

Mrs. McCarthy smiled, and motioned toward the living room. There, he found Little Therese and Evita DuPont awaiting him.

Little Therese ran to him and put her arms around him. They hugged affectionately. Father Callaghan bowed low to Evita.

"To what do I owe having these extraordinary guests?"

"Little Therese has been troubled lately, Father. She says you are her confidante, and counselor, when she is disturbed or confused."

"Father, I have been feeling the conflict of two forces about to collide with one another. I am feeling great tension within me. It seems that all the good that is happening at the Sacred Spring, is in danger. It is as if some hostile force is wanting to take over everything there."

"Have you been dreaming again, Little Therese?"

"No. I wish it had all been a dream. You can wake up from a dream. This terrible, dark foreboding is with me much of the time, now."

Frank decided he had to tell Little Therese and Evita DuPont all of his experiences with Raven over the years.

"So, you see," he concluded afterward, "the threat is real. Raven not only wants to stop the Sacred Spring; he wants to remove all of Joe's legacy from among us. He would have us go back to the way we were, before Joe came to town."

"Do you mean he wants us not to be a Gate of Light City anymore?"

"He never wanted us to be a Gate of Light, in the first place. You remember the Car of Doom."

"How could we not remember it, Father?" asked Evita DuPont.

"The driver is now Raven's assistant. So, you see, all of this is connected. We are Keepers of the Light. Now, we are being called to be Keepers of the Spring. Bread from Stone does not want us to be keepers of anything."

"They want us to leave all of this behind, to forget it, as if it had never happened!"

"Yes, they do, Little Therese," said Father Callaghan.

"Moreover," said Evita DuPont, "Raven wants all of us, but most of all he wants the dear Father here. He wants him dead!"

"We must not allow this to happen," said Little Therese.

"Some of us may have to put our own lives in danger, in order to remain Keepers of the Light and now, Keepers of the Spring," said Evita DuPont.

Then, he said, "Raven will have a plan. This much I know. He always has a plan. And he is very flexible with his plans, because he is very determined to get what he wants, to get his way. He can turn on a dime, so to speak. What you think he is going to do . . . sometimes what *he* thinks he is going to do . . . can suddenly, change.

Raven works in two ways. First, he works by seduction. For instance, I believe Marlene Brooker is under his spell right now."

"You mean, she's having an affair?' asked Little Therese.

Father blanched. Kids knew too much these days.

"I can't say that. But, seduction is not always sexual. It can be about a lot of things. I once knew a priest who had all the attributes of attractiveness, that make up the American ideal of what a man is. He boasted about all the women who came around him and yet, he had never forsaken his vows of celibacy. However, there are many ways to violate one's vow of celibacy. It can be done emotionally, or spiritually . . . a lot of different ways. Yet, even the men loved him, and were not offended, when he flirted, outrageously, and more, with their wives.

"Oh, that's just Father," they said.

"He could get them to do anything he wanted, some of them, at least. There were a growing number, however, that were seeing that he wasn't all that he appeared to be, or claimed to be. They came up against him. Still, his followers would never admit that he was a fraud, even when the embezzlement was discovered; and yes, even when he finally he got a woman pregnant, and the priest accompanied her to get an abortion. Did that make any difference? No, it did not. It was as if the spiritual leader was beyond sin. What was sin for others, was not sin for him."

"Whatever happened to him?" asked Little Therese.

"Surely, he came to a bad end," said Evita DuPont.

"I don't know what happened to him," said Frank. "As far as I know, he is still going. He had the Bishop fooled; or maybe he had something on the Bishop. I do not know. He is probably still doing what he always has been doing, unless some husband, somewhere, has killed him, or he is in prison for theft. Raven will seek to seduce the people by whatever means necessary. He knows human weakness and folly, and he exploits it as far as he can, and then some.

"He will also try to gain his ends through violence. I was going to say, 'where necessary, in order to gain his end'; but, truth be told, he loves violence. It amuses him. He loves to inflict pain, especially upon the good. If he can gain the Sacred Spring by taking the lives of others, either body or soul, he will do it in order to make his report look good when he sends it in to headquarters."

"Yes, and he wants you, Father," said Evita DuPont.

"I know that. It has been ever thus, since my youth, when he sought me out in Rome. But, I cannot allow him to fill me with fear or paralyze me with panic. I must face this challenge with courage and faith, and so must you. We must live our lives each day, always at the ready for a surprise, as long as he is in town."

"Should we have a plan, too, Father?" asked Little Therese.

"Right now, our plan is to put our lives and the soul of our city in the hands of God, and remain vigilant."

Just then, Mrs. McCarthy came in with coffee, as well as juice for Little Therese. She also served small pieces of cherry pie a la mode. Father realized the pieces were from the pie she always baked for dessert when she made him fish and chips for dinner. He hoped that she had not served so much of it to guests that he could not have an extra piece for dinner and then maybe for a 3:00 a.m. snack. He loved his cherry pie.

"It's your besetting sin, Father," Mrs. McCarthy often said.

The three of them ate and drank, in thoughtful silence. When they finished, Little Therese and Evita DuPont went out into the late afternoon sun.

Father sat for a while, fighting back fears, and fiercely, summoning his courage.

Chapter 51

THAT EVENING, CALEB WAS walking across the hospital parking lot, when he was met by Blessed John.

"Are you going out to the Old Eighty?" he asked Caleb.

"I'm free tonight, so I thought I'd go take a walk at the farm."

"Would you mind giving an old man a ride out there? I'd like to take a look at how things are going."

"Absolutely."

As they drove toward the farm, Caleb said, "We really appreciate your drawing the plans for the pool."

"I designed it to look very much like the Pool of Siloam in Jerusalem."

"How do you know what the Pool at Siloam looked like, Blessed John?"

"They only recently discovered the real one, you know."

"Yes, I have seen the ruins."

"I designed yours to match the one from ancient times."

"How do you know what it looked like, then? Were you there?" Caleb joked.

There was a long silence. Caleb looked over at him to see what the expression was on his face.

Blessed John turned toward him.

"My assignment on earth is an extended one. I have been treading the pathways of the world, for many centuries."

They walked together across the farmstead, toward the construction. In the last few days, it seemed to Caleb that, around the pool and the spring, the air was fresher and crisper, and the light was just a bit brighter. The pool area had been hollowed out, and its floor bricked in.

"Impressive," said Caleb. "Impressive, I would say."

"Yes, all is coming along, nicely."

"Maybe they'll finish on schedule."

"I think they might very well do that. Would you like to take a walk up to the old tower?"

"Yes, I'd like that, Blessed John."

"Let's go, then."

As they walked, Caleb said, "You know, Hobe and Georgette say that they don't remember the tower being here and they've lived on this place for the better part of a century."

"It makes itself known to some, and not to others."

"I'm glad you showed it to me. It was really inspiring to see the place for the first time, from the air, so to speak."

"So many things can be seen better from a distance. We like to get up close and figure things out. But, sometimes it's better to move back, so as not to let your own emotions and ideas get in the way. Things take time. Rushed jobs always have to be done all over again. Things know the way they want to be. That's why I don't want you to get in a hurry about how things develop here. The Old Eighty will come along, as time goes on, and its destiny and yours will unfold before you. Do not worry, or fret, or spend your energy trying to push things one way, when they want to go another. Sometimes things are not supposed to happen at all. And some things happen that you cannot imagine."

"I suspect that I have not lived long enough, yet, to know all that you are saying. But, the last part? Yes! When Liz and I bought this place, we thought of only ourselves and how much we would enjoy it. But, it was not going to happen that way. You are right. Things know the way they want to be. That's for sure."

They had reached the tower by now, and scaled its heights easily.

"There it is," said Caleb. "There is Siloam."

"Yes, it wants to be Siloam," said Blessed John. "I'm glad you are open to that."

"It *is* better to see things from a distance."

"Sometimes yes, sometimes no," said Uncle John. "The trick is to know when it is right to look from up close, or from farther back."

"Yes."

"And you will learn how to do this. It isn't difficult, really, dear boy. If one perspective isn't working, try the other."

"So, don't try harder when something isn't working?"

"Do you just try harder when something isn't working in your practice?"

"Hell, no," said Caleb. "Excuse my language, Blessed John."

"Things take their own course," Blessed John continued. "The Creator made humans to be the middle management, so to speak. It's a hands-on task."

"You mean, we take care of the details."

"That's a way of saying it. You also are meant, as your own oath says it, to 'do no harm.'"

"You can bet we're going to take care of things, here," said Caleb.

"I have no doubt of that. And I know you will seek wisdom when you need it. The Wisdom Table at Joe's is an everlasting source of sagacity."

They began their trip down the hill and back toward the pool.

"Siloam! Yes, that's it. Siloam. It seems right," said Caleb.

"'Sent'. It means 'sent,'" said Blessed John.

Chapter 52

FATHER CALLAGHAN WAS HAVING another one of his sleepless nights. He'd never had a wife, but deep inside, he felt that there was a woman, intended for him. He had always doubted that celibacy really worked. He knew too many stories about too many priests, to think otherwise.

He had fallen in love only one time in his life. It was during that summer he spent in Rome, attending the Vatican Council. Three other seminarians and he had taken a bicycle trip to northern Italy. In the small town, where they stayed for a few days, he had met a young woman named Aurora. When he looked in her face, he was stunned, to his core. It was love at first sight, and the two clung to the other, as if they had known one another for all of their lives.

The next year, Aurora had enrolled in school at Sapienza University, in Rome, in order to be near Francis, who, by then, was attending the Pontifical North American University. They were together, constantly.

"My love is so great for you," said Francis, "that I don't know whether I love God or you, the most!"

"God and I don't need to compete!" Aurora had said, laughingly.

But, Francis knew better. The Church demanded of him, a loyalty that would mean that he would have to forego his relationship with Aurora. She knew that, too. Meanwhile, the two pushed it to the back of their minds.

But, the day came when Francis had to decide where his loyalty really was. He concluded that his heart was cracked down the middle. and that, with either decision, it was going to break.

He believed that he shouldn't have to make such a choice, between an intimate life with another human being, and a vow to God. It was not God who made up celibacy. It was the Church. Francis carried, within him, a deep-seated resentment, that he had been required to give Aurora up, in order to live out his vocation. Moreover, he had never lost his love for her. There were times, days, weeks, months even, when Francis buried his feelings. He loved the priesthood, and all that it included. His people loved him and those beyond his congregation, as well. He had developed a jovial persona, which was not phony, but simply, did not reflect the depth of his own being. Except for his spiritual director, he kept everything else to himself.

Chapter 53

SHE CAME TO HIM in a dream, still in the beauty of her youth, it was as if he was seeing her for the first time. Once again, as in bygone days, his knees nearly gave out, and his hands trembled. She reached out to him with her dazzling smile. She came toward him with open arms. He opened his, and they embraced. It was as if they had never been apart.

They walked toward the woods on the Old Eighty, and began to hike up the path, to the watch tower. He hoped the walk would never end. All too soon, they arrived. He went up first, and then turned, and reached for her hand, to bring her safely up to the platform.

He placed his arm around her and felt the familiar curve of her waist. How he loved her! She was everything a woman ought to be. He was filled, completely. There was no lack in him.

She placed her head on his shoulder and he thought he would faint. He held the moment fast. Even in the dream, somehow, he knew this would not last forever.

"What are you doing here, Dear One??"

"We are together. Does anything else matter?"

"No. No, it doesn't. All I want, all I ever wanted, was to be with you."

"But, you chose to follow your vocation. What else could you do? You are a man of integrity. Strangely, if you had not left me, I could not have loved you. If you had stayed with me, you would have always been unhappy, and I could not have respected you as much. I would have wondered if you might turn from our vows, as well. Now that you have become who you are, I love you even more. I love you, even better."

"But, you are another man's wife. I wanted you to be *my* wife. I still do."

"And I want you to be my husband. That will never change. I am happy with your old seminary friend, Gerard. I love him. He is good. He is faithful. He is true. And he loves me."

"But, do you love him? Do you really love him?"

"I am fond of him. One learns to love, Frankie."

She had always called him Frankie. He would allow no other to do the same.

"I have come to tell you something."

"Whatever you want to tell me, Dear One. You know I always love to hear your voice."

"But, are you listening to what I say, Frankie, or are you lost in my voice?"

She smiled.

"I am here to talk to you about the Sacred Spring."

"The spring? How do you know about that?"

"I've been sent to you with a message."

"So, I am being visited by an angel!"

"If you say so, Frankie."

She took his hand.

"Look out over the Old Eighty, Frankie, what it was, what it is becoming, and what it will be."

He placed his arm around her once more.

"I know what it has been. It started with young Mr. Harrison, who had more vision, people said, than common sense and knowhow. He sold it to Bartholomew Grundy, who owned everything else around. Then, Hobe Watson's grandfather bought it, and now, two generations later, it is a proud and well-kept farmstead.

"Ah, but before that!"

"You mean the indigenous people?"

"Yes. Those who were here first."

"Well according to the old Shaman, Roy Legband, the spring was there, as far back as when stories were told for the first time."

"Yes. Then, it dried up when the white men got greedy and cut the native people off, from their source of water. The water flowing from it is precious, Frankie. All water is precious. But, this water is holy. One must come to the spring with intention and purpose. The native peoples will show you. The spring is in their collective memories and lives in their stories. Its restoration is, for them, a reminder that the land belongs to the Divine Being and that no one ever really owns the land.

"The Sacred Spring and the Pool of Siloam is here for all people. Some will come with a creed. Some will come without belief. Some will come with a skeptical spirit. Others will be sure it is a fraud. You must accept all of them.

"That means," she continued, "you must live beyond your own religion."

"You mean, I must be a Christian, and more?"

"That's a way of saying it!"

"What could possibly be better . . .?"

He hesitated.

"or worse?"

"Yes, you have answered your own question, Frankie. The spring calls all people who come to it, to live beyond their beliefs, not to abandon them, but simply to know that there is more than they can possibly conceive of, or ponder, or believe. You are called to live beyond even what you consider to be your best self, and open your heart to become more."

"The Archbishop will never accept this."

"Accept what?"

"He will not accept that I live beyond the Catholic creed. He will tell me I am weakening the people's faith."

"Your heart is fixed, as is mine, upon our own faith. That will never change. But, to live both in and beyond your heart, and to live with all, in peace and affection . . . that is your call."

"So, I am being called to live in my heart, and I am being sent from my heart as well, to live beyond my own understanding."

"Yes, you are being sent, as are all the others. That is the meaning of Siloam, Frankie. Sent."

The words echoed into his waking-up moments.

"That is the meaning of Siloam, Frankie. 'Sent.'"

He heard her words again and again. He reached out to hold her once more, to kiss her, to tell her how much he loved her, but she was gone. He awakened to the smells of Mrs. McCarthy's breakfast cooking. He turned on his other side for a moment and stared at the crucifix on the wall.

He had a deep longing for Aurora, as if he had just parted from her yesterday, He was surprised at this, and full of pain, once more. He thought he had put all that behind him. Clearly, he had not, even though it had been nearly forty years ago. At this stage of life, it probably would never go away. The pain would always be lurking, and sometimes break out, in a spasm.

"That is the meaning of Siloam. Sent."

He heard his beloved's voice for three days. Then, he could no longer hear her. He strained. He struggled to hear the voice once more. She was gone.

Chapter 54

FOUR DAYS LATER, CARMELITA and Marshall showed up at the glass and steel house.

"You have outstanding warrants for your arrest in Indiana," Carmelita informed Homer.

"What kind of warrants?"

"If you must know, you are being arrested for child endangerment, kidnapping, and grand theft!"

"I'm being framed! None of this is true! My spiritual enemies are seeking to destroy me!"

"Of course, you could save us a lot of trouble and money," said Carmelita, "if you would waive extradition, and simply agree to go to Indiana, of your own free will. You're going to end up there, anyway!"

"I'm a man of God!" he protested. "I am a prophet! I cannot sin! I cannot commit a crime. None of what I have done has been for me, but for *Jesus!* It has all been for the souls of men and women!"

"You think over your options, sir!" said Marshall. "You don't have many!"

As Carmelita started the car, Meshach, Shadrach, and Ichabod, appeared from behind the barn, all handcuffed together, escorted by Roy and Jens, who, by now, had been named permanent volunteer deputies.

Homer's eyes widened.

"What are you doing with my boys?"

"They have their own problems!" said Marshall, stiffly.

Carmelita smiled to herself. He was competent but, consistently overcompensated for his own insecurities by doing his Joe Friday act.

Homer was horrified. Would they turn on him? He did not know, and this caused him to panic.

"I must see them! I have to talk to them!"

Carmelita looked back at him through the rear-view mirror.

"You're not talking to anybody, except the judge!"

Homer grew quiet, as he pondered the ramifications.

"By the way, where did you put my Bible? My grandmother gave me that Bible many years ago!"

"Your Bible is now evidence, Mr. Hill!" said Marshall.

"Evidence? The holy book?"

"Yes, I am afraid so!"

"Who gave you the right to steal my precious Bible?"

"I think you better start worrying about your precious ass, Homer!" said Marshall.

Carmelita cast an "if looks could kill" stare at Marshall. He went silent for the rest of the trip to Lincoln City.

Chapter 55

RAVEN WAS LIVID WHEN he learned that Homer and his gang had been arrested.

He sent a text to Marlene: *Come to my office, immediately. Urgent!*

Marlene was miffed. *His* office, eh? She'd see about that. Still, she went, finding him, red-faced, and pacing.

"Homer's gone and gotten himself arrested!"

She wanted to say, "What did you expect? He's a thief, and has kidnapped a young boy!"

Instead, she said, "Oh, that's too bad!"

"It's more than too bad! *Much* more than too bad!"

His eyes were ablaze and threatening.

He continued. "I knew his arrest was inevitable, but, I thought it would take a small-town cop a lot longer to get things moving!'

"Carmelita is very competent."

"Obviously."

"And with his taking a child across state lines, no doubt, the FBI has been of some assistance."

It was during times like this that Marlene knew that he must be talked down. She didn't know what he might do, maybe even call fire down from heaven. She knew his power and who gave it to him. In cases such as this, flattery worked.

"You're the brains of the outfit, Raven. We can always find more help."

He broke out into a smile.

"You always know what to say! That's part of your considerable attraction, my dear!"

He stood and opened his arms.

"Come here!"

This was the cycle. She would flatter him and calm him down. He would, in return, turn on the seduction. She had become aware of how this worked. She had gotten it out of her system that Raven cared for her. She realized he always seduced her to a point and then, turned away. She had been ready to give herself to him from the beginning. He knew this, and capitalized on her vulnerability. Now, she did not respond as in the past.

"We have to get busy with recruiting new help. I'm sure you have some idea of what we should do from here!"

Chapter 56

EVER SINCE THE SUMMER that Joe had been rescued, Lou and Hope had hosted a barbeque and picnic on the first Sunday afternoon in August. The first two summers, the crowd amounted to about fifty people. But the third summer, and then the fourth, the crowd had doubled each year. It had to be moved from Lou and Hope's home to the city park. This year, Hobe and Georgia, along with Caleb and Liz, invited them to have the picnic at the Old Eighty.

Everybody brought something. By now, people began to look for Carla's potato salad, Jeremy and Jason's baked beans, Carmelita's *tacos al pastor*, Mrs. McCarthy's German chocolate cake, Katye's vegetarian chili; the list of expectations went on. It had become a contest, of sorts, as to who could get the most compliments. But, it was all in good-natured fun. This year, there were considerably more present, what with the Unsettlement being just two and a half miles away.

The volunteer community band, was led, of course, by Mrs. Glover. The participants were of varying degrees of talent, which reflected the quality of the band's performance. Every year, new talent was featured. This summer, a young group of women danced an Irish Jig. Maxine sang a solo, to the chagrin of many, and Durwood played his zither, essentially ending all interest in any further performances. The mayor gave one of his ubiquitous speeches, which was strictly limited, by Hope, to ten minutes.

Young and older played a soft ball game. Anybody could participate, making both the game and its outcome, unpredictable. Some, mostly older men, played a game of horse shoe. Many sat and talked, simply enjoying one another's company. Some took hikes in the woods. It was the first time many from Safety Harbor and the Unsettlement had seen the spring. The simple charm of the farm itself and the surrounding beauty of nature, was astonishing.

Marlene came to the scene, late. She helped herself to the buffet. Food temporarily quelled her anxiety, which had increased greatly since she had been living, not only a duplicitous life, but now, she was possibly involved as an accessory to criminal behavior. It had become a vicious cycle of anxiety and eating and she did not know how to get out of it.

She made her way to the largest table where Mrs. Saugus, Georgia, Nate and Sally, Caleb and Liz, and Stewart and Katye were sitting. She was greeted warmly.

"Where is that Raven whatever-his-name-is?" asked Mrs. Saugus. "Don't you hang around with him?"

A chill went through Marlene, which caused her to be defensive.

"No, we don't hang out. I rent him office space."

Liz didn't know why she said it, but she blurted out, "Didn't I see you in Raven's car down at Devil's Churn a couple of weeks back?"

Marlene froze. There was an uncomfortable silence.

"I'm sorry!" said Liz. "I shouldn't have said that. It's none of my business."

"Let's go see the spring!" said Georgia. "I want to leave some prayers there!"

Relieved to have the tension broken, all but Mrs. Saugus arose from the table.

"I'll stay here with Marlene while she finishes her dinner," said Mrs. Saugus. "It's not fair to leave her alone!"

Alone would be better, Marlene thought. Much better. She wanted to call Raven, back out of everything, and throw him out of the office. She began to panic.

"I think you should get away from him," said Mrs. Saugus. "He's no good for you. I know things. He's not to be trusted."

Marlene did not want to talk about it.

"I appreciate your concern."

"He is not for or about this town. I don't know what he wants, but he'll leave as soon as he gets it."

Chapter 57

FRANCIS CALLAGHAN WAS AWAY on personal retreat. He had gone to Our Lady of the Angels monastery at Mt. Angel, for a three-day time apart, where he would be consulting with his spiritual director.

He missed going to the picnic, as much as he was missed. He was naturally gregarious and, going home to an empty house, often, enveloped him in loneliness. But, he had to deal with the storm clouds that were gathering. How could he help the people of Safety Harbor? He knew this: he could not do it alone. It would take a village, specifically, and that village included the sisters at Our Lady, especially his spiritual director.

The drive to Mt Angel was pleasant. He traveled only back roads ,with breathtaking scenes of fertile green farmland and Mt. Hood in the background, stretching toward a deep blue sky. A change of scenery was soothing to the soul; and by the time he arrived, he was all ready feeling calmer.

The sisters invited him to have lunch with them, and he gladly accepted. He spent the rest of the day walking the grounds, breathing in the clear air. He loved the smell of the salt air by the sea, but, it did the soul good to breathe air that mixed with the smell of the freshly-cut grass and ubiquitous flowers that generously decorated the entire convent landscape.

It was a short walk to downtown Mt. Angel, which boasts of a long Bavarian heritage. In the evening, he allowed himself a sausage hot dog, fries, and two glasses of German beer at an outside café.

He slept, fitfully, in one of the inside cells, formerly used by the nuns. Now, with their diminishing number, they were used by retreatants. He never slept well in other than his own bed. He was glad to see the light of day coming through his small window, and the crowing of a rooster in the distance.

A continental breakfast awaited him on a table in the hallway, prepared for all the retreatants who were in attendance. Around the table, he met two women from Switzerland and a man who was from a nearby small town. He was, momentarily, relieved of his brooding, over the issues at home.

He met his spiritual director, Sister Mary Margaret at 10:00, for the first of three sessions throughout the day. He poured his heart out to her, about all that had been happening in Safety Harbor and Siloam.

Chapter 58

ON THE SECOND DAY that Father was on retreat at Mt. Angel, the Unsettlement began Phase Two of their march, from their original location, to their permanent home.

Lou had arranged that the road into Safety Harbor, from the east, be closed, for two hours. There would be no time to lose. Two hundred and fifty plus people and all of their possessions, moving down the road two miles, in that amount of time, would be a challenge.

Lou had suggested that the whole event be a celebration, another parade, of sorts, led by a marching band.

"Thanks, Daddy, said Liz, "but, this is an Unsettlement affair, not Safety Harbor's. I think your idea is a good one, but it has to be the local people that make those kinds of decisions. I'll suggest it, though."

The suggestion of a marching band was replaced by the simple idea of having the children of the community lead the procession. Katye arranged for the members of the staff and faculty of Harbor Community College to be with the children for the two-mile trip, while their parents were busy bringing along their possessions. The entire parade was escorted by Carmelita in her squad car. Marshall brought up the rear in the newly-purchased police motorcycle.

The procession began promptly at 5:00 p.m. Many from Safety Harbor lined the road on both sides to view this unprecedented event in the area. As the children began to pass by them, the people applauded. The children, surprised by the friendly reception, smiled back.

"Wave! Wave!" Katye called out to the children.

And so, they did.

Spontaneously, children broke from the crowd, and began to walk with the children from the Unsettlement. Some of the teenagers came over to Silo, who was walking with Jens and Shirley. They pulled him into their group.

"Come with us!" they said. "Walking with adults is boring!"

Jens and Shirley smiled at each other and joined hands.

A tear rolled down Jens's rugged face.

"Parents, huh?" said Shirley.

Jens squeezed Shirley's hand.

"Look at him!" said Shirley. "He's smiling from ear to ear!"

Chapter 59

EVEN AS THE SECOND exodus of the Unsettlement was taking place, Raven was meeting with the contractors on the BFS property, for the purpose of building a waterpark. Marlene was at his side.

He realized that he was going to need more land.

"How much do you suppose the Saugus woman would want for her property?" he asked Marlene

"Oh, I don't think she'd sell. The house has been in the family for years. She lived with her parents in it, years ago, when she came to Safety Harbor, as a teacher. When she married, she stayed in the house with her husband, just like Hobe and Georgette. They raised their kids. Her husband, Howard, died a few years ago, and she decided to stay."

"Visit her and tell her we'll make it worth her while."

"You will not convince her."

"No, that's your job."

"Don't underestimate her. She is beloved by the whole community. People will fight for her on this one, if word gets out that there is any effort to bully her."

Marlene was surprised that she had spoken up to Raven, who responded with a slight smile.

"Do not worry, dear Marlene. It is not the BFS way to bully. We will simply make our offer too attractive to reject. Now, go see the woman. There is no time like right now."

Marlene drove down the long driveway of the BFS Inc. property. When she reached the road, she found it blocked. She blinked her eyes. A strange kind of procession was making its way down the road. Bikes, trailers, moving trucks, walkers, wheel chairs, pickup loads of what looked like junk, but she could tell was somebody's possessions. The whole strange promenade was led by children and youth.

Who were these people, and where could they possibly be going? When everyone had passed by, she saw Marshall in his squad car, bringing up the rear. So, it was some official thing, she thought.

She decided to follow at a distance. She had forgotten all about Mrs. Saugus. Her eyes grew wide as she saw the whole procession turn into the driveway, of the Old Eighty. Then, it dawned on her. Of course! It was the Unsettlement. They were moving onto the farm! She could feel her stomach tightening. She decided to follow the procession. She parked the car alongside the road, and walked onto the farmstead. Increasing her gait, she caught up with the others. Hobe and Georgette stood in their front yard, waving at the crowd as the ragamuffin pageant passed by. Magdalena and Rock rushed up to Hobe and Georgette and hugged them. All four then joined the moving mass of people.

Where would they be going? Marlene watched as Carmelita escorted them to the right side of the barn, through an open gate, that led into the cow pasture.

"Watch your step!" Hobe called out good-naturedly.

After going around the barn, to her left, she could see the construction taking place at the spring. It looked to be nearly finished. Several people were at the spring, some of them, drinking from it. Others seemed to be praying.

Markers had been placed in the space, between the spring and the forest, behind it. Rock and Magdalena, and George and Hobe directed traffic. Marlene could not help but admire the ways in which everyone pitched in and helped each other out, with great kindness.

The move went on for two and a half more hours. The sun was within an hour of setting. The trees were casting their shapes over the new town. A small utility van from Joe's, driven by Sally, made its way out to the location. It was sandwiches from Joe's. This was something Marlene could help with, and she moved, quickly, toward the van.

"Get into groups of twelve!" called out Mrs. Saugus. She was using her bullhorn that she had employed for many years in high school. "Everybody will get sandwiches, but not until you sit down!"

Those who had gone to high school under her tutelage sat down, setting an example for those assembled, who did not know Mrs. Saugus and her style.

"How can I help?" Marlene asked Nate and Sally.

"You can hand the sandwiches out."

It wasn't necessary at all for Marlene to do this. It probably even took a little more time than if Nate and Sally had done it themselves. Sally remembered that Joe had often worked hard to make people feel significant and give them their dignity. She had seen Marlene's vulnerability, beneath her professional bluster.

Within a half an hour the food had been delivered, all around.

"If you want drinks, you'll have to come and get them for yourselves, people," Mrs. Saugus shouted out.

While they were eating, young Reverend Cecil Bainbridge of the Freewill Holiness Church, accompanied by the Women's Missionary Society, had set up tables, with drinks and desserts, both of which were gone within fifteen minutes.

Magdalena and Rock stood together and welcomed the people.

"There is much left to do to get settled here in our new place," said Magdalena, while Rock stood beside her smiling, with his arm stretched around her waist.

Her words were few before she introduced Hobe and Georgette, who were both reduced to tears by the standing ovation they received.

Caleb and Liz then came and stood beside Mrs. Saugus, who continued to wield the power of the bullhorn.

"We thank you from the bottom of our hearts," said Liz, "for coming to be our neighbors! You are most welcome here! Who knows what the future may bring? We are honored to share this beautiful spot with you, and we hope that you will make yourselves right at home!"

"We have a lot to figure out yet," said Caleb, "but, figure it out, we will."

Sally raised her hand for recognition.

"Joe's will provide complimentary breakfast for a week," she announced. "Nate will bring it each morning in the Joe van."

Jeremy stood. "The coffee shop will provide coffee and other drinks for you as long as Joe's serves breakfast!"

The crowd stood once more, shouting, whistling, and clapping.

Marlene found herself taken in by the whole event. What love and caring these people had for one another, regardless of station or status! She longed to be a part of it all, but somehow, she had never quite brought herself to be open to very many people.

Making her way back to her car, she saw Raven, lurking in a grove of trees near the road. He walked forward briskly toward her. He was obviously agitated.

"What are you doing here?" he asked.

She looked down, unable to meet his eyes.

"I just followed the crowd out here."

"Followed the crowd? Really?"

He raised his voice as he began to rail on her.

"Anyone who works for me doesn't follow the crowd. The crowd follows us! This sidelined you, I assume, from seeing Mrs. Saugus. Was she here?"

"Yes. she was!"

"Did you tell her I wanted to make an offer?"

"No. No, I didn't."

"Why not?"

"I didn't have a chance to do it."

"No chance? How long have you been here?"

"Three or four hours," she said. "Maybe five."

"What were you thinking? What were you doing?"

"It was . . . busy. The Unsettlement moved over here this afternoon from Jens and Shirley's. They moved, then they unloaded, took their lodging assignments, and set up. Then, we had dinner together, a few greetings, and it was done."

"What did you do through all of this?"

"I helped out, where I could."

Marlene thought that Raven was finished. She began to move toward her car.

"I'll see her as soon as I can."

"While you have been wasting your time here, I have found us a preacher who won't get thrown in jail."

She turned around and came back.

"His name is Jimmie Crackers, and he's coming from Branson, Missouri."

"Branson? Isn't that where all the country music entertainers are?"

"Yes, Jimmie was a pretty washed up preacher when he arrived. He once had a big TV show and then got himself involved with his secretary. It's always the same story. The scandal blew up pretty much everything. Before this even happened, he was already sinking. He had robbed people of all the money they could spare, and then some. Quite simply, he ran out of suckers. By this time, most of his supporters were aging, and a good number of them moved to Branson. Jimmie decided to follow them out there and see what he could get out of them again. Many had lost their houses from giving so much to Jimmie and they are living in RVs. Jimmie decided to supplement his preaching by selling some trinkets, and even some food, for 'the last days', as he called it.

"And, do you know, the same people he had bamboozled before, came back to be bamboozled again! But, now they are dying off, and although he had put together a template for a will, for people to give everything to him when they died, there wasn't anything left to give him. Now, he's back to not having enough people to live the way he wants to live. I said to myself, 'This guy is good! All he needs is a new audience. So, I'm bringing him here, along with his wife. They're a team and know how to get what they want. They'll get a following and tear the whole spring operation away from Callaghan and his tribe."

"When are they coming?"

"I'm flying his wife, Minnie Belle, and him out here tomorrow. They'll arrive at the airport about four o'clock. I want you to meet them, and bring them back to Safety Harbor."

"Four o'clock?"

"In the morning?"

"Yes."

"Great!" she said. "Just great!"

Chapter 60

Roy Legband was ancient of days.

Much of the time, his body did not work well for him, so, his spirit often left his body and traveled without it. He had been to many places, and had experienced times other than the present. Sometimes he did not know whether it was now, or some other time. On this particular journey, he was on a high mountain. He looked up and could see the long line of his ancestors in the sky, looking down on him. One of them spoke.

"You are a Keeper of the Sacred Spring Of Peace," said a woman ancestor. "Go, and build your house near it. Claim it as our heritage. The blood and tears of our people fertilize the ground, out of which the spring bursts forth. Your faithfulness to the old ways has earned you a place of honor. You will share it with other holy men and women. Soon, the spring will be under siege. Even now, the forces of darkness are readying their plan, to take the spring and use it for evil purposes.

Protect the Sacred Spring, for your people, for those of us who have passed, for those who live in the present, and for those yet to come. It will be a daunting challenge. You must do this through prayer, humility, and courage. Be strong, when the struggle comes. Know that we are with you, that you have power and strength, that the adversary does not see or know.

"You will have people of good will who will be your allies. Our people and the people of Safety Harbor and Siloam must come together to overcome evil, and the darkness that seeks to pervade this place. The spring is for the healing of those who will come to the waters, and drink of the spring, or bathe in the waters of the pool. Go now to the spring, and do not delay. The futures of many depend upon you."

When Roy Legband came back into his body, he did not wait until morning. He put all of his worldly possessions in his knapsack, and made off, immediately, in the direction of the spring. It was early morning light, when he arrived. The sun was rising in the east, but, light pervaded the place, that was brighter than the position of the rising sun could justify. The old man shed his knapsack, and claimed a place for himself.

After his journey, he was tired, hungry, and thirsty. He cupped his hands, making the palms and fingers into a receptacle for water from the spring. He drank deeply, going back to the spring seven times. Afterword, he sat down by the spring and found that he was refreshed, no longer tired, no longer hungry or thirsty. His fingers, that had been touched by the waters, soothed his aches and pains.

He looked up again into the sky and saw his ancestors. They were well pleased.

Chapter 61

SISTER MARY MARGARET HAD the appearance of an actress, playing the part of a nun. The habit and the years could not hide her beauty. Although her "bubbliness," as one Mother Superior had described it, had been tempered over the years, the twinkle in her eye and the lusty laugh, remained.

"Good morning, Father!"

"Good morning yourself, Sister Mary Margaret! I see you are still avoiding Sister Agnes's coffee!"

"Never! What brings you here, Frank?"

He took the next half an hour and shared with her all that had been taking place, including his dream, in which Aurora appeared to him.

"I must prepare for a bloody spiritual struggle, I am sure, even though I am not certain how Raven is going to choose to attack. He holds vile contempt for me, ever since I did not respond to his call to work for Bread from Stone, many years ago."

They spent two more sessions throughout the day.

Afterward, Frank joined the sisters in the refectory for dinner, Following Sister Mary Margaret's *modus operandi*, he poured a cup of Sister Agnes's thick, black coffee, took two sips of the bitter brew, and poured out the rest, discreetly.

After dinner, he spent some time in the library. He picked up a couple of books, which he intended to read, but, the slower pace at the convent made him realize how tired he really was. He laid his head down on the table in his carousel, to rest for just a moment. It was two hours later, when a library attendant gently awakened him, telling him it was closing time.

The next morning, he had breakfast in the retreat center, and, after saying good-bye to his friend, Sister Mary-Margaret, he drove the rural roads and pastoral scenes, until he reached the Coast Range. Then, making his way through the low mountains, he drove through the Van Duzer corridor. A few minutes later, he arrived at the rectory, where faithful Mrs. McCarthy had made him an early lunch of macaroni and cheese, topped off, she said, "by a very small piece of cherry pie."

He was home. The struggle was enjoined.

Chapter 62

Evangelist Jimmie Crackers, along with his wife, Minnie Belle, arrived, right on schedule. Marlene was at the airport to meet them.

Jimmie's greeting was as effusive as Minnie Belle's was reserved.

"'I will bless the Lord at all times. His praise shall always be in my mouth!' That's from the Psalms, you know. And a good, good morning to you. Marlene, is it?'

Before she had time to respond he said, "Yes. Yes, it is! I am very good with names, you know. Marlene, I want you to meet my wife Minnie Belle!"

Marlene extended her hand toward Minnie Belle, who only nodded. She looked tired.

"We are so happy that the Lord has sent us to you! May he bless the work that he gives us to do!"

"Yes," said Marlene, not knowing what to say.

"We brought a lotta luggage. Minnie Belle doesn't have much, but I've got all my preachin' clothes . . . and my preachin' shoes. Say where are we stayin', do ya know?"

Marlene froze. She hoped Raven did not expect her to host. They picked up the luggage, which Marlene and Minnie Belle struggled to get into Marlene's SUV.

"Brother Sinclair told us we would have a house to ourselves. That's mighty nice of him. We're willing to stay anywhere, until the Lord brings us the abundance he did, back in the old days, when Minnie Belle and I were young. Say, could we get some breakfast, somewhere? I'm starved! How about you? I think Minnie Belle is too, arntcha, honey?"

They drove out of the airport and down I-205.

"Praise the Lord! Oh, Marlene, God is so good. All the time. God is good! Can you believe it? Here we are in Portland! Say! Just look at that

sunrise! And just look at that mountain, Minnie Belle! What's the name
of that big old hill, Marlene? Did you know that if you pray with the faith
of a mustard seed, Marlene, [Marlene, isn't it? Yes, I thought so.] that the
Lord could take that big old mountain and cast it into the sea?"

Marlene could not imagine, for the life of her, what the point would
be to have Mt. Hood removed from its moorings and thrown into the
ocean.

They stopped for breakfast on the way home, where Jimmie Crackers ate voraciously while Minnie Belle nibbled on her toast, barely touching the rest of her food. They traveled on down Highway 99, enduring
Jimmie's endless, ongoing commentary. She sighed, audibly. Jimmie did
not notice.

Chapter 63

RAVEN MET THE CRACKERS in the house owned by BFS Inc.

"We will have the place furnished, by tonight."

"Oh, thank you, Brother Raven! Praise God for his blessings! Isn't this great, Minnie Belle? Everything will be new for us. We're starting over! Praise the Lord of second chances!"

I'll bet you're on your fifteenth, thought Marlene. At least.

Minnie Belle had disappeared. Marlene went looking for her and found her outside, looking toward the woods.

"It's beautiful here, isn't it?"

"Not as beautiful as the children we left behind."

"You have children?"

"Grandchildren too. Five kids and thirteen grandchildren."

"Where are they?"

"They're all grown, with their own families, but now, we're two thousand miles from them. They might as well be on the moon."

She teared up. Marlene handed her a tissue.

"Maybe they'll come to visit. Maybe they'll even move out here! Oregon is a wonderful place to live!'

She couldn't help but think of the possibility of selling houses to all of them.

"Oh, I don't know. We've moved all over the country and the kids aren't going to follow us. They don't know how long we're going to be anyplace. They might come visit, but probably not."

"Surely that's not true."

Minnie Belle did not answer.

"Would you like to go inside?"

"I think I'll just stay here awhile."

"Okay. I'll see you later, then."

Marlene reached out and touched her arm.

Chapter 64

THE SAME MORNING THAT the Crackers arrived in Safety Harbor, at Father Callaghan's request, the Joe Team met at the diner.

Father showed no signs of his usual joviality. Picking up his signals, the group was quiet.

He began.

"My friends, once again, as in the days of Joe, we are faced with a great spiritual challenge. Just as we have been given the blessing of being Keepers of the Light, we are now charged as Keepers of the Sacred Spring.

"But, there are those who would prevent us from our new vocation. Even now, Raven Sinclair is plotting his moves to take over the Sacred Spring."

"I don't understand what's going on out at the spring. What is really happening? Are people really being cured? And, how did we get in charge of it?" a visitor to the meeting asked.

Ruby spoke up.

"Actually, no one is in charge of it. We are just stewards, to take care of it."

Ruby, once again, told the story of the people of the spring and the Siletz people. When she was finished, silence prevailed.

Little Therese broke the quiet.

"The Light from Gemma has been given to us to give us the means to see the things that are, by natural sight, invisible. The Sacred Spring has been given to us to be a blessing to other people. Not everyone can live here, but many can come to visit, experience the Spring, and take home a blessing with them."

"Our stories tell us that the earth rests upon a body of water," Ruby responded. "The water coming forth from the Sacred Spring is from under the land, and holds the earth in place. With the Spring returning, our people are having our heritage, restored."

"Even though the Old Eighty is owned by Caleb and me," said Liz, "we have agreed that the Siletz Confederation will have the right to assemble there, and have first rights to it, for their rituals and events."

"Once it was given to us, our Shaman, Roy Legband tells us, and now it is given to all of us. It will stay with us, so long as we live in peace with one another, and are good stewards of the Spring," said Ruby.

"None of us can know right now," said Father Callaghan, "all that the Sacred Spring means, or will mean in the future. All we can do is to be open to what it will reveal to us about itself in the future. We must not allow factions to divide us. We must live within our own faith, and beyond. Our hearts will come together. The water will heal us, and we will heal one another."

"At the suggestion of Blessed John, Liz and I have decided to call the pool, Siloam," said Caleb. "I often saw the remains of that pool when I was in Jerusalem. Our ancient Jewish spiritual ancestors used it for purification as they arrived in the city for a visit to the Temple. Then, in my own faith as a Palestinian Christian, our tradition says it was where Jesus sent the man to dip in the pool. It was a cleansing and healing place, as we want our own Siloam to be."

Magdalena raised her hand.

"We have decided to name our community Siloam City, since we are near the water. We are no longer unsettled, so the name, Unsettlement, doesn't fit. Siloam City seems right to us."

"Our people will call it the Spring of Peace," said Ruby.

"I have brought us together today to develop a strategy for the oncoming struggle," said Father.

"How will we know what Raven will do?" asked Hobe.

"I have come in contact with Raven, several times before. He and I are mortal enemies, because he has decided that it is so. He has already said, since he has been here, that he wants my soul. I am not afraid of him. I will withstand him to the death. More importantly, it is not just yours truly that he is after. He wants to destroy this community. He cannot stand the light. Now with the spring coming to life again, it is a double whammy."

For the first time that morning, a slight smile came to his face. It was good to see. Barely anyone recognized Father, without his ready grin and joviality.

"Well, that makes me wonder why he would bother with us," said Georgia. "Here we are, a little town. If we weren't near the ocean, no one would even pass through here. How can we be so important to the dark forces? There must be thousands of places more notable than ours!'

Little Therese spoke up.

"To the world, we are unimportant. Joe could have gone to bigger and more glamorous and important places than ours. But, he didn't. He came to us. He knew that it is easier to listen to our hearts when we are not distracted by our own sense of importance. This community is the perfect place for a healing stream."

"Absolutely!" said Lou. "Little Therese is right. We may not be big, but we are a great little town!"

"I don't often speak up since I'm so new," Bartosh spoke up, "but I want to say that this little place is extraordinary. I stayed here at first, for the beautiful Susanna. Now, I have grown to love this village. I would not live anywhere else. I will put forth whatever effort it takes to make us all safe, once again."

Buddy raised his hand.

"Yes. Buddy!" Sally recognized him.

"Maybe the best way to start is to start a group on social media. That way, we can all keep in touch with one another."

"That's a brilliant idea, Buddy!" said Caleb.

Buddy's face showed both surprise and pride.

"If you're not on social media, you need to get on it right away," said Caleb. "If you don't know how to get on . . ."

"I'll help!" said Buddy, empowered by his idea being accepted.

"Buddy will help, and I will too," said Nate.

Caitlin looked at her brother, half embarrassed, half proud.

"I believe one person of the Joe Team should be present at all times at the pool, twenty-four seven," said Carla. That way some of us will need to take our days off and be there. I know I'll do exactly that."

"We could do a group text!" exclaimed Caitlin, not to be outdone by her brother.

"Nate and Sally, you have brilliant kids!" said Rock.

Caitlin beamed, and then looked askance at her brother as if to say, "I am as smart as you, at least!"

"So, once we get word of suspicious activity or something, what shall we do? What can we do, really?"

"We will have to decide that when the time comes," said Magdalena. "We don't know what Raven is up to."

Silo sat observing the meeting. It was such a different place. He never knew there were people in the world like this, who were kind and loving, and who cared for each other like this. He could not keep his eyes off Little Therese. He thought she was fine. Just fine.

Chapter 65

Hobe and Georgette, along with Roy, had not been at the meeting. It was moving day for them. Roy had rented a truck, and had brought a number of his friends to help him. Before the day was over, they had moved six truck loads from the large two-story house, with an attic.

"By golly," said Hobe, "I didn't remember there was that much stuff up here!"

"Most of it was stuff that you couldn't give up after your folks died, honey," said Georgette.

A tear fell from Hobe's eye onto his cheek. Georgette wiped it with her finger.

"Oh, it's just so hard!"

"I know! I know!"

He fell into her arms and sobbed. Not a word was spoken between them. They headed to the front door for the last time.

"I don't think I can do it, Georgette!"

"You have to, honey. We have to!"

"I've failed! I've failed!"

"You haven't failed. We're retiring. We need to have neighbors that are closer than three miles away!"

"I should have been able to persuade one of the kids to take over the farm."

"Kids don't want to farm these days. They want to go out and see the world."

"So, I'm the last Watson on the Old Eighty. I'm bringing it all to an end."

"Hobe, we raised our children here. We gave them a good life and a good start. You took care of the place like you did the kids. You even had names for the livestock! You rotated the crops, so you wouldn't wear out the soil. You trimmed and pruned the trees. You have nothing to be ashamed of. It's just time for us to go."

"The last Watson. The end."

"No, it's not that way."

"But it is! It is!"

"You're comin' back out here to farm the place. I'm sure the kids are all right with you having a few animals on the place."

"Do you think they'll let me mow the lawn with the tractor mower?"

"What do you think?"

"I think they probably will!"

He smiled.

"You always make me feel better!"

"You wear me out, Hobe Watson! You'll be right back out here, tomorrow!"

"Yes, I will! The livestock have to be fed. The lawn needs mowing. And the garden needs tending!"

"Now, let's go down to LeRoy's and have dinner. Then we'll go back to Safety Harbor and try out our new bed."

He smiled.

"I'm glad to try out a new bed if you're in it!

"Hobe Watson, you always were a devil!"

Chapter 66

THE NEXT MORNING, MARLENE took Jimmie and Minnie Belle Crackers to the spring.

"Oh my, this is something!" exclaimed Jimmy. "We can do a lot of work here!"

He went and stood near it.

"We can save a lot of souls who are coming here, from miles around, Minnie Belle! Soon, they will be coming here from foreign lands. Why, we can be missionaries right here in this place! Oh, how the world needs Jesus! I think we can make a good living here, Minnie Belle. Raven has said that we can take offerings here, as often as we want."

"When did Raven say you could start?"

"Why, he said we can start today! No point in waiting around. There are souls to be saved and blessings for us to receive, from those who are generous."

You mean, generous with their wallets, thought Marlene. But, she did not comment.

Instead, she said, "We are due in Lincoln City to pick up a car for you at the BMW dealership. We probably ought to go up there real soon!"

As they drove north on Highway 101 toward Lincoln City, Jimmie chattered on. Marlene discovered she could respond occasionally with a "Yes" or an "Uh-huh" without listening specifically to what Jimmie was saying. This way, she could think her own thoughts.

She was becoming anxious that Raven had taken over so much of her life. All she had done was to rent him office space, and now, she was working for him! How did she get here? She knew. She had responded to his charisma. She was strangely attracted to his darkness. She had gone too far with him. Now, he had something on her that he could reveal any time she did not do his bidding.

Then, there were the people he gathered around him: crooks, ne'er do wells, and vulnerable people, such as herself, Homer and his Sunday School class, and now Jimmie Crackers, obviously, a fraud. It probably wasn't even his real name.

She would wager that Raven never had an honest relationship with anyone, in his entire life. She had to get away from him. She knew that. But, what would be the cost? On the other hand, if her collusion should be discovered, her reputation in the community would be ruined, and, just in practical terms, she would be out of business, on so many levels. They couldn't live on Claude's salary. They would go bankrupt; they could even lose their home.

Chapter 67

Since Raven had all of the paper work finished, there was nothing to do but sign them. Just like that, Jimmie had his car.

"Minnie Belle, why don't you ride home with Marlene! I want to test drive this baby!" said Jimmy.

Marlene was incensed. How impertinent of him! How did he know where she was going? Maybe she hadn't even planned to go back home! How could he dump his wife, just like that? But, she did plan to go back, and willingly, out of pity, she agreed to take Minnie Belle with her.

They rode in silence for a few moments before Minnie Belle burst out, saying, "I don't know how I'm going to take this much longer!"

"Take what, Mrs. Crackers?" asked Marlene, although she knew the answer.

"I can't take the uncertainty, all of the time. We are always short of money. Sometimes, we don't have enough to eat, because Jimmie has gone out and bought another preachin' suit. And Jimmie is such a blowhard!'

Marlene nearly burst out, laughing, but she controlled herself. She didn't know Minnie Belle had it in her. But then, she wasn't expecting Minnie Belle to share so much with her, either. She had the feeling that all of this had been pent up in her, for a long time, and she just couldn't keep it in any longer. She reached over and touched Minnie Belle's hand momentarily. She gripped Marlene's hand as if she would never let go.

'He lies. All the time. He talks about Jesus and he talks about God, but then, he goes and visits prostitutes. He tells me what to do, and sometimes I don't want to do it, but I do it anyway. I tried a couple of times to say 'no' to him."

"What happened?"

"He sent me to my room."

"He sent you to your room?"

Marlene was incredulous.

"You mean, you have your own room?"

"Well, yes, Jimmie and I have our own rooms. He says he doesn't find me attractive any more, and he doesn't want to sleep with me."

"I'm sorry."

"Oh, don't be sorry! I didn't want to sleep with him, long before he didn't want to sleep with me!"

For the second time, Marlene tried to control her laughter, this time, not quite so successfully.

"Do you want to leave him? Do you have anywhere to go?"

"I could go and stay with the kids, but I don't want to be a burden to them, and besides, Jimmie would make their lives miserable, just like he has mine."

They were, just now, coming into Safety Harbor.

"This is a beautiful little town!'

'Oh yes, we love it here! By the way, would you like to stop in at Joe's for lunch? I'm buying!"

As they entered the diner, Minnie Belle was overcome.

"The light! The light! It is so soft and so bright, at the same time."

Sally took their order. Minnie Belle continued to let out her frustrations and fears.

"You know, sometimes, especially now, after the kids have been gone, I sometimes think about how life may have turned out, if I hadn't married Jimmie. I wouldn't give up my kids for anything, but somehow, I would have liked to have had them without Jimmie! I had plenty of boys who thought I was attractive. I wonder what it would have been like if I had made other decisions, if I had married someone else, or if I had followed my dreams of being a nurse."

Marlene reached across the table and squeezed Minnie Belle's hand. This was way too close to home. She didn't know what to say.

"I feel better being able to talk to you," said Minnie. "I don't know why I trust you. I've tried to tell others, and they've gone back and told Jimmie, and he punished me."

"He punished you?"

"Yes, he made me stay in my room unless I was doing housework or cooking his meals."

"He's treating you like a child! Worse! He's abusing you!"

"He has never touched me, never laid a hand on me."

"He doesn't have to. He has battered your soul."

Chapter 68

JIMMIE CRACKERS DID NOT come home, until morning. He expected Minnie Belle to be waiting for him, in their new home, with breakfast cooked, and a change of clothes on the hanger. Instead, he found an empty house. He was alarmed. He called Raven, who did not have any idea where she might be.

"How come you don't know where she is?" he asked. "When is the last time you saw her?"

"In Lincoln City at the car dealership. By the way, Brother Sinclair, that sure is a nice car you bought for me. Praise the Lord for his blessings!"

"Why didn't she get in the car with you?"

"Well, to be honest, I wanted to try the baby out. Minnie Belle doesn't like going in the car any more than she has to, so she went back to town with Marlene. At least, I think she did. I saw her get in."

"So, how did you not miss her earlier? I hope you haven't called the police. We want to keep all of this on the down-low."

"No, I haven't called the cops. As to my not missing her earlier, I'll be honest with you. I didn't come home last night!"

"Didn't come home? Your first night here and you didn't come home?"

"I'll be honest with you, Brother Sinclair. I have a weakness. I love Scotch. I stopped in a bar, up in Seaside. I had a few too many, and this nice lady invited me to stay the night with her, so that I didn't drive drunk."

"You are going to have to be more disciplined, Jimmie Crackers. We can't have any distractions or scandals; if you must drink and . . . cavort, don't do it anywhere close to home. Go to Portland or better yet, Seattle. But right now, you are not going anywhere. You have work to do. Now, get up to the spring and preach like hell!"

"There's still the matter of finding my wife."

"That's your personal issue and has nothing to do with what we are about, here. The stakes are too high for any blunders. Now, I suggest you get to the spring, immediately."

Jimmie really didn't know what to do without Minnie Belle. He didn't know where to begin. Anxiety beset him. He went out to the car, sat in the driver's seat, and drank deeply from his flask. He couldn't get drunk again, not on top of a hangover, and not when he had to preach, right away.

"I know what I'll do, praise the Lord!" he shouted to himself.

He started the BMW, now dangerously close to out of gas, and drove it down to Raven's and Marlene's office. He had a feeling Marlene knew something.

He pulled up in front of the storefront office. She was in. Good!

"She stayed with me last night," Marlene told him. "She didn't want to stay alone in the house, so I invited her to come home with me."

"Where is she now? I need some breakfast and fresh clothes. Right now! I've got some preachin' to do."

"She's still at my place. She was sleeping when I left."

"Well, I'm gonna go get her! Where do you live?"

"She doesn't want to go home right now, Reverend Jimmie. She's tired. She's homesick. She misses her kids. She's just worn out. She needs some time off, and Claude and I have invited her to stay with us, for a few days!"

"Well, I like that! She's my wife and she belongs at home, with me."

"Give her some time, Jimmie. Go on down to Joe's and have breakfast. It's on me. As for your clothes, I don't know what to tell you. Maybe you should go down to Gleason's and buy yourself a shirt and some pants. I'm sure Raven will take it off your expense account."

"Well, I am flat broke!"

Marlene sighed. She could smell liquor on his breath.

She opened her purse.

"Here is hundred and twenty dollars. That ought to buy you a decent shirt and pants. Now, that's all I can do."

"What about my wife?"

"What about her? She's just staying at my house for now. What you two work out between you is your business. Not mine."

"When is she coming home?"

"When she decides to come home, I would say."

"It had better be soon. She is my partner in ministry. I can't do it without her by my side. It's always been Jimmie and Minnie Belle, never just Jimmie or just Minnie Belle. We're one person. One flesh."

"She is tired, Reverend Jimmie. Let her rest. She'll be ready to talk, when she feels safe."

Jimmie Crackers became morose.

"I don't know how she couldn't feel safe. I'd die defending her."

"Minnie Belle and you need to talk. Right now, if you want to keep Raven happy, I think you'd better go and get breakfast at Joe's, buy some clothes, go home, clean up, and get out to the spring with your best sermon in hand."

"I don't even know where my Bible is. Minnie Belle always kept track of that too. I don't have time for such details. What I'm doing is way too important for that."

Marlene could feel the anger welling up within her and manifesting itself on her face, which, by now, had changed to a deep red.

She went into the small lobby and found a Bible that had been given to her by some Seventh Day Adventist missionaries, who had come calling in the office last month.

"Here is a Bible, Reverend Jimmie. Now, you should be pretty well set for the day."

He started to walk out, looking confused.

He turned back to her at the door.

"When will I see Minnie Belle again?"

"I don't know."

His face suddenly became unmasked. His visage was threatening and dangerous.

"I will find her. You can't keep her from me. She is mine. She will come home to me, repentant, and begging me to forgive her."

Marlene did not reply. She couldn't believe what she had just done, what she had just said. She had defended Minnie Belle. She was providing shelter for her. She suddenly perceived her own vulnerability, her own sense of helplessness, her lack of satisfaction with her own life. She was tired of Claude's passivity, and she was tired of demeaning herself with promiscuous behavior, just to feel close to someone, when really, it made her feel worse.

Suddenly, she wasn't afraid of Raven any more. She needed out. She needed to talk to someone, right away, and get out of this tenebrous situation.

Chapter 69

"It's a clique," he said, "and you know it!" Nate teased his stepdaughter.

"Whatever!" said the young teen, who was more impatient with adults, with every passing day.

"You hang with certain people. You decide who can become a part of your little group. All others are excluded. That's a clique!"

"We invite other people! Look at Silo. He's part of us and he's not popular! And Little Therese is considered weird by some people, but she's in our group!"

"True enough!" he said.

He was glad his little girl was doing so well in high school. She was definitely well-liked, by faculty and students, alike. Buddy was doing well, too. He wasn't a leader, but, he was coming into his own, finding friends on the wrestling and track teams.

Most of the time, Caitlin would rather not be seen together in public with her brother.

"He is embarrassing," she said.

But, she would allow Buddy to be with her, if they were both in their groups of friends.

Caitlin's group was headed out to the spring, along with Buddy and a few of his friends. Blessed John caught up with them and walked beside them.

"Where are you kids going?" he asked

"We're going out to Siloam," said Caitlin."

"We're gonna see the spring *and* the pool!" said one of her companions.

"Where are you goin' Mister?" asked Corey, the five-year-old brother of one of Buddy's friends.

"Oh, you can call me Blessed John. I am walking with you, and going where ever you go!"

"That's funny!" said the little one.

His older brother looked embarrassed.

"Sorry, Mister . . . Blessed John. My brother always asks a lot of questions."

"What is your name, son?"

"He's Corey," said his older brother.

"Hey Mister! Can you carry me on your shoulders? I'm getting tired!"

"Can't even walk two miles!" said his older brother, disdainfully.

"You surely may ride on my shoulders, Corey!"

Blessed John lifted him up, placing him firmly on his shoulders.

"Wow!" said Corey. "I can see forever up here!"

"Well, you can't see forever!" said Blessed John. "That's a long way. Why, if you could see forever, you could see past the moon, even!"

"That's a long way, Mister!"

"Yes, it is. But, if you will look over there, you can see the pretty flowers along the creek, and the little waterfalls in the river bed. There is beauty all around us, if we will see it!"

"My mom would like some of those flowers!"

"Maybe your brother and you can pick a few for your mother, on the way home."

Suddenly, from behind, a speeding car came upon them, and passed them, going so fast, it created a tail wind, that nearly blew the walkers off the road, and into the ditch. It was a new BMW. Jimmie was on his way to Siloam, to gather some followers

"Is everybody okay?" asked Blessed John.

"Wow, Mister! That car was goin' fast!"

"Yes, he wasn't looking out for living things, was he?"

"He sure wasn't looking out for us!" said Caitlin.

"It's a good lesson. Slow down and see where you are!"

"Yeah, I'll bet he didn't see the flowers or the stream! But, that was a fast car! I'd like to ride in it!"

"Oh, you can go fast any time you want to," said Blessed John.

"Yeah, even Mom drives fast!" said Corey. "Where do you s'pose he's goin?"

"He's just thinking about where he's going, and getting there fast, Corey," said Blessed John. "He doesn't realize where he is, right now."

"My guess is that he is headed out to Siloam. A lot of people are going there these days!" said Caitlin.

"So are we!" said Blessed John. "But we can also be where we are right now! A lot of you want to grow up fast! There'll be plenty of time to be grown up. But this part of your life is over, very soon. It may not seem like it, but, it's going by quickly!"

"Yeah!" said Buddy. "The school year is long and summer is over, way too quick."

"Quickly, Buddy. Quickly!" Caitlin corrected him.

"When you grow up and become adults, you will always remember this little journey to Siloam, where we walked and talked together, smelled the grass and the flowers, heard the bubbling waters of the creek, and enjoyed each other's company."

"I'm hungry, Mister!" said Corey.

"Well, I just might have a snack for you," said Blessed John. "Shall we stop for a few minutes over there in that little meadow?"

"Sure! I'd like to go there!" said Corey.

As they made their way across the shallow ditch, into the small clearing, that led to forest land, a dog appeared, seemingly out of nowhere.

"Why, that's Ebenezer!" said Blessed John.

The dog rushed up to Blessed John, jumped up on him, and licked him furiously.

"Oh my! He must have gotten loose!" said Little Therese.

"Who is Ebenezer?" asked Corey.

"You're too little to remember, Corey!" said Caitlin. "Ebenezer is the dog they brought back from Gemma, when my Dad and others rescued Joe."

"Yes, he lives with me, now!" said Little Therese.

"Ebenezer is a funny name!" said one of the boys.

"We just call him Ben," said Little Therese.

Chapter 70

"Is GEMMA AN ISLAND from heaven, Blessed John" asked Buddy. "That's what my dad says. Where is it right now?"

"Where ever it needs to be," said Blessed John.

"You mean it moves around?"

"Some say it does!"

"Wow, I'd like to go there!"

"It's never very far away," said Blessed John, "even when it is on the other side of the world."

"How can that be?" asked one of Caitlin's friends.

"Time and space mean nothing on Gemma," said Blessed John. "It can be here, and then, just like that!" he said, snapping his fingers, "it's gone, somewhere else!"

Ebenezer began to chase a rabbit across the meadow, startling a deer that had been spying on the little company.

"Come here, Ebenezer!" Little Therese called out to the dog.

He came bounding over to her, licking her face first, and then slurping as many faces as he could. He pushed Corey over on the ground and licked him, until he giggled.

"Let me up! Let me up!"

Ebenezer had to be pulled off the little boy.

"Come! Come over here and sit by me!" called out Little Therese.

"I'll help!" said Silo, managing to maneuver a place by her.

"Well, now, let's see! How many of us are there?" asked Blessed John, opening his knapsack.

"Twelve!" said several of them, each trying to be the first to answer.

Blessed John rustled through his knapsack.

"Ah!" he said. "Here I have some snacks right here! Let's see, one, two, three, four, five . . . twelve, exactly!"

"Wow!" said Corey. "No one is left out!"

"Look!" said Blessed John. "I even have a dog snack for Ebenezer!"

When the dog heard his name, his tail began to wag, and he bounded over to Blessed John.

"Come here, Ben," Little Therese called to him. "Sit by me."

Blessed John opened a cloth, and then disbursed homemade pieces of bread to each young person. They started to eat.

"Boy! Am I hungry!" said Corey.

Wait! Wait!" exclaimed Blessed John. "We have to bless our food first. Hold your bread high in the air!"

All of the young people raised their hands toward the sky, some raised one hand, some held up both hands."

Then, Blessed John took from his knapsack a large piece of bread, and lifted it to the sky.

"Blessed are you who has created this meadow, this world, and us. You have given this bread. Bless these gifts and bless us too. Amen!"

"Now!" said Blessed John. "Eat all of it! Don't let any of it go to waste!"

Ben began to gnaw on his biscuit.

"Yes!" said Blessed John. "Eat like Ben!"

"Hey Mister! Blessed John! You got anything to drink?"

"Why, yes, I do!"

He took from his knapsack a large bottle of elixir and small cups. He poured the liquid into the cups, and passed them out to each one.

"Looks like gold!" said Buddy.

Blessed John smiled broadly.

"Don't tell anyone," he said. "The drink I am giving you is from Gemma. You can't find it anywhere, except on the island that came from heaven!"

"Wow!" said Corey. "That's good stuff!"

"Drink it all," he said. "We'll wash the cups in the little stream, over there."

"Hey! I never noticed that stream until now!" said Caitlin.

"The earth gives to us everything we need," Blessed John smiled, slyly, "if we have the eyes to see!"

"Can I have another piece of bread?" one of the boys asked.

"Why, you certainly may!' said Blessed John, who tore a piece of bread from the loaf he had lifted to the sky. "Eat all you want! Anyone else? Come up and get another piece of bread!"

Many came and had a second helping.

"Now! Let's go and wash the cups!"

Each of them dipped their cup in the stream, Blessed John dried them off, with a cloth, and put them back, in the knapsack.

"Wow! said Buddy, patting his stomach. "I don't even want no dessert, I'm so full!"

"Tell us a story, Blessed John!" said Caitlin. "Tell us about Gemma, like Joe used to do when he came back!"

Then, Blessed John then told them about the place of unfathomable light, and perfect love.

Chapter 71

BLESSED JOHN AND THE young people arrived at Siloam, just as Jimmie Crackers was at the apex of his sermonizing.

"Who's zat guy, mister?"

"He's everywhere, with a different face and a different name, Corey!"

"Huh?"

"You mean, there are other people like him?"

"You are very astute, Caitlin. That's what I mean."

"What's he doin' here? Why is he here?"

"Money, Buddy. Money. Other than that, I don't know. He hasn't been around here before, that I've seen, although, I haven't been here long, myself."

"I've never seen him." said Caitlin.

Blessed John chuckled.

"Yeah. And we know just about everybody!" said Corey.

"I'll bet you do, Corey! I'll bet you do!"

"Why is he yelling?"

"I've found that, the more people are unsure of what they are saying, the louder they speak."

". . . and that includes you over there!" called out Jimmie Crackers. "Yes, I mean you!"

His piercing eyes met Blessed John's.

"And the young people too. 'All have sinned and are deprived of the glory of God. There is no one righteous, not even one! Not everyone who says 'Lord, Lord' will enter the Kingdom of Heaven.' So maybe you go to church all ready. Doesn't mean you're saved. Doesn't mean that at all. You have to accept Jesus. Goin' to church means nothin', unless you do! And if you do accept him as your personal Lord and Savior, he will reward you financially, and in every way. Then, go and wash in the pool of Siloam, and you will be healed. But let me anoint you first, because without the anointing, my anointing, the water will do you no good! And don't forget your tithes and offerings. Just make your checks out to Brother Jimmie Crackers!"

"*That's* his game!" Blessed John muttered to himself. "I see!"

He walked up close to him. The words coming from his mouth did not match the tired eyes that looked out from his face. He guessed that he had been doing this routine, now, for many years. He had the words memorized. He could recite them, while thinking of something else. But, how did he get here, appearing out of nowhere? Someone was behind this.

"Let's go down to the pool!" said one of the young people.

"That fella said we had to come to him first!" said Corey.

"Well, that fella wasn't here when this all started," said Blessed John. "He is an imposter!"

"What's that, mister?"

"Corey, an imposter is someone who is not who they claim to be."

"Who does he claim to be?"

"He's saying that the water cannot heal people unless they go through him. If that's true, where was he when all the miracles were taking place before he got here?"

"I see what you mean," said Caitlin. "Why do people believe him?"

"People want someone to show them the way. As you grow up, you will be faced with making decisions about things that are difficult. Life is hard, that way. But, when you have someone who is certain, or who seems to be sure of the way you ought to go, it makes life simpler, or seems to, for a while."

"I like to think for myself," said Caitlin. "That makes my dad nervous!"

"Well, it's a hard time for your dad. He wants you to think for yourself, but you still need his guidance."

"Isn't that the same as telling me what to do?"

"Well, no, Caitlin, it isn't. We all need guidance once in a while. That's never over. But this fellow is saying what you should do, for sure. Guidance is giving advice and then letting the person make up his or her mind."

"Sometimes I think my dad is telling me what to do, when he thinks he is giving me guidance."

Blessed John rolled out a big belly laugh.

"Your dad wants what is best for you. He worries about you making a bad decision."

"But, I won't!"

"All of us make bad decisions, Caitlin. We grow up when we can admit that we have not always done the best thing for ourselves and others. The more you can do that, the more you will be grown up."

"Yeah, like the time you sneaked out with that boy!" said her brother.

"Buddy, shut up!"

Caitlin's face turned red.

"All of us here have done or said something we regret. Even Corey!"

Blessed John looked down, smiled, and patted Corey's head.

"I ran away from home, once."

"Oh, yeah," said his older brother, "for about ten minutes, until you got hungry!"

"Let's go down to the pool!" said Little Therese. "I want to dip in it."

"Yes! Let's go!" said Blessed John. It's time!"

Chapter 72

CARMELITA HAD BEEN INFORMED by the Lincoln County Sheriff's Office, that Homer Hill had waived extradition. Meshach, Shadrach, and Ichabod had beat him to it, and were back in Indiana, pleading guilty to robbery and petty theft. For their cooperation, they had managed to have the charge of conspiracy to kidnap a minor taken off the list of charges, with a reduced sentence to five years, each.

When Shirley called from the police station to tell Jens, she told him that Carmelita had said, "Good riddance!"

"I'm sure a lot of people feel that way!" he said.

"Now, the bad news," she said. "Silo has to go back too, for a custody hearing."

"But, CPS has agreed that we can be foster parents, working toward adoption!"

"Carmelita says that, since the crime took place in Indiana, CPS back there, has to be involved. So, he will have to go back to Indiana too!"

When?"

"The FBI will be coming to pick him up, and escort him back."

"For God's sake! The FBI!"

"Homer took a minor over state lines, so it is their thing."

"When? When does he have to go?"

"They'll be here tomorrow!"

"They're going to pick him up *tomorrow*? Who's going to tell him?"

"Carmelita said she would come out to the house and tell him. I told her I would talk to you, but, I thought that you and I ought to tell him."

"Absolutely!"

"And we will need to go back there for the custody hearing, if we want to stand any chance of getting him permanently."

"CPS has recommended us?"

"The Oregon CPS has recommended us, but it's really up to Indiana. He may have relatives that might have first dibs."

"Sounds like we're talking about a piece of property, not a boy!"

"We've got to go back there, Jens!"

"When is the hearing?"

"Two weeks."

"Two weeks!" Jens said, incredulously. "Where's he gonna stay?"

Shirley was tearing up. Jens could tell by her voice.

"He'll have new foster parents, back there."

"New parents? Will they want him, permanently?"

"I don't know."

"What are our chances?"

"We think about fifty-fifty."

"Fifty-fifty! Indiana may want him to stay there instead of coming out to the wicked west coast!"

"Safety Harbor? The wicked west coast?"

"I know. I know! Jens, where are you?"

"I'm dropping off a load in Longview."

"You'll be home tonight, then."

"Yeah, I'll be home, but, I will have to step on it to get there in time to tell him good-bye with you."

"Carmelita says hurry home, but don't speed!"

That night, they told Silo. Tears filled his eyes.

"Can I see my friends, before I go?"

"Oh, of course, honey!" said Shirley.

The night was sleepless for everybody. At three o'clock in the morning, Shirley got up and made pizza. The delicious smell wafted through the house, and Jens and Silo got up to see what was going on in the kitchen.

"Nobody's sleeping," said Shirley. "I figured we might as well eat!"

"This is my favorite thing you make, Mom!"

Shirley had to fight back the tears, turning her back so that Silo would not see her lose it.

Jens, seeing her predicament, said, "Oh, I have several favorite meals that Mom makes!"

"I thought about it, and I would like to do two things."

"Okay. What would that be?" asked Jens.

"Dad, I'd like to see my friends and I'd like to go to the spring."

"Of course!!" said Jens. "I'm off tomorrow!"

"Carmelita has given me the day off too!"

"We'll take you to the spring." said Jens.

"Um, Dad?"

"Yup!"

"I'd like to go to the spring with my friends."

Jens and Shirley exchanged glances. They would hardly see him from now until the time he left.

"He wants to see them more than he wants to see us," Shirley said, when they were finally in bed for a few hours.

"He's fifteen, Shirley. His friends mean a lot to him. He's never had friends before."

"He's never had us before either!"

"Shirley!" Jens said.

He comforted her while she sobbed and sobbed.

Late morning, as Shirley packed his clothes, making sure they were cleaned and pressed, Jens took Silo to meet the Friendship Group for an early lunch at Joe's.

"Everybody get what you want!" said Jens. "I'm buyin'"!

"You may regret that, Jens!" said Sally. "These are teen-agers!"

"I wanna walk to the spring, like we did yesterday," said Silo.

"I don't think there'll be time, Son," said Jens. "Your ride is coming at four o'clock."

"My dad will drive. He's not out in the fishing boat today!" said Caitlin.

Georgia, Nate, and Susanna provided rides for the kids to the spring.

When they arrived, Silo said, "I want to drink from the spring and dip in the pool."

At first, they were lighthearted, laughing and joking with one another, around the spring. In the pool, they splashed and teased each other, piling on Silo.

Finally, he said, "I want to be dipped in the water."

"What do you mean, dipped?" asked Corey, who had come along with his big brother again.

"He means that he wants to feel clean," said a voice from behind them.

"Blessed John!" said Corey, "Get in the pool with us!"

To their delight, the pudgy man came down the steps and walked into the water.

He came over to Silo, and said, "Silo, please allow me to show you how to dip in the pool."

He dunked himself in the water, completely submerged. Then, he came up from the water, shaking his head and his arms, dripping wet.

The kids laughed, but Silo followed suit. He remained under the water so long, that the Friendship Club began to worry.

"Never mind. I can see him. He's fine," said Blessed John.

When he did come up, Buddy said, "Do it again, Silo, and we'll all do it with you!"

It was a somber event, as they all went down into the waters of the pool together and come up together. Then, after a brief moment, they walked out of the pool.

"You kids sit down and dry out!" Jens called out. "Nobody's getting in my pickup, soaking wet."

"I want to go back up to the spring," said Silo. "I want to drink from it one more time. I want to look all around and see everything, so that I can remember!"

Several began to cry.

"All of you come over to the house," said Jens. "I'll call Shirley and she'll have some hot dogs, or something."

Not long later, four vehicles pulled up at Jens and Shirley's house.

The FBI had sent the county sheriff on their behalf. The deputy pulled up right on time, at 4:00 p.m.

"Can't we go to the airport with him?" asked Little Therese.

"Just a minute," said Jens.

He came back and said, "Silo can ride in our car, as long as the Sheriff leads us and Carmelita brings up the rear."

And so, they did, stopping the cavalcade three times between Safety Harbor and the airport, so that Silo could ride with everybody.

When they were parked at the airport garage, the Deputy Sheriff allowed Carmelita to escort Silo to his plane. She did this by holding his hand, as the rest of his friends and the adult drivers walked behind them.

Shirley was overcome with grief.

Time passed with the swiftness of the winter sun. Time passed as slowly as the ticking of a grandfather clock. Carmelita helped Silo get his ticket. Then, there was an interminable wait for an hour, until he could board the plane.

Finally, the time came for Silo to go. Everyone hugged him. There were many tears. The last they saw of him was when he went past the security line, turned, waved, and then, turned back toward the exit, and walked on down the corridor, by himself, to the plane.

"He'll be back. I know he'll be back," said Corey.

Chapter 73

Raven had been called back to Bread from Stone Headquarters.

The creature was not pleased.

"This is not moving fast enough, Raven," he said, as he hissed and writhed on his throne. "You have to move with dispatch, before this thing gets ahead of us."

"But, Your Excellency, we like to get in and out of communities with a low profile. We want to appear as good. It will get us more in the long run, and we will make fewer enemies."

He thought the creature was going to attack him. Instead, he stretched, until his human-like head was an inch from Raven's face.

"So, you think you know more than I do?"

His reptilian eyes were slanted, cold and threatening, and, despite his long tenure at BFS Inc., for the first time, Raven realized he could be fired from Bread from Stone. He knew that the creature had sent many a clerk, laborer, or executive into outer darkness for disagreeing with him, or failing him. He had to be repentant and he had to be fast.

"No, Your Excellency, I do not know more than you know. Actually, compared to you, I know nothing at all. You alone are the mighty one. You, alone, are the Ruler of all. You alone are all-seeing and all-knowing."

"Then, go back and do something and you must do it quickly. And, you must get rid of the old priest. He has been a thorn in my side from the day he was born."

"I'm working on it. Trust me. I detest him as much as you do."

"You failed miserably with Homer Hill. He's in jail."

"Yes, we did not do well with him."

"*We*? What do you mean, 'we'?"

"I did not do well with him."

"You must choose your help from those who, not only have no con-science, but actually can do what you tell them to do."

"I've got a good one, now."

The creature adjusted his position on the throne.

"I don't see your point in employing one of these guys."

"Oh, Your Excellency, they know how to draw a crowd. They know how to get a following, but, they're insecure, and they worry about keep-ing the following. We just leave them at the top and then we manage the situation. Many times, they don't even know what happened."

"But your . . . Jimmie Crackers . . . what is the point in him? He looks pretty much like Homer. Why can't you get someone from a big city who is successful?"

"He's got more potential than Homer. Homer always looked a little bit like he was Mafia. This guy looks a little more like he is on the up-and-up. People will trust him more. As to bringing in some big name or muscle-shirted macho super-sized mega-church, it's impossible to pick one of those off, Your Excellency. They are paid ridiculous sums of money, they live in mansions, they are treated like royalty. They have no interest in coming to a little Podunk town like Safety Harbor. If this were happening in a big city, hell, I could get a whole team of them."

"So, say your Jimmie Crackers is successful, beyond your wildest imagination. Say he draws a big crowd. What makes you think he won't keep his success for himself. How will he help us take the spring?"

"He's got some vulnerabilities. His wife has left him. I can schmooze them back together. He'll be grateful to me. He will feel that he owes me. He can't seem to do a thing without his wife. And if he gets rebellious I'll just remind him of what I know about his drinking and womanizing."

"Drinking and womanizing?"

The creature perked up.

"That gives you some leverage! I still don't get your point of having him there, though."

"If he can get a following, it's our following. We can create such a division in the town. We can bring a whole lot of them to town. Some of them might even join the lowborn at Siloam. We can take over the city. With generous offerings, we can make an offer the Habibis can't refuse. We can buy the whole farm, so to speak.

"It's a long-term plan and we don't have that kind of time."

And, with that, the creature removed his eyes from him, and with-out a word, retreated to his throne, where he curled up around himself.

Raven knew that he was not going to get so much as a fare-thee-well. He was in trouble. He knew that.

That was the evening that Raven crept into Mrs. Saugus's yard, and blew up her house.

Chapter 74

When Marlene came home that evening, she found her entire house had been cleaned. She was amazed. Minnie Belle had been busy all day, sweeping, vacuuming, dusting, and scrubbing her bathroom.

"Minnie Belle! You didn't have to do all this!"

"Oh, I wanted to earn my keep. Besides," she dropped her head, "I miss having a home of my own, to take care of. It's been years."

"How long?"

"I think it's seven years now. No, it's eight. We used to have a nice home in North Carolina. But, Jimmie's preachin' job dried up there, and we lost it. Too much drinkin'. And, he had a woman!"

"Oh."

"The place Raven has given us, well, it's not ours. Jimmie will have itchy feet, not long from now, and we'll move on."

"You're going back to him?"

"I don't know. I've been with him so long, I just talk that way, I guess,"

"Minnie Belle, I've arranged for you to talk with someone tonight."

"Oh?"

"Her name is Meriwether. She has a congregation that meets at the country club, and she's willing to meet you there tonight, after dinner. About 7:30. I figured you ought to talk to a woman about this sort of thing. But, first, let's go down to LeRoy's in Yachats for dinner. Claude will join us there."

"What will Jimmie think? He believes I'm over here with you."

"You'll be with me all evening, at LeRoy's first, and then with Meriwether."

"Will you come in with me, when I talk to her?"

"If it's okay with Meriwether. Otherwise, you know I'll be just out-side. Come on! Let's go to LeRoy's. I'm starved!"

Chapter 75

LOU AND HOPE WERE having dinner at the rectory.

"There's a phone call for you, Father," called Mrs. McCarthy, from the kitchen.

"At this hour?" Hope asked.

"Oh, they come at all hours, Hope."

When he came back, his face was ashen.

"What is it, Father?"

"That was the hospital. It's Mrs. Saugus. There's been an explosion at her house, and she has been hurt. She has been admitted to Harbor General."

"What happened?"

"I asked but they didn't want to tell me."

Lou stood up, abruptly,

"We have to go! Right now!"

"Yes," said Father. "I'll be right behind you in the parish vehicle."

It looked as though Raven had begun his assault.

Chapter 76

FATHER CALLAGHAN AND THE Schofields rushed to Harbor View Hospital. Father was the first to arrive. By the time they reached the lobby, Doctors Bailey and Habibi were talking in quiet and serious tones.

"Frances is critical," said Father.

"Oh no!" said Hope.

Lou was speechless, looking stunned, his jaw slightly dropped. For a moment, he seemed to reel, until Hope put her arm around him, steadying him.

"Yes, she has serious head injuries, from the explosion. We are watching her closely. The damage is critical," said Doc Bailey.

"May we see her?" asked Hope.

"Father may go in, with the family's permission."

"Family?" asked Lou. "We didn't know she had family!"

"Evidently, she has a son, his wife, and three kids, from down in Brookings."

"That close? We never saw them!" said Father.

"They were estranged, I understand."

"Oh, how painful it must have been for her to be that close, and never see them. I can't imagine not seeing Liz, no matter where she is in the world. And grandchildren, too!" said Hope.

"We have Life Flight on the way," said Caleb. "She'll be transported to Portland, as soon as they get here."

"What's keeping them? How long has it been, since this happened?" asked Lou.

"About two hours. We had to get her here by ambulance, then examine her before we called transport," said Doc Bailey. "They're on their way. Should be here in about half an hour."

"I'm going in," said Father.

Five minutes later, Father was back, motioning the Schofields into the room.

"The family wants you to come in," said Father.

It was a strange scene, as the son, seemingly bent over his mother in sorrow, was saying, "I'm sorry, Mom. I'm sorry. Squeeze my hand if you can hear me."

Nothing. No response at all.

His wife had withdrawn into a corner of the room, seemingly unaffected. She did not look up to recognize the Schofields, as they entered. Three children were present, who, they would later learn, were from ages eight to fourteen. The oldest, a daughter, was texting. The middle child, a boy, looked confused. He did not know this old woman, who lay silently on her bed. The youngest, another daughter, was nearly asleep in a chair, close by to her mother.

Since the son did not respond to their entering, Lou turned to his wife, and extended his hand.

"I'm Lou Schofield, the mayor. This is my wife, Hope. We are good friends of Frances."

The woman looked up, seemingly reluctantly.

She did not accept Lou's hand, and, without eye contact, she said, "I'm Lotilla, Bruce's wife."

So, Bruce it was, then, thought Hope. Frances had never brought him up. She had borne her pain alone. A son, three children, and so close. Tears came to her eyes.

Bruce finally looked up and recognized there were visitors in the room.

"Oh, yes," he said, "we wanted you to come in. We know you are her friends."

Lou extended his hand to Bruce, and said, "I'm Lou Schofield. This is my wife, Hope. Yes, we are great friends of your mother's. She and all of you have our prayers."

"I would like to offer her the Anointing of the Sick," said Father.

"I'm not sure she would want it," said Bruce. "We are Christians and are not sure our mother is saved. That's what bothers me, most of all, that maybe she will go to Hell."

Hope thought, "Your mother has already been in Hell, with your living so close and yet so far."

"This is why we anoint the sick," said Father. "Any sins we have re-tained, we ask for forgiveness for sins, and ask that the Lord raise her up, either through healing . . . or the release of death."

"I think Mom was Presbyterian," said Bruce.

"In the last few months, she had been coming to Our Lady," said Father.

Even while Father was performing the sacrament, the EMTs were at the door, waiting, impatiently, to get into the room.

Lotilla broke her silence.

"Move, kids, so the ambulance people can get in!"

Lotilla and the children left the room, along with Lou and Hope. Father remained behind with Bruce. Soon, they exited, as well.

Within five minutes, she had been transported to the helicopter, and it was on its way to Portland.

As the *whop, whop, whop* of the helicopter blades cut through the early morning air, her son, Father, the Schofields, and the two physicians watched it disappear. Lotilla and the kids were in the car.

His wife honked the horn.

"Let's go, Bruce!" she called out. "Let's go, now!"

Bruce did not move, immediately, but stood talking to the assem-bled group.

"I grew up here in Safety Harbor. Went to school here. But, I was estranged from my mother, at an early age. After my sophomore year in college, I never came home again. I've lost track of everybody here. No one would know me, I am sure."

"What happened?" asked Lou.

"It doesn't matter, Lou!" Hope reproved him. "It doesn't matter!"

"I got mad at her about something. I don't even remember what it was, now. But, the years went by, quickly. Mom would always send a card at Christmas, but I never sent her one back. I deeply regret that. Lotilla didn't even want the kids to know about her. But, I insisted they come. It might be the only time the kids see their grandmother. God, how I wish I had swallowed my pride and had come to see her!"

"Maybe, when she gets better," said Hope, "you can see more of one another," said Hope.

'I don't know. I hope so!" said Bruce. "I hope she makes it."

Lotilla honked the horn, again.

"Bruce, come on! It's time to go!"

Chapter 77

Frances Isabelle Saugus died in the helicopter on the way to Portland. She was listed as DOA, upon arrival at Emanuel Hospital. Doc Bailey called Father, and told him.

"Well, she got a head start on getting to heaven, up in that helicopter," said Father, when he heard the news.

"Still and all," said Doc, "it's tragic."

"No doubt. Does his family know?"

"I guess they do, by now."

"How did they know where to find them?"

"At the hospital, she had them listed as next-of-kin."

"After all these years?"

"Yes, she never gave up on them, it seems. How horribly ironic that they have come together in her death, when they were so alienated in life."

"The veil is thin, Doc. The veil is very thin between heaven and earth. We are not equipped to see, as they see. There is no sorrow, no regret, no pain there. Only peace, and joy, and happiness. They see us, and they know that we are not really separated from them, as it seems to us."

"But, oh how hard the exit is," said Doc.

"Yes, I've often thought that those who go on ahead are the fortunate ones, Clyde. '*We feebly struggle. They in glory shine*.'"

"I've seen a lot of them go, in my time. You have, too."

"Yes, I always have more hope that there is a heaven for others, than for myself."

"You struggle, too! I feel as if I've been defeated as a doctor, whenever someone goes. I know life doesn't go on forever, but I'd sure like to make it so."

"So would I, dear friend. So would I."

"We ought to call Carmelita, don't you s'pose, Frank?"

"Yes. I think it's best that you call her, this time. You know more about the details of what happened. I'll call the family, if I can get their contact information, to see what they want for a funeral."

"I've got the information, but who's to say if they even want one!" said Doc.

"Well, the community will want to hold a service, for sure. We'll work that out and they can come if they want to, or not."

"Gosh, I'll miss her!"

"Yes, she is . . . was . . . a beloved icon in this little town."

Father tossed and turned, until the sun began to rise. Then, he went sound asleep at 5:00 a.m. He was awakened by Mrs. McCarthy for breakfast, at seven o'clock.

Chapter 78

MARLENE DROVE MINNIE BELLE to the golf course, just at the north end of Safety Harbor, beyond Pilsner House. There, in the clubhouse, Meriwether was waiting in the lobby. She greeted both women warmly.

Marlene introduced the two women to each other.

"Would you like something to drink? We can get a coke or something, at the bar."

"Oh, if you had some coffee, I'd love that."

"Then, coffee it is!"

For the next half hour, Minnie Belle poured out her heart to Meriwether.

"Oh! I've never had anyone to talk to like this, before!" she said. "Back home, I'd be afraid to talk like this, even to my kids."

"Your husband is an abuser, plain and simple," said Meriwether. "To say it any other way would be to sugar coat things."

"But he's God's man. I know God forgives him, so I must."

"Has he ever said he was sorry?"

"No."

"Well," said Meriwether, "you can forgive him, but if he doesn't get what he is doing, I wouldn't expect any improvement."

"But, he'd be lost without me."

"He'd find himself, soon enough, Minnie Belle."

He'd find another woman, Marlene thought to herself, but didn't allow it to come through her lips.

Listening to the conversation, Marlene began wonder, if they worked on it, could Claude and she make their marriage better? She didn't even know if she wanted it to get better, and she felt guilty for it.

This much she knew. She had to abandon her ways. She had to be married or not married. She had to quit flirting with danger, and sometimes stepping over the line. Her uncontrolled attraction to Raven got her into this participation, with him, in evil, itself. She had to get away.

She had to keep Minnie Belle away. Jimmie Crackers was just the type to stay with Raven. All of that religious gobble-de-gook was just a way to cover up committing fraud and participating in theft, draining well-meaning people of their hard-earned and irreplaceable treasure, as puny as it was. If you can get poor people to give you a little money, and if you can get enough poor people together, you can get a lot of money. And if you can fool them enough, they will even trade their souls.

What should she do? How should she start? She didn't know. Maybe she should have a chat with Meriwether, too.

She was interrupted from her reflection by Meriwether, who said, "We need to make some temporary plans with Minnie Belle. She's going to need a place to stay. We are going to need to get her some supplies. I have some hygiene packs that our church gives away when people need one. She doesn't even have a tooth brush. And we'll need to get over to the clothing store in the morning, and get some clothes. The plane kept some of their luggage. Seems it was only Minnie Belle's."

"But, I have my family pictures in one of those suitcases!" Minnie Belle protested, "All my kids are in there, and my grandchildren."

"We'll get everything eventually," said Marlene. "Carmelita will see to that."

"Who's that?

"She's the town cop," said Carmelita. "You'll like her."

"I'll take you to the clothing store tomorrow," said Meriwether. "I have some time. And we can stop in Ray Ripple's market, too, and see if there's anything you need."

"But, I can't stay with you folks, forever," said Minnie Belle.

"We won't get worried, yet. Susanna may have a temporary place for you, above her art gallery. She has a small apartment where she used to live, before Bart and she got together."

"But I have no money, Jimmie keeps all the money, which isn't much these days."

"We'll see Bart about that. The Cone Foundation sometimes gives small grants to those who need them."

"But, I don't want to be a charity case."

"You aren't at all. You'll be on your feet, in no time. We'll talk to Rock and Magdalena. There might be room for you, out at Siloam."

"Until we get this together," said Marlene, "you continue to stay with Claude and me."

Chapter 79

MARLENE TOOK MINNIE BELLE to breakfast, the next morning, at Joe's. When they arrived, Marlene noticed a "Help Wanted" sign in the window. She had a sudden inspiration.

"Would you like to work here? It looks as if they need either wait staff, or cooks, or dishwashers, or something."

"I've never worked before, except at home, for Jimmie. I went right from my parents' house to make a home for him. Would they want somebody with no experience?"

"Everything's different at Joe's. You'll see! And you've got plenty of experience!"

Room was made, for both of them, at the Wisdom Table. The topic of conversation was the violent death of Mrs. Saugus, the night before. Not everyone had heard, so there was shock and consternation, as the word spread.

When Marlene heard the news, her blood ran cold. She realized that this was Raven's first act toward obtaining Mrs. Saugus's land.

As she dreaded, Raven was waiting for her when she arrived.

"It's too bad about Mrs. Saugus's house."

"Oh! How did you find out?"

"I heard the explosion. I don't know how anybody could have missed it."

"A lot of people must have missed it. It was the topic of conversation, at Joe's, this morning, and many didn't know anything about it."

For the first time, shock registered on the masque that was Raven's face. Then, just as soon as it came, it was gone, followed by a slight smile, that irritated Marlene to no end.

"Well, doesn't the Good Book say, 'All things work together for good?' This could be the opportunity for us to buy up the property. How about we see when the place will be for sale? We can match any offer, and more."

If there had been any doubt in Marlene's mind before, she was now certain that Raven was behind this, and had surely done this himself, single-handedly. He didn't have the Homer Hill gang available, anymore, to do his dirty work, and Jimmie Crackers was too new, to trust with his felonious plans.

"It's a little early, don't you think?"

`"Dear one, [How she hated his patronizing!] it is never too early. It can be too late, but never too early. Who's handling the will?"

"I don't know. There are no attorneys in town, so I suppose it's in the hands of the bank."

"Go down and ask Honecker what's going on."

"I have two houses with interested buyers. I'm going to have to take care of those matters first."

She could sense Raven's surprise, and feel his vexation rising.

"Get to it, today!"

He had always insisted that she do his work, first. He had backed down this time. She felt triumphant. Even with this small step, she had let him know that she was not as afraid of him, as he had thought she was.

Chapter 80

FATHER CALLAGHAN WAS SICKENED by the death of Mrs. Saugus, and troubled with the foreboding that this was the beginning of Raven's scorched earth policy. His very life, too, he knew, was, actively, under threat.

There were only a few people gathered, when he arrived, early in the morning, at the spring. He saw cars in the yard from Illinois, Delaware, and New Mexico. One family was dousing a child with the waters in the pool. Still others were quietly drinking, directly, from the spring. Roy Legband was sitting outside his newly-built cedar plank house.

It was extraordinarily quiet. No one spoke. All that could be heard was the gurgling rush of the Spring.

Father felt the need to submerse himself in the water. He walked down to the pool, far enough away to give the other pilgrims their privacy. Almost instantly, Blessed John was at his side in the water.

Father's focus was broken, and he flinched in surprise.

"I am sorry to have startled you, Francis, but, I wonder if you would mind if I dipped you into the water."

"No, not at all," said Father. "I am grateful for the company."

Ceremoniously, quietly, Blessed John plunged him in the pool.

When he had arisen, and had shaken the water from his head, Blessed John said to him, "You cannot fight this battle alone. I am your ally in the fight against Raven's attempt to destroy what Safety Harbor has become, and to ambush the work, the good work, that is being done here in Siloam."

"So, you know Raven?"

"I have known him for ages upon ages. I will help you. In ways, you must walk this lonely path, by yourself. But, I am very close by, and will not allow you to fall. You will not fail. Raven will be defeated."

"Will I survive this?"

"Even angels do not know the will of God. But, should you not survive this struggle, I will bear your soul to God."

Francis turned and looked toward what he heard as footsteps and quiet voices. All who were at the Wisdom Table, had decided, as a group, to come to the spring.

"We are so glad to see you, Frank," said Lou. "We missed you at breakfast this morning."

"I just wasn't hungry after last night, Lou."

"What a terrible thing to happen to Mrs. Saugus. She didn't deserve to go out that way."

"No, she did not. None of us deserve death, Lou, but it is foisted upon us, anyway. It comes to all of us. How it shall come, we do not know. But, this much we do know, that our passing, at its longest or most painful, is only for a moment. Then, we are at rest and peace."

As Father heard his own voice, he realized he had been reassuring himself regarding his own uncertain future.

"But, it sure is bad for the rest of us, who have to stay here."

Father was aware that everyone was listening to him now.

"Yes, we not only sorrow, but we are starkly reminded of our own death. It is still ahead of us. Once we have gotten through it, it is behind us, not threatening or staring us in our faces, any longer. In fact, we will realize that it does not exist. And, the life we shall have there, is more real than anything here. This life will seem like a passing shadow, when we reach the other shore."

Chapter 81

THAT SAME MORNING, THE people assembled at the Wisdom Table decided to come to the spring. The quiet peace was interrupted by the caw of Reverend Jimmie Crackers' voice.

"Good morning, brothers and sisters! Welcome to the spring, where the water never runs dry, and your healing is guaranteed, with my anointing. It may not be instantaneous, but as you believe, as your faith grows, you will be healed. You may have that blessed assurance in your heart, and 'the peace of God that surpasses all understanding!' Then, before you leave our little community behind, as you continue your journey, I invite you to drive toward town, until you see a sign that says, 'Souls' Harbor Sanctuary.' Construction is starting *today* on a new church *and* a brand-new water park, for the kids. It's my new ministry! Yes, my friends, when the Lord does something, he does it good. The holy water, from the spring, will pass right through my new church, and you can receive my anointing, you can bathe in the water, you can meditate, you can walk through the woods, and all the while, your kids can be playing in the waterpark! This is all thanks to Brother Raven Sinclair, who is donating the property and financing the whole project. What a guy, eh?

"Yes, my friends, and I do mean my friends, come back and see us! Tell *your* friends! It's going to be the premier place to be, anywhere around here! Yes, the Jimmie Crackers' Souls' Harbor and Water Park, will be an entire family experience. But, while we're still here, come and let me anoint you with oil. My hands, which have been blessed to heal all I touch, will bring about complete, and I do mean 'complete', my dear friends, . . . complete healing. Guar-an-teed. 'Is anything too marvelous for the Lord to do'?"

"Oh, he's got to go!" said Liz.

"Who is he?" asked Georgia.

"He is a liar and a deceiver," said Little Therese. "Raven wants to destroy the Sacred Spring and to take over Safety Harbor. He doesn't want us to be a Gate of Light. He wants Siloam. He wants it all. He's using this imposter to help him. We must join the struggle with Father Callaghan and Blessed John."

"Well, I'll take the first step and get Carmelita to throw this guy off the property! He can't come back here." said Liz.

"Hobe and I agree," said Georgette. "We take a lot of pride in this farm, and we love what is happening here. We can't allow this grifter to go on!"

"I think Carmelita is over at Mrs. Saugus's house," said Carla. "We saw her squad car in the yard. We thought she must be investigating."

She was. Marshall was assigned to answer all calls while she was at the Saugus place. When Liz explained the situation to him on the phone, he immediately agreed to meet her at Siloam.

Jimmie Crackers was still holding forth. Marshall listened for a while, then, he said, "I've never heard anything like this!"

"Oh, you have lived a very sheltered life, Marshall," said Lou, who, along with Hope had chosen to stay and support his daughter. "My great grandpa was a revival preacher."

"But, he was sincere man, Lou. This guy is a huckster."

"Well, he's got to be thrown out of here," said Lou. "He's collecting money and everything."

Marshall went, straight away, and arrested him.

"On what grounds?" protested Jimmie.

"I'll think of something!" he said, as he cuffed him. "You have the right to remain silent. And I hope you do!"

Chapter 82

ON HIS WAY BACK to Safety Harbor, Father Callaghan stopped by Mrs. Saugus's place. Surprisingly, most of the house had undergone no damage. Only the bedroom, where she slept, had been completely destroyed.

"She didn't suffer, Father," said Carmelita. "She probably didn't even wake up."

"Well, that's a relief, of sorts, I guess."

"Yes, it's a tragedy, a useless, cold, and intentional act. I can't imagine a motive."

"Oh, I can. I can."

"What's that, Father?"

"Raven Sinclair. He wants this property. He will try to get it, now."

"Why does he want it?"

"He's got big plans. He wants to own all the property from Safety Harbor through to Siloam. He wants control of the spring."

"What?"

Carmelita was incredulous.

"Have you met him?" asked Francis.

"No. I've seen him around town. Marshall has run into him somewhere, and told me who he is."

"I doubt anyone knows who he really is, except for me. Maybe Marlene."

"Marlene? How would she know?"

"He's got her under his thumb, for some reason."

"Think she might know something about this?"

"Just what Raven wants her to know, if she knows anything. But, no, I don't think she knows anything about this."

"Well, we can't arrest anybody until we have evidence."

"You could call him in. Question him."

"I don't want to raise his suspicions, but I'll keep an eye on him."

"I'd watch Brother Jimmie Crackers, too!"

Carmelita laughed at the name.

"Who's he?"

"A preacher who is working for Raven. Marshall arrested him just an hour ago."

"For what?"

"I don't know. Caleb and Liz wanted him off the property."

"They don't have to let anybody on their acreage. I've been concerned about the unfettered welcome they've been giving to everyone. Invites trouble, I think."

"This is all new for all of us, Carmelita. We have no idea what the return of the spring means to our future. But, we do know that Bread from Stone wants it. They'd like to take over all of Siloam, and Safety Harbor, too."

"What can we do?"

"Honestly, I don't know. We've got volunteers at the entrance. I know Caleb and Liz don't want to hire security. It'll drive people away, they think, but, you have to get busy on this investigation, and I have things to do. Mrs. McCarthy gets cranky, when I don't show up in the office in the morning! She thinks I should be working on my homily, so, I let her think I am!"

Chapter 83

MARLENE WENT HOME TO change and to dry her hair, after being dunked in Siloam's waters. She found the house empty. Minnie Belle must be out with Meriwether, getting some new clothes.

She had determined, ahead of time, that, if Raven asked if she had been to see Bartosh about the will, she was going to stand her ground. She would say that she was not going to the bank, until after Mrs. Saugus's funeral.

"It's the only decent thing to do," she told Raven, when he, predictably brought up the subject.

"I told you today! I want it done, today!"

She was shaking inside, but stood her ground.

"No. I'm not going until after the woman is buried. She's not even cold, yet! Do you want to make enemies? Mrs. Saugus is beloved in this town!"

And you killed her, she wanted to say, but she held her tongue. She was surprised that Raven backed down so easily.

"Now, I am going out to sell houses, in order to pay the rent, so that you and I can keep our office open!"

As she drove to Clever, she realized that, even though Raven had promised her $1500.00, for his first month's rent, she hadn't seen it, yet. It occurred to her that she probably never would see it. If she demanded it, he would just threaten to reveal their relationship.

She realized that, in standing up to him, she had crossed a line. She was frightened, and yet, somehow, she was giddy, with happiness.

"Freedom!" she yelled out to herself in her SUV. "Freedom! Oh, freedom!"

She wasn't extricated yet, but, she was on her way!

216

She had two prospective buyers for the house in Clever, and one had made an offer.

As she turned to go, she couldn't help herself. She looked back.

"Jimmie Crackers has been barred from the spring. He was arrested for trespassing yesterday. So, I think he spent overnight in the klink, last night."

The shocked look on Raven's face was a sight to behold. She was on the right track toward escaping his grip. She no longer felt paralyzed and helpless.

So far, it had been a good day.

Chapter 84

RAVEN BAILED JIMMIE OUT of jail, until his trial for trespassing and disturbing the peace. In the time that followed, Raven would put him to work, getting legal matters for construction taken care of at the Lincoln County Courthouse; hanging posters for the new ministry in neighboring towns, and scheduling talks, up and down the coast, introducing Souls' Harbor Church and Water Park. to the general public.

Normally, Jimmie would have welcomed the chance to get on the road, to places where people didn't know him, where he could drink to his heart's content, and find a willing woman. Usually, he could sneak away and then, come home to his Minnie Belle, who would ask no questions. But, this was different. He came back to an empty house, and no supper. His bed was not made. In fact, there was no bed at all. He had a mattress and box springs that the last renters had left behind, when they moved.

Two days after the explosion at the Saugus place, even though county permits were not yet finalized, Raven began construction. He told the earth movers to knock down the property line fence, between the Saugus place and the BFS Inc. property. Since it ran through a thickly-wooded area, it was not visible, to anyone who passed by on the road or at the adjacent property. He would be acquiring the land, soon enough, anyway.

Only a small amount of evidence had been collected at the scene of the explosion. Carmelita was neither pleased nor confident that they had enough, even to consider arresting anybody.

One of Raven's strategies, to soften up potential opposition, was to reign terror down upon the people. Safety Harbor City Hall was burglarized. Lou's office was rifled. He vandalized the lighthouse. He broke into Our Lady, desecrating the church by turning over the confessional, the baptismal font, and the altar. But, he did not touch Joe's, which contained the light from Gemma. This light was what he could not stand. It blinded him. It confused him. It caused anger to well up, within him.

Construction of Soul's Harbor Church and Waterpark continued, at an all-out pace. A significant number of trees, which had provided a backdrop to the once remote house in the woods, had to be removed, to make room for the large facility.

Meanwhile, throngs continued coming to the spring. Indigenous people began to assemble there for ceremonies, some associated with the spring, known, up until now, only by Roy Legband. All of this antagonized Raven to no end, and he vowed to speed up the pace of his plans even more.

Word came back from Indiana, that Jens and Shirley had been unsuccessful in their bid to gain temporary custody of Silo. He would have to go into foster care, in Indiana, indefinitely.

Chapter 85

THE TIME HAD COME. Marlene could put it off no longer. She had to get out. She made an appointment with Meriwether. During a long dinner at the Country Club, Marlene told her all that had happened.

When she had finished, she said, "Honestly, I'm so embarrassed, so humiliated."

"There is no need for that," said Meriwether. "You have been vulnerable for a long time. Raven knew this, and has taken advantage of you. You need support around you. You just need the opportunity to become who you are."

"How do I begin?"

"First of all, you need to quit Raven."

"But, he's in my office. How do I remove him without his spilling the beans on our . . . whatever it is?"

"My guess is that he's bluffing. But, you need to protect yourself, and one way to do that is to tell Claude everything. Get real with him."

"But, we've been so far away from each other, for so long. I don't know how to begin. Besides, I'm so angry at him for . . . sitting there every night, ignoring me and falling asleep. All he knows is going to Ripples, playing with his numbers, coming home, having two beers, and going to bed. And I have not been faithful to my marriage vows. Claude has every right to divorce me."

"Really, would that be so bad? There are worse things in life than divorce."

"Yes, like living my current life!"

"You need to be honest with Claude about everything. Are you afraid he might be violent with you?"

"Oh, no! His problem will be staying awake!"

"Well, don't go home and do it now. Wait for a good time. Be strategic. And as for Raven, if you can handle it, I suggest you play it cool with him. Don't try to kick him out of the office. You will pay a price, and it will tip him off that something is up. The Joe Team may very well be able to use you as a kind of double agent."

"You mean, an informant?"

"Yes. They meet every morning, right now. You could meet with them and keep them up-to-date on what that evil man is up to."

"I'm not sure he is a man, Reverend Meriwether. I'm not sure he is human."

Chapter 86

THE FUNERAL FOR MRS. Saugus was held at the school gymnasium. Still, it was not enough space. There was closed-circuit TV at Our Lady, at the Freewill Holiness Church, at City Hall, and at the Bates Funeral Home. Mrs. Glover formed a community choir. The string quartet would perform.

Many of Mrs. Saugus's former students wanted to say a word. Lou was asked to do the eulogy. The school board provided a collage of photos, that presented her work and presence at Harbor High, over the years. *The Wave* printed funeral brochures. Stores and businesses would close for three hours, out of respect to Mrs. Saugus, so that employees could attend the funeral. The Bates Funeral Home provided the casket. A luncheon was scheduled at Pilsner House afterward. Food would be served by Joe's Diner and Always Sunny. All of these arrangements were made within thirty-six hours of Mrs. Saugus's demise, due to Katye's organizing expertise.

"Frances Saugus was an icon in this community."

Lou's voice was crisp clear, his tone, full of sentiment and melancholy.

"She was beloved to her students, and she was a mentor to many. She put fear into the heart of many a slacker. She did not suffer fools gladly."

The congregation tittered, knowingly.

"She was tough on her students, but that was because she loved them all. She knew the world is a wonderful place, with many opportunities for those who are prepared; but, she also knew that the world is a dangerous place. It eats up those who do not learn how to survive in it. Her discipline was mitigated by kindness. All of the students were her children. She invested herself one hundred per cent, in all of them."

He brought out her bullhorn. Uproarious laughter followed.

"Many of her students recognize this! Actually, many of us recognize it, since she has been herding us through the Joe Parade with it, for the last five years! Who would have recognized her without it!

"She lost her husband, when he was only forty-three years old, and she raised Bruce as a single mother. It was a tough job then as it is a tough job, now. She started as a teacher, here in Safety Harbor, and, in ten years, she became the superintendent and stayed that way, for the next thirty years. I hear the Board made her retire or she would still be working! She always stayed somewhat aloof, she said, because she didn't want to play favorites or make anyone feel left out.

"But, in recent times, since she retired and began to help with the parades, more and more, she came out of herself. She showed herself to be a hero, when she went out to sea, on Nate's boat, to rescue Joe. Now, she has died, too soon, and in a way that she did not deserve. But, that cannot and does not change all she meant to us, and all she did for us."

His voice broke.

"She will always be a part of us. Mrs. Saugus, you did good. Farewell and so long."

There were few dry eyes. Hope gave her husband's hand a squeeze and a tearful smile, as he returned to his seat, beside her.

Long-term residents said they'd never seen such a long funeral procession, any time in the past. Carmelita enlisted the help of the police department in Clever and one highway patrol office, to escort the procession to the cemetery, south of town.

The reception continued on at Pilsner House. By the time the activities were over, the late July sun had disappeared, into the sea.

Chapter 87

AFTER THE FUNERAL, MARLENE made her way to the bank, to do Raven's bidding . . . seeking a listing for Mrs. Saugus's property. Bartosh was not surprised to see her. She would have come, in any case, by this time, in pre-Raven days, to get first dibs on a listing.

"The way the will reads, the property will have to be sold. I am the executor, but I do feel as if I need to consult the family, as a courtesy."

"Of course," said Marlene.

"When do you think that you might be able to do this?"

"I am meeting Bruce at the house . . . or what's left of it . . . tomorrow. We can talk after that."

"There is something you should know."

Sensing from the tone of her voice that this would be important, Bartosh sat back in his chair, and adjusted his glasses.

"Yes?"

"I've been working with . . . well, more like working *for* Raven Sinclair. He is currently building on the BFS property, and has taken out the fence line, between the Saugus land and his. I know he has encroached on the property, because the workmen have been removing earth and leveling out land, so that they can build on it. As the trustee, you have to be concerned about it."

"By all means," said Bart."

"Don't put anything past Raven."

"I'm going to get Carmelita to go out there and tell them to get off the land!"

"Good! I'm glad to hear you say that. You should also know that, if you give me the listing, Raven wants first "dibs" on it."

"Anyone who vandalizes the place can't buy it! Not from me!"

Chapter 88

THE NEXT MORNING, MARLENE reported to the Joe Team that she would be listing the Saugus property for sale, as of today.

"Raven has torn the fence down between the two properties, and is intruding on Mrs. Saugus's land."

"Bart has reported this to me, Marlene," said Carmelita. "I am going out there, right after we are finished here, and give him a cease and desist order."

"He's gone right now. I think he got called back to BFS headquarters. Jimmie Crackers has put himself in charge, on the project," said Marlene. "Can you give the order to him?"

"When will Raven be back?" asked Carmelita.

"I don't know. He never says where he is going, or when he'll return."

"If there's nobody to serve, I'll go out there and shut the whole thing down," she said, "for trespassing, and any other charge I can get to stick!"

"What if Raven makes the best offer, or will beat any offer I get?"

Liz spoke up.

"Caleb and I would love to buy it, but we're financially committed to Siloam."

"What if we all bought it?" asked Georgia.

"What do you mean?" asked Carla. "How would that work?"

"All of us could pitch in and be co-owners!" said Rock. "I like it!"

"It's a lot of money!" said Bart. "That property has become very expensive!'

"Don't we know it!" said Caleb, good naturedly.

"You got a good deal!" Hobe kidded him.

"How much are we talkin'?" asked Nate. "We've got a lot tied up in our houseboat."

"I don't expect that everybody would have the same amount invested," said Bart, "if we do this. You invest what you can, and you will own a commensurate part of the land. Of course, the house, itself, is a total loss. Mrs. Saugus's place is about half the size of the Old Eighty!"

"It's Siloam now, honey!" Susanna interrupted, flashing a smile his way.

"Yes, of course it is! I'll need to get full price for the place, since I *am* working for the estate, and Marlene will need to get her full cut as the agent. It would have to be a cash sale. Getting fifteen loans for fifteen people would be a nightmare! Besides, we'll need to get all the money to Mrs. Saugus's heirs."

"I'll take my cut, as you put it," said Marlene, "and invest it right back in the land!"

There was general applause. Marlene smiled broadly.

"I'll get the papers drawn up, and we can meet tonight if you'd like."

"How about at LeRoy's?" asked Jeremy.

"Good!" said Lou, as if finalizing the deal. "See everybody there at 6:30. I'll call ahead."

"Won't Raven be surprised!" exclaimed Georgia.

"Yes, he will!" said Marlene.

She smiled.

Chapter 89

CARMELITA FOUND RAVEN'S PROPERTY buzzing with activity. Jimmie Crackers was not hard to spot. He came toward the squad car, before Carmelita had time to exit.

"What can I do for you, officer? I'm the Reverend Jimmie Crackers. I'm in charge of this place."

"Well, the Reverend Jimmie Crackers, I am shutting you down!"

His face turned suddenly dark.

"What is the problem?" he asked, in a tight and suddenly reserved manner.

"You're trespassing on the Saugus place."

"We're challenging the property line!"

"Challenge it all you want, but do it in court and not here. I could haul you back to jail, but I won't, if you shut it down right now."

"For how long?"

"As long as it takes."

"What does that mean? I've got to open my church and waterpark!"

"Not until this is straightened out! Now, go shut everything down, and get out!"

Jimmie Crackers began to walk away. Suddenly he turned toward Carmelita again, his face showing his fury.

His filter now completely off, he screamed, "We're gonna get that land, Mrs. Biffle! And the spring too! It's rightly ours. That land belongs to God! Joe was a false prophet and his god is a false god. That spring is a part of my healing ministry. You threw me off that land too, but God will have the last word. One day the stream from that spring is gonna flow right through the middle of my church. I'll baptize in it. I'll heal in it. And, like the Jordan River, souls will walk across it from a sinful world, right into the promised land of salvation! You have given over to the devil. I pray for your soul, Mrs. Biffle, that you will change your ways, and come to the Lord. Hell is a hot place and lasts a long time!"

He walked toward her, extending his arms.

"Let's pray right now, Mrs. Biffle. You can be saved, right here, right now. This is your moment!"

"Back off!" she ordered. "Right now! Shut this place down, and get off this land. I'm sending my deputy to monitor this place, until there isn't a man left here. Now, move!"

Suddenly quiet, he turned, and began to walk toward the crew.

Chapter 90

WHEN EVIL SHOWS ITSELF, most often, it derives from a corruption of the good. People of good intent are especially susceptible to it. Someone declares the good person to be righteous. The alleged righteous person begins to believe that this quality came from himself or herself. Now, it is self-righteousness, which turns into pride, the sin of our first father and mother. Adam and Eve had one choice to make; and the choice they made, got them, and us, driven out of the Garden of Innocence, into a darker and more sinister world, where evil seems to be good, good seems to be naïve; and spiritual pride is the biggest sin of all.

Over the years, evil adapted, so that it could gain power by disguising itself as good. But, there comes a day, when, inevitably, the masque of good is torn away, and the countenance of evil is revealed to be the dark gargoyle that it is.

The Reverend Jimmie Crackers had been through all of those stages, years ago. He ignored the restraining order that prevented him from going on the BFS Inc. grounds. He called back the crew, and construction resumed two days after the eviction. He continued to encroach upon the Saugus property, cutting down trees, and leveling out the land. He insisted that his church receive priority attention. He wanted to preach there in two weeks, he said.

When Carmelita heard of these developments, she went out to the property and told him to shut it down or she would put him in jail.

"Put me in jail," he crowed. "You can't keep me there long, and even if you do, I will run this show from jail. My crew will continue without me."

Concerned that she might create a situation that was larger than Marshall and she could handle, she made a compromise with him. Construction could continue, as long as Jimmie withdrew from the Saugus property. This, he agreed to do. But, of course, he did not. He continued to push across the boundary, tearing out any obstacle that was in his way.

Marlene was stunned when Carmelita stopped by her office to see if she was aware of Jimmie's return to the property.

"This is not really my project," she said. "I don't have the authority to stop it."

"I had the impression that Raven and you are partners. At least, that's the word around town."

"There are some things I need to tell you, but, it isn't a good time," Marlene said.

As Carmelita turned to go, she said, "Don't wait too long!"

"I won't," said Marlene.

Chapter 91

WITHIN THREE DAYS OF their conversation, Bart had collected the money from the Joe Team. The Saugus property would belong to them, within a few days.

Meanwhile, Jimmie Cracker defied Carmelita's order to shut down. His demeanor was becoming ever darker, and his demands for the construction to be rushed, were ever more urgent. The workers seemed to be cowed by the force of his own personality, which was morphing into an ever more malevolent presence.

The construction crew, clearly, had made the church their priority over the water park, and was about seventy-five percent completed. Jimmie was especially proud of the channel created in the middle of the sanctuary, through which the water from the spring was flowing. It would be the very center of his ministry. On Sundays, it would draw big crowds; and during the week, people could visit, and leave a donation. Wherever he was, Jimmie figured out ways to bring in money, although he often spent much of it, more often than not, on gambling, liquor, and in houses of ill repute.

On the fourth day of Raven's absence, Marlene went out to the property to survey what Jimmie Crackers was accomplishing. She was shocked at the progress he had been making.

Jimmie approached her before she had time to get out of the car. She hardly recognized him. He had a swagger to his walk. The modest southern persona was gone, and in its place, was an insolence, accompanied by an air of entitlement and self-proclaimed authority.

"So, what brings you here, Marlene?"

"I might ask you the same thing, since Carmelita ordered this place to be shut down."

"Oh, I promised that I wouldn't trespass anymore!'

"But, of course you aren't keeping your word."

He smiled.

"The earth is the Lord's, Marlene. The world belongs to God."

"And your point is?"

"We real Christians are going to have to take charge of the world. Why shouldn't the Saugus property be ours?"

"Because it isn't!"

"The Lord's work takes precedence. We can claim this property in the name of God, which triumphs over all worldly claims."

"What are you talking about? You're just plain stealing!"

God, she hated that smirk on his face!

"You can't steal something that belongs to you!"

"You know this will not stand. You know that there will be consequences for this, and it will all come to a bad end."

"Marlene, people get by with murder all the time."

She felt a cold chill. Was he threatening her?

"By the way, tell Minnie Belle to pack her things. She's coming home with me!"

"I think that's up to her."

"No, it isn't. She's my wife. I am the head of the house, and she is to be obedient to me."

"I think she may have a different idea about that!"

"It doesn't matter. It's not up to her. It's up to me!"

"She has a job, you know."

"She has a job all ready, and it's at home. I've been suffering since she left. No meals. No ironed shirts. No nothin'!"

Marlene knew she had to get to Minnie Belle right away.

"I am going to leave now. I have work at the office."

"Be sure and tell her. I expect her home! Now!"

She did not respond. She drove down the long lane, leading to Newman Street, turned left into town, and went directly to the police station.

"The first order of business," said Carmelita "is to make sure she is safe. The way we do this, is to go to court, and get a restraining order against Jimmie."

"But, she has to go someplace where he won't find her!"

"That's the second thing to do. Let me work on that. Meanwhile, why don't you see if Meriwether will go with you to Lincoln City, where Minnie Belle can file for an R. O.?"

Minnie Belle was able to obtain the restraining order, within three hours of her application. Before leaving town, the three women celebrated, by having clam chowder, at Mo's Restaurant.

As they were approaching Safety Harbor, Marlene's phone rang. It was Carmelita. Susanna had agreed to allow Minnie Belle to live in her apartment, above the art gallery. When Marlene told Minnie Belle what they had arranged, her eyes filled with tears.

"I'm so sad and so happy, at the same time," she said. "I'm relieved that I have a place to go, but I miss my kids and my grandchildren. And, in a way, I miss Jimmie. I have known him for so long, and we've been through so much together."

"He's put you through a lot," said Meriwether. "I know it's hard, but, this is for the best, right now."

"Maybe we can arrange for you to go back, to be with your family," said Marlene.

"Oh, I don't think that's possible," said Minnie Belle. "I'd have no real place to live, and I would have to move around, so that I wouldn't be a burden to any of them. They would be kind, but they would get tired of me. No. No, I think I'm stuck right here in Safety Harbor."

Marlene patted her on the shoulder, and smiled.

"Well, if you have to be stuck anywhere, Safety Harbor's a great place to be stuck!"

Chapter 92

MERIWETHER HAD NEVER BEEN married, Marlene reasoned, so she did not understand that there never was a "good time" to talk to your spouse about hard things. So much had been left unsaid in her marriage, precisely because of this fact. As a result, she carried around with her a full bag of discontent and resentment. She was tired of it. She decided that tonight was the night.

The way Claude was, there could be no buildup to the main event. The expression of emotions, especially when expressed with passion, frightened him. She had spent their entire marriage, unsuccessfully, trying to figure out how to say things to him. Not much had been said.

Marlene had not wanted to be promiscuous. She realized this was a choice on her part. Really, she was a one-woman man. But, she had human needs for companionship, touch, affection, and yes, intimacy. She wasn't good at being unfaithful. She was not a deceiver by nature and affairs required that you be an accomplished liar and have a good memory for details. She had neither.

She would far rather have an attentive husband that she could spoil and fuss over, and one who would do the same for her. But, this was not the case. She might as well be living with her brother, and an annoying one, at that! She had to say something. It had to be tonight. She had freed herself from Raven. Now, she needed to free herself from a frozen marriage.

She came into the house with the usual scene intact. Claude was sitting in front of the television, waiting for her to come home and fix dinner.

"I've ordered in pizza," she said to him. "We have to talk."

"Okay."

"Turn off the television."

"Just as soon as I see how this western comes out."

"Tape it!"

"What?"

"Record it."

When there was no response, she stood in front of the TV, and said, "I'm going to turn it off!"

Her anger at Claude's slow response, empowered her further and hardened her determination. Claude responded quickly by pushing the pause button on the remote."

She grabbed the remote from his hand and turned the TV off.

Claude laid back in his recliner.

"I need you to sit up, please."

"Oh, it's okay. I'm comfortable this way. When is that pizza coming?"

She realized that his demonstrating a lack of a sense of urgency meant that he had no idea what was going to happen. She might as well be telling him about a new car she liked.

"Sit up!"

His eyes widened and he straightened himself up in his chair.

He remained silent, startled by her words.

She sat down in the rocking chair, that faced their twin recliners.

"Claude, I've been unfaithful to you!"

His jaw dropped. He remained silent.

"And I'm sorry. I know that this hurts you and I never meant to hurt you. But, I have needs, Claude. I'm your wife, not your cook and housekeeper. I need to be able to come home and talk to you, not just about the day's events, but about what is in my *heart*, Claude! I need to lean on your shoulder and know that you understand. I need to be able to touch you and caress you, in our bed, and I need you to touch and caress me. And yes, I need intimacy with you, Claude. Sex."

Silence.

"Have you nothing to say about this? Nothing at all?"

"I was waiting for you to stop. You know I'm uncomfortable talking like this, Marlene!"

"You need to get used to 'uncomfortable', then! We are going to talk this through. Maybe I can give you somewhere to start. I am deeply sorry for being unfaithful to you. I should have addressed all of my frustrations earlier, instead of going out and acting as if I am single. I betrayed you, and I regret it."

"I've known you've been out with other men."

"You have?"

"People don't stay out 'til two, three o'clock in the morning at a meeting, or talking to customers."

"Why didn't you say something?"

"I should have, but I have been afraid of losing you. Instead, it looks as if I've been losing you all along."

The doorbell rang. It was the pizza. Marlene went and got her purse, and paid the delivery boy. She took the pizza to the kitchen, opened the box, got out two plates, took two large pieces of pizza out of the box, placed them on the plates, and took them to the living room. Claude had turned on the television.

Marlene exploded.

"Can't you go for two minutes without that damned thing on? That thing is *your* mistress! You've no time for me. What if I have to use the bathroom? Will you turn it on while I am gone? Yes, I think you would!"

Quickly, he turned it off.

"The only way to talk to you is to be blunt. I'm unhappy, Claude. Very unhappy. Our marriage has reached a cross roads. If we can't resolve our problems, I'm leaving. You have to listen to me and act like you give a damn, about what I am saying. I want to hear from you, too. I want to know what is going on in there."

"In where?"

God, he's so literal, she thought.

"In you! In you!"

"I reckon, not much!"

"Claude, I have too much of my life left in front of me to live like this, forever. If we can't change, if we can't get things together, then I need a divorce. I want to be happy. I need to be loved, and I need to show love. Otherwise, what is there?"

"I know you're unhappy. I've known it a long time."

"Are you happy?"

"I haven't thought about it."

Her frustration rose with his apparent cluelessness, as to the significance of this conversation.

"We need to make a plan, Claude, and we need to make it together. I'm not going to map out our emotional future. This has to be a plan we make together. I want us to see Meriwether for some counseling. If there is any hope, she can help us. And I want you to make the appointment."

"Okay. I'll do that!"

"Tomorrow!"

"I work tomorrow!"

"Do it!"

"Okay."

Marlene was exhausted. She retreated into her home office. It took Claude an hour to get up the nerve to turn the television on again. Most of the pizza went uneaten.

That night, each of them retreated to opposite sides of the bed.

"What's new?" Marlene said aloud. "What's new?"

Claude did not respond.

Chapter 93

IT HAD NOT BEEN a good day for the Reverend Jimmie Crackers.

In the early afternoon, he was the recipient of a restraining order, saying that he could not come within five hundred feet of Minnie Belle. Later in the day, Carmelita came out to the property, and arrested him for trespassing on the Saugus property, for destroying property, and for failure to obey police orders.

"Next time, I'll arrest the whole crew," Carmelita told him, as she slipped on his handcuffs.

The county judge was coming through tomorrow. Jimmie would be arraigned. He was released on bail, provided by a mysterious, anonymous source. His trial would be the next time the judge came through town.

Unrepentant and unafraid, Jimmie went right back to work on the church and waterpark. This time, though, he worked at night. His crew entered the property on an access road that began just south of Safety Harbor. They worked nights, when most people were sleeping. He knew it was risk, but by God, he wanted his church!

"If God is for us, who can be against us?" he said to his men.

"I don't care if God is for us or against us, as long as you pay me," his foreman said.

"Just as soon as Raven comes back, he'll cut your checks."

He brought on a few more crew members. He could finish this up in three nights, maybe four, he thought. He told his workers to stay off the Saugus property. Raven would just have to be unhappy when he came back. This was the only way he could open the church on Sunday

"Sunday's comin'!"

Jimmie Crackers was on the street corner, by Jeremy's coffee and book store.

"We're opening our doors for the first time this coming Sunday at Jimmie Cracker's Souls' Harbor Church and Waterpark. Come to our services Sunday morning and Sunday night. Receive your healing from the spring waters that flow through our worship center, and my anointing, of course! Then, go enjoy yourselves at the waterpark. Bring the kids. Bring the family. Bring your friends. Don't miss it. Grand opening Sunday! We'll have special gifts for all who give a small offering of a hundred dollars or more to support the ministry.

Jeremy came out of the coffee shop to see what the commotion was.

"Can't you take this somewhere else?" he asked.

"Why, where would I take it, young man? This is the best corner in town. Prime property, I tell you. Too bad you're not in the Lord's work, son. This is God's real estate, anyway, you know. The earth is the Lord's. I want to invite you to Jimmie Cracker's, son. Bring an offering, a seed for your faith. Plant it at Jimmie Cracker's and you'll reap a harvest, a hundred-fold. God loveth a cheerful giver, son. Yes, he does."

Jimmie had named the whole project after himself in Raven's absence. He had learned, long ago, about the importance of facts on the ground.

He had bought some advertising time, on credit, on the local radio station, KFSO, and put the account in Raven's name. He had rustled an interview on the local talk show. He proposed to the management that he host a daily show of his own.

Jimmie was filling what he conceived to be a power vacuum in Raven's absence. He had experience with this, back in North Carolina, where he had built his ministry on another man's foundation. The founding pastor was discovered having an affair. Then, news came out about the misuse of money. Jimmie took advantage of this opportunity, and moved in. But, this time, Jimmie Crackers had underestimated his partner.

Chapter 94

A HIGH VELOCITY SUMMER storm came ashore in Safety Harbor, on Friday. It was centered, mostly, on the central part of the Oregon coast, confining the storm damage to towns such as Depoe Bay, Yachats, and Lincoln City, as well as a few miles inland. Safety Harbor was hit the hardest, with severe damage to the buildings on Main Street, including Jeremy's coffee shop. There was window damage at the high school, and minor damage at the hospital. The rectory and the sanctuary at Our Lady's took a beating. Marlene's business was spared. Joe's was not touched. Power lines were down and land-line phone service was interrupted. Some boats along harbor were in splinters. The hospital was overrun with those who needed first aid.

The power was out and almost the whole town would be coming to Joe's, to have breakfast. Joe's had a backup generator, and Sally said the restaurant would stay open twenty-four hours a day until power was restored. Stewart would take the swing shift and Luther take graveyard. Georgia, Minnie Belle, and Katye would cook. Shirley volunteered to help at night. Jens was gone, and with the loss of Silo, she didn't like to be alone. Jeremy's would provide coffee and pastries until their supply was gone. The high school gym, which had suffered no damage, became a shelter, for those who had been rendered homeless.

Caleb and Liz walked up to Siloam, where they found Rock and Magdalena walking through the desolation. Magdalena was in tears. Rock looked grim. They stopped and hugged those who stood outside what was left of their dwellings. There were empty looks on the faces of many, as they experienced the shock of what had happened.

Liz was sickened by what she saw. She had worked so hard to move them to this spot. If they had moved to another location, or even disbanded, this would not have happened to them. A deep sadness flooded her psyche. All of her work, and now, this.

All four joined in mutual embrace.

"We need you now, more than ever," said Magdalena.

"You have us!" said Caleb.

Liz knew that the grant she had received was fast running out, and her work would have to be gratis.

"Has anyone looked in on Roy Legband? It looks as if his little house is intact," she asked.

"Ruby was out here, first thing this morning," said Magdalena. "He is not hurt. He's fine."

"I'm relieved to hear that," said Hope.

"Oh, I wouldn't count him out. He bathes every day in the pool, and his step is quicker, by far, than it used to be!" said Rock.

They saw Bart and Susanna making their way toward them.

"I've come to see how the Cone Foundation can help," he said. "We are prepared to entertain applications for funds. No forms, just an email, saying what you need. We'll do our best to accommodate who we can, with as much as we can."

"You are a godsend!" said Liz.

Magdalena wept.

"You are very generous, Bart," said Rock.

"Not I, Rock. It's Wendell's money. I'm just the steward of it. I know he would want this."

Within three days, power was restored to Safety Harbor and Siloam.

Caleb and Liz began to work on repairing their home. Fortunately, the windstorm did not twist the frame of the house. All that was needed was a new roof. Hobe was there, in the middle of it, working on his old shed, in which so many of his treasures had been stored. Some were wet. Miraculously, none were destroyed. Some had traveled amazingly far, in the gusts of wind, but, he found them all, eventually.

Bartosh had arranged for a generous grant from the Cone Foundation, so that everyone in Siloam who wanted one, could have a Tiny Home. They were being hauled in, at the rate of about ten a day. A local construction community agreed to build a Director's home, complete with office, for Rock and Magdalena.

Meanwhile, activity continued at the spring, and at the pool of Siloam. Tonight, the Siletz Confederation would be having a celebration around the Spring of Peace, and had extended an open invitation to all.

All of Safety Harbor was buzzing with construction. Some were working on their own homes. Some, who needed employment, were put to work at projects around town. The storm had brought a lot of the morbidly curious to town, besides the tourists who had made their plans to be there, before the storm had hit the community. There was a traffic jam during most of the daylight hours, and into the night.

Doc Bailey reported to the Joe Team that there were no fatalities as a result of the storm. The critically injured who had been taken to Portland, were all recovering.

Chapter 95

"GAWWD's JUDGMENT IS COMING down on this wicked community! The storm and the devastation it left behind is Gawwd's way of punishing this wayward city. I tell you, Gawwd's complete wrath will not be held back, forever. Unless you repent you shall perish! Safety Harbor will perish! And Siloam too. They have allowed the Indians in there with their pagan ways! Gawwd will not tolerate the worship of idols. Siloam will be destroyed, unless it turns to our Lord Jesus Christ!"

The terrible storm had done what Jimmie Crackers had hoped it would. People flocked to the opening service in his church. on Sunday.

"Let me tell you, people. Gawwd wants that spring, up the hill. I want you to pray that Gawwd will give us the resources, the wisdom, and yes, the cunning, to get the property known as Siloam. If Gawwd wants us to, brothers and sisters, we will take it by force. We'll go on a crusade. Siloam is not a home for evil people, who worship idols.

"We are so thankful to Mr. Raven Sinclair, from Bread from Stone, who has built this church for us. Our dear brother is elsewhere today, somewhere in the world, challenging the forces of evil and wickedness. When he returns, we will all thank him, personally.

"But right now, today, while Gawwd is present and he is calling you, come, step into the spring. Repent and be healed. Give an offering of thanks to the Lord."

"The best time to get people," Jimmie had always said to Minnie Belle, "is when they are in sorrow or pain or fear. They'll be so grateful that you help them, they'll open up and give you more money than they otherwise would. Giving it to the Lord is the same as giving it to Jimmie Crackers. I'm the Lord's servant. His called. His anointed."

Events couldn't have been more fortuitous for Jimmie's launch day. As a result of the storm, people were in pain, sorrow, and fear, just like he wanted them to be. Many who did not attend church came for the show, and to see the stream that flowed through the church. Some, who were in other congregations in Safety Harbor, and from neighboring towns, flocked into the auditorium.

Jimmie had invited some food trucks to set up, so that, after service, people could stay and eat. He had brought in a generator for electricity for them. For an offering of a hundred dollars or more, they were given a free pass to the still unfinished waterpark. It was meant to be an all-day affair. And, so it was, for many. Happy voices and the laughter and squeals of delight from children, could be heard, until the sun went down.

"This is truly the Lord's work!" exclaimed Jimmie Crackers, to no one in particular.

Chapter 96

No one noticed when Raven slipped back into town. He was giddy with delight, when he saw the destruction.

"Beautiful! Just beautiful!"

He was more than happy to see that his office had not been touched. He would stop in and say hello to Marlene, as soon as he drove by the Bread from Stone property.

His happiness did not last long, when he saw the sign at the entrance of the Bread from Stone property.

"Jimmie Crackers's Souls' Harbor Church and Waterpark, eh?"

He was enraged. His car picked up speed and spun gravel as he went down the driveway. The water park was open and the crowds were growing by the hour. The church was twice the size he had been expecting. Jimmie had changed the plans that he had approved, and had gone his own way.

He entered the church. Jimmie was not to be found. A large steel box, secured to the wall had a sign on it: "Plant your seed money. Receive a blessing!"

"Where is that fraud?" he said in an angry voice.

Finally, he walked behind the church, where he found what appeared to be a private residence, built into the church. He rammed the door with his fist. Jimmie answered.

"What have you done?" said Raven, without so much as a greeting. "What business do you have creating a little fiefdom of your own, Jimmie? You have betrayed me! You have betrayed Bread from Stone! You have changed everything! I want you out! Immediately!"

Jimmie was nonplussed.

"Let me show you something that I think will change your mind, Raven. Here is the bank deposit from Sunday."

He showed him a deposit slip reading $110,786.23.

"One Sunday, Raven. And in this little hick town! It's fantastic, I tell you! People stayed around after church to enjoy the water park and then, some of them stayed for evening service. People are coming from everywhere!"

Raven was still unimpressed.

"Why did you not build on the Saugus property? We had an understanding."

"The police threatened us with a shutdown of the whole project, if we didn't back off. I had to make a decision, in your absence."

"Fool!" Raven raged. "Do you not know that the main goal is to get the spring for ourselves? How has this moved us forward? You are only thinking of yourself. You were given a chance, and you have failed, miserably."

"Look, Raven, I am providing a nice source of income for you and me. Besides that, didn't you notice the water from the spring is coursing right through the middle of the church? Why, we had a splendid time, Sunday! People stepped into the water! Many were saved! It was a real revival, I'm telling you!"

"*I* was supposed to be doing the miracles. I *specialize* in miracles! Nobody should get the credit for miracles than yours truly! We are going to talk about this more as soon as I get settled."

The tone of his voice was not promising.

Chapter 97

JUST BEFORE NOON, RAVEN showed up at Marlene's office.

"I've evicted you. Your things are all in storage," Marlene told him.

She handed him a copy of the official letter of eviction.

Raven was outraged.

"You can't do that!" he screamed.

"Yes, I can! You have not paid your rent at all, and the rent is overdue, for the second month!"

"I have rights! I have to be served a notice of eviction."

"Done and done!" she said. "A process server attempted to serve you papers at your hotel room ten days ago, and then, seven days ago. I contacted you by email, as well. I can't help it if you don't read your stuff!!"

"This won't stand!"

Marlene silently stood her ground. She felt a kind of euphoria rise up in her. She was strong, after all!

When Raven saw that this was not working, he tried the soft approach. He went over and touched her hand. She quickly removed it.

"Don't touch me! You have no right to touch me!"

"Oh, my dear! It is I, your friend, Raven. Allow me to take you to dinner, tonight."

"I'd rather starve! Besides I am going to have dinner with my husband!"

"You are!" he said, in mocking disbelief. "Really! Claude? What has happened to you since I have been gone?"

"A lot. A whole lot. Get out of my office! Now!"

"I'm going to challenge this eviction. You won't get away with this!"

"Here is the key to your storage space. It is in your name, by the way. You better pay them, or you'll be out, again!"

She gave the key to him.

"Don't come back!"

"Oh, I will! I will! And you will regret that you have done this!"

"By the way, Raven, you should know that the Saugus property has been purchased by the members of the Joe Team! I'm the agent, of course!"

"You and this whole town will live to regret this!"

A look of disbelief was frozen on his face, as he walked out the door, without another word, slamming the door behind him.

Chapter 98

FOR ANYONE WHO CARRIED around even a scintilla of free-floating guilt, Jimmie Crackers could evoke a sense, within the soul, that he was right and you were not, that he was righteous and you were not, that you must do for him in order to be a good person, and to be on the God's side. He evoked a sense of spiritual superiority. It defied rationality.

Clearly, he was a crook, but there are forces within the human spirit that are stronger than a sense of logic. He had used his power of persuasion, in order to make a living, over the years. He had made fortunes and squandered them, several times. There had been some dry months, even years, lately. Now, Jimmie had hope that his fortunes were turning. He would hold onto this church and waterpark, at any cost. His flash and pizazz could dazzle some, and he knew, instinctively, just as a snake recognizes vulnerable prey, who they were.

He suspected that Marlene was susceptible to such efforts. Raven had told him that she was unhappy in her marriage, and Jimmie was not above using seduction as access to a person's wealth. He had done this many times, without most husbands ever discovering it; and those who did, he had persuaded, almost to a man, that his relationship with the husband's wife was above reproach, pure, and beyond adultery, necessary as a kind of therapy for her spiritual wellbeing.

Ever since childhood, he had gotten a thrill out of getting away with his actions. His conduct was based upon the deep-seated belief that life had dealt him an unfair blow, that his station in life was a cosmic mistake, that he really belonged among the rich and famous, instead of being the son of a blue-collar worker, a wanderer, who never stayed in any one place for very long. He was disposed to religious sentimentality, and could cry at a minute's notice.

He was confident, this morning, as he headed for Marlene's office, that he could access Marlene's influence in the community. But, the woman that Jimmie met this morning was not the woman he expected.

"I've broken off all connections with Raven. He isn't here in this office any more. I have no sympathy for him, whatsoever."

Jimmie would have to change gears. He moved to evoke sympathy and guilt.

"I know Raven is a flawed person. But then, so are you. So am I. Oh, yes, I am! We all are. I know my shortcomings. Everybody does. We're just here, trying to muddle through things, and find our purpose in life. If God only used perfect people, why, our Lord and Savior Jesus Christ would have been the only servant of God! But, he calls us, too, to do his work. And so, we must. Raven is trying to do something wonderful, here, in this town. So am I. Quite frankly, dear sister, I am surprised that you have, so soon, gone away from us."

"I don't buy your view of the world, Reverend Jimmie. It is possible to change, to improve yourself, to leave your old ways, and to become a better person. If you don't care enough about yourself to make the change, care about it for those who love you!"

Jimmie wasn't finished.

"One of the ways we real Christians look out for one another is to keep our sins within the circle. But, if you are not one of us, if you are guilty of unrepentant sin, then, word of the weakness of those people may well get out to the public."

"If you're threatening me, to expose me, Reverend Jimmie, you may want to know that I have all ready disclosed my collusion with you people to the Joe Team, and I am now fully aligned with them. As for my other imperfections, they are the concern of God, and Claude, and me! Now, get out!"

"That went well," said Jimmie, to himself, as he left her office.

Chapter 99

"RAVEN IS BECOMING DESPERATE to obtain the spring," said Father.

"What can we do?" asked Rock.

"We are going to need to guard it, not with guns or other weapons. We must follow Joe's way." said Father

"What would he do?" asked Hope. "I wonder what he would do?"

"How could we know?" asked Susanna.

"I wish that Joe was here," remarked Magdalena.

"Well, really, he is!" said Meriwether. "We are Joe's presence, now that he has gone from us."

"He would want us to remain calm and centered," said Georgia, "realistic, but not despairing, hopeful, and trusting that all of this will have a good outcome."

"That will be difficult to do," said Stewart, who had joined them. "But then, Joe never took the easy way."

"No, he didn't," said Georgia. "He picked the true way."

"Yes, he would want us to have faith that we are living out our purpose in life, even though it seems, sometimes, that we are not, " said Father.

"This doesn't sound much like a plan to me!" said Nate. "You'll have to admit I'm right."

"So, the best plan is to have no plan?" asked Marlene.

"It's not a choice between a plan and no plan," said Liz. "Sometimes we don't know what to do until we get there!"

"Watch and pray," said Little Therese.

"And wait," said Georgia. "Sometimes we must just wait, and we will know what to do and what to say, when the time comes."

"But, stay alert," said Meriwether, "and ready. By all means, be ready."

"We must love one another," said Little Therese.

"How does that help?" said Nate. "I appreciate the sentiment, but we could love each other, and be dead!"

"If we love one another," said Stewart, "we will look out for the best interests of others as much as we look out for ourselves. I have learned that. We will act together, and not for our own best interests above others."

"And we must not be afraid of death," said Father. "That's what Raven wants. He hopes we will lose our courage."

Chapter 100

JENS AND SHIRLEY WERE notified by the State of Indiana that the final hearing, for custody of Silo, would not be until December 23. Shirley could not imagine being without Silo that long. She called Jens, who was on the road, to tell him. There were many tears. Both decided they must put themselves into their work. It would be a long winter, and an anxious wait. Christmas day would be one of the happiest of their lives or the saddest Christmas day they had ever experienced.

She could stand it no longer. Jens had been on the road for ten days. She was nearly crazy with anxiety and grief. She missed Silo terribly. He had filled an empty spot that she didn't know she had. She desperately needed to call Child Protective Services in Indiana to see if she could, at least, find out where he was. She did not want to go home and do this alone, so she asked Susanna if she would stay, after the Joe Team meeting, and be with her, while she called. If there was bad news, she didn't want to hear it by herself.

"How did it go?" asked Susanna.

"I don't know what I expected. I know what I hoped for, but that was unrealistic. I just want him to come home. Jens and I have learned to love him so much!"

A tear rolled down her cheek.

"What did they say?"

"He's in a foster home until they find his biological parents. The woman who gave him away, you know . . . sold him, is not his real mother. God knows where she got him. They won't tell me where he is."

She bowed her head and tears fell from her face to the table.

"He's been through so much!"

"When will you know something?"

"When they've done all that they can to find his real parents. Even if they don't, we don't know if we'll get him, or not! Indiana will prob'ly want to keep him there."

"Don't think that way! Jens and you make wonderful parents. They'll have to see that!"

"Just keep telling me that, Susanna!"

"Is there anything we can do?"

"They will want some recommendations and some character witnesses."

"You can count on me. Bart, too, I am sure. There are dozens of people who will speak on your behalf."

"You think so?"

"I know so!"

Shirley sighed.

"I have to go to work. I don't want to, but, I must."

"Maybe that will help."

"You may be right, but, I just want to stay here and feel sorry for myself."

"I think you feel sorry for Silo!"

"Yes, I do!"

She choked up again.

They were quiet together for a few minutes, and then, parted ways.

Chapter 101

"I am telling you, brothers and sisters, it's time to begin to take back the world for God! Jesus said that 'the kingdom of heaven suffers violence and the violent are taking it by force'. Enough, I say. Enough! No longer are we going to sit back and take it anymore! Our time has come! We can't take it all back by ourselves, but we can do our part by doing it right here, at Souls' Harbor.

"Why, even now, the forces of the devil are at work, right here, in our fair community! The land right next to us, that we have claimed for God, and is rightly ours, has been taken over by a nefarious outfit that includes heresy and paganism. They are not using it for God, I tell you, but for themselves!

"Listen, folks! God doesn't call you to do anything that you can't do. God wants that property. It's time that we turn the tables. It's time we take it by force. Oh, not guns, people, I tell you. Don't bring guns. This is the Lord's fight. We are just Christian soldiers, doing God's bidding.

"And, while we're at it, folks, there is an even greater threat next door to God's property at the spring! The same ungodly bunch that bought *our land, God's land,* are also in charge of this pagan worship center. As if some spouting of water out of the ground can heal you! Only God can heal, and these days, God is healing through me. These are frauds, I tell you! They are all frauds! This is the very water that is flowing through our sanctuary here. Many have experienced miracles and healing right here at Soul's Harbor, after I anoint them with oil, and they give an offering of a hundred dollars or more! We can't have pagans owning the very origin of these healing waters!

"As if that isn't enough, I have been kicked off the land with the spring, for simply standing up and preaching the Gospel of Jeeeezus Christ! We have to take it for God, I am telling you, brothers and sisters!

We have to take it by force! We can't compromise with the rule of the
devil! Why, I was awake all last night, I tell you. I was praying and I shed
many tears. 'Lord, what do you want?' I asked. 'What would you have us
to do, Lord? What would you have us to do'?"

"'Violence, Jimmie!' the Lord said to me. "Take back my property
by force. The kingdom has suffered violence. No more! Now, it's time to
turn the tables!"

Chapter 102

THE NEXT SUNDAY, AFTER the morning service, the three hundred people in attendance assembled, outside the building.

Jimmie stood up on a small raised platform, and addressed the people.

"It's so great to see such a great crowd here! This is God's work we are doing, and it is so wonderful that you have given up your Sunday afternoon to be a part of it! The Lord will reward you, richly, for your efforts.

"While I'm speaking, the ushers are gonna pass baskets through the crowd for a free will offering. Give generously, and you will have great financial prosperity and success. Remember, the Lord loveth a cheerful giver!

"A few nights ago, I had a vision, folks! I saw a great crowd moving across the grounds here at the church. And the Lord said to me, he said, 'Jimmie, whatever you want is yours. Whatever ground you walk on, is yours. Whatever you ask for, is yours. I will enlarge the borders of your tent, and whatever you do will prosper.'

"Well, folks, our friend and benefactor, Brother Raven Sinclair, has asked us to claim the property next door, known as the old Saugus place, and he wants the spring and all of the land that surrounds it. So, I tell you what we're gonna do, friends. [Ushers, where are those offering baskets? Keep 'em movin'!] Here's what we're gonna do! We are going to walk all over that ground, and claim it for Jesus! We're gonna take it by force, I tell you. God's had enough! We've had enough! No more pagan worship, right next door to the house of the Lord. We won't have it! We're gonna walk right over and through the fences and barriers. We're gonna walk all over that land with the spring. We will drive out the Indians, too! Yes, we will! We'll clear 'em out, just like our forefathers did. They'll worship God, or face the consequences!

"Now, before we start, let's bow for a word of prayer."

But, Jimmie had so stirred up the people that they began to move and drown out his words by their war cries. Somebody started to sing *The Battle Hymn of the Republic*. By this time, the song had found its way through the crowd, like a consuming fire, so that, by the time they got to the refrain, they were singing with all the resoluteness of knights, marching off on a crusade.

They tore through the fences of the Saugus property, and moved on. The crowd became so excited, that some of the older and weaker of them, were in danger of being knocked over and trampled. Babies cried. Children hung on to their parents. Men howled and women shouted.

Jimmy, who had managed to get out in front of the crowd, began to speak, although he could barely be heard by the crowd.

"We're comin'! The Lord's army is comin'! We're marchin' for Jesus, saints! Yes, we are! The Lord will not spare the sinner! The Lord's day of wrath and judgment is coming. It is here, right now! Don't spare those who worship false gods! Keep going, army of the Lord! Keep going! Don't let up, now! We're close to victory!"

By then, the crowd was turning into an angry mob. Some had gone into Mrs. Saugus's house and picked up whatever they could find to use as a weapon. Others ripped away pipes from the plumbing! Someone found a sharp kitchen knife. Now, part of the crowd was armed. No one knew who, among them, had a concealed gun.

There was a wide expanse of about a hundred yards, from the Saugus property, to where the little city of Siloam was located, and beyond that, the pool, the well, and the spring. Like an attacking hoard of hooligans, Jimmie's army of God, raced across the ground toward pilgrims at the pool, and the occupiers of homes. Shrieking and singing, praising and cursing, with someone carrying a Christian flag, they advanced to the edge of the town.

"Stop! Stop!" called out Jimmie, who, by now, realized that he was fast losing control of the crowd. "We're gonna let them surrender in peace, if they will!"

But, the crowd paid no attention. It was a mob, by now. Anarchy ruled. Jimmie tried to regain control over the crowd, but, to no avail.

Some began to beat the residents with what they had picked up at the Saugus house. Someone shot a gun into the air. Everyone began to panic. Screams erupted. The place was completely overrun with Jimmie's now four -hundred-person army of God. They headed into the pool. They invaded the holy area of the spring. They attacked Roy Legband's plank house.

"Come out, Indian! Forsake your pagan ways!" they cried. "Come out, and face the Lord's judgment!"

Roy Legband emerged from his house, standing with dignity in front of it. Someone pelted him with a rock. It hit him on the head. He was bleeding. Someone charged him, shouting out his idea of a war hoop, while those around him laughed. Roy stood there, quiet and somber, awaiting his fate. The aggressor wrestled him to the ground. Some joined the fray, and began to kick him.

Finally, a woman, one of the attackers' spouses, came forward and pulled her husband back. The rest withdrew, partly out of shame, partly because they were spent. Roy Legband was severely wounded.

Someone, who had appointed himself as the leader of this attack, called out, "You women get this Indian to a doctor! The rest of us have to finish claiming this place for God!"

Some had entered the pool. There were those who had come in search of healing, who had frozen in place, out of fear. The invaders jumped in beside them. With mocking cruelty, they dunked them in the pool. They dunked each other, mockingly.

Others approached the barn. Some climbed up on the roof, as if it was a hill to conquer. Others went into the building and let out the livestock.

Someone said, "Burn it down!"

"No, leave it!" said some. "Leave the barn! We can use it!"

Caleb and Liz had heard the commotion, from inside their home.

"I'm going out there!" said Caleb.

"Don't you dare!" said Liz. "They'll kill you! You call Carmelita and I'll call Magdalena to see how things are in Siloam."

One of the pilgrims called 911, and Carmelita was on her way, notifying the state police as she drove to Siloam.

When she arrived, and saw the scene, Carmelita called Shirley and said, "We're gonna need a lot of help, here! I've never seen anything like this! Do what you can! Maybe we can get help. Call everybody We're also gonna need medical from all over! Call Doc, immediately, and get him out here for triage! We're gonna need ambulances and Life Flight. Call Lou! This could be a disaster, if it isn't all ready!"

"We're okay, but it's awful!" said Magdalena to Liz, from their home.

"We're doing our best to get this thing under control," said Liz. "Carmelita is here and other law enforcement. It's going to take some serious crowd control skills. In the meantime, we will do our best to establish our presence."

The crowd began to move onto the front lawn, encroaching upon the house. Carmelita moved her car onto the lawn in front of the entrance. She turned on her siren, got out of the car, and stood in front of it, her hand on the gun in its holster. The police officer from Clever arrived and pulled up beside her. Marshall, off duty, arriving from out of town on his day off, saw the assemblage of cars and people, and smelled trouble. He pulled in and saw more than he had expected.

Jimmie Crackers had retreated behind a tree, where the woods began. Frightened out of his mind, he called Raven.

"It's pandemonium here!"

"What's going on?"

When Jimmie told him of the developments, Raven laughed for a long time.

"Pandemonium! Chaos! Bedlam! I love it!"

"Well, I don't, and easy for you to say!"

"Well, you are behind a tree! What's the difference?"

"How do you know that?"

"Oh, I have a way of knowing things!"

"What would you have me to do?"

"I'd say, get out of there!"

Word had spread of the mayhem at Siloam, and the members of the Joe Team were on their way. Nate and Sally were driving to Siloam, when they saw Jimmie Crackers headed out, down the road, on his way to Pacific Coast Highway.

"There he is!" said Nate. "Let's catch him!"

"No, Nate! Absolutely not! Call Carmelita."

Soon, they saw Marshall coming toward them.

He stopped on the road, next to Nate and Sally, and rolled down the window.

"Which way did he go?"

"We'd have no way of knowing, Marshall, but I'll bet his phone has a GPS."

"I'll get hold of OHP! They can track him!"

"Good idea! Good luck! Now, we've got to get down the road!"

"God be with you," said Sally.

Chapter 103

RUBY CAME TO THE scene as soon as she heard of the beating of Roy Legband, by the hooligans. The paramedics were just loading him into the ambulance. He would be taken to Portland, immediately, according to Doc Bailey.

"I'm going to ride with him!" Ruby said.

"Of course!" said Doc.

Pandemonium still reigned. About half of the crowd had retreated in horror at the scene. The other half stayed, tragedy voyeurs, people trying to be helpful, and thugs looking for more mischief. The law enforcement officers [there were eleven present by now] had formed a cordon around the area, so as to prevent anyone from escaping.

Just then, Blessed John called out from the spring.

"Have no fear, dear people!" he said. "And you who would seek more mischief, stand down. Peace be to all of you. There is nothing that has been done that cannot be forgiven. There is no violence that cannot be taken over by peace. There is no hardness of heart that cannot be softened by grace!"

"Who are you?" some of them demanded. "We have come to take this place for God!"

"God all ready has someone to take care of Siloam," said Blessed John. "Caleb and Liz are the stewards of this land, and they have declared that the spring, and all that surrounds it, belong to the people, especially First Nations people, from whom this place was stolen, so many years ago. They have gifted a place for the little city of Siloam to be settled, so that the people are no longer nomads. The forest and the trees are the watch towers of this place. All of this belongs to God, even now!"

"Not *our* God!" said someone, angrily. "*Our* God allows no other gods, no Indian pagan religion, no new age heresy!"

"That's right!" someone else piped up. "We are Christians! Jesus was a Christian, and so are we!"

"You must turn back from this kind of action," said Blessed John. "After all, do not the Commandments say, 'You shall not covet?' What are you doing, but coveting what is your neighbor's? Now, come away from this, turn yourselves around, open your hearts to love and not to hate. God is merciful!"

"God is merciful," said Carmelita, who had come to stand beside him. "But, you still have to answer to the law! Everyone here is going into the barn, where you will not leave, until you are questioned! Some of you will be arrested. All of you will be given a ticket for trespassing. Those who have perpetuated violence on Roy Legband and those who have damaged property, will go to jail. Anyone who is willing to be a witness, will receive leniency."

"You don't have enough jails to put us in!" someone yelled out.

There was laughter among some.

"There are three buses on their way!" said Carmelita. "One from Portland, one from Eugene, and one from Lincoln City. We will see to it that you have overnight accommodations! Now, every one of you, start marching toward that barn!"

Jimmie Crackers was apprehended in Eureka, California, where he was spotted by a sharp-eyed policewoman, who had just read the BOLO Shirley had sent all over Oregon, Washington, and California. He would be brought back to Safety Harbor the next morning.

It was 10:00 p.m. before Carmelita and the assisting officers had finished questioning those she had corralled in the barn. Fifty were arrested, and the rest were given tickets for trespassing. By 11:00 p.m., the buses were headed to the jails.

Sally offered to open Joe's to provide sandwiches and coffee. The place was soon full of people. All outside tables were filled, and some were seated on the grass in the back yard. Ray Ripple had to open his grocery store in order to provide food to prepare.

The soft light of Gemma, that radiated from the boulder in the diner, emanated peace, and calmed their spirits.

Chapter 104

THE MORNING AFTER THE mob, the Joe Team met with representatives of Siloam City, to survey the damage, and to decide the best way to go about reconstruction. They had not even had a chance to recover from the storm, and now, they were repairing and restoring, again.

After a walk through the damaged areas, they met at Caleb and Liz's house. Stewart arrived with breakfasts for all, from Joe's.

"Bart, you have been generous with the Cone Fund, and we know we cannot continue to ask you for help, indefinitely," said Lou. "But, before we go further, it seems that we ought to know how much you can help us out with, if at all, so we can know how to proceed."

"We can help you out again," said Bart.

"Excuse me, Lou," said Magdalena, "but this really isn't about Safety Harbor. It's about Siloam. We need to be the ones in conversation with Bart."

"True enough," said Lou, "but you're going to have to have an entity to award it to. You don't have any organization."

"Still, it seems that we should be the ones doing, rather than having everything done for us," said Magdalena.

"We can start our own non-profit," said Liz. "It is in my plans for the summer but . . . there's just been so much!"

"I think we churches ought to take up special offerings for Siloam City!" said Father Callaghan. "We can help with funding while the non-profit comes together!"

"I agree!" said Meriwether.

"So do I!" said young Reverend Cecil Bridge.

"Brooker Real Estate and Antiques will make a donation!" said Marlene. "I will shame the Chamber of Commerce into raising funds from their coffers."

"Most generous, Marlene!" said Rock. "Thank you!"

"Count on Argostoli's!" said Susanna.

"The Confederation will help, I am sure," said Ruby.

There was a stunned silence.

Magdalena had tears in her eyes.

"I don't know what to say!" she said. "It is beyond generous, after all that you have been through with the likes of us!"

There was a murmur of general assent in the group.

"The Sacred Spring has brought us together," said Ruby. "As long as we are together, around it, we are as one."

"Which reminds me," Katye spoke up, "how is Roy Legband?"

"He is recovering," said Ruby. "He is as tough as nails, and he will be back in his house, within the week. Someone will have to nurse him back to health, of course. We'll have three shifts of nursing aids right near him."

"Of course!" said Georgia. 'We can help, too, if needed."

They agreed to meet the next morning to report on their progress.

"Meanwhile, "said Nate, "we will start picking up debris today, and hauling it to the dump."

"I'm going to call the City Council together to see if we can have a picnic-in-the-park, or something, for a fundraiser," said Lou.

"Always Sunny will provide evening meals to Siloam City, for three days," said young Reverend Cecil Bainbridge."

"Joe's will cater breakfasts," said Stewart.

"We'll roust something up for lunches." said Jeremy.

"Everyone is most generous," said Magdalena. "We accept your help, gratefully.

Chapter 105

A WEEK LATER, WHAT Nate, playfully, called "Caitlin's Clique," and "Buddy's Buddies" decided to take another hike in the Siloam woods. Little Therese's mother, Ruth, had been in touch with Caleb and Liz, who gave them permission, and agreed to go along, to provide supervision. As they walked, Blessed John joined them again, as he had before, and, on the way, regaled them with stories of places he had been, and people he had known.

"First, before we go to the woods, let's stop at the Sacred Spring," said Blessed John.

The place fairly shone with a sublime light that provided each person there with an immediate sense of peace. All of the children and young people were quiet as they approached the pool and walked down the steps into the water.

After the dip in the pool, they walked through the streets of Siloam, where people were working on rehabilitating their town, from the damage created by the mob. They were greeted warmly by people, along the way.

"The light is here in Siloam City, now," said Little Therese.

"We're taking a hike in the woods!" Caitlin called out to some of the kids from Siloam City. "Wanna go with us?"

"You'll have to ask your parents, first, or whoever is in charge of you, and we will need two adults to go with us," said Ruth.

Fifteen minutes later, a group of a dozen young citizens of Siloam, and two adults from Siloam City, had convened, literally doubling the group's numbers.

Chapter 106

A WEEK AFTER HE was captured, and returned to Safety Harbor, where Carmelita had a jail cell reserved, especially for him, the Reverend Jimmie Crackers was indicted on charges of inciting a riot, trespassing, and conspiracy to do great bodily harm. This time, nobody would provide him bail.

When Minnie Belle heard of his charges, and that he was being bound over for trial, she was disconcerted.

"You must be strong," Marlene encouraged her. "You are lucky to still be alive, after living with this man."

Marlene, Susanna, Meriwether, and Katye had become Minnie Belle's support group, and were having coffee with her at Jeremy's.

"I know, but I still love him! I don't want him to be in jail! He's the kids' father!"

"Minnie Belle, you must stay away from him. He is no good for you. He is going to prison for a long, long time," said Susanna.

"If you see him, it will be worse for you," said Marlene. "He knows how you feel. He'll just manipulate you, like he has before, over and over again."

"I know. I know. I do love him, though."

"We can't help how we feel," said Katye. "But, we don't have to follow our feelings. That can lead to sorrow, and the breaking of a bond that can never be completely healed."

"I'm so lonely!"

"Have you been in touch with your kids?" Katye asked, as she handed her a tissue.

"They've called, but I didn't tell them anything. I just said that Jimmy was away. He was often gone when the kids were growing up, so they weren't surprised."

"But, you must tell them!" said Meriwether. "They can be a great support for you!"

"I know I should."

"Yes, you should! You must!" said Susanna.

"I just don't want them to know how much trouble their father is in!"

"Will they be surprised?"

"No. No, they won't!"

"Do you need to have someone with you, for support, when you call?"

"You ladies are so good to me!"

"We're not ladies!" objected Susanna. "We're sisters!"

Minnie Belle smiled, and reached out for Susanna's hand, joining the laughter that followed.

"Why yes, it would be wonderful if you ladies . . . sisters . . . were with me."

"Why not now?" asked Marlene.

"Yes, why not now?" asked Katye.

"I could call Virginia."

"Call her!" said Meriwether. "God knows the noise in here will cover up anything you say!"

Minnie Belle reached in her purse and got out her new cell phone, that Marlene had helped her purchase.

"I'm not sure I know how to use one of these. Jimmy would never let me have one!'

"You'll learn!" said Meriwether. "Then, you won't be able to put it down!"

Chapter 107

RAVEN HAD CALLED IN a chit on one of the mob bosses in Las Vegas. He needed a few of their action men, he said, to set some fires for him. Four men greeted him the next morning in his hotel lobby.

"Tomorrow will be the perfect day for you boys to carry out my plan," said Raven. "The wind will be just right."

They looked every bit the part of mafia hit men, out of place, with their flash and expensive jewelry. Raven met them in a small out-of-the-way coffee shop in Portland, in order to avoid drawing attention.

"What are we doing?"

"We are burning down the little town of Safety Harbor and everything around it, for four miles. I want it razed to the ground. All of it, including the spring out at the farm they call Siloam. You will need to start the fire in several places in the woods. I have marked the spots. I will show you on a map. Get out there early. I want things hopping by mid-morning."

"We want our pay in advance!"

"Pay? Your boss owes *me*!"

"He said you'd pay!"

"He said wrong! I will tell you what, boys. If you are successful, I will treat you to a night on the town, including some voluptuous women."

"If we want women, we'll get 'em in Las Vegas!"

"You drive a hard bargain, boys!"

"How bad do you want this done, Mr. Sinclair?"

One of them was, clearly, the spokesman for this crew.

"What do you want for this job?"

"Five thousand each."

"Robbery! Five thousand for all of you!"

"We'll be taking the next plane home, then."

Raven's countenance darkened. He gave in to no man or woman. He may promise something, but making a promise and keeping one, were totally distinct matters.

"All right then, five thousand a piece it is."

"And we want it all, in advance."

"That's where I draw the line. You do the complete job, and I'll pay you the five thousand. Fact is, if you finish it as I want it done, I'll double your wages.

"Oh, and there's one more thing. I want you to hit Callaghan."

"Who is Callaghan?"

"He's the priest in town."

"How will we know him?"

"He's hard to miss. He's always wearing a cassock. It's a robe he wears for every-day. It's black and goes down to his knees. You can't miss him. No one else in town wears anything like that."

"How do you want it done?"

"I don't care how it's done. Just do it!"

Chapter 108

MARLENE AND CLAUDE DECIDED to have a trial separation. Surprisingly, it wasn't Marlene's initiative, but Claude's.

Marlene took it hard. She was the one who was impulsive, giving way to desires and dissatisfactions. Claude was the steady one, as if he was the father, and she, the wayward teenager. She wouldn't know how to act any more. She was, for all practical purposes, single. The world did not look nearly so alluring when she no longer had the security of home and hearth awaiting her, with Claude ready to forgive her, when she tired of her flirtations and infidelity.

Now, she would have to come directly in contact with her loneliness, with her resistance to commitment, and her tendency to be vulnerable to the dangerous side. The latter reminded her of Minnie Belle. She knew she saw herself in the wife of the evangelist. It was what made her more sympathetic towards her than she, otherwise, would have been.

She would now be roommates with Minnie Belle, moving, temporarily, into the apartment above Argostoli's. Her privacy, essentially, would be gone, but then, so would Minnie's. She would have to be careful not to allow her housemate to become too dependent. She wanted to be kind, but she had her own concerns.

Stewart told her of his counselor in Portland, but Meriwether thought she should have a woman therapist. She knew of one in Eugene, and Marlene had an appointment for next week.

Moving out of the house was difficult, doubly so, because Claude offered to help her. It would have been easier if he had just stayed away, while she packed. Why did he have to be so damnably nice? Or, maybe the question was, she thought, why did it bother her so much?

"Going on a trip?" a neighbor asked, when she saw the two of them loading suitcases into Marlene's SUV.

"You might say so!" said Claude.

"Where you goin'?"

"Not far," said Claude. "Not far at all."

"Nosey!" said Claude, wrinkling his nose.

"Thanks for staving her off!" said Marlene. "Much appreciated."

"I'll meet you at the apartment," he said.

"No need," Marlene answered.

"I want to make sure you get there safely."

Suddenly "nice" didn't seem so bad, after all.

Chapter 109

SEVERAL PEOPLE SAW THE fire and headed toward Safety Harbor, at the same time.

Doc Bailey was coming back from a house call, in Clever, when he saw a huge plume of smoke, just south of where the Unsettlement used to be. Ashes were falling on his car. Katye saw it, from her view at the college campus. Meriwether was returning from Lincoln City, where she had taken her car, for servicing.

No one saw flames yet, but, it was clear to all who saw the smoke that it was big, and that it was coming their way. All three called in to Carmelita, who, in turn, called the mayor and the county sheriff's office. They would need a helicopter to survey the situation, said the sheriff. The fire department in Lincoln City had one, and she would call and ask the department to go out immediately.

"Those who saw it," said Carmelita to the Lincoln City fire chief, "seemed to think that it was headed toward Safety Harbor. I would agree that, with the wind blowing as it is, this is likely. There are farmsteads and country homes, of course, and there's a rather large settlement, just outside of town."

Lou rushed into the police station.

"Should we evacuate?" asked Lou. "We should evacuate, don't you think?"

"I think we ought to have everyone aware and be prepared to evacuate. But, we don't want people to panic."

"I don't want us to make the mistake of waiting too long. There are only three ways out, and the fire is coming from all three directions."

"I know. I know. Let's get a report, from the Lincoln City fire department, once the helicopter people have taken a look at the situation."

"I'm going to call an emergency meeting of the council, and get their backing for an evacuation; and I'm going to tell Hope to get packing! Call me the second you hear something."

Chapter 110

FATHER CALLAGHAN WAS IN his study, when he began to detect the unmistakable smell of smoke. He was overcome with a sense of dread. So much had happened in his little parish, in the last few weeks. The break-in, the storm, then, the mob. God knows they didn't need anything else. He had known this distinct sickening essence several times in his time in Oregon. It was a forest fire, he knew.

"The wind, the violence, and now the fire! Are we the Egyptians, that you should rain down plagues upon us? How long, O Lord? How long?"

He lifted up his arms, and looked up, as he expressed his complaint.

Mrs. McCarthy heard his loud bemoaning. Pushing on his half-opened door, she asked, "Is everything all right, Father?"

"Do you smell smoke?" he asked

She paused to breathe in deeply.

"Yes, I do. I hadn't noticed it in the kitchen, but you have your outside door open."

She walked toward the door and looked outside.

"No smoke in the sky."

She walked to the large groomed lawn, just beyond Father's office.

"Nothing to be seen out here, Father!" she called out.

She jumped, as she realized that he was standing just behind her.

"Nothing," he said.

Our Lady's was located uphill, from the downtown area, and was surrounded by tall deciduous trees.

"Can't see anything like a building burning. No smoke rising, that I can see," said Mrs. McCarthy, stretching and shading her eyes from the bright sun.

"I think the forest is burning somewhere. Not close, or we'd have smoke around us. But, somewhere."

"Do you think we ought to all Carmelita? She has so much on her plate all ready, with these arrests and prosecutions."

"Surely, somebody knows something," said Father. "If anyone would know, it is our esteemed Chief of Police.

Just then, his wrist watch signaled him that a text was awaiting him. He pulled out his cell phone.

"Maybe this is the news we are looking for," he said.

"Or the news we're *not* looking for!"

He read the text that had gone out to all the citizens of Safety Harbor. He read it.

"They haven't located where it's coming from, but it's close to us. People on the road are not reporting it, until they get within four miles of town."

"That means it's only two miles from Siloam!"

"Yes, it does. This is not good. Not good at all!"

Chapter 111

THE LINCOLN CITY FIRE Department reported that the locations of the fires, and the swiftness with which they were moving, with the prevailing winds, called for prompt and complete evacuation of Safety Harbor.

When Sally read the text on her phone, she was serving diners at Joe's.

"Oh, my God!" she cried out. "My kids! Our kids! All those kids. They're right out by the fire! Maybe they're in it!"

"Where?" asked Georgia. "Where are they?"

"There are fires on their way to town from the east, the south, and the north! We're to get out, immediately!"

Sally told her customers to forget about paying.

Nate was out at sea. She got on her VHF and called him. He ordered both fishing boats in, immediately. Sally called Carmelita to let her know the kids were in the woods.

When Magdalena got her text, she was of the same state of mind as Katye. There were children in danger. The fire was advancing, quickly. She spread the word among the Siloamites, that they needed to leave, immediately.

"Katye, we need you! You're the best organizer we have!"

Lou had called her at the Dean's office at the community college. She was at City Hall within forty-five minutes; and, within another half an hour, she had school buses parked in strategic places, throughout the city, to transport those out of town who had no other way of escaping. Katye had inherited Mrs. Saugus's bullhorn, and sent Roy out to the beach and up and down the residential streets on his motorcycle, to warn tourists. Upon her suggestion, the mayor sent out a text, urging people to head toward Portland, Salem, Corvallis, and Eugene. There would be no motel rooms available anywhere on the coast, during the tourist season. Buses and vans from Our Lady, Always Sunny, and the Shady Rest Retirement Center in Clever, were headed toward Siloam City.

Nate's two fishing boats arrived in town just in time to get his passengers disembarked and out of town.

Katye was on top of every detail and the evacuation. What could have been chaos, was orderly, deliberate, and calm. The biggest problem was the heavy traffic leaving town. Carmelita, Marshall, and part-time deputy, Jens, did their best to keep drivers calm. To any driver who was aggressive, she would get out her ticket pad. She never wrote any tickets, but the pad was an attention-getter.

Within an hour of the mayor's proclamation, the roads were packed with a procession of motor vehicles and bicycles.

Soon, Safety Harbor would be a ghost town.

Chapter 112

FATHER CALLAGHAN DECIDED THAT he must stay and help rescue the children in the woods. He was sure that this was Raven's work. It was all too targeted toward Safety Harbor and Siloam. Other towns were on alert, but had not evacuated. Raven was determined to destroy the spring, and all that is around it. He wanted Safety Harbor too. The fact that it was a Gate of Light, enraged him. Raven blamed Father personally, he knew. Without his influence, Raven believed that the city would never have been chosen. Father was not so sure of that, but Raven was, and that was what counted.

When they reached Siloam, the parents, other family members, and friends, had assembled. About fifty people were there. As Father and the other three members of Our Lady approached, the fire fighters were giving instructions to the crowd.

"Some of you have been in touch with your kids," said the Fire Marshall. "There are several adults with them. We are not going to take any chances. We are going in after them. We want all of you to stay where you are. We know you want to protect your kids, but, this is far too dangerous for amateurs. We'll keep in touch with your Chief of Police. She will keep you informed about our progress. Father is going to give us a blessing, but, make it short, Father. There is no time to lose."

"We bless you on your way," said the priest.

Now, all they could do is wait. He wished he knew where Raven was. He had a strong feeling that he was close by.

Little Therese had been the first to detect the pungency of smoke. It was unmistakable for anyone who had lived around wooded areas.

"This is the lightening I saw, falling from heaven," said Little Therese.

Most did not know what she meant, but, her mother and Evita DuPont knew.

"There is a fire," she said. "Somewhere close, maybe in these woods. We have to head out for home, right now."

Just then, Caitlin received a panicked phone call, from Sally.

"Are you okay?" Sally asked, breathlessly.

"We're fine. We smell smoke, though."

"We've got two helicopters coming to rescue you. Don't try to come down on your own."

What no one knew, was, that, before Raven's fire-starters had lighted a match, they had walked the Siloam woods, spreading accelerant throughout, giving the fire more impetus and strength, turning it, quickly, into a raging inferno.

Chapter 113

RAVEN FLEW HIS PRIVATE plane from Portland to his landing strip near Safety Harbor. On the way in, he took great care to fly over the fire. He was pleased at what he saw. The men had followed his instructions to a "t," and all four fires were melding into one great and overpowering blaze, headed for the coast. Its direction would take the conflagration right through the Sacred Spring and Siloam City, right into Safety Harbor.

Raven smiled. There would be nothing left. The spring itself would be choked over with ashes. There would be no Gate of Light, and no more Keepers of the Spring. The land would be totally scorched. Jimmie's church and waterpark would be destroyed. But, it could be rebuilt.

It was a long wait for each helicopter to deliver the children, one by one, from the area where the fire had them trapped. Parents, grandparents, and family hoped that the next delivery of precious cargo would be their own.

Luther stood, in support, alongside them. Georgette would not be comforted, since Hobe had disappeared into the fire, in his pickup. Liz stood next to her, arm in arm. Meriwether was there, and young Reverend Cecil Bainbridge, too. Magdalena stood next to Sally and Nate. Hope was in tears.

The smell of smoke was heavy in the air. Ambulances stood at the ready. Doc Bailey and Caleb stood at hand, to attend to any who arrived by helicopter, who may need immediate attention.

Katye, Carla, Caleb, and Bart were desperately watering down the old house and outbuildings. Roy and Jens were spraying water on the barn. Jeremy and Samir moved the livestock from the barn, and through a gate into the pasture, farther from the fire. This way, they had some hope of survival.

"I miss Mrs. Saugus and her bullhorn!" said Katye.

"She'd be all over this place!" said Carla.

Chapter 114

JIMMIE CRACKERS WONDERED IF he was losing his mind. Here he was, escaped from the city jail, into a ghost town. The place appeared to be completely abandoned. Not one person walked the streets. Normally, Jimmie would have considered these circumstances to be a gift from God. Everything was available to him. He had but to break in, anywhere he wanted.

He was surprised, out of all the stores available to him, what he wanted was a good cup of coffee. He didn't know what kind of rotgut Shirley made the coffee out of, down at the police station, but, he was sure he could do better, himself, even though he had never made coffee. Minnie Belle had always made it, and if it wasn't to his liking, he would make her throw it out and brew a new pot.

He broke into Jeremy's, but, he was disappointed. There were too many fancy machines for him, to know what to do. A plethora of choices of coffee drinks were offered on a sign on the wall, behind the counter. Doesn't anybody just make coffee anymore?

He stepped outside the front door of Jeremy's. Earlier, he could definitely smell smoke. Now, he could see that it was heading, toward town. He had to save his church. He began to run up the Main Street, looking up and down the side streets for a vehicle with the keys in it. The Lord had not left even one old truck in town for him. It was a trial of his faith.

He decided to hoof it. He walked and ran, until he was exhausted. Three times, he fell to the ground, until he could catch his breath. He did not know it could be so far from Safety Harbor to Siloam. The church and the waterpark were intact.

"Thank you, Jesus!" he said out loud. "Thank you for saving the church. 'I will bless the Lord at all times. His praise shall always be in my mouth'. Yes, indeed! Thank you, Lord!"

He walked in the front door. Awaiting him there, was Raven.

"I see you made it out of town!"

Jimmie had grown to hate the mocking grin on Raven's face.

"Yes, I did, praise the Lord! This is an awful fire. I hope we can save this ministry. It's the Lord's will that I stay right here for the rest of my life!"

"However long that is!"

"You started this fire. You can end it!"

"The spring, and all that is around it, must be destroyed, above all!"

"That's awful close to the church."

"You are right. It is."

"So, are you going to save it?"

"It depends."

"Upon what?"

"You mean, upon whom!"

"Okay! I'll bite!"

"It depends upon you!"

"Why me?"

"Because you're here! You're available!"

"What do you want of me?'

"Come! Sit down!"

He sat in the row of chairs, behind Raven, who turned around and stared at him with those penetrating eyes. Jimmie was somewhere between mesmerized and terrified by his look. I want you to help me utterly destroy Frank Callaghan!"

"Why?"

"Never mind why!"

Jimmie had never killed anybody before, although he would have, if the Lord had asked him to do it. If he had to hurt somebody, he wouldn't mind if it was a Catholic priest. They were tools of the devil. Everybody knew that. They worshipped idols, and Mary, and the saints, and left Jesus out of it, entirely.

"Will you save my church if I kill the priest?"

"I will."

"How will I do it?"

"He's up in the woods, right now. He's surrounded by fire."

"Then, that should take care of him."

"Don't underestimate Frank Callaghan. If you do this, I promise you will prosper the rest of your life. But, you must prove your loyalty to me. I'll be watching you."

Chapter 115

JIMMIE MADE HIS WAY across the waterpark and then, onto the old Saugus place. He could hear the drone of a helicopter, not far away. He looked up and saw one descending. He went a little farther He saw a large group of people, waiting in front of the helicopter that had just landed. He didn't know it, but it was Buddy, Sally and Nate's boy, climbing out of the helicopter, and running toward his parents.

"Gotta be some kind of rescue," Jimmie muttered to himself. "Maybe I should go and see if anybody knows where Callaghan is."

He approached the group.

"Anybody seen the priest?"

"Who are you looking for?"

"Callaghan."

"I haven't seen him," said Magdalena.

"Has anyone here seen him?"

No one.

"The last I knew, he was searching for the kids," said Georgia.

"Maybe he's with them now," said Hope.

Sally called Ruth.

"No, he's not there!"

"Good grief!" said Susanna. "I hope he's not out there in the fire, somewhere!"

"Anybody know his number?" asked Nate.

"I've got it!" called out Magdalena.

The priest did not answer.

Francis Callaghan, in fact, had gone, on his own, into the fiery hills. He was now fighting for his life, in a forest, alive with fire. Ahead, he saw that there was an open walkway, framed in fire, between two rows of trees. The fire made an arch, through which Francis thought he could

walk. It was dangerous. A burning limb could fall, and kill him immediately. He did not know what awaited him on the other end, indeed if
there was an exit. He could very well walk into a wall of pure flame. But,
he saw no other choice or chance. If he walked into his death, well then,
he would die, trying to save the children.

"When you walk through the fire, you will not be burned, nor will
the flames consume you!" Francis fairly screamed, "Do not be afraid of
those who can kill the body!"

But, who did he see ahead? Or, what did he see? Why it was Ben,
Little Therese's dog, the one that the adventurers had brought back from
Gemma! He was coming toward him, in the fire! The little fellow must
have strayed off, somewhere. Ben came toward him. The dog seemed
overjoyed, to see him. He stood on his hind legs, and put his front paws
on Francis's shoulders.

"Whoa, boy! We don't have time for old home week! We've got to
get out of here!"

At once, as if he understood him, the dog turned, and began to lead
him. It had been Frank's plan to make his way through the arch of fire,
but, Ben began to lead him toward the right, and a solid bank of fire.

Just as he had done on Gemma, for Rock and Nate, he sat down, and
looked back, as if to say to the priest, "Follow me!"

Frank followed him, but only to try coax the dog, away from the fire.
He would not be persuaded. When he came toward Ben, as if to rescue
him, he walked even farther, toward the wall of flame.

Father went to turn back, but, he could not keep himself from trying
to rescue the dog. Mother 'o God! Ben was going to walk right into the
fire! He could not bring himself to go back, now. He would follow the dog
into the fire and die with him. Logic no longer counts in situations such
as this, when, suddenly, the sanctity of all life comes into clear view.

Father cried out in fear, and, as he did, he thought he could hear
the trees and all of life around him, shrieking in anguish, moaning in
death throes. He began to pray the Our Father, as the suffocating heat
of the flames bore down upon him. He staggered and fell, nearly losing
consciousness.

Ben came back and nosed him with some urgency, as if to say,
"Come on! We have no time to lose!"

He struggled to get up, and, as he did, he would have sworn that
someone took him by the hand and pulled himself to his feet, although
he could see no one. Still farther they went, until the priest wondered if

he were all ready in Hell. He looked down and saw, to his horror, that his cassock was on fire. He threw it off and watched, as it was, immediately, immolated.

Suddenly, Raven was standing in front of him. He could not tell if Raven was impervious to the flames, or if they were exuding from him. He was framed in fire, unhurt, seeming to thrive in it, as if it was his natural habitat.

"We've got to quit meeting like this!" Raven smiled. "Whatever happened to your jacket?"

"Get out of my way, you son of Satan!"

"Why, I'm not standing in your way. You're standing in your own way! You have but to join Bread from Stone, and the flames will cease! Just think of all the lives you may be saving! Don't you tell everyone every Sunday about the one who gave himself so that others would not die?"

Father remained silent. Ben, sensing he was in trouble, came back to get him.

Suddenly there was a look in Raven's eye that Father had not seen before. It was fear.

"The damned dog from Gemma!"

"Yes, from Gemma. You are afraid of him!"

Father recognized the absurdity of standing in the midst of burning trees as a backdrop for a colloquy with the messenger from Satan. He could feel the flames, ever hotter, singeing his hair.

Ben began to tug at Francis's leg as if to say, "Time to go! Time to go!" He looked up and saw that Raven had disappeared.

"Resist the devil, and he will flee from you!"

Now, Ben was once again, out ahead of him; and, once again, Father resisted, as the dog was leading him in the last direction he would go.

Now, they approached the wall of fire. He could not walk into it. He wouldn't. Maybe the dog was an apparition, a trick of Raven's to send him to his death. He turned around. What had once been an arch of fire, was no longer there. Trees were fast falling. If he had stayed back there, it would have been certain death for him. There was nothing to do, now, but to follow the dog.

Smoke clouded his eyes. Someone had him by the hand. He looked up.

"Are you the angel of death?" he asked.

"No. I am your brother, Blessed John. I walk along with people on their journeys, no matter where they are going."

"Where are we going?"

"We shall see. We must follow Ben."

Francis could see, now, that Blessed John was protecting him from being immolated. The angel walked right into the fire, keeping Francis always to his left and away from the holocaust. He could not see, but all he could envision was the Red Sea parting in front of the Israelites so that the water did not harm them.

". . . when you pass through the fire . . ."

For what seemed to Francis to be an eternity, Blessed John led him through the hellish heat, with kind and gentle direction. Not once, did he feel the overwhelming heat. Not one time, did the fire burn him. Suddenly, he was at the clearing, where some of the children still awaited rescue, by the helicopter.

"Father!" called out Ruth. "How did you get here?"

"The Lord's angel," he said. "Blessed John."

Chapter 116

SOME OF THE CHILDREN were afraid to ride the basket, that lifted them up into the helicopter. The group below decided to send Nate and Georgia up to the meadow, to help bring them home. Georgia had a soothing and grandmotherly presence that children trusted. Nate was a sailor, and a kind of hero to many in Safety Harbor, especially since he was piloting the boat that brought Joe home, a few years ago. Between the two of them, they would manage, both to comfort and to inspire. Word that Father Callaghan had been seen, crawling out of the burning forest, reached the little waiting group. They were overjoyed. All but Jimmie Crackers, who had been given the task of getting rid of him.

On one of the trips back up the mountain, Jimmie slipped into one of the helicopters, telling the pilot that he was a doctor, and that he was going up to help with the children. When he arrived, he looked around for the priest. His ample frame and dark clergy clothes were hard to miss. Crackers had no plan at the moment, but, in his hardscrabble life, he had been accustomed to seizing the moment. Some opportunity would present itself.

He noticed Corey, the youngest child there. He would be easy prey. If he could get him aside at the right moment, he would snatch him away into the yet unburned forest. Callaghan, ever the do-gooder, would be one of the party that would come and rescue him. It would be a close and calculated call, avoiding the fire and, at the same time, making sure Callaghan got toasted. He would have to do this by the seat of his pants. But then, that's how Jimmie had lived all of his life. It wouldn't be different. The boy may have to be sacrificed, but, if it would save his church, then it had to be God's will.

Jimmie went up the child and said, "Hey kid! Wanna see a bear, over there in the trees?"

"A bear?" Corey asked. "Sure!"

"Come here!" he said. "I'll show you, but we have to be quiet, because the bear will get mad, if he sees us!"

They walked up a path that took them into a part of the woods yet untouched by the flames.

"Hmmm. He was here a few minutes ago. We may have to go farther into the woods to see him."

They walked for about five minutes.

"Still no bear!"

"Maybe he went that way!" said Corey, pointing to the left.

"Maybe he did!" said Jimmie. "Let's go!"

After another five minutes, Jimmie said, "I'm afraid we're lost, kid!"

"You mean, you don't know where we are?" Corey wailed. "I thought we came here to see a bear!"

"He is still out here, somewhere. Let's keep looking!"

"No, I want to go home!"

"Somebody will come and find us. That Callaghan fellow. I have a feeling he'll be along, soon!"

Chapter 117

No one had seen Hobe in a while, and Georgette was panicking. The helicopter pilots had been asked by Doc Bailey to keep a lookout, for him. So far, there had been no sightings.

Corey, who had been promised he could get on the helicopter with his brother, because he was afraid, would go aboard the last chopper, with his brother, before the adults came down; but, when they looked around for him, he was gone. At first there was general panic.

"Okay folks, think!" said Georgia. "Who saw him last, and where?"

"When I came out of the woods, he was right with the rest of you," said Father Callaghan.

"Well, he's not here now!" said Corey's brother, beginning to cry.

Georgia comforted him.

"If he's not here in the clearing, he's in the forest. There are no other choices," said Nate. "I'm going in for him."

"I'll go with you!" said Father Callaghan. "I must! I have to confront Raven. I am who he wants and he won't rest, until we have our last confrontation. Most importantly, we have to find that child. Corey knows me. He greets me, at the door, every Sunday, after Mass."

"Before we all get carried away, let's make sure Corey didn't slip down in one of the helicopters, when we weren't looking," said Nate.

"I'm pretty sure he didn't," said Georgia. "I'd have seen him. Besides we have a list, and there's no check mark behind his name. But, I'll call, just in case."

Chapter 118

DURING THE RESCUE, RUBY and a few others from the Confederation, had returned with Roy Legband. His little house was still intact, untouched, as of yet, by the fire.

"Boy, am I glad to see you!" said Lou to Ruby. "We have been worried sick about Roy."

"He was anxious to get back into his house," said Ruby. "We wanted to keep him on the Res, for a while, but he says the Sacred Spring is where he belongs."

"I believe he is right!" said Liz. "Caleb and I feel that way about being here."

"We have arranged," said Ruby, "to have some of our young people and our well-abled older adults come and protect the Spring. They will stand around it, at the ready, to put out any fire that may encroach upon the spring and the pool."

Liz began to cry. Caleb and she were under tremendous pressure to save their farmstead.

"The spring belongs to all of us, to everyone," said Liz. "Our open heartedness is the reason the spring has burst forth again. We are grateful."

"Here they come now!" said Ruby. "We're going to do it the old-fashioned way. We went to the hardware store in Lincoln City, and bought all of the buckets they had; and we brought along all the buckets we could scare up at the Res. They'll spread water from the pool all around the edge of the spring to prevent the flames from coming any further. This will also protect the barn and the house, and the other outbuildings, at least, if we have the time to do the job before the fire arrives. We will do our best. Roy Legband will come out and bless the efforts, before we start."

Katye's phone rang. It was Ruth. She was panicked.

"Is Corey down there?"

"Just a minute."

"Is Corey here anywhere?" she called out to the group who stood by. Word came back.

"No, he's not down here, Ruth," said Katye.

"His brother and he are to be the last to come down. Now, we can't find Corey. He's just vanished into thin air!'"

"They've lost Corey!" said Katye to those next to her. "Gosh, the little fellow is only five or six."

"Allow us to help!" said Ruby. "We'll send a few of our young people up to look for him."

Chapter 119

ALTHOUGH IT WAS DIFFICULT, Father Callaghan and Nate were persuaded to wait until the Siletz crew could get to them, by helicopter. Frank wanted to go in, right away. So did Nate. Time was of the essence. The fire was now burning at its hottest. But, it was not wise to go, helter-skelter, into the breach, either. They would need a strategy.

From the helicopter, it looked as if about three-quarters of the timber on the Old Eighty was burning. The fire was closing in fast, on the rest. This would be where they would most likely find Corey, who, by now, everyone assumed, had been taken, by Jimmie Crackers.

The Confederation spokesman organized the search, sending his own crew and Nate into the deepest part the forest, while ordering Father Callaghan, Marlene, and Lou to go into the forest, only to the older growth of trees.

It had been Jimmie Crackers' plan to take Corey to his church and hide him there. This way, he would both draw Callaghan into the burning inferno, but he, himself, would be safe. His plan didn't go well. Soon, he was hopelessly lost and didn't know one direction from the other. He was out of shape too, and soon, he was exhausted by walking over uneven ground and dragging a protesting child along with him. Back and forth, he went. Back and forth, like an ant on a match stick, that is burning on both ends.

He could not keep this up much longer. The kid was growing more frantic and had gotten away from him, once. On his sixth trip from north to south and back again, Father Callaghan, Marlene, and Lou, found them. Corey was crying and Jimmie no longer had the stamina to keep his hand over Corey's mouth and flee, at the same time. When he saw Callaghan, Jimmie reached for his knife. It was now or never. He let Corey go, who ran toward the three adults.

"Come here to me! Come here, Corey!"

"Father!"

The little boy ran to his open arms.

Jimmie took this opportunity to charge him, and cut him with his knife. He went at Father again, but this time he lost his balance, and fell back into the fire. His eyes widened in fear.

"Help me! I'll burn up!"

"Get back, Corey!" said Father.

"I'll get him, Father, although God knows I want to leave him there," said Marlene.

She placed her hand in Jimmie's outstretched hand, that was, even now, being burned in the flames.

Jimmie let out a horrifying shriek.

"Hurry up, woman! I'm dying, here!"

She took off the jacket of her suit, and beat out the flames that were curling around Jimmie.

"I'll call Doc Bailey, and let him know we've got two patients!" said Lou.

Father took the phone.

"Doc, put Mrs. Clifton on."

"Mrs. Clifton, we're bringing him out of the woods into the meadow!" said Father. "We will need life-flight."

"For Corey!"

"No, for Jimmie Crackers, his kidnapper."

"Let him die!"

"We can't do that, Mrs. Clifton! It would not be Joe's Way!"

When Georgia and one of the helicopter pilots, saw Corey walking out of the woods, surrounded by Father Callaghan, Marlene, and Mayor Lou, and ten young people, from the Siletz Confederation, they were overjoyed. Suddenly, Corey felt no fear, and allowed the helicopter crew to bring him up out of the meadow, with great ease.

Within an hour, the meadow was cleared, Crackers had been taken to Portland via Life Flight, and Marlene was being treated for burns by Doc Bailey. The members of the Siletz Confederation stood guard, around the perimeters the spring and the pool. The members of Siloam City stood alongside. All would come to the rescue of the tiny homes, campers, and tents in the little village should the fire come from that direction.

The fire burned all night, lighting up the area for miles around. To an onlooker, the streets of Safety Harbor, lighted dimly by the flames, looked like a village on the moon.

Chapter 120

By mid-morning, the fire had overcome the last of the trees' protecting Siloam City. The bucket brigade had soaked the ground beyond it, to hold it back, from coming any farther.

Just as the last flames had been extinguished, Blessed John came walking up the driveway, and made his way to the spring, where people were now gathered round in conversation. Overnight, such comeraderie had been created, that, now that the danger was over, they did not want to leave.

"Thanks be to God! Nothing was lost!" said Blessed John.

"Where were you when we needed you?" demanded Lou, who was exhausted and sick with worry about the wellbeing of Safety Harbor.

"I am charged to accompany people on their journeys. That is my sole assignment in the world."

"Well, this has been quite a journey!" said Lou. "You could have been a bit more liberal with your interpretation. Stewart has let us know there are still flames licking at the outskirts of the city. The fire departments from Clever and Corvallis are there, even now, and they have been successful in their efforts, so far. I'm going back to town!"

"So am I!" said Marlene.

Several others assented in agreement.

"Come for breakfast, all of you!" said Sally. "It's on the house! Joe's will be open, in half an hour. It may take a little longer to get the coffee made and the stoves warmed up!"

"I guess that means I'd better get back, too!" said Luther.

"I'll call Stewart," said Katye, "and let him know he is expected."

"I'll be there to help," said Georgia.

"Is there something I can do?" asked young Rev. Cecil Bainbridge.

"Come, help set the tables!" said Sally.

Bart and Susanna hurried back to the gallery, where they picked fresh flowers to decorate the diner tables. Parents collected their children, playing as if they had not been rescued, just hours before. Within an hour, a party, that would make Joe proud, was happening at the diner. Laughter was loud and spirits were high, as breakfast was served. No one was left out.

Several were not present. Doc, Caleb, and Ruth were at the hospital. Father Callaghan and Marlene were being attended there. Sally smiled. It was the first time anyone from the Siletz Confederation besides Ruby had been inside the diner.

Liz had stayed behind and was in her house, finally able to break down. She was shaking and sobbing.

"We almost lost it all, Momma!"

Hope took her in her arms.

"Yes, but you didn't. We are all here, thanks God!"

"Not all of us! I am scared to death for Uncle Hobey!"

They heard a groan from upstairs.

Both women went up the steps cautiously.

They found Georgette in Caleb and Liz's bedroom, prostrate on their bed, crying as if her heart would break.

"I'm sorry Liz. I have no right to be in here. It just makes me feel closer to Hobe. I'm so afraid he's gone!"

Liz and Hope took Georgette with them, to the diner.

"We can't find Uncle Hobey," said Liz. "Aunt Georgette hasn't seen him since he started out in his pickup, to rescue the children. We need to go looking for him."

"I agree!" said Lou, who had been presiding at the wisdom table, as usual. Carmey, Marshall and you need to get on this!"

"I don't think it will take long," said Marshall. "There's only so much ground to cover and it's all burned over."

"Damned fool!" thought Carmelita.

She still hadn't been able to teach him the basics of diplomacy. By now, she doubted he would ever learn.

Chapter 121

IT DIDN'T TAKE LONG to find Hobe. His totally burned-out pickup stood out, along the old logging road. What was left of his charred body, had been rendered unrecognizable, by the fire. His remains were taken to the hospital, for an autopsy, although the cause of his death was pretty obvious. Then, his body was turned over to the Bates Funeral Home.

Georgette went into deep mourning. Two days later, her children arrived.

Hobe had known many people during his seventy-plus years, right here in the area, on the Old Eighty. He had worked at the lumber yard, for years, and was beloved by many of his customers. They all came from far and wide, to honor and to remember him. Liz invited Georgette and her family out to their Old Eighty, to help her plan for Hobe's memorial service.

"I didn't know I'd be such a mess!" she said to Liz. "I've always been the strong one," she said.

"You are strong, mother!" said Rhonda.

The boys were uncomfortable with the conversation.

"I'm going out to walk the old place," said Bernard, the oldest.

"So am I," said his brother.

When they had gone, Georgette said, "I don't know how to begin. If you'd ask Hobe what religion he was, he'd answer, "A little bit of everything and not much of anything.""

"Uncle Hobey was a very spiritual man," said Liz. "He didn't have to try to be kind. He *was* kind. He loved children. He loved his land. He loved everything God loves. He loved his family. He was devoted to you, Georgette. He may not have fit into any of the artificially drawn categories of religion, but he was more religious than some of the self-proclaimed pious I have known!"

Georgette began to cry. Rhonda went behind her mother and hugged her. They were sitting around the kitchen table.

"Come here, Momma," said Rhonda. "Give me a big hug."

Her mother stood and the two embraced. Liz joined them. After they all had a good cry, they got back to planning.

"I can't think but that the memorial can be anywhere but here, on the land," said Liz.

"That is a very gracious invitation," said Rhonda.

Three days later, at the opening of the outside ceremonies, Ruby burned sage, and the Siletz Confederation honored Hobe with a dance, led by the ancient and revered Roy Legband. Each of his children paid tribute. Georgette remained silent, dignified, and deeply sorrowful. The choir from Always Sunny sang an anthem. Marlene had just joined them in recent days and they were surprised when her voice stood out among the others.

Meriwether, who had often given Hobe a ride through town in her chili-red Mini, read a poem, that she had composed, just for him. Mayor Lou, always ready for a public appearance, made a small speech about Hobe as good citizen and God-fearing man. Mrs. Glover, ever at the ready, led the crowd in some of George's favorite hymns. Father Callaghan eulogized him.

Appropriately, lunch and refreshment was served in the old farmhouse, provided by Joe's and Always Sunny Church. Liz was sensitive to step aside and allow Georgette and Rhonda to host the occasion. The sons remained silent and stoic, throughout.

Stanley Bates transported Hobe's body to Willow Township Cemetery. A fresh grave could be seen nearby to Hobe's, with the newly-laid marker declaring it to be the resting place of Frances Saugus. Each of the clergy were allowed a part in the graveside ceremony. Young Reverend Cecil Bainbridge surprised them all with his eloquence, as he led everyone in the closing prayer and benediction. Afterward, Joe's was open with complimentary coffee, cold drink, and desserts. People lingered for hours.

No one had noticed the dark figure, halfway behind a tree, observing it all.

Chapter 122

THE CONFLAGRATION HAD LEFT desolation in its wake. The foothills that provided the backdrop of the new Siloam City, had been completely consumed by the flames. Black and grey covered the hills, with the occasional burned tree stump still emerging, from the detritus. The sickening smell of wet ashes pervaded the air.

The morning after Hobe's service, Sally called a meeting of the Joe Team.

"I have talked with Caleb and Liz," said Sally, "and I want to recommend that we help with putting Siloam back in shape."

""What can we do, Sally?" asked Lou.

"The big thing," said Liz, "is to get the trees replanted. Besides being an awful sight," said Caleb, "we need to prevent soil erosion and restore life once again on the hills. We don't expect financial help. We have the funds to buy the seedlings, but, to plant them all ourselves would be an overwhelming task.

"Then, there is the whole business of the old Saugus place," said Jeremy. "We've got to decide what we're going to do with that property, if anything."

"What's the status on the church and water park?" asked Carla.

"No one knows," said Father, "that I know of."

"Where's Raven?" asked Meriwether.

"He's around," said Marlene. "He won't leave, with his business unfinished."

"What business?" asked Nate.

"To destroy my life, one way or the other," said Father.

"That's not going to happen!" said Suzanne.

"The whole community will fight for you!" said Katye.

"Unfortunately," said Marlene, "Raven doesn't work that way. He's sneaky. Cowardly."

"He needs to leave town," said Samir.

"It will take a confrontation," said Father. "As long as he can stay in the shadows, he can continue to do his dirty work. We will have to draw him out into the open."

"If you're thinking about being the bait, don't, Frank," said Lou.

"I can bring Roy on as deputy until we have taken care of Raven, Lou," said Carmelita.

"That's a good idea!"

"What about Jimmie Crackers? Is he still at large?" asked Carla.

"I have to take responsibility for his escaping jail, during the fire," said Carmelita. "In my haste to protect everyone else, I wanted to make sure the town got evacuated. I intended to come back for him, but he got out, before I could get back. He was burned pretty badly in the fire, and he's at Emanuel hospital in Portland. He's likely to be there for a long time, but, once he gets out, he'll go to the Lincoln County jail."

"Let's get busy on the tree planting!" said Katye. "We can't live in fear, waiting for Raven to strike."

"Say, you know what? I don't know why I didn't think of this before!" said Lou.

Hope put her head in her hands, anticipating one of Lou's off-the-mark ideas.

"We ought to dedicate the spring. Bring everybody together. You know . . . one of those ecu . . . "

"Ecumenical?" asked Father.

"Why, yes, ecumenical. I mean, include everybody."

"It's certainly in the spirit of Joe," said Nate.

"Yes, I think he'd like that," said Little Therese.

"Since it's Siloam," said Magdalena, "it would be our job to plan it, along with Caleb and Liz," said Magdalena. Then, she added, diplomatically, "But, of course, we'd like to invite Safety Harbor, to help us out!"

"On behalf of all the citizens of Safety Harbor, I accept being your partner!" said the Mayor.

"We will ask our friends of the Siletz Confederation to join us," said Rock

"Or, perhaps we should ask if we may join them," said Magdalena.

Chapter 123

IF YOU ASKED ANYONE on the streets of Safety Harbor or at Siloam how they felt, their answers would vary. Shock. Devastation. Relief. Gratefulness. Sorrow. Thankfulness. No one knew how or what to feel, so they felt different ways, at different times.

The fire had changed everything. It had taken Hobe's life, while he tried to rescue children from the fiery furnace. It had left behind, a sorrowing widow. It had threatened Father Callaghan's life. It had nearly burned up old Jimmie Crackers, although no one felt much sympathy for him. It had destroyed all visible life on the hilly forest of the Old Eighty, and had created a scar on the face of nature, that was hard to look at, or to look away from.

Unfortunately, the final days of the Watson family on the Old Eighty would become, for them, bitter herbs, as their husband and father perished, on the land he had so loved. They would build a shrine to him at the point where he died, trying to rescue the children. Rhonda wanted Georgette to come and live with her, but Georgette said that she would stay anchored at Safety Harbor, where her friends were. She would make short visits to each of her children.

Hovering over all the emotions of the people of the little twin towns was a feeling of disquiet, as if the fire was not the end of things, that more was to come. What it would be, they could not imagine . . . all but the Joe Team, who knew that Raven was still lurking around, seeking to destroy Father Callaghan's life. No one had seen him, but, everyone could feel him nearby, somewhere. Marlene had his office furniture removed, and put in storage. She changed the locks on her office doors and on her home. She turned all of his papers over to the county sheriff, upon the advice of Carmelita.

In the midst it all, everyone tried to return to some semblance of normalcy, although, because of their own anxiety, they could not manage it.

Raven, himself, had retreated to the old glass house, once owned by Homer Hill. He had purchased it, under an assumed name, from the realtor in Clever, who knew nothing of him or his works. It was delicious, he thought, hiding in plain sight. In the middle of the night, he would reconnoiter in Safety Harbor. He would haunt the streets near Our Lady and the rectory, to see if a plan to off the old priest would come to him. On one of his midnight visits, he saw a figure walking down the street. His heart leaped. He thought, for a moment, that it was Callaghan. He could nab him, put him on his plane, and take him to Headquarters. But, it was not Callaghan. It was that Blessed John fellow, who, Raven highly suspected, may be an ambassador-at-large, from Gemma. He bore watching.

On the third day after the fire, Raven decided to go into town during the daytime hours. He did this, just to be seen, just to keep those who knew him or of him, on edge. He walked up one side of Main Street, down to the Harbor Mall, and then down the other side of Main. He was sure Marlene saw him, when he walked past her office. He loved the shocked look on her face. He also took a little walk past Joe's, but it was mid-afternoon, past closing time. He had to look away from the Gemma light shining from the stone. He was especially sensitive to it, and if exposed too long to it, he felt that he couldn't breathe. He kept moving. Carmelita was just getting in the squad car when she spotted him. He moved quickly into the shadows behind Jeremy's bookstore and coffee shop.

There. Enough people had seen him, that the word would spread. But, before he left town, he could not resist walking past Our Lady and the rectory. Mrs. McCarthy saw him, straight through the kitchen window. Her face resembled Marlene's when she saw him. He smiled and waved. Now, he could go. That old busy-body would make sure everyone knew. Callaghan too. The Papist would regret saying "No" to him. The opportunity was not present yet, but it would be, in due time.

Chapter 124

A NEW WORLD HAS been forming on the planet, underneath the old system, that is rotten to the core, and collapsing in on itself. While evil seemed more and more to prevail, thin places, such as the Gate of Light in Safety Harbor, were providing a foretaste of what the world would, eventually, be. The more the underground of spirituality grew, the more frantic became the powers of darkness. Rather than trying to weaken and compromise the forces of good by, taking advantage of the frailty of human nature, BFS Inc., more and more, attempted to destroy, both spiritually and physically, every setting, where the new Spirit of goodness appeared on the earth.

Human beings often mistake the big for the important. Big cities. Big money. Big houses. More is . . . well . . . more. Small things are . . . small. What humans fail to see is that it is not places where more human beings gathered, or more money was invested, or more status was given to where humans lived, that mattered one whit, to the forces in the battle between good and evil. Centers of spirituality were strategic. They could be in any place in the world, small by human standards, or great. In the spiritual world, the thin places become the battlefields. Transformative changes took place. Pilgrims gathered.

Safety Harbor had become doubly dangerous, since the healing spring had reappeared, a sign that, indeed, peace had arrived here, and bubbled up from the earth, in a place now called Siloam. "Sent." Not only was the little coastal village host to a thin place, now, people came to the Sacred Spring, for spiritual healing and physical relief. Then, they departed, went to their own homes, and spread the news about this place. Over time, tens of thousands would journey to this and other thin places around the world where the old mythological human curse of a flawed nature could no longer prevail in the human heart.

Ever since Raven had come to town, the battle for the hearts and minds of the people had been enjoined. He had made every effort, either to claim the Sacred Spring for Bread from Stone, or to destroy it. In addition, he had made a commitment to Headquarters and a promise to himself, that by the time he left Safety Harbor and Siloam, Father Callaghan would not be on the planet, one way or another.

What had seemed to him, at first, to be an almost effortless assignment, had become one of the most difficult he had undertaken, if not the most difficult of his life. Contrary to the opinions of humans with whom he had come in contact, he was not all darkness, not all evil, not totally depraved. He did have a good side, he thought. It was just that, in order to do this work, the dark side had to prevail. Any hint of kindness, and the whole act would be over. He would be recalled, and cast into outer darkness, with other damned souls. Over time, he had forgotten how mercy, fairness, and compassion felt. He moved ahead with what he had to do, without hesitation, and sometimes, with outright pleasure.

Up until the present moment, every attempt Raven had made to destroy the spring and to obliterate the priest, had failed. Even the fire had not done it. Instead, a person he had not intended to kill, Hobe Watson, had died, and one of his own, Jimmie Crackers was in the hospital, burned critically. He had failed, not only to obtain the Old Eighty, he couldn't even get the property next to it. A woman had died there. Necessary collateral damage. He could not go back to Headquarters. Not with these circumstances.

Raven saw the whole world as a kind of drama, in which he was the hero. All others were mere backdrop, lesser actors in the play. Hubris would not allow him to admit his mistakes. They were only miscalculations and ultimately, the fault of others. His plans always worked, if someone else did not get in the way. Some humans, inevitably, failed him. Many were never quite evil enough to stay with the program.

There were exceptions to this, of course. Some were even heads of state. Those who had left the planet were now employed at Headquarters. Where were these people when he needed them? Too often, he felt, the creature left him to do his work alone, as a solo act.

He would pull his own sword from its sheath. He would enjoin the battle, alone. The lines were drawn. Francis Callaghan and the Joe Team stood in the way of his getting out of this provincial little town, and on to more interesting and exotic places.

There was no going back, now.

Chapter 125

AT THE MOMENT, RAVEN determined that he would not try destroy Safety Harbor, nor would he destroy Siloam. For now, he would simply take out the Joe Team and Callaghan. The rest of the details, regarding the spring, could be worked out afterward, when their influence no longer held sway over the community.

The strategy was to find the Joe Team all together in one place, and destroy them all at once. The challenge was, that, most of the time, the team met at Joe's, and he couldn't have anything to do with Joe's. Just the thought of the light from Gemma inside the diner made him anxious. He would have to keep his eyes and his ears open. This wasn't easy, either, because Marlene had quit him, and Jimmie was in jail. This would be a solo affair.

He would read *The Wave*. The little neighborhood newspaper included both real articles of news, as well as who visited whom, who poured coffee, and who served sandwiches or cake. He bought himself a copy at *The Wave* office.

He was in luck. There would be a small marker placed for Hobe Watson, at the place where he died, in just two days.

The only access to that location was the old lumber truck road, that would not be easy to navigate. It was a dead end, and to turn around on the road took some considerable skill. It was even more of a challenge, now, since, after the fire, there was nothing to camouflage the steep drop-off that most did not normally see, because of tall trees and undergrowth. Now, there it was, starkly dangerous, staring anyone on the road in the face.

He became even more excited when he learned, eavesdropping in Joe's parking lot, that the Joe Team would arrive in one bus! What luck! He wouldn't have to send a number of cars careening off the cliff. Just one would do it. Package deal. Gone. Just like that. It would be a matter of timing and skill. Nobody could survive the drop-off.

He would need some assistance. The mob had done good work for him in starting the forest fire. He had worked with them, on and off, for years. They could be trusted. Their work was quality, although they demanded big favors in return. Times, such as these, called for taking no chances.

The trick would be to ram the bus, just at the right time, and just at the right place. Done successfully, it would be the end of this Gate of Light business, and the growing interest in the spring. Safety Harbor could get back to what it once was, a harmless, small town on the coast, leading a quiet life.

Suddenly, Raven was feeling good. It was the first time he had put together a plan, that he thought could actually work!

He went to the hotel bar and had a whiskey sour, to celebrate.

He missed Marlene.

Chapter 126

On Tuesday morning, for the last two weeks, after Minnie Belle's counseling session with Meriwether, Marlene and Susanna joined them for a late breakfast, at Joe's.

"I can't seem to get away from this place!" she said, as they had breakfast together at Joe's for the third Tuesday in a row. "Even when I'm not working here, I'm here, anyway!"

"Many of us find ourselves dropping in at Joe's, sometimes even more than once a day. For instance, I'll be joining Bart here for lunch," said Susanna.

'Oh, I wish I could join my husband here for lunch," said Minnie Belle, with a stricken look on her face.

"I wish I could join *my* husband here for lunch," said Marlene. "But, Claude and I are separated. Sometimes our imagination of the ideal is not what is real. He may not be the man for me, even though I have wanted him to be, for many years."

"Jimmie's in jail, Minnie Belle. He's not coming out, soon. We are better off not hitching our fates to the unpredictable tides of our relationships," said Meriwether. "We need to have plans of our own."

"I would agree with that," said Susanna. "I thought I'd never love again, after my husband died. But, here we are. I'm furiously in love with Bart."

"Oh, I don't think I could ever begin again," said Minnie Belle.

"But, you are starting over, right now! You have a job for the first time since you worked in that drive-in when you were sixteen."

She managed a smile.

"Why, yes, I have! I've started over, haven't I?"

"We need to get you a car, Minnie Belle," said Susanna. "Fact is, I've got one in my garage that I barely use any more, Bart and I are together so much. How would you like to buy it?"

"Oh, that's such a nice offer, but I could never afford to buy it!"

"What if we made you an offer you couldn't refuse? What if we worked out payments so that you could actually afford to buy it? Remember," said Susanna, with twinkling eyes, "I'm engaged to a banker!"

"It's been so long since I've driven," said Minnie Belle. "Jimmie never wanted me to work, or to drive a car."

"Those days are over!" said Meriwether.

"And they should be!" said Marlene.

Chapter 127

A SENSE OF UNEASE pervaded the air, at the Pool of Siloam. The sun was shining, yet, it seemed cool, even cold. Pilgrims noticed that when they got out of their cars and walked toward the pool, the air seemed, quite suddenly, to change, penetrating them with a biting frigidity. Some went back to their vehicles, to pick up a jacket or a sweater.

Roy Legband emerged from his house, and stood at the end of his small porch, looking first, to the east, and then, to the west. A few people from Siloam City ventured down to the pool, sensing that something was not right.

Some would say, later, that the earth shook. Those who were at the pool, or in it, said that it was the water, itself, that was disturbed. A light breeze stirred the air. Dark shadows appeared, went away, and came back again, as if clouds were passing in front of the sun. Except there were no clouds in the sky. Angry voices could be heard as arguments broke out among friends, families, and strangers. Children cried. Confusion reigned.

Suddenly, Raven appeared, standing at the platform of the spring.

"Come forward, now, and I will perform miracles!" he called out. "Whoever is sick among you, come to me. I will heal you. Come to me, and I will give you peace. No money is needed. But, nothing is free. You must, in exchange, give your soul to me. If you do, your life will always have good fortune and you will be free of many of the troubles of this world."

Suddenly, he was surrounded with a strange light, that, at the same time, appeared as darkness. It was uncanny.

"It's an angel!" someone called out.

The wind was picking up, now, and pilgrims had to steady themselves, standing. Some of the more desperate among them began to come forward, toward Raven.

Now, Roy Legband approached the spring. He said nothing. He simply stood nearby in silence. Raven was visibly unnerved by the presence of the holy man, but he continued to invite people forward.

Rock approached Raven.

"What do you want?"

"Give me Callaghan and I will go away. You will never see me, again."

"That's not going to happen," said Rock.

The others, including Roy, joined the confrontation.

"Everything can go back to normal. Just hand over the priest. Then, you can go back to the way everything was.

"Ghost demon out!" cried out Roy Legband.

Suddenly, Raven faded, as if he were some kind of video image. Then, he was gone.

Chapter 128

WORD SPREAD THAT RAVEN had come out of the shadows and had made a bold appearance at the Pool of Siloam. The next morning, when the Joe Team met, there was further concern about Father's well-being.

"I don't think you should go with us when we set Hobe's marker, tomorrow, Frank," said Lou.

There was all-around assent from the group.

"I will *not* allow Raven to set my course!" said Father. "I must not live in fear. I won't!"

"We don't want to be without you, Father," said Meriwether. "You and I have formed a good relationship over the past few years. I can't imagine serving here, without you!"

"Hear! Hear! So, say we all!" said Nate.

"I am to dedicate this marker, and I will not cower before evil. I will fulfill my promise to Georgette to do this!"

"We knew you wouldn't agree to it, Father," said Hope. "But, we had to try."

The next morning started with the Joe Team and the Confederation sharing breakfast at Joe's. Zeke, still the bus driver for Always Sunny, pulled up in front of the diner.

Nate went out to get him.

"Come in and eat with us! We've got time!"

"Sure thing! I'll take you up on that!"

He got a standing ovation.

"I understand breakfast is free, too!" said Hope.

"Thanks to Nate! Thanks, everybody, for such a warm welcome!"

Georgette was smiling and laughing, with the group. It would be difficult later. For now, she would enjoy the support of friends.

An hour later, the Team was on its way to Siloam, and up into the burned over fields of annihilated trees. It was sickening for the group to see such beauty, turned to ashes; and it was horrifying to know that one of their own had died, so painfully, in his noble attempt to save children.

"He didn't deserve this!" said Liz. "Uncle Hobey didn't deserve it."

"He didn't. That's the truth," said Carla.

"We're going to park the bus soon!" Zeke called out. "You will need to watch your step when you exit, because the drop-off is only about ten feet away!"

"Maybe we ought to get out of the back-emergency door!"

"If you feel unsure of yourself, please do that. I'll open it up!"

Many exited the back of the bus. Nate, Carla, and others who were in good physical shape left by the side door.

They approached the marker that had all ready been established, firmly in place, It read,

Hobe Watson, Lover of Children, Animals, the Land, and All Things Beautiful

No dry eyes remained, after reading the inscription. Everyone remained in silence. A visual reminder of his passing put many of them back into the shock they experienced, when they first heard of his death. Georgette stooped down and traced her fingers over the lettering of the monument, sobbing quietly. Liz and Caleb walked up behind Liz, and placed their hands on Georgette's shoulders. They could feel the quivers throughout her body, as she wept.

Little Therese, Mayor Lou, Liz, and Magdalena gave brief eulogies. They sang *Amazing Grace*. Meriwether offered a prayer. Sally opened a picnic basket, producing small pieces of Georgette's recipe for spice cake, that Hobe had loved so much. Water from the spring was poured on the parched land, by Liz and Caleb.

Within half an hour, the little band of pilgrims had finished their rituals. They lingered fifteen more minutes, while Georgette grieved, and then, regained a modicum of control over her emotions.

Zeke produced a small ladder so that most could board the bus through the back door. When they all had been seated, Zeke started up the bus and began to turn it around, very carefully. He didn't have much maneuvering room, and the drop off loomed, not far away.

Suddenly, from behind them, a large tow truck came up over the hill, toward them.

"It's not stopping!" said Carla, who was the first to see it.

Zeke had just maneuvered the bus to the point, that the front end was heading, directly, toward the drop-off. This coming attack was, clearly, a planned move by someone who wished them no good. The truck connected with the bus and pushed it ahead. It backed up and shoved it, again. And again. The front end of the bus now hung, precipitously, over the edge of the cliff.

"Everyone move to the back of the bus!" Rock called out.

Marlene opened the back door and let herself down.

"No one else do that!" Nate said. "One wrong move could put us over the cliff!"

Marlene closed the door behind her, and stood between the bus and the tow truck, which, even now, was backing up to strike again.

"Marlene! Don't!" Georgette cried out.

The truck was coming again.

Raven was riding on the passenger side of the tow truck. He had to see the end of the Joe Team, especially Francis Callaghan.

"That damned woman!" exclaimed Raven. "What does she think she is doing?"

One of Raven's Las Vegas Mafia friends, who was driving the truck asked, "Do you want me to take her out, boss? One more hit and that bus will be gone!"

"No! Hold off!"

The driver looked at him, incredulously.

"We're almost finished here!"

"Hold off!"

Suddenly, Raven realized he could not bring himself to end Marlene's life. He hadn't seen too many people willing to lay down their lives for their friends. He admired that.

"You've hit the bus enough times. It's going to go over the edge. There is no way the bus can back up. Its front wheels are touching air. It'll be over soon. Let the woman live. You've got to admit, she's got guts!'

"Whatever you say!"

He backed the truck up.

"I'm sure you'll wanna stay close by and watch!"

Raven was suddenly filled with a sense of sadness. The challenge that had fueled his life, that had stirred up his adrenalin, was all going over the edge of the cliff. There had been no worthier opponent, than Francis Callaghan. Now that it was all over, he almost regretted that his plan had worked.

"Yes, let's watch and see what happens!" Raven said.

"We have to get out of here!" said Georgia.

"Everybody move to the back of the bus!" said Carla.

She spoke with the authority. Everyone listened.

"Zeke, move carefully!" Carla said. "You're closest to the front, and the most likely to take us over the edge!"

The precarious balance of the bus was interrupted, momentarily, and it seemed that it was going to fall. But, as Zeke moved toward the back, it righted itself. There was a sigh of relief.

"Open the door! Carefully!" Nate called out to Ruth.

Slowly, she moved the latch downward, and cracked open the door.

"The ladder is folded up, under the back seat!" Zeke called out.

"Mother 'o God! Pray for us!" Father prayed aloud.

Carefully, Carla reached under the seat and brought the ladder out. One false move and all of it was over.

Set it up!" said Carla, as she handed the ladder to Marlene.

Georgia and Georgette were the first passengers to get off, safely. But, with each loss of weight, within the bus, the chances increased that the bus would go over the edge. Nate, Carla, and Rock had become a team, as they worked to get the oldest and most vulnerable among them off the bus, first. Soon, only the three were left on board.

They decided among themselves that they would all go through the back door at the same time. The problem was that the door was too narrow. Two could crowd through and one would be left behind, to get off alone. They decided to hold firmly to one another's hands and pull the last one off at the last minute. They didn't have long. It was clear that the bus was going to give way to gravity any instant. They moved quickly.

Carla and Rock exited the bus and in a kind of coordinated dance turned around immediately, to pull Nate out of the death trap. As they did, the bus began to fall.

The sounds of the crash were heard by all, followed by a deafening silence.

Everyone was dumbstruck at what they had just seen and heard.

Chapter 129

ONE OF THE CITY busses had been dispatched to pick up the stranded pilgrims. Raven and his Las Vegas mob thugs abandoned their truck, and headed, on foot, through the burned over forest, getting lost three times, before they found a back way onto the Bread from Stone property. Raven sat in the auditorium of Jimmie Crackers' church, wondering what he had done, and why. At the last minute, he had backed down. All he had done was to destroy a bus. Callaghan got out, unscathed. Everything he had planned, he cancelled, by a momentary hesitation. He was no farther along than he had been, before he started. He was worse off, really, because now, he would have to admit to the Creature, that he had lost his nerve. Worse yet, he had backed down from a woman. Well, he would not go back to Headquarters empty-handed. Callaghan was still in his cross hairs.

Marlene was taken to Harbor View Hospital for observation. She had no physical injuries, but Doc Bailey had said she was to have no visitors. He was unable to hold off the throng, once they had heard of her heroism. Her room was filled with flowers, candy, and balloons. She had not received such an outpouring of love and appreciation, in her life. Even Claude came by to see her, after work.

In the early evening, Carmelita came by.

"Do you have any idea of who was in the truck?" she asked.

"It was Raven. I know it!"

"But, did you see him?"

"I could make out enough."

"Weren't the windows tinted?"

"Yes, but they got pretty close."

"How close?"

"I'd say they came within three feet of me."

"How do you know it was Raven for sure?"

"Can you imagine anyone else who would want to do this?"

"No, I can't. But, that isn't enough to arrest him. I have to have some evidence."

She hesitated.

"I'm going to come back in the morning. Maybe, by then, you will remember more about this. Meanwhile, Marshall and Roy are up on the mountain, going through the truck, looking for evidence. I'll let you rest. By the way, you're a hero, you know! You're my hero, too! Thanks for saving so many lives!"

Marlene blushed.

"Thank you," she said.

Chapter 130

AFTER TWO DAYS, MARLENE was dismissed from the hospital. The next evening, a dinner celebrating her heroism took place at Joe's.

"This won't be enough!" said the mayor. "I nominate Marlene to be the Parade Marshall next summer!"

"Hear! Hear!" said Rock.

The others joined in.

"Hear! Hear!"

There was laughter and clapping.

"Thank you all, very much!" said Marlene.

She teared up.

"I don't deserve this!"

"Oh yes, you do!" spoke up Minnie, who had was pouring coffee. "Remember what you told me about me?"

"Yes, I do!" said Marlene. "Okay, I deserve it, and I'm grateful!"

"There's no way of thanking you, for saving so many lives," said Hope.

"I just did what came naturally to me. I'm no hero!"

"All heroes say that!" said Georgia.

"You all are so wonderful!" said Georgette. "You all risked your lives to honor my Hobe!"

"But," Jeremy said "no one can hold a candle to what Marlene has done, for all of us!"

"I wish Uncle Hobey and Mrs. Saugus were here with us," said Liz

"Yes, how we miss them!" said Carla.

"Very much!" said Hope. "Very much, indeed!"

Chapter 131

Two nights later, as Raven nursed his psychological wounds, with a Tequila Sunrise, at the hotel bar, he felt a tap on his shoulder. He turned around, and nearly lost his balance, on the barstool.

"Surprised to see me?"

"I suppose I am."

"Can we talk, somewhere else?"

Raven led Father Callaghan to his usual table in the restaurant.

"To what do I owe this honor?"

"I think you know why I am here."

Raven feigned puzzlement.

"I am here to offer myself to you."

"It's a little late in the day, don't you think?"

"I don't mean I am here to serve you. I am here to offer you my life."

"Do you mean that you are willingly making yourself a victim?

"Oh no! I am not a victim! I am here of my own volition, and I have a quid pro quo that accompanies my offer."

"What do you want, Francis?"

"I want you to leave the people of Safety Harbor and of Siloam alone. I want you to give up your ambitions for the Sacred Spring, and I want you to donate your land to the people of Safety Harbor."

"Why would I do that?"

"You would have the satisfaction of my life on this earth being over. I will never trouble you again."

"I'm not going to let you off the hook that easily."

"What do you want?"

"I want you to suffer a fate worse than your own death. I want you to renounce your vows, and live in exile."

"I wouldn't know who I am without my vows. They are my life."

"That's the point, don't you see? It will be a kind of living death."

Raven had Francis in a catch-22. If he did this, to keep his friends from being hurt or killed, he was turning his back on the divine call. If he did not, the harassment by Raven would continue, and would likely result in his own death and the demise of the whole Joe Team.

"Why should I trust you? The world is full of stories of those who made a deal with you and ended up worse off than before."

"You will just have to trust me."

"The souls of the damned can testify, otherwise."

"You have a very one-sided view of things, Francis. We are a humanitarian organization. We do a lot of good. Our efforts to control the world are only altruistic. We only break our agreements, when it is best for all concerned."

"What good does it do me to give my life for my friends, if you go back on your word?"

"I'm going to be after you, Francis, one way or another. I may appear without warning, and take your soul."

"My body, maybe. Not my soul."

"That's the chance you'll have to take."

"I'll take my chances, then."

With that, Father was up, and out the door.

Chapter 132

THE NEXT DAY BROKE with a blanket of gentle fog, snuggling the little town of Safety Harbor into its nest. It did not reach Siloam, although those visiting the spring could feel dampness, in the cool morning air. Not many people had assembled there, this morning, and Liz, looking out the bay window of the big farmhouse, wondered if things might be slowing down, a bit. She felt guilty at the relief that surged through her, when she thought this might be true. This feeling did not last long. Soon, the place was beginning to fill up with visitors. Liz was grateful that Hobe's father and mother had seen fit to plant enough trees to give the house its privacy. The burned-over land, with its protruding stumps amidst the black and grey ash, provided a stark contrast to the still peaceful and beautiful site of the spring. It would be a long time before the hills were covered with trees and the wild underbrush that accompanied it.

Workers had arrived by 8:30 a.m., to begin construction of two sprawling greenhouses, just west of the new Siloam City. They would contain the seedlings that would be planted early next spring, when the fire-scarred hills had begun to repair themselves. The project was providing work for some of the unemployed, who lived nearby. Liz knew this was a good thing. Still, she could not help but imagine this morning, what it might be like to live in the quiet, peaceful setting, that they had once envisioned.

Although it had not been that long ago, when Caleb and she had walked onto the place, during the auction, it seemed to be in the far distant past. The bucolic setting was what had attracted them in the first place. The struggle, she could see, would be to keep it that way, offering a place of solace, rest, and healing for those who came to drink from the stream, and bathe in its pool.

Today, Rock, Magdalena, and she were to meet with the city council of Safety Harbor, for a discussion about bringing the residents of Siloam City into the city limits so as to provide city services. She felt ambivalent about this, knowing that even the actions of the most well-intended among them could contribute to the loss of the Arcadian setting with which Caleb and she had fallen in love.

Her thoughts were interrupted by a rapping on the door. It was Susanna.

 Got any coffee?" she asked

"Sure! Come on in!"

"Sorry to come out so early in the morning!"

"It's not early or late here. Seems there's always something going on, all hours of the day and night."

She poured two cups of coffee.

"Let's go sit on the porch," Liz invited her guest.

The sprawling trees had begun to cast long shadows, as the sun made its way through the morning sky. The breeze rustled through the leaves, and birds were singing in their branches.

"So much beauty here, and so much pain," observed Susanna.

"Yes, it hard to believe that Uncle Hobey died such a terrible death, just over those hills. He had lived on this land, and loved it. I'm glad a marker has been established where he died. My heart breaks for Georgette, though. I don't know what she'll do."

As soon as she said this, she was horrified. Susanna, too, had lost her husband in a tragic car accident, several years before.

Sensing her embarrassment and chagrin, Susanna said, "It's all right, Liz. You just do what you have to do. You get up every morning and the first thing that happens is that the loss hits you in the face. You feel a wave of deep sadness coming over you, even before your feet hit the floor. Sometimes, you want to just turn over and go back to sleep. Sometimes you can, but, mostly, you can't. And if you do, it may haunt you in a dream. I managed it by pouring all that I have into the art gallery."

"Aunt Georgette doesn't have anything like that, though."

"What matters is that you pour yourself into something that is bigger than your sadness. Grief will consume you. You can't send it away, and sometimes it is overwhelming and paralyzing. But, you just go on, because, well, because you have to."

"I've wondered if there would be room for her to cook at Joe's. That's what she's done for her whole life, just cook for Uncle Hobey and her kids."

"I don't know. There are a lot of customers at Joe's these days. It would make sense if they could work her into the schedule. Sometimes I wonder if we need another Joe's, or if the present one should be expanded. Since the spring appeared, I understand business at Joe's has tripled."

"What brings you here, my good friend?"

"Bart and I have decided to tie the knot!"

"Oh, Susanna! Congratulations! I'm so glad for you two!"

Both women got up, and embraced.

"We would like to have the wedding here, at Siloam, if that would work for Caleb and you!"

"We'd be honored!"

"Are you sure you don't need to talk to Caleb?"

"I can ask him, but he all ready knows the right answer to that question!"

They both laughed.

"Thank you, Liz!"

"When do you plan on this august occasion taking place?"

"Next spring, we hope."

"Oh, that would be perfect! We would have the seedlings planted on the hills by that time."

"New life emerging from the ashes," said Susanna, "just as Bart has brought new life to my own heart."

Chapter 133

On his way back to Safety Harbor, driving through Amity, Father saw a man, walking along the road. It was Blessed John. He pulled over and rolled down the window.

"Care for a ride, Blessed John? I'm on my way home."

"Well, if it isn't too much trouble," he said.

"Not at all. Having someone to talk to, right now, would be a relief."

Blessed John opened the door and let himself in.

"I was going to stop here in town and have a cup of coffee and a piece of cherry pie. Do you mind? Mrs. McCarthy is cutting me way back on desserts, and I have to get them on the sly, now."

"Yes, a cup of coffee would be great!"

"My treat!"

"Well, thank you, my good man!"

They didn't have cherry pie, so Father had blueberry instead.

"Where have you come from, if you don't mind me asking?"

"I've been to see Raven to offer myself in exchange for his leaving the good people of Safety Harbor. But, the offer went bad, when he tried to change the terms of the contract."

"Oh, yes, that's just like him, and even if he didn't try to change the terms, he'd make up his own terms anyway. A contract with Raven is no contract at all."

"How do you know him?"

"I've known him, for let's say, a long period of time."

"Me too."

"He's been after you for a long time, hasn't he?"

"How did you know?"

"It's part of my task to keep track of his goings on, while I'm here on assignment."

"Then you know . . ."

"Yes, I know everything."

"He's really after me right now."

"That's his nature, Francis. He's like a black widow spider whose bite brings death. He can't not do it. He has come to this world to steal, to kill, and to destroy. That's what he does. That's who he is."

"I don't know why he has singled me out."

"Who knows why evil dogs some people, more than others? But, even if we knew the answer to that question, it wouldn't change anything."

"Sometimes Raven gets me to thinking. Sometimes I think I'm living the wrong life, really. I keep wondering if I hadn't made this decision or that bad judgment, where I would be."

"At such times, Francis, you must resist that kind of thinking. It's not good for the soul. You are where you are, both because you have made some good decisions and some not so good. Your destiny is not so much being in one place or another, or being one person or another. What matters is the wellbeing of your soul, Francis. It's all about what's going on in the heart."

"Yes, I know, but I need to be reminded. I know if my life had followed another trajectory, that there would have been disappointments as well, maybe even bitter ones. As it is, I've bet my whole life on God. That's a big bet, because you only get to do this, once."

They traveled the rest of the way into Safety Harbor, chatting, good naturedly, as if they had been long-time friends.

Chapter 134

THAT NIGHT, FATHER CALLAGHAN dreamed that he was on the widow's walk of the lighthouse, with Raven.

"All of this you could have had if you had just joined forces with me."

The messenger from Hell stretched out his hand. Father looked, and from this point he could see Amsterdam, London, and Helsinki. He looked another way and he saw Abu Dhabi, Amman, and Istanbul. Then, Raven pointed out Moscow, Beijing, and Ho Chi Minh City.

"See, all of this would be yours to rule over, and more. The whole world would be yours. Instead, you're stuck here in this poor excuse for a town, unknown and unsung, living hand to mouth with pitiful people, who keep you on a starvation stipend. What a waste you have made of your life!"

Father stirred. When he awakened enough, he could see that his dream had melded into reality. He actually *was* on the widow's walk. His hands were zip-tied to the railing of the platform that, for him, stood between time and eternity.

He looked up to see Raven.

"How did I get here?"

"Simple. Those leftovers you got up in the middle of the night and had for a snack? I can always bet on your healthy appetite, Francis. They were sprinkled with a tasteless drug. I didn't think you were going to get back to your bed, before you collapsed. I carried you here on my shoulders, and brought you up the ladder with me. It was quite a task. You've had too much of Mrs. McCarthy's cooking, I'd say!"

Raven smiled. He had a look of triumph in his eyes.

"If you are a man of faith," he said, "throw yourself down from this place. Don't you have a guardian angel to catch you? Most people do, I understand. And where are your people, now? Why, they are still in bed, catching the last few delicious moments of sleep! Your friends have forsaken you, it seems. But, it's not really a fair fight, is it, you with your hands tied, and all. Here, let me set you free. Then we can go at it, *mano a mano*. You can even call your angels, if you'd like. But, I think they may be on a journey, maybe even a long one. You can try, though. Maybe Blessed John will come and save you; or, you can cast yourself down, of course, and see what happens. That's always an option."

Raven loosened his hands from the barrier that went around the widow's walk.

"What do you want from me? I've offered you my life in exchange for these good people, and you have rejected it!" Father screamed.

"Actually, I brought you up here for a little theatre. I love the theatre, don't you?

It was Nate who first saw Father on the widow's walk as he walked down to the shore to get his fishing boat ready for the day. He called Carmelita, right away.

"There's a man up on the widow's walk!" he said.

"Who is it, can you tell?"

"No, I can't for sure. But, it looks like Father Callaghan's profile.

Chapter 135

MARLENE HAD COME INTO the office early. From her front window, the lighthouse was in sight. She thought she saw two figures out on the widow's walk. Couldn't be. Nobody went up there, anymore. She went outside to get a closer look.

Sure enough, two figures, dark against the gradually lightening sky, could be seen. She knew who it was, instinctively. Oh, God, no! It could not have come to this! Raven wanted to take Father out, but she could not have imagined it would be this way. A wave of guilt came over her. She knew she wasn't directly responsible for this, but what if she hadn't given into Raven's wiles? Maybe this whole thing would have been over earlier.

She called the police station. Shirley told her that seventeen calls had called come in, before hers. She began to walk down to the lighthouse; and, as she did, she noticed a number of people gathered, while others were on their way. By the time she arrived, about a hundred people had assembled to view the spectacle.

"Out of the way, folks!" said Marshall. "The mayor is here! Make way!"

Lou parked, gave the keys to Marshall, and said, "Move my car if you need to!"

There had been a number of people, over the years, that had gone up to the widow's walk, and threatened suicide. Fortunately, they had all been talked down. But, never had there been a scene quite like this. People who knew Father Callaghan, knew that he had vertigo, and would not climb to such heights, on his own. Someone had taken him there against his will.

"It's Raven with Father Callaghan," said Marlene to Lou. "He's taken him up there to kill him!"

"I know," said Lou. "I know. We have to figure out what to do about this, and quickly."

Thanks to Carmelita, the Lincoln City Fire Department was soon on its way with a life net to place near the lighthouse in case Father was pushed or chose to jump, in order to escape Raven. The Swat Team from Portland would be here as soon as possible. They would both try to talk the situation down by negotiation, and they would attempt a rescue of Father Callaghan by force, if necessary.

"The trick," said Lou, "is to keep things on an even keel, until then."

While all of this was happening, Stewart had come before all of this started, to the observation deck, for his morning reflections, unaware of what was happening above him. He sat down on a blanket, spread on the floor. He poured coffee from his thermos, and began to quiet his mind.

He was disturbed by voices from below. He stood up and looked out the window that opened toward land. He could see a growing crowd. Someone saw him looking out, and pointed upwards. Was something going on above him? He wondered. He began the two-floor ascent to the widow's walk, up the spiral staircase. Lifting the hatch door, he climbed out onto the platform. He never liked this part. There was a moment when both hands were not touching anything, as he transferred them from the staircase to the handles that pulled him up onto the floor.

Raven greeted him.

"Welcome, Stewart! It is good to see you! It is most fortuitous that you are here. Father Callaghan and I have been talking theology, you might say. I insist that Francis cast himself down and that the angels will save him, but, he is reluctant. It seems that, since he has come to this great height, his faith has dwindled."

Father was standing at a distance, near the edge of the platform. As Stewart looked at his face, filled with fear and concern, he realized the gravity of the situation.

Below, someone in the crowd said, "Now, there are three of them."

Magdalena looked through her binoculars up at the lighthouse.

"It's Stewart!" she said. "Oh, my God, Katye! It's Stewart!"

Katye, who stood nearby, responded, "Oh, Lord! I wish he hadn't done that!"

The crowd grew restless, as they saw a new figure had appeared, near the top of the lighthouse.

Stewart rushed toward Father.

"Come back from the edge, Father!"

"I can't. Raven wants me here. I am no match for him!"

"Well, I am!"

"Remember, Stewart, 'Resist the devil and he will flee from you'! Don't play into his hand. He wants a wrestling match, so that he can cast us both over the edge!"

"Now, there are four!" Rock cried out.

The growing crowed gasped.

"It's Blessed John!" said Magdalena, still looking through her binoculars.

"I hope he can help!" said Ruth.

Joe's had closed its doors, in the light of this development. The staff had made its way to the lighthouse. Many of the members of the Joe Team found each other, and stood together.

"Where is that Swat Team?" Lou worried aloud.

"They are still eighteen miles out!" said Marshall.

"They need to hurry! How many others are going to appear up there?"

"Blessed John! How good of you to come!" said Raven. "We were just talking about you! I assume you are here to rescue the priest!"

"It is not in my purview to rescue. I accompany people on journeys, both physical and spiritual. I have come to see how I may be of assistance."

"To me?" Raven mocked him.

"I doubt you would want my help,"

Raven turned toward Father. "It looks as though no one is going to rescue you! Too bad! I was hoping for a challenge."

Father was now paralyzed with vertigo.

"Oh, Francis!" exclaimed Raven. "Do look over the edge. You are perfectly protected! Why, if you die, Blessed John will accompany you on your spiritual journey!"

"He could call ten thousand angels, if he wanted!"

Raven twirled around.

"Who is this?" he demanded.

"Little Therese! What are you doing up here? How did you get here?" Stewart cried out, with alarm.

"I climbed the stairs, like the rest of you!"

"Little Therese! You shouldn't be here!"

"I had to come, Father. I am needed here."

"Well, be careful."

"Don't worry about me, Father. My eyes can't see, but my heart can!"

"Please, Little Therese! Go back down!"

"I cannot."

"Then, please get yourself inside, where the light house lamp is, where you are safer."

A gust of wind suddenly hit the lighthouse, and knocked Father off balance. The crowd was watching and stirred. He sat down. He could not do this much longer.

A strong overwhelmingly strong voice, within him. said, "Just get it over with! Jump!!"

For a moment, he seriously considered it. Everyone else could climb down, then, and be safe. Raven only wanted him, after all. But, he couldn't bring himself to do it. He couldn't even move, let alone jump.

Little Therese said, "Come, Father. We're going to go now. Raven can stay here, if he wants, but, the rest of us have other things to do."

"Not so fast, little girl!"

"I'm no girl!"

"Whatever you say, dear!"

"I'm not a dear, either. I am a prophet and you are my adversary!"

Suddenly, the hatch opened again. It was Marlene.

"Good Lord, Marlene!" said Stewart. "This is the *last* place you should be!"

"How about you, Stewart?" she asked. "I might ask why *you* are here?"

"Now, there are five up there!" screamed Lou. "This is getting out of hand!"

"The SWAT team is here, Lou!" said Hope.

"There's just one problem with the life net!" said Lou. "The other side of the lighthouse has only rocks and the ocean below. If Raven wants to push him off, he'll push him off on the ocean side. Frank would have to jump in order for the safety net to be of any use."

The SWAT team leader addressed Lou and Carmelita.

"We're going to see if we can talk them down. In the meantime, we will be prepared to carry out a rescue. We will take Raven Sinclair out, if necessary."

"I think you might have trouble with taking him out, as you say. He is no mere mortal," said Rock

"How are you going to do this without endangering everyone else with him?" asked Georgia.

"We deal with these kinds of things all the time," he said. "I can't say anything more about our strategy."

Stewart reached down to the vertigo-stricken priest.

"Come on, Father. "We're going to get out of here."

Suddenly, Raven's visage changed, morphing into a reptilian appearance.

"You two are not going anywhere!" he said. "I'll tell you when to move."

"You have no power over us," said Little Therese. "We resist you!"

By now, Ruth had arrived on the scene. She was stricken when she saw her daughter in imminent danger.

"She's really gone and done it now!" she said, her eyes wet with tears.

"We're doing all we can, Ruth. The SWAT team knows what they're doing. We'll get her down."

Lou wished that he was as confident as he tried to sound. Hope put her arm around her. Georgia stood alongside her.

Stewart helped Father to his feet. Raven attacked them both. The force with which he struck was far beyond the abilities of a man of his size and stature, knocking both of them to the floor, and against the railing. Old and in disrepair, it bent, at the weight of both of them, against it. The widow's walk was intended only for the lighthouse keeper. The rail was never built for strength.

Little Therese went and stood by both of the fallen men.

"You will need to come through me to go against these men. Do you want to be known as a somebody who caused the death of a young woman?"

"It matters not to me, a whit!" he said. "I don't have the weakness of worrying about what people think of me. Collateral damage knows no age. I am known for bringing death all over the world. An early death is even better. It gets things over with! You know what I mean?"

"All too well, Raven. All too well," said Father. "I have stood at the grave of many a child and young person. I have buried those who suffered, mightily. I have seen murderers live long lives while their victims have their lives cut off. I know that you view this world as belonging to you. I know you rejoice at death and chaos. And you are happiest, when you have put fear in the hearts of human beings."

Just then, another gust of wind hit the lighthouse. Father held, ever more tightly, to the railing.

"Let go of it, Father!" Marlene called out. "It will fall and take you with it!"

But, he could to bring himself to do it.

"It's not secure, Father!" Marlene persisted.

"Take my hand," said Little Therese.

He let go of the railing, grasped her hand, and held it, tightly.

Raven stepped up his attack. His face further contorted into serpentine likeness, his breath emitted a sibilant sound, which caused all of them to retreat. He picked up Marlene, and dangled her over the side of the rail.

"If I throw you off, Marlene, you will never get up. Your bones will come apart on those rocks below and your corpse will float out to sea."

He held her by the neck. She could barely breathe.

"Jump, Father!" Marlene called out to him. "Jump into the life net!"

"Others go first!" said Father.

He truly did want the others to go ahead of him. At the same time, he was frightened in so many ways of doing exactly what he had always feared he would do, to fall over the side of a high place.

"No! You must go first, Father. He is after you."

"I can't!"

"You must, Father! You must! He will throw you off the other side, and you will die, for sure!"

"I'm going to push you, now, Father," said Stewart, gently. "You have to go!"

With that, Stewart tipped him over the side, directly over the life net.

Father had always imagined what it might be like to fall that far. Before a thought could enter his head or a feeling pass through him, he had landed. He bounced on the trampoline-like surface. Strangely, he could count the bounces. There were four. The onlookers clapped and cheered. Then, immediately, he was snatched away by EMT's, who took him to Harbor View Hospital.

Up on the platform, Marlene wrestled with Raven. He continued to choke her, and to threaten her.

"Go!" she said to Stewart and Little Therese. "He is going down. I'm not going to let loose of him."

"'Fear not those who can kill the body, but cannot kill the soul'!" said Little Therese.

"Here, Little Therese," said Stewart, lining her up with the life net. "You may go now!"

With that, she slid off the side. People would say, later, that she fell gracefully, floating in the air like a winged bird.

Only Stewart and Blessed John remained to watch the fearsome struggle between Raven and Marlene. They watched in horror. One or both of them were going over the side. If they intervened, they would end up on the rocks below, as well. There was nothing they could do. Stewart could not say, later, how long they watched. It was as if everything was in slow motion.

The spell was broken, as they saw the side rail break open. Did Raven fall or did he jump? Hard to say. Stewart suspected the latter, as he watched Raven leaving the widow's walk. He appeared, for a moment, to fly. Then he fell . . . or flew . . . right into the ray of light in the lighthouse lamp, the light that was from Gemma.

People heard a loud pop, as if it was a backfire from the tail pipe of a motor vehicle. Some thought it sounded like a fire cracker. Others thought it was a gun. Stewart, who witnessed this phenomenon, said that, when Raven fell into the light, he disappeared into thin air, as if annihilated.

Marlene could not regain her balance, and was the second to fall. Stewart was sure that she had gone to her death. He looked around. Blessed John was nowhere to be seen. He must have fallen too.

As if on cue, six members of the SWAT Team appeared on the platform.

"Too late," said Stewart. "It's over."

He knew he was too exhausted to climb down the metal stairs, and so, he allowed himself to fall backwards, into the life net.

Chapter 136

No one had seen Blessed John leaving the platform, but he was gone. In fact, he had descended just on the north side of the cliffs, over craggy, slippery rocks, down to what would have appeared to any witness, to have been the remains of Marlene Brooker.

Facing the loud crashing of ocean upon the shore, splashing up, threatening to take both what remained of Marlene, and him, into the strong undulating of the waves, Blessed John reached down, and, lovingly, picked her up. Staggering, as if almost to fall backwards into the sea, he righted himself and began the long, dangerous ascent, from the chaos below.

He reached dry land, just where the crowd had assembled below the lighthouse. Like a god rising from the sea, Blessed John walked toward the still-assembled crowd. At first, there was stunned silence. Then, an outpouring of cheers. Someone spread a blanket and he lay her down, tenderly, upon it.

"Get an ambulance!" someone called out.

Blessed John knelt down by her, and breathed, quietly, into her nostrils.

The paramedics arrived, and crowd parted in front of them, until they reached Marlene.

"She's still breathing!" one of them called out.

Just then, Claude appeared at her side, and accompanied her in the transport, to the hospital.

All of those who had jumped or fallen to safety in the life net, were examined by Doc Bailey, on the scene, and pronounced to be in good condition, while Caleb attended Marlene at the hospital. She was barely alive, insomuch that Caleb was concerned that any movement at all could further injure her. He placed her in a drug-induced coma, so that she could be examined, x-rayed, and tested. After twelve hours, she was taken to Portland.

Her prognosis was uncertain.

Chapter 137

THE CONVERSATION THE NEXT morning, at Joe's, was subdued.

"It is actually difficult to believe that all of this really happened," said Jeremy.

"I wanted to go up there and help," said Meriwether. "But, it was dangerous for those who were up there, and I would have only made it more so."

"Those of us who were up there were largely helpless, too. All we could do was to try to save Father Callaghan while staying alive, ourselves," said Stewart.

"Lou and I are proud of all of you," said Hope.

"This could have had a far worse outcome," said Lou.

"What I don't get, is how Blessed John got down from the lighthouse without any of us seeing him go," said Stewart.

"He has always seemed a bit strange to me," said Georgia. "Not quite like us, I'd say."

"Not *anything* like us!" said Carla.

"He was amazing in his rescue of Marlene," said Rock. "He saved her life, I am sure."

"Where did Raven go?" asked Magdalena. "That's what bothers me."

"He went into that light, and disappeared, just like that. I've never seen anything like it!" said Stewart.

"Very strange," said Lou. "Very strange, indeed."

"I saw it too," said Little Therese. "I can see in the Gemma light. All at once, there was a flash, and for a moment I could see Raven; and then, 'pop', he was gone!"

"I don't get it!" Roy said. "I don't get it at all! How could one guy get down from the lighthouse without descending the ladder, or falling into the life net? That's only one thing. How could somebody just disappear into the glare of the light?"

"Frank!" said Lou, as Father Callaghan came through the door. "Good to see you!"

Everyone at the Wisdom Table got up immediately. Little Therese ran to hug him! Everyone in the diner joined in the applause, although some had no idea what all of this was about. Everyone at the table insisted upon a handshake or a hug.

"Sit down! Sit down, Frank!" said Lou, offering him his chair.

"Oh, my!" said Father. . .

"You've got your old smile back, Frank!' said Lou.

"Good heavens! Such a welcome!" said Father.

Just then, Sally came to the table, with a family style breakfast.

"One more plate for the priest!" said Lou.

"Has anyone heard how Marlene is doing?" he asked.

"She's still alive," said Liz. "Caleb and I were in to see her last night."

"Susanna and I are going in to see her after breakfast. I'll report back," said Meriwether.

"And I'll go into Portland after classes today," said Katye.

"I'd like to go along," said Magdalena.

"Maybe we can work out a schedule so that she is not alone," said Minnie Belle, who had been pouring coffee. "I used to do that for Jimmie, when he was . . . when he was a real minister. I'd go and stay with sick people for hours and hours."

"That is a good idea, Minnie Belle," said Hope. "Let's you and I work on this together."

"Jeremy and I can help," said Samir.

"Good!" said Father. "Now, you want to know what happened yesterday. My friends, we have been in the presence of evil itself, since Raven came to town. He has wanted to kill me, yes, but what he was sent here for, was to obliterate Siloam and take over the Sacred Spring. This is why he blew up Mrs. Saugus's house, and killed her. That is why he started the fire."

Georgette began to cry.

"He killed my Hobe!" she wailed.

Susanna, Rock, and Magdalena comforted her.

"How do we go on?" asked Bart.

"What do we do?" asked Carla.

"We go on living," said Meriwether. "Hobe and Mrs. Saugus want us to."

"Will Raven be back?" asked Shirley. "I hope not."

"Whether he comes back, or not, evil will always return in some form," said Father. "Meriwether is right," said Carla. "We must pick ourselves up and live our lives."

"Life is short," said Georgette. "We are going along, and suddenly, it is over. I wish I could help younger people understand. They think that a long time is the same as forever. I am grateful for every day that Hobe and I had together. He was a pain in the neck sometimes, and in his later years, he was always underfoot, it seemed. But, I wouldn't have traded him, for one minute, for anybody else. His memory will sustain me, until I join him. I don't know whether he went to Heaven or Hell, but I want to be with him, wherever he is."

Father smiled.

"Oh, he'll be in Heaven, by then! Why don't you just plan on going there!"

"I think we must continue with our plans to dedicate the Sacred Spring," said Katye.

"I certainly hope so!" said Liz. "We have constructed two huge greenhouses to get seedlings ready, for next spring. We are going to need all of you to get the seedlings in their containers, and lined up, inside."

"There will be plenty to eat that day," said Ruby. "We will be bringing some of the best food the Siletz Confederation can offer."

"Beautiful!" said Father. "And we look forward to your participation in the whole day!"

"Well, let's get ready, then!" said Liz. "Ruby, Liz, Magdalena, and I will be planning it!"

"Hey!" said Samir. "I'd like to help!"

"Great!" said Liz.

Just then, Caleb came in, smiling.

"Marlene is awake, and talking. The docs are optimistic!"

"I wish Blessed John was here, so we could thank him!" said Shirley.

"He'll be back," said Little Therese. "I know it."

The group left the diner with lighter hearts.

Chapter 138

THE DAY OF THE dedication of Siloam dawned, sunny and beautiful. The whole place had been spruced up, trees trimmed, grass mowed, flowers were blooming, and there were well-placed flower pots throughout, evidence of Katye's and Susanna's handiwork. Corey, and his friends were selling lemonade in Liz and Caleb's front yard. Roy and Jens directed cars to their parking spots. Greeters from Siloam City and the Siletz Confederation met people on the path, by the barn, handing them a program for the day.

Katye's organizational skills were obvious. The day would be long. She knit the entire schedule together, with that in mind. There would be no room for the mayor to drag out his comments. Children would be involved, song and dance, work and play.

The burned-over forest land stood out, in stark contrast to the beauty of the fields and farmland around them. But, hope would spring from this day, as participants would be involved, later, in planting seedlings in small containers, to be stored in the greenhouses that stood, new and proud, just to the west of the pool. The next Spring, they would be planted on the now bereft hills.

A temporary platform had been raised for the occasion, between the pool and Siloam City. In front of it, lay a wide expanse of open field, providing a gathering place for the assembly. Local talent provided music as people gathered. Ben, Little Therese's dog, had appointed himself as an exuberant greeter of anyone who would give him attention.

Rock, Magdalena, and Ruby opened the ceremonies, for the day. Katye and Liz had to explain to Mayor Lou, that, since this was not Safety Harbor, his speech would need to come later in the program, along with others. Lou had protested, but he was outvoted by Liz and Hope. Still, he could be seen, glad handing and back slapping. He never stopped campaigning.

Ruby went first.

"We are pleased to gather with all of our friends today, around the Sacred Spring, denied to us by the invaders, who came and took our land, tried to eliminate us and our culture, and to absorb us into their way of life They murdered our people, stole our children, and denuded the hills of the trees that once had stood, tall and proud, some of them for centuries. They took this place, this spring, from us, as well. It was a place of peace, a refuge for those who were sick, lonely, or longing for a spiritual vision. But, when the invaders came and took it, it dried up, and no matter how hard they tried, even going so far as to dig a well, they could not bring it back.

"Now, discovered by a child, the spring has been restored and brought to life, again. The descendants of those who were once enemies, the invader and the invaded, gather here today, as friends. The spring has been restored because we, as people, have decided to put old resentments aside, and to live in different way, in the new and out breaking world.

"Our children and grandchildren will grow up with this spring as their heritage. We can begin to be healed, to walk together, while respecting our distinct histories and ways of life. We can celebrate together, eat together, dance together, and live our lives, side by side, as we are doing today.

"Our wise man, Roy Legband, has said that the water flowing from the spring, is a sign of a new era, a new time, free from the old hatreds, suspicions, and ignorance of the past. On behalf of the Confederation, I extend our greetings and our friendship."

Liz spoke next, giving tribute to Hobe.

"He lived on this land all of his life," she said. "And he gave his life, on this land, to save the children of our communities. There is no honor great enough to give him, for his selfless love."

Music from a couple of groups from Siloam City played, next. Many more people were coming onto the grounds, some of whom did not know anything about the program. They had come to drink of the spring and to take a dip in the pool. Some of them joined the festivities after they had accomplished their mission.

Ruth was sitting by Father Callaghan, as the music played. A tear rolled down her cheek.

"Why isn't my little girl cured of her blindness, here, at this pool? She is a loving child, a spiritual child, who has given up so much of her life as a child and a young person, in order to do the work that she believes she is called to do."

They saw Little Therese and Ben sitting beside Caitlin and Buddy, and their friends. She was laughing and talking up a storm.

"Why can she not see all of the beauty and the people, like other children. What did I do? Is she being punished for my mistakes?"

"Of course not, Ruth. It's difficult, especially when someone we love is going through such an experience as Little Therese. But, I do believe that God is working a purpose out. Our poor dim human brains are not evolved enough to see what that purpose is. God is an alchemist and turns our mortal bodies and our longing spirits into gold, that will last for eternity, which is longer than a long time. So, we just live from day to day, doing our best with what we have been given, and consider it all a gift. It takes a lot of trust, and a faith that some people would call foolishness."

"Sometimes I'm afraid to believe that much, Father. Besides that, I want my daughter to be able to see, now. I would give my own sight for her. People say, 'Well, she has spiritual sight beyond the rest of us'. That's easy for them to say."

"I understand how insensitive people can be," said Father. "But, it is important to know that Little Therese is perfect, just as she is. After all, how many times have you said that she is just perfect? Her pure spirit can see things that those of us who are distracted with physical seeing, very seldom, can see. Her insights are what makes her a prophet. It is her calling, her vocation. Contrary to what some may think, I have very few answers. I can sympathize with you, empathize with you, and offer you the wisdom I have been given."

"That is all I need, Father. Thank you."

It would not be a community gathering without Mrs. Glover leading the crowd in the songs that were familiar to many, which she was doing as Father and Ruth talked.

Afterward, the Confederation performed two of their native dances, followed by the Community College chorus.

The mayor was next. Expecting that he would wax long, Katye had arranged for Hope to come to the platform and pull on his coat tail when he went overtime, which he did, and she did. Much laughter followed, as the mayor turned around, in surprise. Hope gave him a kiss on the cheek.

"Oh, all right, all right! In conclusion, then . . ."

The crowd roared in laughter at the scene, and Lou threw up his hands. He began to laugh good-naturedly at his own long-windedness, and was escorted off the stage, by his beloved Hope.

Shirley followed the mayor, to pay tribute to Mrs. Saugus.

"How many people here knew Mrs. Saugus?"

Half the crowd raised their hands.

"Such a tribute to our beloved friend, whose life was cut short by violence. She clearly had a great influence on so many of us. We have many fond memories of her and we shall miss her. Let's stand now, and for you who know it, let's all join in the Harbor High school song!"

Half of the people rose and began to sing. Then, many others stood, and did their best to mouth the words.

"Let's hear it for Mrs. Saugus!" someone shouted out.

The applause and clapping lasted for ten minutes.

Liz then addressed the crowd.

"It is a real blessing for Caleb and me to be able to share this land with you, this wonderful spring, which is bringing healing to individuals, to our communities, and between communities. We don't know what this spring shall mean to us, in the future. But, we do know that we are its keepers, we are its stewards. We do this by caring for it, tenderly. by caring for our own souls, and by honoring one another, preferring the other, before ourselves."

Blessed John made his way up the driveway and onto the grounds of the pool. He stood by the side of the crowd, observing children playing. He heard laughter. He experienced human kindness. These mere mortals could not know what awaited them in the future. Some would die early, some would suffer, lose children, and be betrayed by their spouses, all of the things that make up human life, bitter-sweet and hopeful. Being here almost cured his restlessness and made him want to settle down, right here, in this place. But, he would have to move on, soon. Others needed him more, now. Safety Harbor and Siloam had come through their trials, and would be given respite, for a time. No one saw him leave, as he moved across the fields, toward his next assignment.

The time had come for the dedication of the spring, and the pool. Father Callaghan, Meriwether, the young Reverend Cecil Bainbridge, Roy Legband, Ruby, and Little Therese all gathered behind the spring, as the crowd, estimated by Lou to be three hundred, moved toward them. Each one spoke or prayed or sang.

"Liz has it right," said Little Therese, the last to speak. "We are Keepers of the Spring. We have been given great responsibility and great blessing. We are witnesses that there is healing for all, both those who will come here, and those who live here. We are being healed and we are healers."

After the ceremonies, many of the people stayed to plant the seedlings, and place them in the greenhouses. Next Spring, they would plant them in the dark, fire-scarred land, signaling a new start, a new era.

Joe's, Always Sunny Freewill Holiness Church, and the Confederation served a free meal afterward. Many stayed until late in the afternoon.

Marlene would recover, completely, and return to her work and to her husband. Minnie Belle would divorce Jimmie Crackers, and move into a small cottage, by the sea. Eventually, two years later, the land claimed by BFS Inc. would be declared abandoned, since no one knew who to contact. It would be purchased by the City of Safety Harbor, which would open it to the public as a waterpark. Jimmie Crackers' church would become an event center.

But, for now, just today, the people who had come, ended their time together by drinking from the spring, or taking a dip in the pool. Becoming Keepers of the Light and Keepers of the Spring had not come without considerable cost to them. They could not know what was in store for them, in the days ahead. But, this much they did know. They had withstood a terrible trial and had come out of it, not unscathed, but stronger. They had undergone terrible losses, but they had also been changed for the better. They had been through sorrow's gate, and had, inexplicably, found joy, deep within.

Keepers of the Spring. Yes, that's what they all had become. Keepers of the Spring.

Epilogue

SUMMER TURNED INTO AUTUMN. Before people knew it, Christmas was upon them.

On Christmas Eve, thirty people stood waiting, at the Portland airport, for a passenger to deplane.

"He's late!" said Buddy. "When's he gonna get in?"

"He's called," said Shirley. "They've landed. The one you are waiting for always comes off last, you know."

In the distance, a familiar figure could be seen, now, nearly running down the walkway. The closer he got, the clearer it was, that it was Silo. Jens and Shirley had been deemed, by the State of Indiana, to be his foster parents. They had begun adoption proceedings.

A roar came from those who were waiting. He was running toward them, now. He rushed into Jens and Shirley's arms, and hugged them.

Liz and Caleb began to sing, 'For he's a jolly good fellow'. The rest soon joined in, as Silo went from person to person, and received a warm welcome. His friends were literally jumping in the air, for joy. Silo chose to walk with them down the walkway to baggage claim.

Jens and Shirley looked at one another.

"That didn't take long for him to abandon us," said Shirley.

"He's a teen-ager," Jens said. "His friends are everything!"

"I know," said Shirley.

The mayor and the city council had permission for one of the city busses to be used, so everyone could ride home together.

"Merry Christmas, Silo!" said Little Therese. "We're so happy to have you home, where you belong!"

Lou led out on "Hark! The Herald Angels Sing," but his voice was off-key. Mrs. Glover over rode him and began to lead, in a clear voice.

Everyone joined in the singing. Some shouted out their favorite carol, and then, at least one verse was sung, all the way home.

The bus turned in to Siloam. Liz and Caleb's home was decked out festively, in lights, and candles marked the driveway, from the road to the house.

Georgia, Carla, Jeremy, Samir, and Mrs. McCarthy had stayed behind to prepare the large meal that awaited the crowd when they arrived. All the way from the bus to the old farm house, the crowd sang, "O, Come All Ye Faithful!"

Mrs. McCarthy met them at the door.

"Glory be!" she said.

"Look!" said Shirley. "'This son of ours was dead, and has come to life again! He was lost, and has been found'!"

Silo stood between Shirley and Jens. Phones came out and the moment was captured on camera.

"We are so glad you are home, Silo!" said Caitlin.

"What is Christmas, but coming home!" said Little Therese.

"Dinner's on!" called Mrs. McCarthy. "A traditional Christmas Eve dinner. All kinds of fish, deviled eggs, lasagna from Joe's, and all the trimmins."

"Any cherry pie for dessert?" asked Father Callaghan.

"You'll have to eat that when you get home!" said Mrs. McCarthy, with a playful evil eye.

"I'm going home with Frank!" said Lou.

"Try it!" said Hope.

As they sat around the table, they ate and drank together, and talked, animatedly, while a small group from Always Sunny sang Christmas carols, in the background.

Nate stood and raised his glass.

"I offer a toast!" he said, "to Silo!"

"To Silo!" everyone said, as they raised their glasses.

"To the new family!" said Hope.

"To the family!"

"Silo wants to say a word," said Jens.

Silo stood, and raised his glass, "To my new forever parents, to my friends, and to this place by the sea, that I love, and where I will live, forever!"

"Forever!" they all said. "Forever!"

www.ingramcontent.com/pod-product-compliance
Lightning Source LLC
Chambersburg PA
CBHW051132030726
47504CB00004B/835